THE NEXT ONE TO FALL

FORGE BOOKS BY HILARY DAVIDSON

The Damage Done

THE NEXT ONE TO FALL

HILARY DAVIDSON

A TOM DOHERTY ASSOCIATES BOOK

NEW YORK

THE NEXT ONE TO FALL

A Forge Book
Published by Tom Doherty Associates, LLC
175 Fifth Avenue
New York, NY 10010

www.tor-forge.com

Forge® is a registered trademark of Tom Doherty Associates, LLC.

Library of Congress Cataloging-in-Publication Data

Davidson, Hilary.
    The next one to fall / Hilary Davidson.—1st ed.
        p. cm.
    "A Tom Doherty Associates book."
    ISBN 978-0-7653-2698-0
    1. Travel writers—Fiction.   2. Americans—Peru—Fiction.   I. Title.
PS3604.A9466N49 2012
813'.6—dc23
                                                2011024968

First Edition: February 2012

Printed in the United States of America

0 9 8 7 6 5 4 3 2 1

For my husband, Dan—my first, my last, my everything

ACKNOWLEDGMENTS

If I started a novel with a character who's deeply in debt, you know he or she would end up burying a body, committing a heist, or participating in some mayhem. In my own case, I'm forever indebted to a long list of amazing people, and I consider myself blessed. My editor, Paul Stevens, never ceases to amaze me with his brilliant insights, gentle humor, and thoughtful ways. The entire Tor/Forge team deserves a round of applause for all their hard work, especially Miriam Weinberg, Aisha Cloud, Patty Garcia, Edward Allen, and Ragnhild Hagen. I'm grateful to many at Macmillan, in particular Talia Sherer. A big thank-you to my agent, Judith Weber, and to everyone at Sobel Weber Associates for all their work on my behalf and for their ongoing assistance.

I'm so grateful to all the bookstores and libraries that have supported my work. Special thanks to Barbara Peters at the Poisoned Pen in Scottsdale; Lesa Holstine at the Velma Teague Library in Glendale, Arizona; Marian Misters and J. D. Singh at Sleuth of Baker Street in Toronto; Bobby McCue and Linda Brown at the now closed—and very much missed—Mystery Bookstore in Los Angeles; Allison Robinson and Dustin Kurtz at McNally Jackson in New York City; Mary Alice Gorman and Richard Goldman at Mystery Lovers in Pittsburgh; Scott Montgomery at BookPeople in Austin; Ed Kaufman at M Is for Mystery in San Mateo, California; Charline Spektor at BookHampton in East Hampton, New York;

and Sally Owen at the Mysterious Bookshop in New York City. A big thank-you to the entire staff at Partners & Crime in New York City, where I had the launch party of my dreams. I'm sorry I never got to meet David Thompson in person, but I'll be forever grateful for his sweet enthusiasm when I contacted him about reading at Murder by the Book in Houston; my thanks to McKenna Jordan, Kinley Paisley, and everyone else at the store for their warm welcome.

Publishing fiction has shown me just how many people are in my corner, and I'm amazed at their efforts, awed by their tenacity, and humbled by their belief in me. Linda Fairstein has astonished me time and time again with her generosity and kindness. The Crimespree family—Jon and Ruth Jordan and Jennifer Jordan—has been unfailingly helpful and wise. Steve Weddle has been a one-man promotion machine, interviewing me in print and audio, hosting a contest, foisting my work on countless strangers, and doing so much more. Jen Forbus has overwhelmed me with her support of my work. Susan Shapiro has been a longtime source of wisdom and encouragement. I'm also thrilled that an incredible group of writers—including Megan Abbott, Ken Bruen, Reed Farrel Coleman, Ed Gorman, Jane Stanton Hitchcock, and Dennis Tafoya—took the time to read and blurb my work.

The support I've had from the crime-fiction community has been incredible. Some of the many I need to thank: Patti Abbott, Jedidiah Ayres, Nigel Bird, Judy Bobalik, Aldo Calcagno, Rebecca Cantrell, Lisa Cotoggio, David Cranmer, Elyse Dinh, Barna Donovan, Margery Flax, Cullen Gallagher, Kathleen Gerard, Jack Getze, Christopher Grant, Chris F. Holm, Kate Horsley, Fiona Johnson, Vince Keenan, Ray Adam Latiolais, B. V. Lawson, Sophie Littlefield, Maggie Lyons, Erin Mitchell, Lauren O'Brien, Dan O'Shea, Brad Parks, Keith

Rawson, Todd Ritter, Todd Robinson, Peter Rozovsky, Kathy Ryan, L. J. Sellers, Robin Spano, Julie Summerell, Sarah Weinman, Chuck Wendig, Holly West, Elizabeth A. White, Lina Zeldovich, and Dave Zeltserman. I'm also thankful for the support of my fellow members of Sisters in Crime, Mystery Writers of America, Crime Writers of Canada, International Thriller Writers, and to my pirate crew of fellow bloggers over at 7 Criminal Minds. A special shout-out to my wonderful friends on Twitter and Facebook, who keep me (passably) sane.

Others who deserve my deepest thanks: Darya Arden, Tom Best, Margaret Cannon, Suzanna Chang, Joan Chin, Beth Russell Connelly, Carolyn Cooke, Stephanie Craig, Barbara DeMarco-Barrett, Jessica DuLong, Leslie Elman, Alice Feiring, Alyson Gerber, Stacey Gibson, David Hayes, Amy Klein, Jenn Lawrence, Martin Levin, Pia Lindstrom, Helen Lovekin, Louisa McCune, Michael Mejias, Ellen Neuborne, Dorri Olds, Bethanne Patrick, Tony Powell, Rich Prior, Ilana Rubel, Jenna Schnuer, Rita Silva, Trish Snyder, Charlie Suisman, Alex Robertson Textor, Kate Walter, and Royal Young.

Heartfelt thanks to all my family and friends, who have been supportive of me from day one. A special thank-you to my mother, Sheila, for never complaining about the countless pages I send her way; her sharp eyes and solid editing instincts are invaluable to me. My father, John, is a one-man cheering squad, and I apologize to everyone he's tackled and forced to buy my work. My husband, Dan, manages to encourage me while giving great criticism, a rare feat.

Finally, thank you to everyone who has come to a reading or contacted me online after reading my work. I can't tell you how much that means to me.

THE NEXT ONE TO FALL

1

Standing at the edge of the mountain, I imagined what it would feel like to let go. There were thousands of feet between me and the valley of the winding Urubamba River. It was lush and green and oddly inviting. I stared down, feeling an exhilarating combination of anticipation and trepidation tugging at me.

"Say cheese, Tiger Lily."

The voice shoved my dark thoughts aside. "Not another photo." I looked at Jesse. "This is my fourth day in these clothes."

"It's only day two for that shirt. I'm pretty sure you changed yesterday." Jesse tousled my hair. "You're always so glamorous. It's kinda fun to see you roughin' it. Like Ava Gardner in *Mogambo*—you know, the scene where she tries to feed the baby elephant and gets mud all over her? That's so cute."

For a split second, I pictured the scene, and it almost made me smile. But the memory faded almost instantly, as if it were a relic of another life. I went back to studying the valley. "How high up are we?"

"Eight thousand feet. You breathin' okay, Lil?"

"Not bad. It's easier here than it was in Cusco." I didn't add that I'd felt like death in Cusco. For the past three months, I'd barely slept, unless I knocked myself out with sleeping pills. In Cusco, even the pills hadn't worked. The combination of thin Andean air and shallow breathing left my lungs starving for oxygen, and my body's panicked self-preservation mechanism kicked in every time I lost consciousness. A terrifying jolt of adrenaline would shock me awake, leaving me gasping and bolt upright in bed, as if I'd had a nightmare, though I rarely slept long enough, or deeply enough, for dreams anymore.

"That's 'cause Cusco is over eleven thousand feet above sea level," Jesse said. "We started at the top."

When we arrived in Peru, we'd headed straight to Cusco, the ancient Inca capital, and we'd started hiking the Inca Trail with a group the next day. It had sounded like an exciting plan when Jesse suggested it on the phone. In reality, I'd overestimated my abilities and my resilience. Now that we'd completed the four-day hike, all I could say for the Inca Trail was that it had worn me down to the point where I didn't care to see another moss-covered ruin again. I was so weary, it would only take the slightest gust of wind to knock me over and down and out for good. I wouldn't have cared.

"Hey! You payin' attention to any of this?" Jesse asked suddenly.

"Any of what?"

"That's what I thought! Here I am, tryin' to get you up to speed on Inca architecture, and you're starin' down there like a big magnet's pullin' you in."

"You should go back to the group. I'm such bad company right now." Not sleeping had left me dwelling permanently in twilight, and I couldn't shake myself out of it.

"I'm sorry, Lil. I'm just blabbin'. I know you're not yourself, for plenty of reasons." He didn't mention the obvious one, that my sister's funeral had taken place in January, three months and two days earlier. Instead, he cleared his throat. "I'm to blame for draggin' you here. Thought it would be good for us to spend time together, and to travel. Hell, I thought you'd be writin' stories and I'd be takin' photos to go with 'em. But I rushed you into this trip."

"No you didn't. I wanted to come." I couldn't remember why I'd agreed to do it. Jesse had talked me into it, of that I was certain. My friend could be very persuasive. He'd gone on about how the trip to Peru would pay for itself with work assignments for both of us—me as a writer and Jesse as a photographer—and that was probably true. But the real reason I'd agreed to the trip was that I had nowhere else I wanted to be. After Claudia's funeral, I'd drifted around New York, my hometown, in a daze. Then I'd returned to Spain, where I'd been living for the past year. My Barcelona apartment seemed hopelessly empty—even though I'd already been living there alone—and I felt like an inept ghost stumbling through it and bumping into walls. It had been a relief to go along with Jesse's plan. But I was just as miserable in Peru as I was everywhere else. The awful part was that now I was dragging Jesse down into quicksand with me.

"That's my girl." He put his arm around me, and I rested my head on his shoulder. For a minute, we were both quiet. "You hear that?" Jesse asked.

Straining my ears, I could hear a man speaking English with a local accent. "Now, I will tell you of Emperor Pachacutec, who built Machu Picchu. Did you know conquistadors never discovered the site? Everything is *exactly* as the emperor left it."

"That's Diego, isn't it?" I said.

"Yeah. Let's just hope he doesn't figure out we went AWOL and skipped out on his group."

Diego had been our guide through our four-day hike along the Inca Trail to Machu Picchu. He was a sweet man, but he had an unfortunate tendency to make everyone stand in place for an hour at a time while he described the history of a site and the mythology and folklore around it. I got more than enough of that from Jesse.

"He'll be upset when he finds out we're gone."

"But by then, we'll have had the fun of exploring Machu Picchu while it's almost empty," Jesse answered. "Those trainloads of tourists won't start arrivin' for an hour. We got the run of the most beautiful sight on earth. C'mon. Let's get a good head start on everybody else. So long, suckers."

He led me away from the ledge. My waterlogged hiking boots squished every time I put a foot down on the stones of the winding pathway. It had poured every day since we'd flown in to Cusco—no surprise, given that it was rainy season in the Andes. But now the sun had burned off the layers of mist and fog that had shrouded Machu Picchu as we'd hiked in through the Sun Gate. We didn't speak for what felt like ages, and then Jesse said, "It's gonna take Diego and everybody else a donkey's age to catch up with us here."

"Where . . ." I started to ask, but the question died on my lips. As we'd walked, I'd kept my eyes on the stone pathway, still slick with rainwater. Now that I lifted my eyes, I was breathless again. We were standing on the edge of the Inca city. On our left was a wall of perfectly fitted stone; below us, on my right, were endless layers of terraces, which resembled tiers of an epic cake. Ahead, there were more Inca walls, with triangular stone buildings perched atop them, row after tidy row. In the near distance, I could see another mountain, thin gray fog covering its peak like a veil.

"It's beautiful," I whispered.

"Told you it'd all be worth it, didn't I?" Jesse surveyed the city with satisfaction. "We have it all to ourselves for a little while."

He spoke too soon. A man's voice swept by us, faint but angry. "You lied to me."

"How dare you judge me!" The woman's voice was shrill.

"I was trying to help you."

"Leave me alone! I wish I'd never come back."

Jesse rolled his eyes. "Apparently there's no such thing as peace and quiet 'round here anymore."

"Paradise lost?" I tried to smile. "Was it ever really as good as you remember?"

"First time I came here, we were still in college. I'd never seen anyplace so beautiful. I love the mythology of it, too. How the Spanish looked for it but never found it. How Hiram Bingham was led here by farmers in 1911. Wish I could've seen it then." Jesse squinted, as if imagining the stones overgrown with vegetation. "You know we're standing in an earthquake zone, right? This has been here for five centuries. Nobody can figure how the Incas built the walls, how they made them so perfect." Jesse ran his hand over the stone wall. "You're touching what they made, not a reconstruction of it."

I touched the wall, surprised that it wasn't flat. The Incas hadn't shaved the stones to make them even, and looking at the differently sized and shaped pieces, I couldn't figure out what held them together.

"There's no mortar," Jesse added, as if reading my mind. "I'm not kiddin' about nobody today understanding how they put this together. It's like the biggest jigsaw puzzle on earth."

When I looked at the panorama of the city on the mountaintop, all I could think was how much I wished Claudia could have seen it. My sister had never cared much for travel, and she'd mocked me for flitting from place to place, but this would have impressed even her. My chest constricted when I thought of her, to the point where it sometimes became hard to breathe. It was as if her memory could strangle my heart. Then I heard a short, sharp shriek and felt a jolt of adrenaline crackling through me with the force of electricity.

"Did you hear that?" I asked Jesse.

"Sure did. C'mon, it was from this direction, I think."

We followed the stone path and heard another scream. Both of us rushed to the top of a steep staircase. At the bottom, completely still on the stone landing, was a woman's crumpled body.

2

Jesse ran down the steps and I followed him, almost tripping on a silver cylinder. There was nothing to grab to steady myself but the wall. Taking a deep, shuddering breath, I looked down and saw that Jesse had almost reached the woman. There was a noise behind me and I turned my head, catching sight of a man at the top of the staircase. His head was covered by a woolly Andean cap with ear flaps and pompoms. He was pale, and his chin had an unruly overgrowth of black beard. In the split second he was there, our eyes met, and then he ran.

"Lily!" Jesse called. I continued down the steps, holding the wall for support. As I got closer, the woman came into focus. Her long red hair cascaded over the cold, wet stone. She was wearing a black satin raincoat and black trousers, but only one foot had a shoe, a black patent wedge heel. The other must have gone over the side of the mountain. Her eyes opened suddenly, shocking me and making me hug the wall even closer. For a moment, I'd thought she was dead, but Jesse was saying, "You're gonna be okay," to her, over and over. Her lips were painted bright red, and they were moving, muttering words I couldn't make out. She was alive, but her skin had a grayish pallor, as if the color of the surrounding stones were seeping into her, and she pressed one hand against her chest.

"I gotta get help," Jesse said. "You stay with her, Lil."

"Please," the woman moaned. "Don't leave me."

My heart trembled. I didn't want to stay with a woman who looked as if she were about to die. "I'll get help," I said.

"You'll get lost, Lil. You stay here, keep her conscious." Jesse ran up the steps, his long legs taking them two at a time. At the top he vanished around the corner without a backward glance.

"Is this what a heart attack feels like?" the woman whispered. "Am I going to die?"

"Just hold on. Jesse's getting help. You're going to be fine."

"He made me drink something. At first, I didn't think it was doing anything but then . . ." She closed her eyes and her head drooped to the side.

"No! Stay awake!" I yelled.

Her eyes opened wide, as if I'd startled her. She stared, as if seeing me for the first time. "Who are you?"

"Lily." I knelt beside her. "What's your name?"

"Trista. Are you really here?"

I looked her over. She was about my height, with long, wavy hair dyed a dark burgundy red. Her body was skinny, even bony, suggesting that her prominent breasts, jutting like twin peaks through a thin T-shirt, might be as fake as her hair color. She could have been my age, thirty, or a little older. "What are you on?" I asked her. "Some kind of drug?"

"Go away." Her eyelids fluttered and shut.

I grabbed her hand and her shoulder, gently shaking both. "You need to stay awake, Trista." Her hand was sticky, and when I looked at it, I saw my own was now red with blood.

"What happened to you?" I tried not to panic. How badly hurt was she? I turned her hand and saw a gash in her palm. There was blood on her wrist, too. I tugged up the sleeve of her black raincoat to see the damage. The red was just a smear that must have come from her hand, but I noticed something else that made me catch my breath.

Track marks. The telltale trail of the junkie ran from her wrist into the crook of her elbow. They didn't look new, but they weren't that old, either. I knew, from long experience with my sister, exactly what scars they left behind, and that some of them never healed.

"What are you on right now?" I asked.

"Nothing!"

That was obviously a lie. I pulled back a little but she grabbed my wrist, as if suddenly alarmed I really might leave.

"Where's Len?" she whispered. Her nails dug into my wrist.

"Who's Len?" She didn't respond. "Was he the man you were fighting with?" With no one else around, I assumed that this woman was one half of the pair that had been fighting minutes earlier.

Her grip on me tightened. "You heard us fight?" Her eyes were open now, intense and lucid and fixed on mine. She was breathing hard. "What did you hear?"

I'd thought she was out of it, tripping on some drug, but suddenly she seemed wild and predatory, and I wished I'd kept my mouth shut. "He said you lied to him, and you said you wished you'd never come back," I admitted.

"What else?"

"That's it. My friend and I were talking . . ." My voice petered out as I watched her face. Her tongue was flicking at the corners of her mouth and her eyes were on the sky.

"Bastard. This is all his fault. He hates me." Her eyes were pale blue, and they seemed watery, as if she were about to cry. But she didn't; she blinked and took a few deep breaths as if girding herself up for something terrible. She grimaced and her eyes took on the hardness of flat stones. For a split second, I was less afraid for her than I was of her. "Doesn't matter. I hate him, too." She gritted her teeth as she spoke.

She was coherent and responsive, I had to keep her talking, but I didn't want to upset her any further. "There was a man at the top of the stairs. He had a Peruvian hat—the kind with the pompoms—and a black beard. Is that him?"

"Yes." Her breathing was ragged, and she let go of my wrist and pressed her hand to her chest again. "This is his way of getting rid of me."

"Rid of you?"

"Always knew I'd die young, but I didn't think it would end like this." She closed her eyes, but she wasn't drifting into unconsciousness. Her face contorted; she was obviously in pain.

"You're going to be okay, Trista. My friend went to get help. He'll be back any minute."

"I can't believe I was ever in love with that bastard. I threw away the best years of my life on him. But don't worry, I'm getting even." Her eyes opened and stared into mine with an urgency that both drew me in and made me want to back away. "Listen to me. Len made me drink something that made me sick. Then he pushed me down the stairs. Tell the police. Promise me."

"If you can't, I will. I promise."

"Don't let him get away with what he's done. If he didn't have daddy's money, Len would be in jail right now. But the money makes him untouchable."

I touched her cheek and the heat of her skin scorched my fingertips. Whether it was from a drug or a fever, she seemed to be burning up, and I could feel the pounding of her rapid heartbeat drumming through her.

"He's already crazy, so it wasn't hard to make him crazier."

Her eyes bulged and her mouth was open as she gasped. Whatever thin oxygen there was at this altitude wasn't enough for her lungs. She desperately needed help. "Maybe you should just rest right now."

Her head moved from side to side. "Do you hear the snakes?"

"Snakes?"

"The hissing." Her glassy eyes floated to my face again. She was raving now, mentally moving away from me and the mountain and—I hoped—the pain she was in. As long as she kept talking, there was hope. The risk with a concussion—which she had to have—was passing out and never waking up.

"I don't hear them," I said.

"Len said there'd be snakes," she said, panting. "He abandoned me before. After everything I did for him. Then he crawled back, just like Tina said he would."

She was getting agitated again. "I can hear people coming, Trista." There were footsteps, and the rumble of a voice, though still too far away to be distinct. "You're going to be fine."

"No I'm not." Her face twisted. "I'm going to die here."

"You'll be fine, Trista. I promise!" I was desperate to believe it myself.

"You can't promise me that," she whispered. Her lips moved again but no sound came out. I put my face close to hers, trying to hear her, but there was only the hiss of her gasps for breath.

"Everything's going to be okay." I forced myself to say the words, even though I could feel her pulse pounding at a furious rate. I was repeating them when her whole body started to tremble, then convulsed, and went still.

3

Jesse came running back with a security guard in tow, then disappeared again. The guard rushed down the steps, made sure Trista still had a pulse, and spoke in rapid-fire Spanish into a walkie-talkie. When Jesse returned, it was with a man, heavyset and in his mid-fifties, who took the steps at a painfully slow pace. The wind lifted tufts of white hair so that they waved around his head like a halo. "Well, what have we here?" he asked. His voice was deep and might have been reassuring in a hospital setting, but he spoke in a blunt tone that suggested he didn't approve of this interruption to his vacation.

"My friend and I heard her scream," I said. "We found her lying here."

"Unconscious?"

"No. I tried to keep her talking, so she would stay conscious. Some of what she said made sense and some of it . . ." I didn't know how to explain what I'd heard, and I let the words trail off.

"Hmm." He lifted Trista's eyelids and listened for her heartbeat. "It's like a pack of racehorses galloping in there. Did she mention having any medical conditions?"

"No, but she said she drank some kind of drug. I don't know what it was."

"Well, she's obviously an addict." I'd left Trista's sleeve rolled back, and the doctor spotted the track marks just as I had. But what had, for me, been a shock of recognition was, for him, a reason to dismiss her. "No wonder she collapsed. Taking drugs at altitude magnifies their impact. Her blood pressure is out of control."

"She said a man made her drink it, whatever it was," I insisted.

"Really? Did he make her shoot up with heroin, too?" The doctor's face was impassive. To him, she was already a lost cause.

I tried to keep my voice even. "He pushed her down the steps."

"What, these steps? That's ridiculous."

"That's what happened. She told me."

"Look, the steps go up, what, two hundred feet? Her head would have smashed open."

"Look at her hands," I insisted.

"Oh?" He examined the cut. "Bloody mess."

"That must have happened when she fell."

He raised his shaggy eyebrows at me. "She might have tripped and cut her hand on the edge of a step." He peered at her more closely.

I was about to snap back at him when I remembered my own hand. I'd held Trista's, and her blood was on me. For a second, the vibrant green of the valley and the harsh whiteness of the stones swirled around me. I thought I was going to pass out, but a hand touched my shoulder.

"Best we get outta the way," Jesse said in a soft voice. "They're comin' over with a stretcher to carry her out, and from what I can make out they're gonna do a medical evacuation. Kinda hard to tell what they're sayin' in Peruvian Spanish, though."

He led me up a few steps, then foraged in his pocket until he found a foil packet that contained a lone towelette. "This might not get it all off, but try it till we get to the restroom."

I rubbed it between my palms. There wasn't a lot of blood, but it had dried in enough to be difficult to remove. "Did you see the man she was with?" I asked Jesse.

"Who?"

"We heard them fighting. His name is Len. Peruvian hat, black beard."

"Nope. He must've gone to get help. Maybe they're making arrangements to evacuate her now."

I turned and looked down at Trista. At even this short distance, she'd become blurry. I could make out her red hair and black coat. The white-haired doctor was still kneeling beside her, but there was nothing urgent about his movements. I dropped down onto a step, feeling nauseated. Jesse continued to stand, rubbing my neck and back. I tried to take deep breaths and wished I could stop shaking. When I closed my eyes, it was Claudia whom I saw instead; she was lying on the floor of my apartment after overdosing on heroin. She'd almost died that time, but I'd managed to save her. Then, not long ago, I'd failed her and she'd died.

"C'mon. Let's go up a little farther." Jesse's voice cut into my thoughts.

We climbed till we got near the top. I was having trouble breathing again, and I kept my eyes on the steps, focusing my attention on not tripping. I'd forgotten about the silver container that had almost made me lose my footing, but I spotted it again and grabbed it.

"What's that?" Jesse asked.

The cylinder was small, less than four inches long, rounded

except for one flat edge. The initials *MBW* were engraved on it in an ornate script. "It's a lipstick case," I said, popping it open. Some shards of its mirror fell out.

"That's some serious bad luck. What's *MBW* stand for?"

"I don't know. She told me her name is Trista." I pulled the lipstick tube out, careful to avoid any glass fragments. It was made by Chanel, and *Excessive* was written on the bottom. I opened it and saw a fiery red, as startling as blood.

"Maybe somebody else dropped it," Jesse suggested.

It looked exactly like what Trista was wearing, but I couldn't get the words out. Instead, I stared at it for a moment, then shut the case and thrust it at Jesse with shaking hands. "Would you hold it?"

"Sure. You look a little green around the gills, Lil."

I was leaning against the wall for balance. The lipstick had brought to mind the queasy memory of the blood on Trista's hand, and on my own. I wasn't phobic about blood, but I was badly shaken by what I'd seen and heard.

"You think you can make it up the last few steps?" Jesse asked. "We're gonna have to clear out so they can get a stretcher through here."

I looked up, seeing the growing body of onlookers crowding at the top of the staircase to peer at the scene below. At that moment I felt frozen, unable to go up or down. But the moment passed and a shout from below made me look down. Trista was convulsing again. I was too far away to make out the expression on her face, but the twitching of her head and arms was obvious. Suddenly, she stopped, and I knew what the doctor was going to say before the words came out of his mouth.

Even though the guards tried to shoo onlookers away, the crowd kept growing. Jesse dragged me away, so we didn't see Trista's body being carried up on a stretcher. He led me to what he called the central plaza, a flat rectangle that could have doubled as a football field. There were llamas grazing on the green grass growing there, and Jesse tried to distract me, calling one over and feeding it trail mix. The animal was a curious mixture of tame and wild: domesticated enough to expect to be fed, but not enough to allow anyone to pet him. Jesse took pictures of the animal while I paced and bit my lip and wished desperately for a cigarette. Smoking was another thing that became very difficult at high altitudes, unless you enjoyed the sensation of gasping for air after a couple of drags. I'd been indulging heavily in my old bad habits—nicotine and alcohol—since my sister's funeral, and part of me suspected that Jesse had lured me on the trip to get me to quit smoking and drink less. There was a giant lump in my throat, as if I'd pulled a hunk of rock out of the Inca wall and tried to swallow it. I heard a choked cry and realized it had come from my mouth.

"You okay, Lil?"

"I just can't believe it." Dimly aware that I was in shock, I tried to put my thoughts in order. Trista's fight with her boyfriend had led to her death moments later. An hour before that, maybe they'd been a happy couple, excited about seeing

Machu Picchu. No, I realized suddenly, what Trista had told me was quite the opposite. *He hates me. Doesn't matter. I hate him.* It hadn't felt like the heat of a fight, but something cold and hard and bitter. What had she been doing here with him, anyway? "One moment, she was alive, and then..." Her track marks flashed in front of my eyes. Her arms were pale and slender, like Claudia's, and scarred in the same horrible way. Trista was a complete stranger to me, yet I felt that I knew her in a way too intimate to put into words.

"I know. It's an awful shame."

"Her boyfriend hasn't come back." I'd been watching for Len's return, but he hadn't made one. I couldn't explain why my stomach had dropped when I'd seen him at the top of the stairs. When he ran, I'd assumed he had gone to get help. But where had he ended up, and why hadn't he come back? It was hard to come up with an innocent explanation for that, especially since Trista had said, *This is his way of getting rid of me.* Hairs started rising on the back of my neck as I realized she might have meant it literally. He'd given her something to drink—drugging her—and he'd pushed her down the stairs. No, not the whole flight—the doctor was right, no one could have fallen that distance, on solid stone, without becoming a mass of bruised, open wounds. But maybe he'd pushed her when she was already near the bottom landing . . . or tried to push her off the mountain?

"He's probably talkin' to the guards or some officials right now."

"He poisoned her."

"Lil?" Jesse's face registered surprise and concern. "Calm down. You don't know anything like that. That's a terrible thing to do, accusin' some fella of that."

Trista's words echoed in my head. *This is his way of getting rid of me.* Then, later: *He's already crazy so it wasn't hard to make him crazier.* I was silent, turning them over in my mind.

More and more people were surging toward the staircase. Many of the tourists wore cheap, brightly colored rain ponchos, in shades of pink and yellow and green that made them look like an electric rainbow. People who hadn't seen any part of what had really happened were lining up to talk to the police. They'd have some story to tell their friends back home.

I sagged against a wall. Everything around me was surreal, as if the scene were playing on a giant movie screen. The setting was perfect for an old CinemaScope film. Now that the sun was shining brightly at Machu Picchu, the site was revealed in its magnificence. I was standing in a city made of stone, built over the crest of a mountain. Something I'd once read had claimed that New York, my hometown, would be flooded within three days if people vanished, and that within two years it would start to collapse. But for the better part of five hundred years, Machu Picchu had been empty, and yet it was as solid as if it had been lovingly tended all that time. The smell of it was earthy and damp from the onslaught of the rainy season, but to my eyes it was grandeur and majesty, especially the peak of Huayna Picchu that loomed over everything just beyond the city. I looked at it as if regarding a postcard: I saw it, but I wasn't really there. The people around me chattered away, mostly in Spanish or English, though there were a few German voices I heard, too. Just background noise until, occasionally, the words whipping around me did sink in.

"I heard that a gust of wind blew her down, right over the side of the mountain," a man said.

"That couldn't possibly happen," a petite gray-haired lady who seemed to be his wife corrected him.

"I didn't say I *saw* it, that's just what I *heard*," the man groused.

"My neighbor came here the time they had those giant mudslides, when they were evacuating people by helicopter. Whole bunch of people died here that time," another woman added.

It felt ghoulish to listen to them, but I couldn't tune them out. Listening to the other so-called witnesses was like hearing a game of Telephone brought to a crime scene. Everyone had a different take, and rumor and conjecture took the place of facts.

I was the last person the officer spoke with. "Did you see the woman?" he asked. His question was routine but the way he asked it sounded as if he were genuinely interested.

"Her name was Trista," I told him.

He raised his eyebrows. "And her family name?"

"I don't know that," I admitted. That was the paradox: I knew intimate things about her that some of her closest friends likely didn't, and yet I knew next to nothing about who she'd been.

"Have you seen her, before this morning?"

"No."

"Very well. Tell me what you did see."

I took him through it: the snippet of an overheard argument, Trista's screams and our discovery of her, and what she'd told me on that cold stone landing as I'd held her hand. "You have to find the man she was with," I said. "His name is Len. He's white, and he has a black beard. I saw him for a moment at the top of the staircase, and then he ran away. Trista said he wanted rid of her and he pushed her down the stairs."

His eyebrows crept higher. "The doctor said she did not fall. She was an addict." He must have seen something in my face that made him think I didn't comprehend what he was saying, because he pantomimed injecting a hypodermic needle into his arm.

My tongue seemed stuck to the roof of my mouth. "The man she was with gave her a drug," I said, but my voice came out shaky, a faint protest. The officer wasn't listening; he was already closing his notepad.

"People like that can't be trusted. If she was fighting with the man, she may be trying to get him into trouble."

The offhand, dismissive tone of his comment hit me as hard as the words themselves. People like that? My sister had told me, many times, how people pretended not to see her when she was homeless. *They don't think a junkie deserves to share the same sidewalk as them,* she'd said. I knew from experience that an addict could lie about anything to get a fix, but that didn't mean they didn't know what the truth was, or wouldn't tell it in other circumstances. "The fact that Trista used drugs doesn't mean that her statements are meaningless or untrue. Where did that man go? Why hasn't he come back? Why aren't you looking for him?"

"We are." His tone was curt, as if he resented my question.

"Hey," Jesse said, coming up behind me. "You done, Lil?" He smiled at the officer. "Hope you fellas got something that'll help."

"No one knows who that woman is or where she came from." The officer shook his head. "It is frustrating."

"Maybe that silver case we found on the steps will help. Fingerprints or somethin', right?"

"It's strange about the initials. *MBW*. Odd if her name really was Trista." The officer gave me a sly look that suggested he thought my story was less than credible. Maybe he thought I was an addict, too.

"I thought everybody checking into a hotel in Peru had to show ID, and the hotel keeps a copy. That right?" Jesse asked.

"Yes. By law in Peru, each tourist checking into a hotel must show identification—their passport and tourist card. But we have not found her hotel. Not yet."

The officer took down my name, then asked if the hotels I would be staying at in Machu Picchu and Cusco were the same as Jesse's. After the officer and guards left, Jesse put his arm around me.

"Did you hear our conversation?" I asked him. "Did you catch any of his comments on addicts?"

"Oh, *that*'s why you were gettin' so worked up. I saw you come up all hot and bothered. Thought you might sock the guy, so I ducked in."

"I'm not worked up. Not *that* worked up." I amended my claim when Jesse gave me a who-are-you kidding look. "I know what Trista said. Maybe she was confused about some things . . ." And raving about hissing snakes, though I didn't add that aloud. "But she was fighting with her boyfriend and next thing she's dead."

"You think he killed her?"

"He ran off and he didn't come back. That's some kind of admission of guilt. What do you think?"

He rested his head on top of mine. "I think we should head on down to our hotel. No one's got the heart for a sight-seein' tour right now."

"How do we get down the mountain?" The thought made me a little bit desperate. I felt trapped up there.

"There's buses up and down."

"Buses?"

Jesse walked a couple of steps down the stairs. There was no railing for support or security, and so he held his hand out for me, and led me into one of the huts. The ones closest to the entryway had thatched roofs over them, but this one was open to the sky. Jesse pointed through the tall window on one side. Through it, I could see white scars on the mountainside. These weren't terraces; instead, they were two rows at intervals, obscured at both ends by vegetation. "Those are the switchbacks up the mountain," Jesse said. "The trains arrive in the valley, then you gotta take a bus up thataway."

"That just doesn't look like a good idea."

"Just hope you're not scared of roller coasters, Tiger Lily."

"That's not . . . that's not how we get down from here, is it?" I wanted off the mountain, but I was afraid to go down. Considering the trip down the mountainside made me lightheaded with vertigo. That was stupid, I chided myself. I'd gone ziplining in British Columbia and rock climbing in Rai Leh in Thailand, so why did I feel paralyzed at the idea of taking a bus? Since Claudia had died, my perception of the world had changed. I didn't feel adventurous anymore; instead, I felt as if I were marking time until my own funeral. Death seemed to trail after me. When I left New York to return to my rented apartment in Barcelona, it tagged along in my suitcase. It was subtle, wary of getting too close too soon, but I felt its taunting presence. It was like a chilly draft that brushed across my throat every now and then, just to remind me it was always close.

I didn't have any more family for it to steal away. My father, mother, and sister were gone, and there was no extended family that I was in contact with. So death skulked around the edges of my world. It peered into my mind, drinking in the strange, inappropriate thoughts I was having. A few weeks earlier I'd climbed to the top of Sagrada Familia, the unfinished cathedral Antoni Gaudí had designed for Barcelona.

Standing on one of its catwalks, exposed to the elements, I looked down and wondered what it would feel like to fall. Vertigo made me feel as if I were about to pitch forward, and for a split second, I thought the ground was rushing to meet me, and I jolted back.

It would be so easy to let go, said a woman standing behind me, in English. Dressed in chic black, she was staring down as well. I wasn't sure what made me pull back that day, and why that night, when I'd talked to Jesse on the phone, I'd agreed to go with him to Peru. I'd doubted my decision ever since. Now, a woman was dead and I felt the weight of it on my shoulders. Rationally, I knew it had nothing to do with me, but that didn't stop the pressure I felt under my rib cage, bumping up against my heart.

"If you don't want to go down now, we don't have to, Lil. If you don't want the bus, there's a staircase we can walk down. That would take maybe an hour to ninety minutes, dependin' on how you're feelin'. Whatever you want, we'll do." Jesse shrugged his backpack off and set it on the ground. "We can stay here long as you like. There's a snack bar by the tourist entrance—you didn't see that yet 'cause we hiked in through the Sun Gate. And there's the Sanctuary Lodge. It's kinda ritzy, but on account of what's happened I bet we'd be able to—"

"Jesse," I said suddenly. "Can we go back to where Trista fell?"

"Why'd you want to do that?"

"She told me she fell. I know she wasn't bruised up, but that cut on her hand was bad." The truth was, I wanted to go back and look for evidence that could back up what she had told me, before a steady flow of visitors swept it away. "The doctor said it wasn't a fall, and the police believe him. But the doctor didn't hear what she said."

"You want to prove the dead girl right, don't you?"

"I just want the police to take her death seriously. Do you think that's too much to ask?"

He looked at me, and I wondered if he saw Claudia's ghost in my eyes, because his handsome face looked grim. But he answered, " 'Course not. Let's go."

5

The crowd had dispersed when Jesse and I returned to the staircase. There was no police tape, or any marker roping it off. There were people around, but no cluster of poncho-clad tourists holding their collective breath while waiting for the next scene in the drama unfolding in front of them. That was such a cynical way to think, I chided myself, but deep down, I felt that no one had cared about Trista. Did her boyfriend even care? Where was he now? Other people had been curious, and being a witness to a tragedy would just be another souvenir collected on the trip.

There was a huge, broad-shouldered man with a shaved head moving slowly down the stairs, step by step, as a billowing black raincoat flapped around him. I wondered if he was having trouble with the altitude and the thin air. If he was overweight, he was probably having a very difficult time, I realized. But he bent down suddenly and stood again in a swift movement that made it clear he had no disability.

"So what are we looking for?" Jesse asked, jolting me to attention.

"Anything we missed before."

"So, needle in a haystack, but we don't know what all the needle looks like," Jesse said.

"You've got it."

"Well, okay. The best way out of a difficulty is through it."

"Did you just quote Robert Frost?" I asked.

" 'Course not. Will Rogers." He looked vaguely insulted. "Let's get to it."

On the stairs, I didn't feel any vertigo. Somehow, I'd expected to, because they were so steep and there was nothing to grab to steady myself if I tripped. It was a long way down, but my sense of purpose outweighed my anxiety. Jesse went ahead of me, surveying each step. I followed, studying the scene for anything we'd missed earlier.

Forty steps down, a passageway branched off from the stairs. "Now that's interestin'," Jesse said, stepping onto it.

"What is it?"

"Hold your horses. I'll be right back."

Patience wasn't a virtue I possessed, but I bit my lip and I continued down the steps, looking at each one for . . . something. A hint, a clue. No, that wasn't quite true. I was looking for blood. Trista's hand had been bleeding. Had that happened when she fell, or was it possible that there'd been some physical violence between her and her vanished boyfriend?

I took the steps carefully, looking for any sign. There was nothing. A wave of disappointment crashed over me. What had I been hoping to find? Had I really thought there'd be a clue about Trista's identity, or about the man she was with? That was a childish fantasy. What was I going to discover that would convince the police to look at her death as anything other than an accident involving an addict? Maybe that was wrongheaded, too. After all, the fact that I'd spoken to exactly one officer who didn't seem to care much didn't mean that no one on the police force would investigate.

All of these thoughts disappeared as I lifted my gaze from the steps long enough to catch sight of the hulking man jumping off the side of the landing. One moment he was there, and in the next he was gone. Had I just witnessed a suicide? I screamed and ran down the remaining steps to the landing, peering over the edge. I'd expected to see the side of the mountain; instead, the drop down was about ten feet, onto a grassy terrace. The man was moving from a crouch to a standing position, making a show of dusting his clothing off with his hands, but I saw the glint of silver as he put something in his pocket.

"Did you scream?" he called up to me, looking faintly amused. His face startled me. He was in his late thirties and a thick scar stood out, pink against his well-tanned skin. It ran vertically from under his eye to his chin. He spoke English, but his husky voice had an accent. "I'm sorry. I didn't mean to scare you, *mina*."

"*Mina?*" I was baffled. In Spanish, that meant a mine.

He smiled more broadly, but the scarred side of his face didn't move. "In my country, *mina* is what we call an attractive woman."

Even though I spoke Spanish fluently, and had no trouble living in Spain, traveling in Spanish-speaking parts of South America was a challenge. Each country had its own distinctive take on the language, with different pronunciations and local vocabulary. "Why did you jump down there?"

"Why not?" He shrugged. "The view from here is very good. Come down. I'll show you."

"Are you crazy?"

He laughed. "Maybe. Don't be scared."

"I'm not leaping down there. There's no way back up."

He looked around, taking note of that fact for what seemed to be the first time. "*Estoy jodido.* Always leaping before I look. Hold on, *mina*."

He walked along the terrace, away from me. About a dozen yards away he found a ledge and pulled himself up to it. He wasn't overweight at all; the reason that he'd appeared to have no neck was that he was corded with muscle.

"You okay?"

I turned at the sound of Jesse's voice. My friend was rushing down the steps toward me.

"You heard me scream, didn't you?" I said. "False alarm. I saw someone go off the side of the landing. Turns out it's not such a big step down."

Jesse stood next to me and peered over the edge. "In some places it's a sheer drop, then in others you get these terraces. That's how the Inca farmed. They'd flatten parts of the mountain so they could grow crops up here. Genius. You're gonna see these terraces all over the place in Peru. Just wait till we hit the Colca Canyon."

"Sounds like you're on the grand tour of Peru, *mina*."

I turned and saw the man had pulled himself up from the ledge to the edge of the landing. He was breathing hard, but it was still an impressive feat. He smelled of cologne—not unpleasant, a little like a smoky wood fire, but also too heavily applied.

"I still can't believe you did that," I told him. "What did you find down there?"

"Find?"

"You picked up something silver."

He laughed. "You are sharp as well as beautiful. How's this: I will show it to you if you tell me your name, *mina*."

Jesse spoke suddenly. "You happen to know that a woman *died* on these steps today?"

The man looked at him as if noticing him for the first time. He and Jesse were about the same height, but Jesse's lean body looked slight next to his. The man nodded solemnly. "This staircase? Yes, I heard someone died. What a tragic accident."

He looked at me again and smiled, completely unconcerned about Trista.

"What's *your* name?" I asked him.

"Bastián." He paused, then added, "Has anyone ever told you that your eyes are the color of emeralds?"

"She's heard that plenty," said Jesse.

"I'm sure she has. How could she not? They are startling and very beautiful." He started to say something else, but Jesse interrupted him.

"Where you from?"

"Chile."

"Chile? Hey, I love Chile," Jesse said. "You know what I go to see when I'm there? The Monument to the Disappeared. You know it, don't you? In Santiago's Cementerio General, a stone's throw from the Pinochet family mausoleum."

Bastián's face was sour now; the scar made his expression almost threatening. "It is popular these days to reject what General Pinochet did for his country."

"The abducting, terrorizing, and murdering, you mean?" Jesse's voice was hard and sharp without its folksy charm. Hearing him pronounce each syllable sharply made me realize how annoyed he was.

"Without him, Chile would be in as sad a state as Peru." Bastián crossed his arms. There were scars on his hands, crisscrossing his knuckles.

Jesse's hand settled on my shoulder. "Sweetheart, I just remembered, we left the camera bag back at the gate," he said. I didn't understand what was bothering him so much, but I wasn't leaving until I saw what Bastián had found on the terrace.

"Ava," I said suddenly, glancing at Bastián. "Now you have to show me what you picked up down there."

"Like the actress, Ava Gardner? How appropriate." He put his hand in his pocket and held up a silver compact. It looked doll-sized in his hand, and it was surprisingly plain, without any engraving or even a scalloped edge. Bastián started to put it away, but I touched his hand and he stopped. But the moment I tried to lift it out of his palm he pocketed it again.

"I'd best turn this over to the authorities," Bastián said. "How do you say it, the sooner the better?" Abruptly, he turned and headed up the steps, his feet thudding heavily on the stone. He stopped and turned. "I'll look for you later, Ava." He continued up the stairs, departing without a backward glance.

"Why'd you talk to that creep in the first place?" Jesse asked.

"I wanted to know what he was doing." My mind was on the silver compact.

"That guy was a thug for the Pinochet regime."

"How can you possibly know that?"

"Let's just say that the Monument to the Disappeared is a divisive issue. You know how people stand on the dictatorship by what they think of it. The scars on that fella, he was either tortured by Pinochet's men, or one of them himself."

"So that's why you brought out the guard dog routine," I said. "He was just trying to flirt."

"Will you promise me that you won't pick up any more thugs on this trip? Last thing you need is a droolin' psycho making eyes at you."

"He wasn't that bad."

Deep down you're pretty superficial.

For a fraction of a second, I thought I heard my sister's voice. Claudia loved paraphrasing a line of Ava Gardner's and shooting it at me. And she was right. I was standing in the place where Trista died, and yet I was superficial enough to turn that compact over and over in my mind, as if it had some special meaning.

"Why did you go running off?"

"I found a path back up, and I wanted to follow it. I was thinkin' on what you said about that guy. Maybe that lady fell from that landin', and he ran to get help and got all confused. This place is like a maze, only it's spread over a mountaintop." Jesse shrugged. "I dunno. It's hard to figure if that's important. Probably not." He frowned at me. "What's wrong?"

"The compact," I told him. "Bastián held it up, but he wouldn't let go of it."

"Yeah, so?"

"He was holding up the bottom. That's why it was so plain. The engraving was on the other side. What do you want to bet the initials *MBW* are on it?"

"Maybe he thought you were gonna take it away from him?" Jesse suggested.

"Don't you get it?" I asked. "We came here looking for anything Trista might have dropped this morning. That's exactly what he was doing, too."

On the bus barreling down the side of the mountain, Jesse and I were both subdued. My friend sat beside me, staring out the window. I tried to not think about Trista herself, and instead focus my brain on my frustrating conversation with the police officer and my vaguely flirtatious exchange with the man who called himself Bastián. Was that even his real name? Not that I had any right to judge; I'd told him mine was Ava, after all. But the more I pushed Trista's face away, the closer her shade got, until she seemed to whisper in my ear. *I always knew I'd die young, but I didn't think it would be like this.* Then, a moment later, *I'm going to die here.*

Why had I promised her she wouldn't? Another lie from my mouth. It reminded me of how my father used to promise me everything would turn out all right. I'd always believed him, and then one day he was murdered and nothing was ever right again with my family.

I was jolted out of my guilty thoughts by the bus driver jamming on the brakes and suddenly reversing. I grabbed Jesse's arm. "What's going on?"

"These switchbacks are so narrow, two buses can't pass each other," he said. "We just met another bus head-on. We could play a game of chicken . . . or we could do the responsible thing. That's why we're backin' up to the last elbow to let them pass."

The bus's slow, backward progress made me shiver. "There must be accidents on the mountain all the time."

"Nope. The drivers are real good." He patted my arm. "Try to relax, okay? I know that's not your strong suit, Lil."

Everyone was silent as the bus rolled back, waited for its twin to pass by, and continued down the mountainside. It was only then that I realized I'd been holding my breath.

"Surely it's incredibly rare for a traveler to die at Machu Picchu," the woman in the seat behind me said. Her nasal voice was much too loud for a confined space. "I wonder if it really was an accident or, you know, foul play."

"Really, Gemma, you have the most overeager imagination." Her male companion was quiet and unamused.

"I read that there's a terrorist group in the jungle. They sometimes kill tourists."

"They're called Shining Path," the man answered. "They were Marxists until they discovered how profitable the drug trade is. And no, I don't think they came down from the jungle in the north to kill a tourist here. You've got to stop reading those blasted Agatha Christies."

"I don't read her, I read Walter Mosley and Dennis Lehane and Val McDermid," the woman answered. She was huffy now.

"Well, pick up some nonfiction for a change. It will do you some good."

"For the record, I do read nonfiction. As a matter of fact, maybe you should read some of what's on my shelves."

"Such as?"

"*The Animals Are Innocent.* That's a book that will teach you a thing or two about taking the official story of a tourist's death at face value."

The title of the book hit a bull's-eye in my memory. I'd

never read the book, but I remembered the older travel journalist who'd recommended it to me. I'd met her on the very first press trip I'd ever taken, a junket to Barbados; at the time, I thought she was bitter and mean. I'd been thrilled to come to the island, and I'd annoyed her with my gullible innocence. *You need to understand something, newbie,* she'd told me. *Tourism boards are paid to lie to you. That's their job. Stop thinking you're so lucky to be here. Every dollar they spend wining and dining you gets them a hundredfold return when you write an article. And, newbie, if anything bad happens to you while you're on the road? Just remember they'll sweep you under the rug with the rest of the trash.*

She'd written *The Animals Are Innocent* on a cocktail napkin and put it in my hand. Then, when I'd see her at dinner, she'd repeat the phrase. All that had done was made me avoid her, but now that I heard the phrase again, I had to know what it meant.

"Excuse me," I said, turning around in my seat. The man and woman were in their late sixties, wearing identical blue rain ponchos. "I heard you mention *The Animals Are Innocent.* I know I've heard of it . . ."

"Oh, yes. You wouldn't be likely to ever forget it," the woman answered. "It was a real-life case. This poor girl— oh, what was her name?—well, she was a wildlife photographer who was murdered in Kenya. But the government tried to pretend she'd committed suicide, and then, when that was shown to be completely false, they pretended she'd been attacked by wild animals."

"I remember that," her companion said, snapping his fingers. "Nineteen eighty-eight. Julie Ward. Her father fought for more than a decade to get justice for her. Poor girl had been completely hacked to pieces, but it was all cleanly done. It was obvious from the beginning she was murdered, and equally obvious that the Kenyan government was going to lie about it to protect their growing tourism industry."

"That's horrible," I said. "Did they ever catch—"

"Well, yes and no. They got the man who did it, and there was a trial a decade after her death. But he was acquitted." The man shook his head. "Tragic business."

"Yes." I sank back into my seat. "Thank you."

"In case y'all weren't depressed enough already," Jesse whispered, patting my arm.

We sat quietly as the bus arrived at the foot of the mountain. It continued on over a short bridge and stopped in front of a pedestrian pavement with tourist cafés and shops. The doors opened, our signal to depart, but no one moved very swiftly. My legs felt like jelly, and I suspected that wasn't uncommon, given the combination of the endless staircases at Machu Picchu and the gut-churning drive. Jesse went ahead of me, stepped off the bus, and held his hand out to help me disembark. Normally, it would have just been a sweet, courtly gesture, but I was so shaken that I needed the help.

I looked around. This wasn't the town's plaza, but it looked like the main drag in a very small town. There wasn't much to it but a slightly raised pair of concrete sidewalks that sloped upward, past boxy two- and three-story buildings. Most of the structures were gray, but a few were painted yellow or orange or blue, and most of them had colorful banners flying out front, advertising a restaurant or a hostel. "Hold on for a minute, Jesse." I let go of his hand and walked up to the nearest police officer, who was staring at his phone, texting. He wasn't the one I'd spoken with that morning, but he looked familiar, as if he might have been part of the police contingent that had taken statements. "Perdón," I said. "Puedo pedirle que—"

"Hi. Can I help you?" he answered in English.

"My name is Lily Moore. I was one of the people who found the woman who died on the mountain this morning."

"Yes, a very sad case."

"I wanted to ask you if you'd found out who she was yet."

"We are still investigating." He sounded formal, but he looked almost too young to be wearing his uniform.

"In other words, no."

He glanced around, as if making sure no one else was listening. "We have checked all the hotels, and we haven't found any record of this woman. No one admits knowing her."

"I'd like to talk to the investigating officer. Can that be arranged?"

"You know something?"

"Let's just say, I've seen a few strange things. There was a man there when she fell, and it doesn't sound like he's come forward." I told him where I was staying and watched him text a note. "Thanks," I said, starting to walk away before I remembered something else I wanted to ask about. "Wait, did a man turn in a silver compact?"

"Silver com-pact?"

"It's for makeup. About this big." I held up my index finger and thumb. "A man found it near the woman's body. He said he would turn it in."

"I will ask, but I don't know about this com-pact."

Of course not, I thought. Bastián had found exactly what he was looking for.

"You wanna tell me what that was all about?" Jesse asked as we headed toward our hotel. Since Aguas Calientes, the little town at the base of the mountain, lacked amenities such as sidewalks away from the center of town, we were making our way along the train tracks. To the right of us was a long string of market stalls, some shiftier looking than others, all of them hawking knitted caps, brightly colored bandanas, embossed shot glasses, and other junk tourists never needed but were willing to buy as keepsakes while away from home.

"You heard everything, didn't you?" I glanced sideways at him. Jesse was a hopeless busybody who had no shame about opening my mail or listening in on phone conversations. The idea that he'd missed my conversation with the officer was unlikely. "I just wanted to talk to someone about that woman. About Trista, I mean." It felt disrespectful to refer to her as *that woman,* as if she'd lost her identity as well as her life.

"Yeah, I heard that. But talk about *what*?"

"Bastián and the silver compact, for one thing. Also Len, the amazing disappearing boyfriend. Where the hell did he go? Why hasn't he come forward?"

"The cops are already lookin' for him, Lil. You don't need to tell them again. And about the compact . . ."

"What?"

"I'd say let sleepin' dogs lie. I gave them the lipstick thing we found. *MBW*, who knows what that stands for? But it's up to them to figure it all out."

"The cop I talked to this morning was already writing off Trista's death as an accident, because of her track marks." I shook my head. "I just feel that somebody has to take her death seriously. I need to talk to the police."

"But why should that someone be you?" Jesse's face was serious. "Thing is, Peru is not a place where you want more contact with cops than absolutely necessary."

"Why not?"

"Pretty doll for you, miss!" called out one of the hawkers, a woman about my age. She stepped into my path, carrying a foot-tall doll dressed in a colorful Andean costume, complete with broad-brimmed hat. She thrust it forward so suddenly she almost smacked me in the head with it, and I was annoyed as I ducked back and around her. Then I glanced into her stall and saw two toddlers playing with a baby. The woman's aggression suddenly seemed more like desperation, and I felt stirrings of guilt. With all of the places I'd been to, many of them countries poorer than Peru, you would think I'd have developed a tougher skin. But what I was used to was people begging. In Mumbai, there was no end to the mutilated people sitting next to begging bowls. In Bangkok, children literally wandered into traffic to beg from tourists in taxis and tuk-tuks. While I was often sheltered when I traveled—public relations people usually charted my course, steering me to the scenic and primly sidestepping the seedy—it was impossible not to see hardship in so many parts of the world. I had yet to actually see a person beg in Peru; instead, people were determined to sell you things. There was a kind of pride about it that I found hard to resist.

"How much?" I asked her.

"No!" Jesse said, tugging my arm. The woman looked crestfallen, but the tone of my friend's voice didn't leave room for debate.

"Why not buy something?" I whispered.

"Look, there are good markets with handicrafts and all that, like Pisac. Some of this stuff was made in other countries and imported for sale here."

"That happens everywhere," I pointed out. "Remember Mr. Ika?" Mr. Ika was an Easter Island native Jesse and I had encountered when we were traveling a couple of years earlier. On our first day there, the group we were with had bought every carving and necklace he was selling on his pair of folding card tables. *It's going to take me a month to make more things to sell,* he'd told us. Then we'd seen him the very next day with a table full of the same trinkets he'd sold the day before. *Bet it took him all night to take the "Made in China" stickers off that stuff,* Jesse had said at the time.

" 'Course I remember Mr. Ika. I never forget anybody who takes me for a ride," Jesse grumbled. "That's what I got against this place, too. I mean, look at it." We both stared ahead. Along the train tracks, there were stalls, and hawkers, and children.

"It's depressing."

"Lemme give you a down 'n dirty history of Aguas Calientes," Jesse answered. "A few decades ago, there was nothin' here 'cept a tiny railway workers' camp. Then they found some hot springs a little north. After that, some bright light got the idea that since all tourists who see Machu Picchu have to come through here, it's the perfect place to fleece 'em."

"That's harsh."

"That's just the truth. This ain't some slum like they got

ringed around Lima. This is a place folks set up just to take advantage of rich tourists. That's its whole purpose."

"We're obviously not rich. We've been hiking for four days. If we were on a street in New York, people would think we're homeless."

"You're not gonna make me explain why you're a rich tourist, are you?"

"I'm rich because I was rich enough to get here in the first place," I quoted. We'd had this discussion before. We both traveled the world, but Jesse refused to go on press tours, preferring instead to strike out on his own or with a friend. Next to him, my trips were tame, and they were usually underwritten by luxury hotels.

"Right. The really rich folks are stayin' up in the clouds at that Sanctuary Lodge. That costs upward of eight hundred a night, American dollars. Down here, you can stay at Gringo Bill's for under a hundred. But that's still an awful lot of money in a country where per-capita income is on the underbelly of nine thousand dollars."

We got to the train station, which sat at the edge of the town. While the track itself seemed to be used as a walkway by locals, the station itself looked like a ramshackle fortress. It was really just a bit of track covered with a peaked roof of corrugated metal; the platform was a slab of concrete, maybe six inches above the track, with yellow safety lines painted on it. The perimeter of the station was marked with a tall wire fence and uniformed guards at every entry point. They wouldn't let us walk through the station, even though the entrance to our hotel, the Inkaterra, was just on the other side. Instead, they pointed to some concrete steps, which took us up to the shops and a small bridge. A couple of porters in khaki uniforms emblazoned with the hotel's name asked if we needed help, and one of them led us on a quiet path out the opposite side of the station. There were no stalls and no hawkers here, just lush trees and hanging vines.

"Where is everyone?" I asked Jesse.

"We've just left Aguas Calientes. This here is all Inkaterra property. Used to be a tea plantation."

We passed some whitewashed buildings with pueblo roofs of terra-cotta tile. The porter took us into what looked like a large manor house. The central atrium was open, with sand-colored sofas scattered around.

"Buenas tardes," Jesse said to a pretty girl in a suit. "We're checking in."

"Welcome to the Inkaterra," she said, sounding genuinely glad that we were there. "What are your names, please?"

After we told her, she asked if she could bring us tea, then disappeared with our passports. The hotel in Cusco had done the same thing; obviously there was a record of Trista's visit somewhere, I thought, as Jesse and I took seats on a couch.

"How's your breathin', Lil? You feelin' okay?"

"Fine." I smiled at his mother-hen routine. "How about you?"

"A shower's all I need." He yawned. "Well, maybe a siesta."

"I need to wash all this dirt off me before I talk to the police," I said. "Maybe then they'll take me more seriously."

Jesse rolled his eyes and sighed dramatically just as the receptionist returned with a tray, poured us two cups of tea, and disappeared again. I took a drink and choked on the bitterness of it. "Coca tea," I said, remembering something Trista had said.

"You had it in Cusco and on the trail, Lil."

"I know." I hadn't liked it any better then. "Coca—that's the same plant you would make cocaine from?"

"Same plant, but a world of difference. Usin' coca leaves is as traditional here as turkey on Thanksgiving in Tulsa. More than that—they been doin' it a lot longer."

"Trista said her boyfriend made her drink something that tasted awful," I pointed out. "Is it possible to make coca tea so strong that it would make someone dizzy or sick?"

"Nope. The tea is about as stimulatin' as the caffeine in a can of Coke, no matter how long you brew it. Plus, it helps you fight altitude sickness. If that's what the boyfriend gave her, he was helpin' her out, not hurtin' her."

"He definitely wasn't doing anything to help her this morning."

"Look, if he was there, the cops will find him."

If, I thought. If? "You . . . you don't believe me? You heard them fighting before we found Trista, didn't you?"

"'Course I did," Jesse answered, his voice a shade too hearty and bright. "But you need to stop playin' it over in your head like a movie. It's all up to the police now, and it's gonna play out however it's gonna play out. There's really nothin' you or me can do here."

I stared at him, wondering how he could be so unfazed by what had happened. But Jesse had been the one to run for help; I'd stayed with Trista, held her hand, and listened to her. *This is his way of getting rid of me,* she'd said about her boyfriend when we were alone on the mountain. Now it felt like I was the only one who believed her.

After we checked in, another porter took us out of the main house and along a stone path, to an area where small cottages were set together in neat row after row. The porter unlocked the door and gestured for us to go inside. The little cottage was much grander within than without. Its high ceiling was constructed from logs, giving the room the rustic feel of a cabin, but everything else was luxurious, from the pair of queen-sized beds with wrought-iron headboards to the plasma-screen television. There was a fireplace and a large sofa with a finely woven, colorful throw blanket elegantly set across it.

I was ready to pick up our discussion where we'd left off, as the porter closed the door behind him. But Jesse had other ideas. "You want to take the first shower?" he offered.

"Are you sure? I know you wanted one."

"Sure, go ahead."

The bathroom was huge, with the same rough-hewn ceiling but the floor and walls covered in pale granite and tilework. Small, triangular windows were placed near the top of the walls to let in natural light. It seemed impossible that only a few hours had passed, and yet so much had happened. I couldn't help but feel guilty that I'd moved on into luxurious surroundings while Trista had been carried off the mountain, dead. Where was her body now? What would happen if no one claimed it? It was a lonely, unbearable thought to me, not least because it made me think of my sister's death. I managed to keep myself together until I got into the shower. Then, once the water was pounding down on me, I started to cry.

The guilt I felt over Claudia's death wasn't something I talked about with anyone. That twinning of shame and secrecy had made me feel completely alone wherever I went after her funeral. It was even worse than the guilt I'd felt over my mother's death when I was eighteen. At least in that case, I could honestly tell myself that it had been wrong of my mother—immoral of her, even—to threaten to kill herself every time I did something she objected to. She'd been drunk and furious when I'd finally gone away to college in New York City, and when I'd come home for Christmas, she'd decided I was home to stay. The last words she'd said to me were, *You only care about yourself, you selfish little bitch.* She'd hurled them at me when I'd left for the bus back to New York. Then she'd committed suicide that night.

Her death left me horrified and shattered, but it also made me angry. After it happened, I'd felt cut off from much of the world, though more closely linked to certain people, like Jesse and Claudia. But my sister's death had put me in another place entirely. Now, I was untethered, not in the sense of being free, but in terms of having no roots at all. Even Jesse, the person who knew me best in the world, didn't know what to do with me anymore. My reactions baffled him and occasionally upset him, and I couldn't find the words to explain myself to him. I couldn't get past the fact that, when Claudia was alive, I wanted rid of her. Now that she was gone, I would have done anything to bring her back.

I scrubbed the sweat and mud of the Inca Trail off myself, then soaped up my hands again. And again. Trista's blood wasn't on them anymore, but there was some trace of her on me that I couldn't get rid of. Deep down, I wished that I hadn't held her hand. Thinking of Trista's mad, throbbing heartbeat made me dizzy again, even though it wasn't so different from my own at that moment. *It was folly to grieve, or to think,* I recited silently. My sister would have understood the quote—it was from Edgar Allan Poe, whom we'd both loved. Thinking of Claudia made my heart hammer even harder against the cage of my chest. Her memory stung like a taunt, and it made something simmer underneath my skin. Now that she was gone, I was left with feelings too big and too painful to fit inside me.

When I stepped out of the shower, I bundled my hair into a towel-turban and pulled on a white terry-cloth robe. In the steamed-over mirror, I couldn't see myself clearly, though I knew a sad-eyed wraith was lurking behind the fog. I was a moving blur, a phantom you caught sight of in your peripheral vision. That was a perfect description for me, I realized. I was a ghost haunting my own life, without purpose or meaning.

"You finally done in there?" Jesse asked when I came out. His back was to me, and I wondered if he was annoyed. Or maybe he'd heard me crying—or just suspected tears—and was trying to give me some measure of privacy.

"I'm sorry. I left it kind of steamy in there."

Then Jesse turned around, and I realized he'd been planning to surprise me. There was a room service tray with three covered plates on it, as well as bottled water and glassware. "Ta-da," he announced, pulling the cover from one plate.

"You're amazing, but I don't think I can eat anything right now."

"No dice," Jesse said. "You didn't eat breakfast today. Don't gimme that look! I'm watchin' you like a hawk." He reached behind him and flourished a bag of plantain chips that he'd kept out of sight. "These, I know you'll eat," he said, waving the bag in the air, as if luring me to grab it. "That's your reward for bein' good and finishin' this nice, healthy salad."

"Sneaky." I sat on the edge of the bed and he joined me.

He handed me a plastic bottle. "I have to be sneaky. Look at the company I keep."

Before he handed over the chips, he forced me to eat half of the salad. "What would I do without you?" I asked him. Even if I couldn't explain my thoughts to him properly, having him in my life was probably the greatest blessing I'd ever had.

"You don't want to find out," he answered. Then, quietly, "How you doin' right now?"

"I'm still in shock, I think. And I can't believe that Trista's dead."

"The way you say her name, it's like you knew her."

Biting my lip, I realized that I thought I did know her. What was more intimate than being with a person as they lay dying?

"You're all riled up, Lil."

"What are you talking about?"

"This," he said, touching my hand. I looked down and realized for the first time that it was bundled into a fist. I unclenched it, feeling as if I'd been caught doing something wrong.

"Sorry. I didn't realize . . ." My voice trailed off. I stared at my wrist. Jesse had convinced me not to bring the silver Irish scrollwork bracelet I treasured to Peru. Normally, it never came off my arm, except in the shower, but now it was sitting in his apartment in New York. Memories of my father, who'd given it to me, and of my sister, who'd once stolen it, were inexorably linked to it. My arm felt naked without it.

"Things are gonna get better, Lil. I promise you that. It just takes time. And a better trip planner. I can't believe I dragged you here to take your mind off death, and then . . ."

"That's not your fault. No one could have known."

He held my hands in his. "How d'you think Claudia would feel if she could see you right now? 'Cause, I promise you, she's watching you from heaven."

I rolled my eyes. "From a fluffy cloud, no doubt."

"Oh, ye of little faith." Jesse stared at me. "I'm not gonna pretend I have a hotline to heaven. I don't have a clue what it looks like, or what it means. But Claudia's there. She can see you. She can hear you. I bet she kicks your ass now and then, too."

He'd done what he'd set out to do. I smiled, and my heart got a little bit lighter. If there was such a thing as an afterlife, and Claudia could watch me from it, I had no doubt that she wanted to kick me.

There was a knock on the door. When Jesse answered it, I saw the young police officer whom I'd spoken to in the town square standing there.

"I apologize for disturbing you," he said. "The train from Cusco has arrived. The investigating officer is most eager to speak to you."

My meeting with Felipe Vargas began without a handshake or even a proper introduction. All I'd been told about him was that he was from Cusco and that he was the investigating officer, but the way he stood—broad shoulders squared, back ramrod straight, hands behind his back—shouted "military" to me. He wore a dark olive uniform that reinforced the impression, even though it had no army insignia on it. Combined with his close-cropped iron-gray hair, thick neck, expressionless face, and dark, intrusive eyes, he looked formidable.

"Your name is Lily Moore, yes? Tell me *exactly* what you saw," he demanded in English. The way he spoke was abrupt and guttural, not like a native Spanish speaker. The young officer who'd walked me from the Inkaterra's reception area to a small concrete building just off the town square in Aguas Calientes closed the door behind him. I suspected he was very relieved to make his escape.

"Well, my friend and I were walking—"

"No! From the beginning."

"Where would you like me to start?" I asked him.

"When did you arrive at Machu Picchu?" The way he pronounced it sounded like *Matu Pixtu,* but he spoke rapidly and I wondered if I'd misheard him.

"Before dawn. My friend, Jesse, and I were with a group of hikers on the Inca Trail. We watched the sunrise with them."

Vargas stared at me. "Why did you and your friend leave your group?"

"Jesse has been to Machu Picchu before, and he wanted to get to the royal city at the center of the site before tourists started coming in on the train."

"Go on."

"We heard a man and a woman arguing. He said that she'd lied to him, and she told him to leave her alone." When Vargas didn't respond, I went on. "A few minutes later, we heard a woman scream. When we found Trista, she was lying at the bottom of a long staircase."

"How did you know her name?"

"She was still conscious then. Jesse ran to get help and I tried to keep her talking so that she wouldn't lose consciousness."

"What else did she tell you?"

I froze for a moment. My exchange with Trista was over so quickly, yet, at the time, it had felt like forever. And it wasn't without its contradictions: she'd told me she was on a drug, then denied being high. That had come across like the reflexive denial of a junkie, though; lying about using was second nature to the ones I'd known. "She said a man named Len made her drink something that made her sick. He also pushed her down the stairs. She made me promise to tell the police. She was sure that she was going to die."

"I have already spoken with the doctor who attempted to save her. He said that she couldn't have fallen down those steps. She would have been dead before she hit the landing. Even a slight fall on the stone would have resulted in cuts and bruises."

"One of her hands was badly cut," I argued. "Did the doctor mention that?"

"Yes. From what the men at the scene said, she appeared to have cut her hand on the edge of the bottom step." The fact didn't interest him, or at least, that was what I inferred from his cold tone. "Did she say anything else?"

"She said, 'This is his way of getting rid of me.'"

"So, in her raving, she was convinced that a man had deliberately caused her death?"

"She wasn't raving," I insisted. "She was lucid and coherent, even though she was in pain. There was something wrong with her heart—she said something about feeling like she was having a heart attack."

"Lucid. Coherent. I do not believe those terms normally apply to a drug addict."

That stopped me cold. There it was again. I wasn't naïve enough to pretend that I didn't understand why hard-core drug users were routinely dismissed in life and in death. Their willingness to alter reality by tempting death was both frightening and infuriating. They were incomprehensible, and yet who hadn't felt that impulse to blur the harsher edges of the world?

"Drug addict?" I said. "I saw the track marks on her arms, too. They weren't fresh."

"Oh, you are an expert on drugs, Miss Moore?" Vargas's eyes narrowed. "Did you know this woman was high on cocaine?"

"How could you *possibly* know that already? You haven't had time to do a toxicology screen. Those tests take days, some of them weeks." I was tempted to say more, but I held myself back. Everything I knew about tox screening was recent knowledge, earned while searching for my sister. I wasn't about to admit that, not to him.

"The evidence of long-term addiction was obvious to the

doctor, as was evidence of recent usage." There was something even sharper in his tone now. It wasn't just a harsh manner; it felt more like contempt.

"Evidence of recent usage? Meaning what?"

"There was cocaine under her nails."

"Her nails?" I thought about how her heart had raced as I held her hand. Maybe cocaine explained that. Was the drug her boyfriend made her take cocaine? If I'd misunderstood that, what else had I gotten wrong? Even though what Vargas said made a certain kind of sense, the force of her anger was powerful in my memory. *Bastard. This is all his fault. He hates me. Doesn't matter. I hate him, too.*

I opened my mouth to tell that to Vargas, but I noticed him studying my hands. Even though I'd showered, they still looked grubby, with black dirt trapped under the tips of my fingers. "How do you know so much about track marks, Miss Moore?" he asked.

The idea of opening up about my sister to this reptilian character was unthinkable. But I didn't want to lie and end up having to deal later with more personal, probing questions. "I knew someone who was a heroin addict," I said. "I could often tell from the marks I saw whether she was using drugs or sticking to methadone."

"I am sure that in America you must know a great many addicts."

"Excuse me?"

"Depending on drugs is the American way. They have a medication for everything. They cannot sleep, they take a drug. They are unhappy, they take a drug. They are shy, they take a drug." He took a step closer to me. "America, land of the quick fix. And when Americans come to my country, they believe they can indulge in illegal drugs here."

"That's a sweeping generalization to make."

"Not all Americans, of course. But many. I think you might be surprised by how many, Miss Moore."

"I hope you don't allow your personal feelings about Americans to overshadow your investigation into Trista's death." I watched Vargas's face, noting how his jaw continued to tighten as I spoke. The effect my words were having on him wasn't good, but I went on. "There was a man there this morning, at the top of the staircase. He stopped and looked down at us, then ran away."

"From what I have been told, you are the only person who saw him. Your friend, Jesse Robb, did not."

"Jesse had run down the stairs to help Trista. I was following him, but I almost tripped and I stopped to steady myself. That was when I looked up and saw the man."

"Your description of him is completely generic. White. Black beard. *Peruano* knit cap. How many men at the site today would that fit?"

"He was only there for a second. I didn't notice anything else about him."

Vargas kept his eyes on me, but he didn't say anything. I'd spent enough time around cops to know that they loved nothing better than to give a person the silent treatment, in the hope that person would cough up more information. Sadly, I had nothing else to give him.

"That is all?" he asked finally.

"No. Jesse gave one of the officers a silver lipstick case we found. It had the initials *MBW* engraved on it. Also, a Chilean man named Bastián found a silver compact. He said he would hand it in to the police."

"I haven't seen either item yet. I will ask about them. Thank you for coming to see me, Miss Moore."

I wasn't ready to be dismissed yet. "I'd be happy to stay to identify the man I saw. I know I didn't give you a very detailed description of him, but I know I'd recognize him if I saw him again."

"I don't think that will be necessary."

"Why not?"

"This is a very simple case, Miss Moore. A drug addict died this morning. Perhaps we do not know all of the drugs she was on, but there is clear causality between her drug use and her heart failure. Her death could have happened anywhere. It is not a shock."

"But the man she was with ran away!"

"Very likely he is an addict, too. It is unfortunate that he has not come forward, but unsurprising. He is, undoubtedly, aware that he would be arrested for drug possession and possibly trafficking."

Vargas had arrived in Aguas Calientes less than an hour earlier, yet already had the case wrapped up with a neat and tidy bow. No need for an investigation that might disrupt the tourist trade. No, it was better to blame Trista for her own death than consider the odd angles and shadows of the actual case. I had to tamp down my urge to scream at him.

"Doesn't it seem suspicious to you that Trista's boyfriend made her drink something, and it made her sick?" Before Vargas could answer, I barreled on. "And how did she wander so far into the site if she was sick? Trista said, 'This is his way of getting rid of me.'"

"She *also* said she fell, when she did not."

"She might have meant that she fell down on the landing, rather than on the staircase," I admitted. "Maybe I misunderstood that part. But she said, several times, that Len wanted rid of her."

"Do you suggest that this woman was killed, Miss Moore?"

Something else Trista said flashed through my mind. *Don't let him get away with what he's done to me. If he didn't have daddy's money, Len would be in jail right now.*

"Yes. It's still murder if someone gave her something to make her ill, then took her to a place where she couldn't get help. It's a coward's way of killing someone."

Vargas studied me for what felt like an uncomfortably long time. Finally, he said, "Tell me about your background."

"My background?" For a moment, I thought he meant family background, and I hoped that my expression didn't give away my anxiety.

"What is your vocation, Miss Moore?"

The question was a relief. "I'm a journalist."

That earned a nod from him. "Ah, I see. Like Angel Paez."

"I don't know who that is," I admitted.

"You are a journalist visiting Peru and you do not know of Angel Paez?" His surprise seemed genuine. "Paez founded the first investigative reporting team in Peru at *La República* in nineteen ninety. He has exposed government corruption, international drug trafficking, and concealed warfare. He has written for papers from Mexico to Japan."

"Oh. He sounds like someone I would like to read." It was embarrassing to admit how little I'd prepared for this trip. Normally I did a lot of research, but in this case, I'd floated along in my hazy state, trusting that Jesse knew enough for both of us.

"What do you write about?" Vargas asked.

"Travel."

"You are on staff at an organization?"

"I freelance. And I write travel guidebooks for Frakker's Travel Guides."

If he'd been vaguely interested in my profession before, he was completely dismissive of it now. "Guidebooks?" He frowned. "I see tourists here and in Cusco, their noses buried in those guidebooks. So you are one of the people providing them with a superficial, stereotypical picture of my country? Those books are horrible. I remember seeing one that told travelers to avoid Lima, that it was dirty and there was nothing worth seeing there. The capital of my country!"

I knew exactly which guidebook he was talking about, and I was just glad it wasn't by Frakker's. Not that Vargas would care; to the average person, one guidebook was pretty much interchangeable with its competition.

"This isn't about my work," I said. "I want to make sure that Trista gets justice. I promised her I would."

"Then, please leave this in my hands. I will contact you if I need anything else. I will speak with your boyfriend as well."

"Jesse is my friend, not my boyfriend."

"He is your male friend whom you share a room with," Vargas answered. "If he is not your boyfriend, what is he?"

"That's none of your business."

Vargas blinked at me. I turned to leave, opening the door and bumping into a tall, fair-haired man who'd been standing just outside the room. He was wearing a dark suit and a beige trench coat.

"I'm sorry," the man said to me. "I didn't mean to get in your way." He looked at Vargas and took a deep breath. "I need to speak with you, Mr. Vargas. I've been told that my friend Trista Deen fell on the mountain this morning."

10

The man in front of me was definitely not the one I'd seen at Machu Picchu. Even though I'd only glimpsed the other for a heartbeat, I knew that he was shorter and slighter, with dark hair and a beard. This man reminded me, just a little, of what Gary Cooper had looked like in his late thirties, when he'd filmed *Desire* with Marlene Dietrich. His hair was much lighter, almost blond, but there was something coldly formal about him. He studied me briefly then turned to Vargas.

"I apologize for the interruption," he said. "I can wait out here until you're done. But I'd like to speak with you as soon as possible." His voice was deep, but there was tension in it. Under his eyes were purplish half-moons, making him seem exhausted. His expression hinted that he was steeling himself for an unpleasant encounter.

"*You're* Len?" I stared at him, dumbfounded. If he was Len, who was that other man I'd seen?

His head snapped around and he stared at me, obviously surprised that I knew his name. His eyes were striking, with one blue iris and one green. His mouth set in a grim line, as if he were holding back a question.

"Please excuse us, Miss Moore," Vargas said. "I would like to speak with Mr. . . . ah . . ."

"Cutler," the man filled in for him.

"Mr. Cutler. I would like to speak with you now."

"Of course." My mouth moved, but I was rooted to the spot. Part of me was dying to ask him questions, or at least to listen in on his conversation with Vargas. But outside the office was a room that served as both reception area and office to the Aguas Calientes police officers. Instead, maybe I could prompt him to explain what had happened. "I just wanted to say that I'm so sorry for your loss, and . . ." And what? That I knew he'd made Trista drink something that made her sick? That it had taken him one hell of a long time to step forward? Maybe Vargas was right about the drug stash and Len's need to get rid of it first. I stared into the man's oddly matched eyes and couldn't bring myself to articulate what was in my thoughts.

His face was neutral. Unreadable. "Thank you."

"Thank you, Miss Moore." Vargas didn't sound grateful at all. "Now please leave."

The man stood back so that I could pass him. When I did, he slipped inside swiftly, shutting the door behind him with a solid click. The officer who'd walked me over from the hotel to the police station sat at a desk, watching me. He'd introduced himself on the way over and I knew that his name was Angel, he was twenty-one, and he was originally from one of the slums that ringed the city of Cusco, the capital city of the province.

"Se enteró de que . . ." I started to ask him, then remembered he spoke English. "Did you hear what that was about?

"I did. That man has a great deal of explaining to do," Angel answered. "For example, where has he been all of this time? But he looks rich, so I am certain he has a good alibi."

I liked this kid's cynicism, even if he didn't look old enough to shave. Moving closer, I perched on the edge of his desk.

"Alibi or not, how is he going to explain away the drugs? Or the fact Trista said he wanted rid of her?"

He shrugged. "If the woman took drugs, perhaps that was her choice. Perhaps her rich boyfriend did not know. It is possible." He gestured at the door. "He can afford the best justice. You can find an excuse for anything."

Angel's comment, delivered in an offhand, casual tone, tensed up my stomach. Trista had told me Len was rich, very rich. *If he didn't have daddy's money, Len would be in jail right now. But the money makes him untouchable.* I had first-hand experience with exactly how money could shape justice. I'd seen that with Claudia's death. Admittedly, justice was a complicated concept there, because the circumstances around her death were murky, and that let defense attorneys have a field day presenting alternate theories of the crimes involved. Two of the guilty were dead. One was in a mental institution. Others who *should* have been behind bars were walking around free, because they had money. My former fiancé, Martin Sklar, was at the top of that list. Sometimes, that fact made me so sad that I felt as if I'd just lost Claudia all over again. Occasionally, I found myself believing in karma, and wishing that it worked more quickly. Injustice was a galling thing to live with, especially since most of the world barely shrugged at the consequences.

I couldn't say any of that to Angel. "What was her name again?"

"Trista Deen. That is what Mr. Cutler said. He showed me her passport. She was from Toronto, Canada. Thirty-five years of age. No children, he said."

That was a small mercy, but I supposed it was something to be grateful for.

"I should walk you back to your resort," Angel added. "Are you ready to go?"

No, I'm not, I wanted to say. I didn't want to leave the little police station, with its concrete walls and low ceiling. I wanted to stay and find out what happened with the boyfriend. I wanted to watch the austere Mr. Cutler's mask slip. I wanted to see his reaction up close and probe his reflexes for clues as to his real motives. But I had no excuse to stay back. "Is there a place we could get some coffee?" I asked him.

When we walked out of the station, the sun was blazing. "This is what I love about the Sacred Valley," Angel said. "It might rain all day, but when the sun appears, it makes you forget the damp."

I wasn't sure he was right about that. It had rained every day while Jesse and I were hiking the Inca Trail, so much that my friend had started cracking jokes about "rainy Pago Pago," a reference to the Joan Crawford film *Rain*. Forgetting that would be hard, even if the sun was determined to show its face, as if it could burn off the sadness of the day with the mist and fog.

I bought us coffee at a little café that sat between the police station and the train station. Actually, *coffee* wasn't quite the right word—it was Nescafé, which had been oddly popular in Cusco, too. Since the café had no chairs, we stood outside, watching the hawkers try to sell their wares to mostly blasé travelers. The train station itself stood empty. Around four o'clock, a train rolled into the station, but no one disembarked.

"That is one of the trains to Poroy," Angel said. He'd been explaining bits and pieces of life in Aguas Calientes to me, though he'd only lived there for six months. "In a few minutes, they will let people board. It is the same time, the same routine, every day. Even in low season, there are fifteen hundred tourists at Machu Picchu every day."

"Have you seen a tourist die before at Machu Picchu?" I asked.

He gave me a suspicious glance beneath his long lashes. "Are you going to write about this?" After I shook my head, he went on. "My first week working here, a Quechua man who worked as a guide fell and died. He was taking a picture of a group. It was very sad. Many people here knew him. A few weeks ago, another man died."

"Did he fall as well?"

"No, he had a heart attack. Seventy-four years of age. Perhaps he should not have come to the mountain. You see all kinds of people here, some very old, some very frail, and sometimes you think, perhaps this visit is not a good idea for you. Still, you cannot say that. We have strict rules about who can climb Huayna Picchu, though."

"Hmm?" I was distracted by a man standing at the gated area outside the train station. He was hopping from foot to foot, as if desperate for a bathroom, but the guard wouldn't open the gate for him.

"That is the sacred peak. When you were on the mountain, you must have seen the taller peak? That is Huayna Picchu. It is where the Temple of the Moon is. Now we only allow four hundred people each day to climb it. It is *not* for the weak. We have the authority to tell people they cannot climb it."

There was obvious pride in Angel's voice, but I wasn't paying attention to him anymore. I only had eyes for the small, skittish man. He was wearing a trench coat that looked too big for him. A line was forming behind him, a Japanese tour group, with members still in plastic rain ponchos; each member had a matching rolling carry-on bag. But the Caucasian man with the curly black hair had no luggage, except for a messenger bag large enough to hold a laptop. He looked around, taking in the people around him, as if he were watching for someone.

That was when I recognized him.

He looked so different from the way he had that morning. For one thing, he'd shaved his beard and lost the brightly colored knit cap that had made him look like a backpacker. He'd been casually dressed when I'd seen him at the top of the staircase. Now, he'd somehow found a set of more formal clothes; the fact that they didn't quite fit made him look as if he were playing dress up.

What I recognized was the expression on his face. When I'd first seen him, he'd seemed like a startled animal, with wide-set eyes that veered between haunted and hunted. He looked the same way now, furtively glancing over his shoulder, then returning to his argument with the guard. He pulled out a piece of paper and waved it in the guard's face.

"That's him," I said.

"Who?"

"The man I saw this morning. The one who ran away."

"He does not look like the man you described," Angel pointed out. "You said he had a beard."

I moved toward the station, hoping Angel would follow. The concrete riser was maybe five feet above the train tracks, and it gave me a view of what was going on at the gate. The first guard was joined by two others, who opened the metal gate, but they still wouldn't let the man through. He was arguing with them in Spanish. I hurried down the staircase and caught bits of their exchange.

"Ningún billete, ningún tren." *No ticket, no train.*

"Tengo un boleto. ¿Ves?" *I have a ticket. See?* He wasn't a native Spanish speaker, that was instantly clear from his accent.

"Sí. Para mañana. Vuelve mañana." *Yes. For tomorrow. Come back tomorrow.*

One of the guards waved the leader of the Japanese group to come forward. She did, handing him several pages.

"¿Mira, qué se requiere?" *Look, what will it take?* the man demanded. I was only a few feet behind him now, and I saw him hand something to the guard. Folded bills; I couldn't say how many. "¿Suficiente?"

I'd found the man, but what was I going to do about it? There was a big gap between spotting him and getting him to the police station, and I didn't know how to fill it. Hoping that Angel could take over from here, I turned to look for him and saw that he was still up on the concrete riser, watching me with a skeptical expression. The problem was entirely in my quivering hands.

I took the direct approach. "La policía quiere hablar con usted." *The police want to talk with you.*

The man glanced at me for a fraction of a second and turned back to the guard. "¿Suficiente?" he repeated.

"Maybe I wasn't clear enough the first time," I said loudly, speaking in English. That was what Trista had spoken, and I was willing to bet this man did, too. "I know what you did. The police want to talk with you, right now, about a dead woman."

He moved forward, trying to go through the gate and onto the train, and I reacted reflexively, grabbing his arm. The man instantly turned and shoved me so hard that he knocked me off my feet. I crashed backward into a mass of tourists and luggage and fell flat on the ground.

11

I was down, but I wasn't out. When I lifted my head, I saw the man was running for the train, his oversized trench billowing behind him like a cape. One of the guards grabbed the fabric and pulled it, jolting the man so that he snapped backward like an elastic. He tripped and fell, going down on all fours.

"Espero que esto sea algo más serio que una pelea amorosa," another guard said to me. *I hope this is about something more serious than a lovers' quarrel.*

"Felipe Vargas, el inspector de policía, quiere hablar con él." *The police want to talk with him.* I was embarrassed enough at being knocked over by a man who was barely taller than me and so skinny he probably weighed about the same. The idea that anyone would mistake him for my boyfriend was almost as bad.

"That was crazy," Angel said. Suddenly he was beside me, looking excited. "You grabbed him. And then he pushed you. It was like a movie!"

"Could you go arrest him now, before he tries to run away again?" I asked, dusting myself off.

"Oh. Okay."

"I'm so sorry," I told the group of tourists. They were talking and pointing and looking startled. Turning, I saw the man get to his feet. His face was red and he was cursing in English and Spanish and possibly a couple of other languages.

"You need to come with me to the police station," Angel told him. "There are questions for you to answer."

"Is that where I go to swear a complaint about *her*?" The man shot me a look of pure loathing.

"What is your name?" Angel demanded. "Let me see your identification."

"I don't have to—"

"When the police ask for identification in Peru, you must provide it."

The man dug into his trouser pocket, pulling out a navy passport case and handing it over. I assumed it was American, but as I stepped closer, I saw an imperial coat of arms in gold, with CANADA emblazoned above it.

"Leonard Wolven," Angel read, his accent making it sound like *Lee-o-nard Wool-ben*. Standing next to him, I read *Leonard Eric Wolven* before Wolven grabbed the passport back.

"I want this crazy woman arrested, right now. She accosted me and threatened me."

"That's ridiculous," I said. "All I did was tell you the police had to talk to you. I only grabbed you because you tried to run."

"I want to press charges," Wolven said loudly.

"You can't do that. I'll press charges against you!"

"We will all go back to the police station to sort this out," Angel declared. "Let's go."

Angel asked one of the guards to accompany us, and they made us walk ahead of them through the gate and up the stairs of the concrete riser.

"Who the hell do you work for?" Wolven whispered, staring straight ahead. "Who hired you to do this to me?"

The question was so bizarre I didn't have an answer.

"Is this about money? Because whatever you're being paid, I can double it," he added.

"What are you talking about?"

"Stop talking!" Angel commanded. I looked over my shoulder, giving him an incredulous look that was supposed to say, *Are you talking to me?* His face was stony, and I suddenly understood why Jesse wanted to minimize his interaction with the Peruvian police.

"Look, I saw you on the mountain this morning. You were at the top of the staircase, and then you ran away."

"That was you?" he whispered back, checking me out from the corner of his eye. "I didn't recognize you."

"You left Trista to die there."

"No, I didn't! I went for help."

"You're a liar. You never came back."

"But I—"

"I told you both, stop talking!" Angel yelled. He was really grating on my nerves, but I didn't say anything. We got to the police station and went inside. The door to the office Vargas had questioned me in was closed, and Angel knocked on it.

Wolven leaned forward. "Is Trista okay? Have you seen her?" His brow was furrowed in an incredibly realistic show of concern. He was a good actor, I thought suddenly. Even though he was cleaned up, the schoolboy role didn't quite suit him: his dark eyes looked like they hadn't shut for a good night's sleep in a week.

"Are you going to pretend you don't know she's dead?" I whispered back.

"Dead? Trista?" His voice cracked when he said her name, and his mouth hung open as he stared at me.

Impossible as it sounded, I wondered for a second if his

reaction could be real. Was it possible that he really *had* gone for help, and that he didn't know Trista had died? But Trista's own words ran through my head, pushing those doubts out. *If he didn't have daddy's money, Len would be in jail right now.*

12

"I'm not gonna say you're in a bad mood, Lil," Jesse said. "But I'm kinda concerned lightning bolts will hit if I look at you the wrong way."

I glared at him and took another sip of my drink. After sitting in the police station's reception room for forty-five minutes while Vargas questioned Leonard Wolven behind a closed door, I needed a cocktail. And I needed a *second* one for what Vargas had said to me afterward. He'd stalked into the reception area and stood in front of me with folded arms. *One question, Miss Moore. Do you think you can behave yourself for the rest of your stay here?*

"It was one of the most humiliating experiences of my life. Vargas acted like I was a toddler having a tantrum."

"Good thing Vargas didn't see you when you're real mad. He might've locked you up overnight to keep scenic Aguas Calientes safe."

He was trying to make me smile, and it was almost working. I took another gulp of my pisco sour. I'd already developed a taste for pisco, a Peruvian wine that was supposed to be made using mysterious pre-Inca techniques. When mixed with lime juice, egg white, simple syrup, and bitters, it made a potent cocktail. The bar at the Inkaterra, where we were sitting, made a particularly good one. It also offered a great view: through floor-to-ceiling glass windows, I could see lush vegetation outside, and a faint shroud of mist. Strutting peacocks paraded in the dusk.

"I'm just glad you're not in the clink," he added. "That woulda been twice in three months."

"Stop trying to pretend I was arrested." While Jesse found the idea of me lurching into trouble amusing, I found it embarrassing. Three months earlier, I had been arrested, and the memory of the episode made my stomach churn. If my sister knew that I was getting into this much trouble, she would have been thrilled. When Claudia was alive, she'd always savored the role of the bad girl. She was the black sheep of our family, and proud of it. Now that was a mantle I was wearing, whether I wanted to or not.

"Okay, but you were detained. That's almost as good. Or as bad." He shook his head and took a drink. "I told you not to get into anythin' with the cops here."

"Trust me. I don't plan on having anything else to do with them." I'd already given the police a sworn statement about what I'd seen on Machu Picchu, and what Trista had said to me. It was up to them to do something about Leonard Wolven. I'd exhausted the meager list of things I was capable of.

"Don't get me wrong. I *love* a man in uniform."

That earned a smile. "I know. What do you think they'll do with Wolven?"

"Depends on the drug angle, I reckon."

I took a long drink. "Vargas was obnoxious on that front. To him, Americans are all drug addicts." How had he put it? *Depending on drugs is the American way. They have a medication for everything.*

"He's not completely off base, Lil. Plenty of people come to Peru for the drugs."

"Cocaine, you mean? Because of all the coca growing?"

"Peru doesn't get so much of the coke crowd. That's more of an export here." Jesse took a sip of his pisco sour. "Peru's known for its psychotropics. There are places, most of 'em in the Amazon jungle, where you go and, uh, partake of certain chemicals to expand your consciousness."

"What do they take to do that?"

"Don't know exactly, but I've heard it called natural LSD. Main thing is that it's not cooked up in labs, it's all from plants in the Amazon. The thinkin' is it's gotta be healthy if it's natural."

"Nightshade is natural, and it's a deadly poison."

Jesse grinned. "I've pointed that same fact out to folks. Great minds. The drug situation is weird here. The psychotropics are legal. So's marijuana. But tourists who get caught with drugs, even legal drugs, can end up in the clink."

I stared out the window, trying to make sense of what Trista had told me. She'd talked about Len, and she'd talked about a boyfriend, and from my second visit to the Aguas Calientes police station, I'd learned that those were actually two separate things. Her boyfriend was the tall man who'd reminded me of Gary Cooper; his name was Charles Cutler, and he happened to be traveling with a couple of friends, one of whom was Leonard Wolven. Len? That's what I assumed, but I'd made wrong assumptions before. Maybe she was involved with both men. Maybe they'd both played a role in her death. Maybe there was someone else involved that I hadn't even encountered yet.

Maybe I should just mind my own damn business. I'd promised Trista that I would tell the police what she said, and I'd done that. There didn't seem to be anything more I could do for her, sad as that made me feel.

"Earth to Tiger Lily. You keep zonin' out there."

"I'm sorry. I just keep thinking about what Trista said, trying to make sense of it. She said someone made her drink something. I'm wondering whether she meant . . ."

"*Made* her. Let me point somethin' out. Like I *made* you come to Peru? Meanin' that I bugged the heck outta you till you said yes."

Taking another drink, I tried to see his point of view. "I guess you could take it that way. But what if someone really was determined to get rid of her?"

"She was on drugs, Lil. Maybe that paranoid stuff she said was just crazy talk."

That hit a nerve. Claudia had looked down on what she called chippers, people who dabbled with different drugs. Even a heroin addict needed someone to disapprove of, I guess. *Nothing makes you paranoid like cocaine,* she'd told me.

"Leonard Wolven is completely paranoid, too. He knocked me down when I grabbed his arm. When we were taken to the police station, he wanted to know who I was working for."

"Like attracts like. What are the odds he's another coke-head?" Jesse frowned. "To be completely fair, rich folks and kidnapping go hand in hand in some places, like PB and J."

"And South America would be on that list of some places. I know." Maybe I had scared Leonard Wolven, and that was why he overreacted when I tried to hold him back. Still, a big part of my brain was trying to work through the knots of the problem, and I wasn't satisfied with the answers I was coming up with. "What if someone deliberately brought Trista here to die?"

"Why would anybody do that?"

"The police are useless. There's no hospital nearby. You can't get out quickly if you're sick. Ninety-nine percent of the people here are tourists who are going to be somewhere else in a day or two. Wouldn't that make it perfect for a murder?"

"Never thought I'd say this, but you have watched too many movies." Jesse reached out and put his hand over mine. "You remember hearin' the name Natalee Holloway?"

"She was the American tourist who was murdered in Aruba." In the back of my mind, I could see a photograph of her that had circulated in news accounts: a beautiful blonde with a warm smile. I remembered that, and the fact that she was only eighteen when she died.

"By a man named Joran van der Sloot. That ring bells?"

"Yes. He went on to murder another woman."

"Yeah. Stephany Flores Ramirez. Only that time, he committed the murder in Peru. You know what place you don't want to pick to commit a murder? Peru."

"Why?"

"Because even though they don't have the death penalty here, they got the world's worst jails. I'm not kiddin'. From what I've heard, they make the Siberian gulag look like a church picnic. They also got real cops who can solve crimes. Sure, some of 'em are on the take, but that's different from incompetent."

I was still unsettled by everything that had happened that day, but I had to push it out of my mind. There was nothing else I could do for Trista. Just like there was nothing else I could do for Claudia.

Jesse was definitely ready to move on. He picked up the little folded menu card on the table. "Can you believe we gotta wait till seven for dinner? I'm hungry enough to eat an alpaca right now."

"You mean those cute, furry creatures that look like a cross between sheep and llamas? How could you eat one?"

Jesse rolled his eyes. "I've seen you tuck into lamb, y'know."

Behind me, a voice said, "I hope I'm not interrupting."

I turned around in my seat. Charles Cutler was behind me, staring down at me with a bland expression that still managed to unsettle me.

13

"We haven't been properly introduced," he continued. "But I know from the police that your name is Lily Moore. I wanted to meet you. Charles Cutler."

He reached for my hand and shook it, slowly and formally. There was a stoic calm about him that I'd sensed when I saw him at the police station. He seemed completely unflappable, even in the worst of circumstances. It was impossible to tell how broken he was by his girlfriend's death, but he had the steady balance of a man able to shoulder heavy burdens. I could see how that quality would inspire confidence, but it made him seem cold in my eyes.

Jesse stood and extended his hand. "Jesse Robb. Pleased to meet you. My condolences on your loss, Charles."

"Thank you for that. Please call me Charlie." He looked at me. "I was hoping to speak with you."

"Let me go and spruce up before supper," Jesse said. "Our hikin' group has only seen me in a rain poncho. Gotta surprise 'em tonight. You never get a second chance to make a good last impression." Jesse was already dressed for dinner in jeans and a striped teal shirt, but as nosy as he was, he had gracious manners. Not that he was actually getting up from the table.

"No, please stay," Charlie said. "You and Lily were both there this morning, from what the police said. I'd love to speak with both of you, if I may."

"Well, in that case . . ." Jesse stood and borrowed a chair from the empty table next to ours, so that Charlie could sit. "We're just havin' some drinks before dinner. Meetin' our Inca Trail buddies at seven."

"Is that a pisco sour?" Charlie asked. "I need a strong one." He waved the waiter over and ordered.

"This your first time at Machu Picchu?" Jesse asked.

"No, we've been here before."

"You and Trista?" I asked. Her name came out so softly it was almost like a sigh, but Charlie caught it.

"I've been here a couple of times with Len, but never with Trista."

"How long are you visitin' Peru?"

"I'm on an extended stay here."

"Really? For business or pleasure?" Jesse asked.

Charlie frowned slightly, but he answered. "Business. And my friend Len seems to have set up house here."

The waiter brought over his drink and set it on the table. Charlie took a long swallow and put the glass down.

"Must be nice to live here," Jesse said. "This is my fifth trip to Peru. I love it."

"I think I like Chile better," Charlie said. "The company I work for has major mining operations there. Some in Peru, too, but Chile's where the action is. Santiago's a great city."

"I'm pretty fond of Lima, myself," Jesse said.

"The slums don't depress you?"

"Every city's got its ghettos. Lima's got more than its share. But it's also got a grandeur most other places can't touch. And while I kinda hate the conquistadors for tearin' up Inca temples and palaces and cities, Lima was one place the Spanish founded and built from scratch."

"City of Kings," Charlie murmured. He was relaxing now

that the conversation had shifted from the personal to the historical.

"Right. Everything there was built on the grandest scale. The Plaza de Armas, the cathedral . . ." The look on Jesse's face was dreamy, and I knew that even though he was sitting at the table, it was Lima that shimmered in front of his eyes.

"There's a church there I love," Charlie said. "Santo Domingo. Calling it a church isn't right—it's a basilica and convent and I don't know what else. But it has these peaceful chapels and gardens."

"I know it. They got the skulls of Saint Rose and Saint Martin on show there. Made my skin crawl, first time I saw 'em."

"It's a shock, looking at something like that, coming face-to-face with death. The ultimate memento mori."

"Remember your death," Jesse translated from the Latin, voicing what was in my own mind. "You a Catholic?"

Charlie seemed surprised by the question. Jesse's matter-of-fact curiosity could be disconcerting to strangers. Still, he answered, "Yes."

"Thought so. Lily is, too."

"Lapsed," I put in.

"My family is very strict about it. But I'm on the lapsed side, too." Charlie took another drink and signaled to the waiter. "Another round," he said. I was waiting for him to introduce the subject of his girlfriend. By mentioning Trista's name, I thought I'd given him an opening, but he'd talked about Lima with Jesse instead. Was he being sneaky, by avoiding the obvious while chatting about harmless topics, or was he working up the nerve to ask something about his girlfriend's last moments? His mind seemed to be very much on death, and I felt more sympathy for him than I expected to. It was difficult to picture this somber, contemplative man on a drug binge.

The waiter brought more drinks. When he left, I asked, "Did Trista like Lima?"

"I don't know. I mean, she just flew in a week ago. I don't know that she had time to really experience much of the city." Charlie gulped down half of his pisco sour; stoic as he appeared, he was tense. "Trista and I had been apart for a long time. I went back to the U.S. a few weeks ago and saw her; that was the first time in a couple of years. She just flew down to Lima last week. We . . . we weren't that close, I suppose, but she was a lovely person."

"She told me that you two had broken up and gotten back together," I said.

"She . . . what?" Charlie's oddly matched eyes stared at me. His expression was inscrutable, but the intensity of his gaze wasn't. My words had caught him off guard.

"Trista told me that you jilted her to marry another woman." My voice was so quiet that Jesse leaned forward so as not to miss anything. "She said you'd called her when your wife left you."

"That isn't . . . that's not how I would have described it." He took a drink and grimaced. "May I ask you what else she said about me?"

He already seemed wounded, and I didn't want to hurt him more than I had to. "She talked about her boyfriend, but she never said your name. She only . . . the only name she mentioned was Len."

"Len?" He picked up his glass, swirling the liquid inside instead of drinking, before setting it down again. "What did she say about Len?"

"She said he'd made her drink something, and that he'd pushed her down the stairs." As I considered that again, Jesse's paranoia theory made some sense. She hadn't been pushed down that staircase. Suspicious as I was, I had to admit that. That must have been paranoia talking.

"Trista's been a drug addict for a long time," Charlie said, his eyes on the table. The way he spoke was so soft that I wasn't sure he wanted me to hear him. "All she ever wanted to do was party with whoever would give her pills and coke and anything else. Her closest relationships were with drugs, not with people."

That remark hit home. It could have described my sister, too, for much of her adult life. Claudia's relationship with heroin trumped everything else. Yet, she'd tried to move past it, over and over, and for a time, she'd succeeded. But the drug was always there in her peripheral vision, beckoning her.

"Did you try to change her?"

"I've been to hell and back with this," Charlie said. "You can't help an addict who doesn't want to stop. I don't know where the off switch is, and I could never find it for her. Or for anyone else."

There was a painful honesty in his words. I shifted gears. "Did the police tell you that I saw Len at the top of the staircase where Trista fell?"

"Yes. They were satisfied by his answer and let him go. We talked about it. Len didn't see Trista collapse, but when he heard her scream and discovered what was going on, he ran to get help. Only he got lost and confused and he panicked. When he finally found the entryway to the site, they already knew about Trista and they told him a doctor was with her. He had his own seizure after that, caused by some combination of dehydration and a migraine, I think."

"Really? Did anyone see him experience this seizure?"

"Yes. It happened at the entryway to the site. A couple of the workers actually carried him over to the Sanctuary Lodge. I was with him after that. He isn't a well man. Hasn't been in the years I've known him. I was so worried about Len that it never occurred to me that anything might have happened to Trista. For hours I had no idea."

There was something calculated about Charlie's story that didn't sit well with my gut. It was as if he'd self-consciously constructed the perfect alibi for his friend. "Could Len have given Trista drugs?"

"Absolutely not. Len would never do such a thing. This misunderstanding with the police has been straightened out. Len is from a very wealthy family, and so he can be a bit paranoid. Or a lot paranoid. He feels terrible about what happened with you and wants to make it right." Charlie turned his strange eyes on Jesse. "Did Trista happen to say anything to you?"

"Just 'Don't leave me.' I ran up the steps after that to get help. It was so early, there was almost no one around. I had to run to the front gate to get help."

"Thank you for doing that," Charlie said, touching Jesse's forearm. "I appreciate everything you did. And Lily"—he turned to me—"I can't tell you how much it means to me, that you stayed with Trista. The police told me you kept her awake. If there had been any way to save her, it would have happened because of what the two of you did."

"Have the cops been able to tell you anything about why she died?" Jesse asked.

"They took her body to Cusco. The doctor's report called it a hypertensive crisis."

"Hypertensive what?"

"There's only a preliminary report, but Trista's blood pressure shot up suddenly and she suffered a series of ischemic strokes," Charlie explained. "They don't give a cause, but that answer is probably drugs. Trista used cocaine, and she was on some prescription antidepressants and other drugs that could interact badly, especially at altitude."

"Do they know what made her hallucinate?" I asked.

Charlie turned quickly to look at me. "Hallucinate?"

"She asked me if I heard the snakes hissing. She also wanted to know if I was real or part of the trip."

"They'll be running tests for days, from what they said. I'll be going to Cusco tomorrow and staying there while we wait for results. She won't be buried until after that."

"What about her family?" I asked.

"She doesn't have any."

"Not anyone?" That shocked me. I didn't have any family anymore, either, but that didn't make the situation seem any more normal.

"Trista grew up in foster homes. She didn't have anyone she considered family."

Charlie's words made my heart sink. Drug addicts came from all strata of society, but people who had family and friends they could trust had a real chance of getting their lives back one day. Someone who was all alone in the world had nothing to anchor herself to. I was acutely aware of that as I went through my days now. It wasn't the same thing as loneliness; it was more like an emptiness that could never be quenched. Even when I was with other people, it gnawed at me.

"This is going to sound very awkward, but I'd like to thank you both for your help today," Charlie went on. "I don't know what would be best—I could make a donation to a charity of your choice, or I could write a check to you to do with as you wish."

Jesse and I looked at each other, equally stunned. "That's not necessary," Jesse said. "We were both just glad to help. Right, Lil?"

"Exactly. I wouldn't feel comfortable with anything like that."

"You don't have to decide now," Charlie said. "Give it some time. I'll be in touch later. If you want to contact me, I'm staying at the Inkaterra tonight. We...I...my friends and I felt that it would be a good idea to switch hotels after what happened."

"From the Sanctuary?" I couldn't understand what he meant exactly, since Trista hadn't died at the hotel. Was there some other reason?

"Yes. Well. Thank you, both, again, for everything you did today." He shook Jesse's hand again, and mine, then stood and walked away.

"What a thoughtful gent," Jesse said, staring after him. "Kinda old-fashioned. Don't meet many like him these days."

I was watching Charlie, too. He spoke to a waiter, slipped him some cash, and left the bar. I wasn't thinking how thoughtful he was. I felt as if someone had just tried to bribe me.

14

"Are you feelin' okay?" Jesse asked me as we walked to dinner. This time we were avoiding the path of the train tracks, instead taking a concrete bridge that led directly from the Inkaterra into the heart of Aguas Calientes. *Bridge* wasn't quite the right word. To the left, we had an elevated view of the train tracks; to the right, there were shops. Not the homely stalls that we'd seen earlier in the afternoon, but actual shops. Their windows were filled with many of the same tchotchkes that the hawkers were selling down below. It was a quieter route, though, and no one stepped into our path to push us to buy something.

"I'm fine. Why do you ask?" I felt a little as if I were being watched by an unfailingly loyal, sweet raptor. Jesse noticed everything, and sometimes I wished he didn't.

"Well, you seemed to be in a bad mood back there, in the bar. On account of that cop, Vargas, right? I didn't get to tell you what he asked me."

"What was that?" I'd forgotten that Jesse had spoken with him as well. He'd gone to the police station before I did, but I hadn't seen him before I talked to Vargas.

"Well, after he got through grillin' me about what I saw of that poor lady who died—not much—he wanted to know about my relationship with you."

"You're kidding. What did you tell him?"

"I said you're my best friend. Then he asked when we're

gettin' hitched. I'm all, hello Oprah or Dr. Phil or whoever he thinks he is."

"He asked me about you, too," I admitted. "To quote, 'If he is not your boyfriend, *what* is he?'"

"Holy hell. He's such a yeti."

That made me laugh. "You mean yenta."

"Yeah, that's it. Love them funny New York words." He grinned. Mostly, he was pleased with himself for making me laugh, I think.

"What did you think of Charlie Cutler?" I asked, turning serious again.

"Interesting fella. Real polished, nice manners. I liked how thoughtful he was. Got the sense he was someone who really thinks things through. Kind of made me wonder why he'd be with someone like Trista."

"Why's that?"

"Oh, I know you can never get inside other folks' heads and really get why they do what they do, but why would a serious, sober fella like that take up with an addict?"

"Maybe she reminded him of his mother," I said, making Jesse laugh. "Who knows? Maybe she'd just come out of rehab and was clean when they first met. Maybe he was looking for a damsel in distress."

Jesse nodded. "That I could picture. Kinda made my heart ache when he talked about Trista and the drugs."

"I know what you mean." When Charlie had spoken about that issue, his words had resonated with me. *You can't help an addict who doesn't want to stop. I don't know where the off switch is, and I could never find it for her. Or for anyone else.* He was absolutely right about that, and he spoke with a gravity that made me believe he really had been to hell and back. It was the same journey I'd had with Claudia, and ultimately it had ended the same way. Still, that didn't mean that I believed everything Charlie had said. "But there was something strange in the way he reacted to questions about his friend Len. It was as if he couldn't consider the *possibility* that Len would do anything wrong."

"It's clear they're close. Who knows? Maybe Len's got an issue with drugs and Charlie's tryin' to hide it."

"Why would he do that? His girlfriend is dead because of drugs."

"Let me refer you back to our earlier talk about Peruvian law," Jesse said. "Aside from Bit Part and Martin Sklar, there's nobody I've met I'd want to hand over to them." Bit Part was an actor that Jesse's former boyfriend had cheated on him with; Jesse's feelings about my ex, Martin, were at least as intense as my own. " 'Course, I'd love it if they dragged in every murderer and creep who hurt a kid. Serve 'em right. But short of that, nope."

"Len had to have given Trista drugs. From what Charlie said, she'd only been in Peru a few days. It's not as if she had a dealer here."

"Let it go, Lil." Jesse's voice was tender. "However we feel about this, we gotta step back and say this is really none of our business. You know that, don't you?"

"I do. It's just hard to shake off the feeling that there should have been something I could have done for her." I didn't have to close my eyes to see Trista's agonized face before she'd died. Many times over the past few months I'd imagined my sister's last moments. Now I felt as if I'd witnessed something similar, and it left me shaken and horrified.

"I can understand that." Stopping suddenly, he said, "Will you look at that?"

Following his gaze, I saw what I took at first for a waterfall, but I realized that was a mistake. The sun had gone down behind the mountains a couple of hours earlier, but the sky wasn't dark, just a shade of deep blue I'd never seen before. There was enough light to see the gleam of white rocks, and I could hear water running around them.

"Is it a river?" I asked.

He snorted. "*Should* be a river. This is an offshoot of the Urubamba. You could see that snakin' through the valley from where we were this mornin'." He shook his head. "It gets uglier each time I see it. It's too dark to tell now, but the water's brown."

There was a distinct scent of sulphur in the air. "Do people dump their garbage in it?"

"It's not as bad as that, Lil. We could follow it up to the hot springs. It ain't far, but it's uphill." He moved to rest his arms on the railing, still staring at the water. "Don't know why, but it depresses the hell outta me," he said.

"Maybe because you expect it to be beautiful." I leaned on the railing, too, noticing the decrepit arch of a rusted-out metal bridge farther up and into town.

"It's extreme here. You get bowled over by this beautiful, majestic, imposin' stuff, and then suddenly you're in the gutter, and you can't even figure how you got there." He chuckled. "Would you listen to me, spoutin' off like a philosopher. We better get goin' or we'll be late to supper."

"I like it when you get all thoughtful like that."

"Yeah, you bring that out sometimes. Which just goes to prove Will Rogers was right."

"About what?"

"A man only learns in two ways," Jesse said. "One by reading, the other by association with smarter people." He put his arm around me. "Secretly, I'm after your brain, y'know."

. . .

Dinner was at a pizzeria in the center of town. We'd forgotten the name of the place Diego had told us to go to, which was unfortunate; all we remembered was pizzeria, and it turned out that every restaurant-café in that stretch was a pizzeria.

Fortunately, Aguas Calientes's main drag was small enough that, after a bit of wandering, we found the right spot. Diego saw us first, and waved us over. We'd been hiking with a group of fifteen people—not including the agile porters, who ferried the cooking gear and other necessities from one campsite to the next with shocking speed. The porters weren't there, and neither were six members of our group. I vaguely remembered that some hikers were planning to take a train back to Cusco that evening. After four days together—well, three, since today hadn't counted—I was embarrassed to say that I didn't really know their names. I hadn't spoken with anyone in the group, beyond simple pleasantries, except for Jesse and Diego.

I sat at the outer edge of a rectangular table, letting Jesse do all of the talking for both of us while my mind wandered. For most of the trip, I'd been lost in a fog, mentally playing out pieces of my sister's life and our many fights. But my mind was stuck on Trista now . . . and Len and Charlie, and how they fit together.

"Have you seen any, Lily?" asked the man sitting across from me at the table.

"Excuse me?" I mumbled through a bite of pizza.

He leaned forward, putting his face closer to mine. He had matted blond hair styled into dreadlocks and pale eyes. A pair of binoculars hung around his neck. "UFOs," he answered.

"Are you joking?"

"Why would I be joking? Peru is ground zero for UFOs."

I glanced at Jesse, but he was busy regaling the table with a story about the time he was attacked by a herd of vicuña while photographing them.

"You know about the Nazca Lines, of course?" the man asked.

"I've heard of them."

"Fifty miles of geoglyphs in the Nazca Desert," he clarified. "They were carved into the earth sixteen hundred years ago. Drawings of animals, birds, fish, people. They couldn't have been created without help from aliens."

"Interesting." Setting my pizza down, I looked at Jesse again, hoping to catch his eye.

"I've had a UFO sighting every time I come to Peru. Except on this trip, so far. Thought I saw one on the second night we were camped out, but it was just a little flash in the sky. There, then gone. So I don't know for sure."

"I see."

"But tomorrow night I'm going to Lake Huyapo. It's outside Cusco, and if you want a guaranteed sighting of a UFO, it's the place to hit. You should come with me . . ."

"Excuse me. I'm going to find the bathroom," I said, pushing my metal chair back and standing. That caught Jesse's attention.

"Bathroom's over thataway," he said. "These places don't have their own. You gotta pay, too."

"Thanks." I made my escape. I passed one restaurant after another, all of them serving pretty much the same thing ours did. With the captive crowd below Machu Picchu, I guess it didn't really matter. People needed to eat something, and it made sense to create simple, cheap offerings that could be steeply marked up.

While I was waiting in line, my gaze fell on a man wearing one of those funny-looking Peruvian caps with the earflaps and pompoms. He had a slight build and dark beard, and I did a double take. He looked not unlike the man I'd seen at the top of the staircase that morning, even though I knew it wasn't him. The cap, which was dark red with a bold pattern in orange and blue looked just like the one Len had been wearing. He was with a couple of other men wearing similar headgear, and one of them noticed me staring and nudged his friend in the red cap, who turned and checked me out.

"She's kind of cute, for a goth," he muttered, and I felt mortified. Worse, he took a few steps in my direction. "Hey, did I see you up on the mountain today?"

Well, duh, I thought. When you went to Machu Picchu, was there anywhere else you would go?

"That is such a great hat," I said. "I'd love to get one like it for my boyfriend. Would you mind telling me where you bought it?"

His face turned a little bit sullen at the mention of the boyfriend, but he said, "Would you believe a dude came up to me and gave it to me?"

"He was walking around selling hats?" I asked.

His friends laughed. "No, seriously, this guy came right up to him and asked him if he wanted the hat," one of his friends said.

"It's not cheap to get a *chullo* like that, either," the other friend chimed in. "I've been backpacking for a while and I've lost a couple. Right now the one I've got is shit. The good ones are made from alpaca, and they really keep you warm. I was all, like, whoa, I'll take it. And the dude just stared at me. He was freaky."

"That was funny," the one in the red hat chuckled. "It was meant for me!"

"Who was this guy?" I asked. "Did he tell you his name?"

"No. He just handed the hat over and walked off. It's funny how stuff like that happens when you travel. That would never happen in St. Louis."

"I'm going back up there tomorrow and I am going to look for this guy giving out hats," I said, trying to sound light even though there was something off about this picture.

"Look for the dude with the crazy eyes," the friend who lost out on the hat said.

"Crazy eyes?"

"Not crazy. Mismatched, I mean. They were different colors."

"Wait, the man's eyes were different colors?" I repeated. "Which colors? Blue and green?"

"I don't remember exactly, but it was freaky to look at."

15

"Let me see if I got this straight," Jesse said as we walked back to the Inkaterra. "You think Charlie Cutler looked for a guy who kinda resembled Len, and gave him Len's hat?"

"How many people walking around here have different-colored eyes?" I asked.

"Lil, those college kids you were talkin' to were high as kites. *Your* eyes probably looked like kaleidoscopes to them."

Jesse had hunted me down when I didn't come back from the bathroom and found me still talking with the backpackers. While it was sweet of him to come after me, it was unfortunate that he'd actually encountered the boys, as their drawly, sleepy voices and vague words would have marked them as stoners even if their clothes hadn't smelled of skunk. Worse, they'd followed us back to our table and got into a conversation with the UFO aficionado. Roswell and government cover-ups were cited a few times. When we'd said good night to them, they were debating a visit to mythical Lake Huyapo with its little green men.

"Don't you think it's bizarre that Charlie would give Len's hat to a kid who resembles Len?" I demanded. "Doesn't that suggest some kind of weird intent to you?"

"That fella probably thinks Santy Claus gave him the hat along with a bong," Jesse groused.

He wouldn't listen to me, and when we got back to the

serene grounds of the Inkaterra, we parted ways. Jesse had made a plan to photograph some night-blooming flowers, and a horticulturalist from the resort was waiting to take him to a couple of sites at the foot of the mountain. He went to our room to get his camera gear, dropping me off at the resort's spa and telling me to get a massage. But I didn't want to relax. Or maybe it was just that I couldn't let myself relax when so many issues were niggling at me. So I stood outside, trying to calm my mind and think clearly. Instead, my brain was taunted by the lovely but mysterious scent that floated over the resort's grounds. Earlier in the day, I'd noticed orchids and attributed the sweetness to that. But in the dark, the scent seemed stronger. It was familiar and made me think of citrus fruit, yet it was like nothing I'd encountered before.

"That is *montelimón* and heliotrope," the woman at reception told me when I asked about it there. "They grow well in this part of the Andes. We grow the plants here and use them at our spa." She smiled. "Any other questions?"

"Just one. Where can I get Internet access?"

She directed me to a building at the edge of the property. My laptop computer was back with our luggage in Cusco, but that didn't mean that I had to be cut off from the world. As I followed the path, the ground sloped down and I found myself walking across the train tracks. There was no barrier or warning, but I supposed they didn't need one. A few trains came in early in the morning, and the same trains left in the evening.

A few feet away was a small hut that glowed with artificial light. There was no one else inside, but there were four computers. The one I sat down in front of had a relatively new monitor, but it was an old PC, and it loaded pages at a snail's pace. True, I was in the middle of nowhere, but I was still impatient. When my e-mail in-box finally opened, it was clogged with messages, many of which I deleted without reading. There were press releases that I had no use for, e-mail alerts I couldn't be bothered to read, and spam.

Then there were several e-mails from a friend in New York, a police detective named Bruxton. I'd gotten familiar with his style while I was in Barcelona: no greeting, no sign-off, just a line or two that sounded as if he were in the room with me, speaking. I could count on him to send at least one e-mail each day, even if it went like this: "You really leave for the Inca Trail today? Can't imagine you roughing it." Or: "Just read about people getting robbed on the Inca Trail. ??? Why did Jesse think this was a good idea?" Or: "You still taking altitude sickness meds? Looked them up, side effects sound like a horror movie."

He also forwarded me articles to read, usually without a note. I let those sit unopened. It was nice to have such a reliable correspondent, even if there was nothing remotely romantic about his messages. Not long ago, he'd seemed interested in being more than just my friend, but when I left New York and went back to Barcelona, it seemed as if that moment passed. I had no idea whether he was dating anyone, and I wasn't about to ask. I'd invited him to come visit me in Spain, but he'd turned that down immediately. "I hate flying. You think I'd survive crossing the Atlantic without smoking?" he'd written back. Still, he kept in touch, even when I didn't instantly write back to him. I wanted to now, but didn't know what to say. I could tell him that Jesse and I were at Machu Picchu, but I couldn't imagine leaving out what had happened to Trista Deen. The truth was, I didn't want to write the words. My hands hovered over the keyboard, but I couldn't decide what to say. *Later,* I promised myself. *I'll write to him later.* But that didn't seem right, either. Finally I hit reply, and wrote: "Arrived at Machu Picchu. More later. Four days of hiking the Inca Trail = lots of bug bites, no sleep, great photos when it's not raining. P.S. It's always raining. P.P.S. Hope you're well."

There was another e-mail that caught my eye. The sender's name, Anna Mallory, had turned up in my e-mail before and I dreaded seeing it. She'd started sending me messages after Claudia's story hit the newspapers in January. I'd heard from so many strangers then that it had barely registered. But Anna Mallory had, apparently, attended my sister's funeral. Bruxton and Jesse and other friends had kept strangers away from me that day, knowing that there were plenty of reporters trying to get "exclusives" with me. The story had died down after some New York governor's scandal had knocked it off the front page, but Anna Mallory kept writing every week. The subject of her e-mail was "Hope things are better." Reluctantly I clicked on it.

Dear Lily,

I hope that time is making things easier for you. I can only imagine how tough everything has been. I don't know whether you're in New York now, or if you're traveling somewhere, but I'd really like to talk with you. We've never met, but my mother used to be friends with your mother when they lived in Woodlawn Heights.

Best wishes,
Anna Mallory

There was nothing alarming about the e-mail, but even if it was true that our mothers had known each other, that didn't seem like much of a reason to get in touch. I'd encountered plenty of people who claimed to have a "special connection" with me since Claudia's death, and most of them were nutty. The others obviously believed that I had insurance money from Claudia's death. None of them were people I wanted to deal with. I deleted Anna Mallory's e-mail.

There was a little chill that ran through me. It was the second time in an hour that I'd had an unwelcome reminder of my mother. It seemed harsh to say that I had no good memories of her, but it was true. When I thought back to my childhood, before my father died, my mother always seemed to be sick. It made sense later, when I found out about the miscarriages she'd suffered. *Your mother needs quiet,* our father would tell Claudia and me. *I think it's high time I take my favorite girls out to the zoo.* We lived in the Bronx, so our outings were often to the zoo or the botanical gardens, though when Claudia and I discovered the Edgar Allan Poe Cottage, we demanded repeat visits. It wasn't so much the tiny alabaster-white cottage with the black doors and shutters that caught our imaginations, as the fact that our father would recite Poe's poetry to us. He'd told us that Poe had composed "Annabel Lee" while living there, and I could still hear his lilting Irish accent dancing over the lines. *I was a child and she was a child, In this kingdom by the sea; But we loved with a love that was more than love—I and my Annabel Lee.*

"*Mina?*" The deep voice made me jump. Turning, I saw the man with the shaved head and scarred face I'd last seen on the staircase where Trista had died.

16

As tall and muscular as he was, he'd managed to creep up behind me without my noticing. That rattled me. "What the hell are you doing here?"

He smiled, which made the scar that ran down his face shiver and stretch slightly. "I'm sorry. I didn't mean to frighten you."

"You didn't," I said, feeling both silly and defensive. "If you want to make me nervous, make another leap off the side of a mountain."

"If it would impress you, I would." His smile broadened, at least on one side of his face, revealing perfectly even, capped teeth that were bleached bone white. There was scar tissue over his nose, and a long scar along one side of his jaw. He looked like a boxer, though not a very successful one. "I think you are what an American would call a tough cookie."

I didn't want to smile back at him, but he was making it hard not to. Rough as his appearance was, he had an easy manner and a quick smile. "You speak English really well. Better than I do Spanish."

"I lived in America for a couple of years, and in Australia for one. And I've traveled everywhere. When I am at home in Chile, people tell me I talk like a foreigner now." He pulled out the chair at the computer next to the one I was using, and sat down.

"It's hard to ever go home again." I paused. "By the way,

did you ever manage to hand that silver compact you found over to the police?"

He raised his eyebrows. "Are you going to rat me out?"

"Probably."

"Now you are making me nervous. Do you mind if I smoke while you interrogate me?"

"Not at all. But wait . . ." I was about to point out that you couldn't smoke in the thin mountain air, when I realized we were at the foot of the mountain.

"What's wrong?"

"It just occurred to me that I haven't had a cigarette in six days because of the altitude."

He held out the pack to me, then lit my cigarette with a gold lighter. "You were in Cusco?" I nodded, inhaling blissfully. "I hate Cusco. But there are cafés there where you can smoke. They use hookahs for tobacco." He lit his own cigarette and dragged on it. "This is so much better than a stupid hookah," he sighed, exhaling. "But beggars cannot be choosers."

"So why did you keep the compact?"

"We haven't been properly introduced." His eyes wandered over me, lingering on my breasts before moving back to my face. His eyes were dark and, for a moment, uncomfortably intent. Then he put out his hand. "Bastián Montalvo. It is my distinct pleasure to meet you, Ava."

I remembered my lie from that morning as we shook hands, and I felt my face get warm. That had been childish of me. I was about to apologize for the lie, when he added, "Or should I say, Lily Moore?"

"How do you know my name?"

"You're more famous than you realize."

I got to my feet. My encounter with Bastián on Machu Picchu had been relegated to one of the less-strange events of a heartbreaking day, but the idea that he'd dug up my identity on his own disturbed me. Perhaps he had gone to the police after all, and that was how my name came into it.

"Don't look so upset, *mina*. Sit down. I'll tell you, but you won't like it."

I took my seat again, feeling wary. "How did you find my name?"

"Len Wolven has a great many resources. Or at least his family does. The moment you and your friend Jesse became involved in his business, one of his family's minions looked you up."

What was it that Trista had said? *If he didn't have daddy's money, Len would be in jail right now. But the money makes him untouchable.* "What's your connection to Len Wolven?"

"I work for the Wolven family. Just as Charlie Cutler does."

"What?"

"More accurately, we work for Len's father, who is also named Leonard Wolven. He holds all of the purse strings in that family. Everyone, including his children, refer to him as Mr. Wolven. I do not believe any of his wives would have dared to call him Len. The father has everyone's respect. The son is barely tolerated."

The silence stretched between us as I stared at him. "Charlie said Len was his friend."

"Ah, funny choice of words. Charlie and I are tasked with keeping Len on the straight and narrow path. It is the most difficult, unrewarding, thankless job I have ever had. I've worked with men I despise, but . . ." He took a heavy drag on his cigarette and exhaled toward the ceiling. "Charlie told me he had spoken with you. He was authorized to give you money."

"He offered money. I said no."

"I would advise you to take it. The Wolvens like to buy up assets. What they don't own, they are happy to destroy." He stood. "If I were you, I would take whatever is offered. Ask for more, if you like—Mr. Wolven would not have a problem with that. He is honorable about his contracts. His son, on the other hand . . ." He grimaced, and seemed to bite words back. "The less you have to do with him, the better for you and for everyone else."

Bastián moved toward the door. "Wait. Are you suggesting that Len hurt Trista? Did he push her or . . . or . . ." My mind reeled at the possibilities.

"I am not suggesting anything. I have no idea what happened between Len and Trista," Bastián said. "I was sound asleep at that hour. But Len and drugs? They are inseparable."

"Would he have given her something? Or forced her to take a drug?"

He took a business card out of his pocket and wrote a number on the back of it. "I would love to see you again, *mina,* but the next few weeks will be a rough time. After that, though . . ." His scarred face looked almost dreamy. "I will be back in Chile. Maybe I can convince you to come see me there. You are a travel writer, after all." He set the card next to the keyboard. "But unless you wish to create a great deal of trouble for me, please do not tell anyone what I have told you tonight. Not Len and not Charlie. I don't trust either one."

17

After Bastián left, I was glued to my terminal, clicking away as fast as the ancient computer would let me. That there were actually two Leonard Wolvens was suddenly an inconvenient fact, because everything I found was about the senior one. Papa Wolven had come from family money, but had created a global empire that made him one of the richest men in the world. His reach appeared to span everything from the mining of raw resources to computer software, and he appeared to run an online-gambling company that was growing by leaps and bounds by setting up operations in developing countries. I didn't understand how there could be money made by bringing virtual gambling operations into poor countries, but apparently Wolven did, which explained why he was the billionaire and I was the footloose journalist.

While the same corporate filings and press releases kept showing up in my search, it was impossible to get anything very personal—until I typed Trista Deen's name into the search engine. That got results: "Vegas Showgirl Strikes Gold With Billionaire's Son." There was a flurry of stories from six months earlier, all on rather questionable-looking blogs. The Vegas showgirl in question was a woman named Marianne Bargeman. Judging from the photos, Trista and Marianne looked alike—red hair, slim bodies, dramatically enlarged breasts—but Marianne was a decade younger and her face looked natural, not a concoction shaped by nips, tucks, and fillers, which was what Trista's looked like in the photo.

According to inside sources, the heir to the throne of global powerhouse Wolven Industries married in haste last week in Las Vegas. While the city's motto may be "What Happens in Vegas Stays in Vegas," it looks like the sudden wedding of Leonard Wolven, 27, and busty Texas-born showgirl-on-the-make Marianne Bargeman, 23, has survived the 55-hour Britney mark. Bargeman has a reputation as a notoriously popular party girl. She was once arrested for check kiting, but sentenced only to probation.

I'd never worked for a tabloid, but I knew how the sausage was made. This kind of story usually had only nebulous, unnamed sources, and everything had to be stated in a way that would survive a lawsuit. The check-kiting charge was almost certainly true; a flat-out claim like that had to be backed by facts, unlike the "notoriously popular party girl" label, which suggested a drug-addled whore but left the inference to the reader's imagination.

The notably tacky nuptials surprised some observers, who say that Wolven's inheritance might be revoked by his notoriously controlling and reclusive father, Leonard M. Wolven, 72. "Wolven has been grooming his son to run the business from the day the boy was born, but Len won't settle down," said one intimate. "With Len going from crisis to crisis, it's time for Wolven to change his succession plans." The likely replacement would be Len Wolven's half-sister, Augustina, 37, who has been her father's right hand for years.

That was interesting. Crisis to crisis—what did that mean? Bastián had made it clear that drugs were an issue, and that Len was a difficult charge to manage. What else had he been involved with? And why was he the heir to the family business when he had a sister who sounded like she wasn't a screwup?

Len Wolven, according to one intimate, abandoned his longtime girlfriend Trista Deen, a model and actress, to marry Bargeman after a whirlwind courtship.

That stopped me dead. Trista had been *Len's* girlfriend? I could picture Charlie Cutler, sitting in the hotel bar with Jesse and me that evening, and hear his voice. *Trista's been a drug addict for a long time. All she ever wanted to do was party with whoever would give her pills and coke and anything else. Her closest relationships were with drugs, not with people.* At the time, his remark had resonated with me, because it could have described Claudia, too. I hadn't paid attention to the coldly analytical, almost clinical, tone he'd dissected Trista with. No wonder he hadn't betrayed any emotion at her death. Charlie had been more concerned with Len Wolven's reputation when I'd asked about drugs. He hadn't cared about Trista; she'd just been an addict who was dating his boss's son—and, presumably, one of the reasons Len kept getting into trouble.

Everything shifted into crystal-clear focus suddenly. Charlie was covering up for Len. The moment I'd asked him if Len could have given Trista drugs was the only time I saw him lose his cool façade. *Absolutely not. Len would never do such a thing. And his misunderstanding with the police has been straightened out.*

That one puzzle piece sliding into place changed everything, I realized. Was Charlie pretending that Trista was his girlfriend to keep suspicion off Len? Far out as it sounded, he really *had* looked for a stoner who resembled Len and given him his red alpaca-wool cap. Just how far was he willing to go to cover up for Len? The timing of his visit to the police station wasn't accidental, I realized; he'd gone there while Len had made his way to the train station, trying to get the hell out of Aguas Calientes a day early. It was Charlie's job to stay behind and clean up after Len.

My pulse raced at the possibilities. Was Len responsible for Trista's death? She had blamed him, and even if part of her claim hadn't held up to scrutiny, there was no arguing with the fact that she was high. Even if Len hadn't pushed Trista, he'd be criminally responsible for her death for drugging her, or providing her with drugs. No wonder Charlie was lying through his teeth for him—his boss's son was in danger of landing in jail in Peru, something that would undoubtedly affect Len's ability to take over the multibillion-dollar family business.

If he didn't have daddy's money, Len would be in jail right now. But the money makes him untouchable.

It all made so much sense suddenly, and I realized that I needed to talk to Jesse. I needed to talk to Vargas, too—where was he staying in Aguas Calientes? Would the local police tell me? I was shaking with nervous excitement and almost missed the last line of the tabloid piece.

Deen had nursed Len Wolven back to health after his apparent mental breakdown over the death of his first wife, Kirsten.

18

I couldn't find Jesse anywhere. Running back to the room, I saw that the lights were off. Thinking he might have just gone to sleep, I eased the door open, saw that both beds were empty, and closed it again. It was almost ten. Could he still be out taking photos? That was hard to imagine, given our predawn start to the day. Maybe he'd stopped at the bar or the reception area? I checked both places and started to panic. What if something had happened to him?

Stop it, I told myself. Just go back to the room and wait for him. I did, and that was when I found his note. *Want to come see the Spectacled Bears?* it read. Not having a clue what he was talking about, I took the note with me to the reception desk.

"Of course, the Spectacled Bears!" said the young girl behind it. The people who worked at hotels in this area acted cheery no matter what time of day it was. "You will love them. We have two. Such amazing creatures!"

"But what are they?"

"Um, bears. You know. *Bears.* This kind is a special Andean bear. They have, um, patches around their eyes. Like spectacles." She held the thumbs and forefingers of both hands over her eyes, in case the explanation wasn't clear. "Our bears are from rescues. One from a circus, one from a fire. They are nocturnal. If you go now, you might see them play."

She gave me directions to the conservation area, where the

bears were housed. I crossed the grounds quickly. There were a few couples strolling around, and a couple of exotic birds that crossed my path, but otherwise the night was quiet. I spotted Jesse's lanky form standing alone. He wasn't watching the birds or bears; instead, he was staring at the night sky.

"Jesse, you won't believe what I found out—"

"Hey, Lil. You take a look at the sky tonight? Clear as a bell."

"I don't care about the sky. Listen. Bastián found me in the Internet café they have here and—"

"Who's Bastián?"

"The big guy with the shaved head. We ran into him this morning on the staircase where . . ." The sentence drifted off; I didn't want to mention Trista's death again. "You started getting into it with him about Chile's government."

"*Former* government, thank the Lord." Jesse jolted to attention. "Was he buggin' you? That guy's a thug if I ever saw one. I'll clean his clock right out."

"He didn't do anything. We talked. You're not going to believe this, but both he and Charlie Cutler work for Len Wolven."

"They *what*?" Under the starlight, I could see enough of his expression to know he was as incredulous as I'd been.

"More accurately, they work for a giant multinational corporation owned by Len Wolven's father. Len's the heir to a billion-dollar fortune. Bastián knew Charlie was offering us money. He really was trying to bribe us not to say anything."

"But what the hell could we say? We told the police exactly what we saw. It's not like we tried to hush it up."

"Trista wasn't Charlie's girlfriend. She was Len's. I looked her up online. There are stories about how he'd jilted her when he got married."

It took a moment for that to sink in. "So Charlie was just lyin' through his teeth at us? I never would've taken him for such a low-down no-count . . ." His words trailed off. I understood how he felt, because I'd also taken Charlie at face value. He'd seemed trustworthy somehow, handsome and reserved yet bracingly honest. But it was all put on, and all Charlie turned out to be was a very convincing actor.

"That's just real disheartenin'. So, lemme guess, Trista and Len were high as kites at Machu Picchu. She dies, and they don't want the rich punk mixed up in the mess, so Charlie takes the fall for it. Which makes sense, 'cause if the cops test him for drugs, he's gonna come through clean as a whistle." Jesse turned his face to the sky again. "I try to see the best in everyone, y'know. I really do. But sometimes it feels like the whole world's out to let you down. They must think the cops are big chumps. Us, too."

"There's more," I said. "Something else that was in the story. Len Wolven's first wife died, too."

"Holy hell. This gets worse every second. She fall from a mountain, by any chance?"

"I don't know. I couldn't find anything about how she died." I'd typed her name, or what I assumed it was—Kirsten Wolven—into a search engine, and had come up with nothing. When I'd tried adding Len's name to hers, I found mentions on a few sites to his "collapse" or "breakdown" after his wife's "sudden death," but not a word about what had caused it. It was as if her life had been wiped away, not only in reality, but virtually speaking, too.

"This is crazy," Jesse said. "How many women who've been with this guy have died?"

"Two, by my count."

Under the starlight, Jesse's warm, kind face had strange shadows playing on it, making him look oddly fierce.

"We need to go to the police," I said. "We have to tell them about this."

"Fine. First crack of dawn, that's what we'll do. But if the rest of our trip consists of us sittin' around jails, I'm blamin' you, Tiger Lily."

19

When Jesse and I finally retreated to our room, I felt frustrated and defeated; judging from Jesse's stormy expression and clenched jaw, his mood matched mine. How would the police react to the news about the death of Len's wife? Would that make them look at Trista's death differently, or would it be explained away or ignored outright? Vargas's cold, arrogant demeanor hadn't given me the impression that he cared about finding new evidence. If he'd already written Trista off, I was going to have a hell of a time changing his mind.

The phone was ringing as we came in the door, and Jesse picked it up. "Hello?" Then he stared at it and set it down. "Someone just hung up on me."

"Wrong number?" It was hard not to feel that something was a bit off about it. Was someone trying to check if we were in our room? To do what, exactly?

Jesse seemed to read my mind, because he pulled a chair away from the desk and propped it against the door. "Now I got the creeps," he said. "I hate that."

He went into the bathroom and shut the door. A moment later, the phone rang again. My hand hovered over it for a moment, and then I picked it up. "Who is this?"

There was the sound of heavy breathing on the other end. Just when I was about to hang up, a man spoke. "Is this

Lily?" The voice was slurred, and almost certainly drunk, but I recognized it.

"Leonard Wolven?"

"It's Len. Please. Don't hang up."

The bathroom door opened. "What do you want, Len?"

"I need to talk to you. About Trista."

"Okay." Jesse was beside me now, his head touching mine as we shared the receiver.

"Can you come meet me?" Len's drunken voice was almost wistful.

"No!" I answered with more force than I meant to. "You can ask me what you want on the phone. It's late."

"Okay. I'm sorry. It's just . . ." There were a couple of gulps and a huge sigh. "You were the last person to talk to her. Can you tell me what she said?"

"You tell me something first, Len. Why did you pretend you didn't know Trista was dead?"

"But . . . I didn't. I didn't know."

"How is that possible?"

"Because Charlie's a fucking liar. He kept it from me. He lied straight to my face. He said she was fine, but they had to take her to Cusco by helicopter. I'd passed out and I . . . I thought it was true. I wanted it to be true. I'm so sorry."

"Why did you think I was working for someone?"

"Because of what you said!" This was the first time he sounded anything other than slurry and despondent. There was anger simmering underneath.

"What did I say?"

"I know what you did."

I waited for him to say something else, but instead there was sobbing. Jesse moved his head a few inches away and whirled his finger in the air beside his ear, the universal sign of crazy.

"Len, I thought you hurt Trista. She told me you made her drink something, some kind of drug."

"I was trying to help her," Len said. "But she was a liar. She told me she wanted help. I was trying to be her friend. But she . . ." He started sobbing again.

That had been part of their fight, before Trista collapsed. And that was what Len had said on the mountain. *You lied to me.* Trista had answered, *How dare you judge me!* And then Len had said, *I was trying to help you.* Maybe there *was* some truth in what he was telling me now.

"Len, what did Trista lie to you about?" I asked him.

"I can't tell you," he sobbed. "I don't know what to do. I'm responsible. She lied to me, and I didn't know, but I'm still responsible. I brought her here. This is all my fault."

He was breathing hard, and then there was a slurping sound that made me suspect he was still hitting the bottle. "What did you want to ask me, Len? Why did you call."

He burped a couple of times. "Did she . . . did she say anything about me? When you talked with her, I mean."

I swallowed hard. What Trista had said about him was awful, but in daylight I wouldn't have hesitated to repeat it. At midnight, with him drunk and crying, I thought twice.

"It was bad, wasn't it?" he demanded, his voice agitated and angry.

"She was furious at you," I admitted.

"What did she say?"

"She . . . she said you were crazy. She blamed you for making her take drugs."

"What else?" He was almost yelling now.

"She said you should be in jail, would be in jail, if it weren't for your father's money."

There was total silence on the other end of the line.

"Len? Are you there?"

"She's wrong. She's wrong. Wrong. Wrong. Wrong!" He ranted. "I shouldn't be in jail. I shouldn't be anywhere. I don't deserve to live."

He slammed the receiver down and the line went dead.

20

Jesse took the receiver out of my hand and set it down. "We're gonna have a lot to tell Vargas in the mornin'," he said.

"This can't wait till morning." I picked up the phone and dialed the reception desk. "Please connect me with Len Wolven."

"We have no guest under that name," the girl answered. That must have been for privacy reasons.

"Charlie Cutler then."

"He is in one of our private casitas. They have their own reception desk. I will transfer you."

I bit my lower lip while I waited. Then a man's voice came on the line. "May I help you?"

"Yes. I need to speak to Charlie Cutler, please."

"I am sorry, señora. He has left instructions not to forward any calls. I can take a message, if you like"

"This is urgent!"

"I am sorry—"

I hung up before he finished speaking. "I'm going over there."

"The hell you are," Jesse said. "Len Wolven's got two skeletons in his closet, that we know of. I ain't lettin' him lure you in there, too."

"You heard him on the phone. He's drunk. He was crying. I think he might really try to hurt himself."

"So what?"

Looking at Jesse, I knew that I couldn't admit part of me believed that Len was genuinely shocked Trista was dead. Charlie was a liar; he'd lied to us, and maybe he really had lied to Len as well.

"Lil, this is the guy who knocked you down at the train depot. He's a sick puppy. If you think I'm lettin' you run over there, you got another think comin'."

"Jesse, do you know what hesitation marks are?"

He frowned at me.

"Before someone kills herself—or himself—they often make these marks. They cut into the flesh of their forearms, trying to work up the nerve to cut deep enough into the vein."

"That's awful, but why—"

"My mother had them all over her arms. She was always threatening to kill herself. People who do it talk about it first. They threaten. Hardly anyone kills themselves on the first try, not without beginner's luck." I gulped. "It's a process, Jesse. People build up to it. Len saying 'I don't deserve to live' to me? That's a hesitation mark."

"Okay, we'll go over there and talk to Charlie. Make sure this punk doesn't OD or whatever. But we're not holdin' his hand or anythin'. And no matter what, you aren't goin' off alone to talk Len off the ledge. I don't care what he threatens. Got it?"

"Got it."

Grabbing our jackets, we hurried outside. Following the footpath in the moonlight, we came to a fork that pointed us toward the villas. The closer we got, the more it felt like we were stepping into a dark jungle, with tall trees above blocking the moonlight. There were tiny lights set along the path to guide us, like a trail of fairy tale breadcrumbs. The whole section of the property felt oddly remote from the main building and the cottages, which already felt so secluded from the haphazardness of Aguas Calientes.

"Well, now, this is how the other half lives," Jesse commented when we got to the reception area. The man behind the desk looked wary. "Charlie Cutler, please."

"I apologize, sir, but—"

"I don't want to hear it. A fella just called us, sayin' he would take his own life. We are good and ready to go bangin' down every door in this place if you don't point us to the right one."

The clerk's eyes bulged. "Well, in that case . . . Rafael!" He called to a bellman. "Show these people the way to Señor Cutler's villa."

Rafael led us outside and along a path. There were footlights to guide us, though he turned and warned us to watch our step as we came to a stone staircase. Unlike Machu Picchu, these steps were smooth, with a lighter-colored mortar to keep them even. As we walked up, the night sky vanished behind a canopy of trees.

"Very secluded, very romantic," he said. "Good for honeymoon."

He led us to a villa that sat alone in a clearing. It had to be an illusion, I thought. There had to be other villas nearby. But this one felt perfectly isolated from everything else.

"We'll take it from here," Jesse said. "Gracias."

We knocked on the door and waited. "Who is it?" called Charlie.

"Jesse and Lily. Open up. We need to talk."

The front door swung open. Charlie had taken off his suit

jacket, but not his tie. His expression was severe. Maybe he was recalculating what getting rid of us would cost. Whatever it was, it didn't include pleasantries.

"What do you want?" he asked, stepping back for us to come inside. Jesse strode in boldly, but I felt suddenly as if I should hold back. Charlie hadn't had any time to plan anything, so it wasn't as if we were walking into a trap, I told myself, forcing my feet over the threshold. Not unless Len had deliberately lured us over . . .

I looked around as Charlie shut the door and locked it. The carved wooden furniture and warm, neutral colors were the same as in our cottage, but set on a giant scale. This living room had a ceiling that was two stories high. The fireplace was aglow with burning logs, clearing the room of the damp chill of the evening. Several room-service trays cluttered up the otherwise serene space; each looked as if it had been barely touched. There were beer bottles on the tables, all of which looked open, but what permeated the room was the smell of scotch. I didn't see any bottles, but it smelled as if someone had emptied one over the room and the wood had drunk it in.

"Is this about money?" Charlie had his game face on. "I told you earlier, my offer stands. If you've decided what you want, go ahead and name it."

"Money?" Jesse said, his expression incredulous. "You think we came running over here in the middle of the night over money?"

"Look, let's be adults about this," Charlie said. "That would be the decent thing to do."

"You're gonna tell us about decency? After lyin' to us about that girl today?"

"What lie did I tell?"

"She wasn't ever your girlfriend!"

"I have been circumspect in my choice of words," Charlie shot back. "I have not referred to Trista Deen as my girlfriend. If you or anyone else inferred that, that is your mistake."

"What are you, a lawyer or somethin'?"

"Yes, I *am* a lawyer." He looked from Jesse to me. "You assumed that Trista was my girlfriend. Vargas did the same thing."

"Right now, I don't care," I said, finally finding my voice. "Where's Len?"

"Why do you want to know?"

"What do you think you are, his bodyguard?"

"I'm his friend."

"He's your boss's son," I said. "And he just called me. He's incredibly upset."

"Upset about what?" Charlie asked, crossing his arms.

"About Trista, what else?"

"Len is sleeping right now, so he obviously didn't call you," Charlie said. "It's time for you to go."

"You're a liar!"

We all turned toward the source of the outburst. Len stood on the second-floor landing, scowling down at us. He started down the stairs, and I saw that he was barefoot, wearing only jeans and a button-front shirt.

"Len, you should put some shoes on." Charlie's voice was quiet. "You don't want to hurt your feet, do you?"

"In case any glass is still lying around from that bottle I broke? Shut up, Charlie." Len surged toward us on wobbly legs. His eyes were swollen and his face was blotchy and red. He was obviously very drunk, and I realized he hadn't been putting on an act when he called me. "All of you, shut up. You're making my head hurt. I'll make sure someone shuts you up. I can do that."

"All right, we're done for the night," Charlie said. "Jesse, Lily, I don't think we have anything else to talk about, but if you think we do, we'll speak tomorrow morning."

"Why did you come here?" Len's eyes were on me. Then before I could answer, he added, "Do you hate me?"

"Of course not."

"Do you think I hurt Trista?" There was a plaintive, whiny quality in his voice. The overlap of that and his bloodshot eyes made it hurt to look at him.

"I don't know, Len. Maybe you didn't mean to hurt her, but you did. Maybe it was all an accident."

"That's enough, Lily." Charlie's voice was stern. "Leave. Now."

"Shut up, Charlie! You don't give the orders here. I do. You're just an employee of my father's, and you're here to do whatever I fucking tell you." Len shook his head, like a fighter who'd just taken a punch, and rubbed his eyes. When he spoke again, his voice was soft and quiet. "Lily, please believe me. I wanted to help Trista. She called me and told me she needed help. That's why I flew her down here."

"She called you for help?"

He nodded quickly. "She was in a bad place. I was, too, but I thought I could help—"

"Len, you need to go rest," Charlie said, moving next to him and putting his hand on Len's arm. Len shrugged it off roughly.

"Lily, tell me more about what she said."

"I told you that already. Charlie's right, you should go get some rest now."

"I need to know." Len's voice was a childish plea. "You have to tell me."

"How about this, Len. I'll talk to Lily while you get some

rest," Charlie suggested, using a patronizing voice as if he were negotiating with a particularly willful two-year-old.

"So you can report back to my father and lie to me about it?" Len snapped. He turned back to me. "Why did she say I should go to jail?"

"I don't know, Len. She was sick and sometimes she had a hard time talking. But—"

"What? What is it?"

"I don't know. Maybe it was because of your wife," I said.

Len's jaw dropped, and he took a step back. His face was draining of color and his shoulders were hunched up. He was staring at me with a look of pure bewilderment and pain, as if I'd just reached out and slapped his face.

Charlie stepped forward. "Len's not himself right now. He's very upset. I'm sorry, but you need to go."

That was when all hell broke loose. As Charlie moved toward the front door, Len rushed to the fireplace, threw the grille aside, and reached into the flames. "Len!" Charlie yelled, running to him and pulling him back. Len resisted, leaning farther in, and I tried to imagine what he was doing. Was there evidence in the fireplace, something he was willing to walk through fire to make certain that it was destroyed? He flailed his arms and hit Charlie as he was pulled back. But it was too late. The fire had leaped onto Len's shirt and was encircling his torso. Len screamed and flapped his hands, making the flames jump.

"Roll on the floor!" Charlie yelled. He was trying to push Len down, and the flames shot up his own arms. They were beginning to engulf him, too. I was frozen in place, unable to do anything but watch in horror. Only Jesse had the presence of mind to grab the giant tapestry down from the wall and throw it over Charlie and Len. He beat down the flames, extinguishing them. But by then, Len lay on the floor, unconscious.

21

We waited at the villa until the police came. Vargas showed up with a couple of officers, but I didn't see Angel. Charlie's statement to them was brief. "Len tried to kill himself. It's not the first time. He suffers from severe depression."

Vargas told Jesse and me to leave, and said that he would speak to us in the morning. When we left, Len was being given oxygen and a medical evacuation was being arranged. Later, when we were back in our room, we heard the distinctive whirr of a helicopter coming in for a landing.

"That was a hell of a thing," Jesse said. He was lying on his bed, staring at the ceiling. I was sitting beside him, my back against the headboard. We hadn't said much after we'd left the villa; I think we were both dazed by what had happened.

"Yes, it was. I still can't believe it." I wondered where Bastián had been. The villa had certainly been big enough to house him, too, but he hadn't appeared until the police did. He'd nodded at me but hadn't spoken.

"You think he'll be okay?" Jesse asked.

"His eyelids started fluttering when they gave him oxygen. He had some burns but I don't think they were that bad." Thinking of the burns reminded me of how the room had smelled when the flames were spreading. I think it was singed hair that made me feel ill.

"No, I meant Charlie. One of his hands seemed to be

burned pretty bad." He was quiet for a minute. "Imagine havin' a job like that, takin' care of someone crazy."

I glanced down at him, wondering if he'd forgotten about my mother. That was how I'd felt about my relationship with her. Claudia's heroin addiction had made her impossible to deal with, but as painful as that was, it was never as awful as being a teenager forced to prop up a drunk, crazy mother who was hell-bent on her own destruction.

"You catch the reference to the bottle Len smashed?" Jesse asked. "That's why the place reeked of booze when we went in."

"I noticed that, too. I guess those trays of food were from Charlie trying to get him to eat. But I don't know if Len is crazy or not. He'd been drinking. Maybe he was high on something, too."

"You heard what Charlie said. Len's tried to kill himself before. It . . . it was like you said, about hesitation marks."

"Yes." It was a horrible irony. I'd gone over to Len's villa because I thought he might hurt himself, but it was only when I kept on talking to him that he acted on his suicidal impulse. If I'd hoped to avoid guilt, I'd made a horrible mis-calculation.

"That was real brave of Charlie, grabbing the little creep the way he did."

"That's his job, obviously. Protecting Len from himself."

"You can't pay someone enough to do that," Jesse answered. "I don't like the fact Charlie lied to us, but you gotta respect character, you know?"

"I don't think it's character to cover up for someone else."

"He doesn't even like Len. You could tell from the way Charlie talked about him. He thinks that punk is a piece of trash. But he still risked life and limb for him."

Shaking my head, I realized that even though we'd witnessed the same scene, we weren't going to see eye to eye on it. Even though I willed it not to, part of my heart went out to Len. Whatever he was guilty of, whatever he had done, he was truly tortured by living with it. Charlie, on the other hand, struck me as cold and calculating, a machine who didn't feel remorse. He was looking less and less like Gary Cooper to me, and more like the character Claude Rains had played in *Notorious,* a Nazi who decided to slowly poison his wife when he realized she must be an American spy.

"Why are you always so determined to see the bright side of everything and everyone?" I asked Jesse suddenly. "You know the world isn't really like that."

"The world's a funny place, but most of what's in it is good. But the bad stuff, it's what grabs for your attention."

"You were sounding pretty cynical earlier tonight," I reminded him.

"That was then, this is now."

"I don't understand you." I shifted position so that I was resting on one hip and could watch him more easily. "How can you have gone through what you have and still be so positive about life?"

Jesse's neck tensed up. A shadow passed behind his eyes and a muscle in his jaw clenched. We had been midway through our freshman year of college in New York when Jesse's father had killed his gravely ill mother and then turned his gun on himself. It happened the same week my mother had finally succeeded at killing herself. His tragedy was something he never brought up voluntarily; the few times we'd talked about it, I'd raised the subject.

"Why would you bring that up?" he asked me.

"I'm sorry. I . . ." I wanted him to tell me that the darkness dwelled in his mind the same way it did in mine. I could deal with him being better at hiding it, but I wanted to know that I wasn't alone. Deep down, I felt that I'd been marked by the deaths of my father, mother, and sister, that each loss had taken a toll on me, leaving me less than I had been before, and irrevocably damaged. Claudia swayed at the edge of my thoughts every waking moment, but I was afraid to let her any closer, in case the darkness she carried with her consumed me. I couldn't see any way out. "I shouldn't have said anything."

When he didn't answer, I felt chilled. The thought of causing him pain was intolerable to me. "I didn't mean to make you uncomfortable. I don't understand how you can live with something like that and still be happy."

"They wouldn't let me see their faces," he said suddenly. "Closed casket, y'know. A service and right into the family plot. But when I was there I . . . I had to see 'em. Not even see, just . . . touch."

"You never told me that," I whispered. "Was it awful?"

"Their faces were covered. That was okay. I didn't want to see . . . you know. But I got to hold my mama's hand while I talked to her some." He was quiet again for a while. "I felt like she was there. It wasn't just like talkin' to her spirit, like when I pray. It was just more connected somehow." He sighed.

"What about your father?"

"I was angry at him. I mean, Mama was so sick and in pain, and I understood what he did, in a way, but I was still mad. So was Grandmama. Furious with him. She still is, truth be told. But she went back and forth about whether he should wear his weddin' band to the grave. She took it off him, then we talked, and we put it on again, and, well, we went back and forth like that. It was kinda like we were fightin' with him, I guess." He cleared his throat. "You still fightin' with your sis?"

"I'm scared to. Every time I start to really think about her, it's like I can't breathe."

There was more to it than that. I was afraid Claudia would drag me down into the pit of suffering she and our mother had sunk into. They were both addicts, even if their substances of choice were different. The point was that you could lose yourself with alcohol or heroin. What scared me was this: sometimes, I hurt so much that I wanted to disappear, too. There were times when I thought I would give anything to make the memories that haunted me go away. I couldn't do it on my own, and I couldn't imagine living the rest of my life with them swirling around me, jabbing at me no matter which way I turned. Now that I was completely rootless, lacking family or a real home, I seemed to be standing at the edge of an abyss, ready for a fall of my own.

"You have to find a way to remember her that isn't painful," Jesse said. "It's okay if it hurts sometimes, but you're torturing yourself too much."

"Is there a right amount?" I asked. That made him smile.

"Lil, you got some dark thoughts runnin' through your head. I understand why they're there, but you got to push them away when they start crowdin' in on you. Otherwise they'll take over."

They already have, I thought, but I couldn't say the words.

22

Jesse's serious mood didn't last long. It had mostly evaporated by the time we heard the helicopter leaving. He sat up, as if that would help him hear it better. "I hope Charlie'll be okay and all, but otherwise I'm thinkin' good riddance to bad rubbish."

"What do we do now?"

"We let the police sort it all out. Honest, Lil, I wish we'd never got involved. Bad enough I brought you to a spot where you had to watch a lady die. Then you had to watch Len freak out tonight. I owe you a refund, plus damages. Promise me you won't sue."

"How about you just come visit me in Spain next month? That would be better."

"You sure you'd want me around? I'm like a wacko magnet these days." He gave me his most wicked smile. "Y'know, I'm from a whole long line of crazy folks."

"Look who you're talking to," I reminded him. "I'm the last in a long line of insane people."

"That sounds like somethin' from a novel. The last of the ancient race of the Ushers."

"Now you're quoting Edgar Allan Poe?" I stared at him in disbelief. "Did we travel to some alternate universe?"

"That's what you get for leavin' a pile of stuff at my apartment, Tiger Lily." His smile now verged on smug. "Us Okies can read and everythin'. You lay books in our path and watch out."

"I didn't mean to make a mess of your apartment. I should put that stuff into storage." Back in January, I'd packed a couple of boxes of personal items and mementoes from the Lower East Side apartment I'd once shared with my sister and moved them to Jesse's. Then I'd e-mailed everyone I knew in New York and told them to come over and take what they wanted from the place. Right before the locusts descended, I had a panic attack and swept through the rooms, piling some clothes and books and other things I'd decided to give away into trash bags, which I'd also deposited at Jesse's. I'd turned my friend's lovely, airy Greenwich Village apartment into a setting that could have been mistaken for the pawnshop in the Humphrey Bogart film *Conflict*.

"It's okay. I let the boxes alone, but I figure whatever's in the trash bags is fair game."

My friend was the kindest, warmest, person I'd ever met, but his devotion came with a price. He was also the nosiest man in the world. When we'd lived together, he'd thought nothing of opening up my mail if he didn't recognize the return address. His snooping was part of the package, and I could hardly complain that he'd gone through what I'd left in his home. "So that's how you discovered Poe?" I asked. "Does this mean you're going goth on me now?"

"Yeah, get ready to meet my dark side," he said.

"I can hardly wait."

It took me a long time—and a hot bath, and a warm glass of milk—to fall asleep that night, but I finally did. And, for the first time in weeks, I had a dream. Or at least a dream I remembered.

I couldn't say how it started, but I was walking into a dark room, and someone pulled back a heavy velvet curtain, and suddenly strobe lights were dazzling my eyes. There was a gigantic mirrored disco ball hanging above, and it swayed wildly, like a massive pendulum, through the room. There were people everywhere, and lights flashing constantly in all directions. It was like being in the middle of a violent lightning storm, only instead of thunder, there was disco.

"I can't believe I was ever in love with that bastard," said someone beside me. I turned and saw Trista. Her red hair flowed around her face like a mane, and she was wearing a low-cut dress that displayed her huge chest. "I threw away the best years of my life on him. But don't worry, I'm getting even." She wasn't looking at me, but at the dancers, her head swiveling from side to side. We were standing on a platform that was slightly elevated, and she took a step down. I felt a sudden panic, sure that she would fall, but she moved down the steps smoothly, disappearing into a crowd of dancers that swallowed her up whole. I stepped after her and tumbled down, somersaulting past far more steps than Trista had taken. I landed on my back and opened my eyes, but I was blinded by the strobe lights.

"This is not your scene," said a voice beside me. "You have to keep one eye on the exit, Honey Bear." A hand touched mine.

The next thing I knew, I was sitting bolt upright in bed, patting the blanket around me for Claudia's hand. She was the only person in the world who'd ever called me Honey Bear. *You were dreaming,* I told myself. I lay back, torn between sifting through the details of the dream and pushing the whole thing out of my mind. If there was one kind of music I hated, it was disco. It brought back memories of my mother, who used to play the same records over and over, often singing along with them, chiming in on the chorus with her gin-soaked voice. "Heaven Knows," that Donna Summer song, was playing in the disco in my dream. That had been a favorite of my mother's, who'd emigrated from Ireland to America when disco was still king. The echo of it made me queasy.

Reaching down next to the bed, I grabbed my knapsack, rifling through it and pulling things out until I found my iPod. Jesse's snoring wasn't enough to drown out the disco, but Frank Sinatra's cool, crisp voice did. I listened to "I've Got You Under My Skin" with my eyes closed, drinking it in. I loved how you could hear him enunciate every syllable, yet his breezy style made the words feel effortless. We weren't supposed to bring extraneous items on the Inca Trail with us, but Sinatra was essential as far as I was concerned.

I turned on the bedside lamp, praying that it wouldn't wake Jesse, but he was dead to the world. In front of me was a mess of tissue and gum wrappers and other junk. Then I found what I was looking for, a photograph of two little girls in front of a Christmas tree. Both Claudia and I were grinning, clearly anticipating joy in the wrapped boxes beneath it. The sight of our younger selves made me smile, even though I knew that what was ahead of us was grim. A couple of days after that photo was taken, our father was dead, and our mother disappeared into a gin bottle.

Gently tucking the photo away, I lay back, still listening to Sinatra. "I'm a Fool to Want You" was playing now, the melancholy love song he'd written for Ava Gardner. It usually brought to mind my ex-fiancé, but I was obsessed with the dream I'd just had. It didn't take a psychoanalyst to see how I'd blended Claudia and Trista in it. The drug connection was an obvious one. Two addicts trying to leave the embrace of a lover who wouldn't let go. Popular culture pretended that a drug addiction could sink a soul in a matter of weeks or months, but I knew that a habit could be sustained for years, growing until it had consumed everything else in a person's life. When a person got to the point where nothing else—no relationship, no love—was as important as the drug, she was lost. Neither my presence nor Claudia's had ever got in the way of my mother's drinking.

I closed my eyes, but there was something that nagged at me, something important I couldn't quite grasp, much in the same way I'd tried to grab my sister's hand before she vanished. There was a part of the puzzle I hadn't consciously processed, even though some part of my brain had picked up on it. I lay awake, trying to force it to the surface, but it kept escaping, just like Claudia. Then, just as I was falling asleep again, I realized what it was. Marianne, that was the name of Len Wolven's second wife. The stripper from Texas, the check-kiter. What hit me suddenly was this: when I'd said to Len, just before he threw himself into the fire, *Maybe it was because of your wife,* I'd been referring to Kirsten, who seemed to have died under mysterious circumstances. But where was the Vegas showgirl that Len had married six months ago, and why wasn't Len traveling with her?

23

Jesse and I woke up very early the next morning. My friend was determined to get a look at Machu Picchu as the sun rose over it, precisely the vista we'd been partially denied by the fog the day before. Part of me wanted to stay in bed; hearing my sister's voice in that dream had unsettled me, but it had also left me longing to catch a glimpse of her again. Claudia had always been like a cat: when you went looking for her, she was impossible to find. But Jesse's enthusiasm, coupled with Vargas's promise to show up first thing at the resort, got me up and into the shower. Then Jesse dragged me to the dining room, a space with floor-to-ceiling windows looking out onto a drizzly morning. But inside it felt fresh and crisp, and it was brightly lit for the predawn crowd.

"Hey, look at this spread! Now that's what I call breakfast."

There were mounds of food on long, curving tables. Even from the doorway I could see platters of fresh fruit and bacon and bowls of yogurt.

"Boy, that bacon smells good. They cook eggs in the kitchen and bring 'em to your table." As usual, my friend's mind was on his stomach. He handed me a plate and started filling his own as well as mine. "You gotta try the potatoes. Did you know there are five thousand varieties of potato in Peru? And that the potato came from Peru in the first place?" Jesse's enthusiasm was boundless, especially where food was concerned.

"They'd better have real coffee," I grumbled.

"Better than that. Nescafé!"

"Not again . . ." I stopped speaking and stared at the open doorway. Felipe Vargas walked into the dining room and headed straight for us. Two steps behind him was a handsome man I'd never seen before. He was tall and slim and looked more Italian than Andean. He had wavy black hair that shone like patent leather, a generous mouth that curved up at the corners, and long-lashed dark eyes.

"Buenos dias," Vargas said. "Allow me to introduce Hector Alcántara. A detective. From—"

"A *police* detective," Alcántara corrected him.

"A police detective. From Lima." Vargas's tone left no room for doubt. Apparently, the only thing worse than being an American was to be from Peru's capital city. "Allow me to introduce Lily Moore and Jesse Robb, of New York."

"Delighted. *Li-ly*," Alcántara said, drawing out the two syllables as if he were curling them around his tongue. "What a beautiful name. Just like a flower."

"Thank you." His warm, almost flirtatious manner surprised me. Vargas's face was blank, but he shot me a glance. It was not an approving one.

"Your parents chose a very appropriate name for you. Is it a family name?" Alcántara asked.

"Yes. My father's mother was called Lily." I'd never met her; from what my father had told me, she'd died when he was young. But he'd adored her, and so I was given her name.

"Ah!" Alcántara smiled more broadly. "I love family traditions. Myself, I am named for my grandfather. Custom in Peru and America is not so different, is it?"

"Maybe not."

"Are you returning to the mountain today?"

"That's the plan," Jesse answered. Alcántara glanced at him and then back at me.

"Good, good. I pray that you will have a good day there, one that will push the sad memories of yesterday from your mind." His cocoa-brown eyes were almost liquid with concern. But his sympathy was undercut by the way his eyes occasionally darted around the room, as if there might be someone more important for him to speak with.

"It's a long trip for you to get here," Jesse said. "All the way from Lima? Wow. What brings you to these parts?"

"What an excellent question," Vargas said. "Why not enlighten us all, Hector?"

The friction between them was palpable. Vargas was openly antagonistic, but Alcántara was restrained. He gave Vargas a sour smile, as if he'd bitten into a lemon but was determined to pretend his tongue easily tolerated its tartness. "You know very well why I am here, Felipe. But, unfortunately, I am not at liberty to discuss it. Of course, you could have saved me the trip here had you informed me that the men I needed to interview had already gone to Cusco."

"How was I to know that you would arrive here in the early hours of the morning?" There was acid in Vargas's tone. "Such eagerness. It almost makes me believe in the existence of that illegal road from Santa Teresa that I'd heard about. I will have to investigate that sometime. I have never seen you investigate any other crime with such vigor."

Alcántara brushed that off with a little shake of his glossy head. "The events of yesterday are most shocking, I am certain we all agree. Felipe has been kind enough to give me your contact details in Cusco. I will have questions for you both, but first, I would like to ask some questions about Leonard

Wolven and Charles Cutler. I trust I will have no difficulty reaching you both tomorrow?"

"We're happy to talk whenever you are," Jesse answered.

"Excellent. My best wishes to you both for a perfect day on the mountain." Alcántara nodded at us both and walked out, ignoring Vargas. I looked at him and he shrugged.

"I know no more about his visit than you do. All I can say is that his eagerness to get here speaks volumes."

Vargas's gruff frankness startled me. "Is there any news on Len Wolven or Charlie Cutler?" I asked.

"They are both in hospital in Cusco, but neither case is critical. They will be released in a day or so." He lowered his voice. "Mr. Cutler gave me his version of last night's events, but I am curious about yours. All you said was that Len Wolven telephoned you. I still do not understand why you were at the villa."

"Len called because he wanted to know what Trista Deen had said about him before she died," I admitted. "I told him that she said he should be in jail, that only his father's money kept him out of jail. Len got upset and told me he didn't deserve to live. He hung up, and I couldn't get him back on the phone. Jesse and I went over because we thought he might harm himself."

"You were certainly correct about that."

"There's more. Len Wolven's first wife died under strange circumstances. I don't know the details, but—"

"You are referring to Kirsten Wolven, I presume?" Vargas said.

"How did you know?"

"There is this marvelous invention called the Internet, Miss Moore. It even works in Peru." Maybe I looked suitably chagrined by my stupid biases, because Vargas went on. "Mr. Cutler explained it to me. Leonard Wolven was driving a car while drunk, and he ran it off the road. His wife died, but he did not. A tragedy."

Charlie's propensity for lying made me wonder if that was the full story, but I didn't say anything.

"One more question: what do you think of the relationship between Mr. Cutler and Mr. Wolven?" Vargas asked.

"Charlie works for Len's father. Len was contemptuous of him," I said.

"I think Charlie's doin' his level best to keep Len out of trouble, and Len resents the hell out of him," Jesse added.

"Interesting," Vargas murmured. "I had suspected some sort of love triangle, but it appears Trista Deen was not involved with either man."

"*Not* involved?" I asked. "What do you mean? She was traveling with them."

"Ah, not *romantically* involved, Miss Moore." Vargas cleared his throat.

"How d'you know that?" Jesse asked.

"There have been, ah, tests. There were no signs of, ah, recent activity." Vargas's own answer was delivered with an uncharacteristic fiddling with his collar. Talking about sex—or even the lack of sexual activity—clearly made him awkward and embarrassed. "I will likely have more questions for you later," he added. "Perhaps after I learn what my well-styled counterpart wants. Either way, I will be in touch in Cusco. Good day." He inclined his head slightly and departed as well.

"That was an interestin' show," Jesse said. "Wonder if it's always fireworks when Cusco meets Lima, or if there's more to it than that."

My mind was turning on Trista's sex life, or lack of one, and Vargas's discomfort at discussing it. "I don't know."

"Why would a Lima cop come all this way?" Jesse shook his head. "My argument before about stayin' out of this mess? That goes double now."

"Can you imagine a bluer sky? It's bigger than Oklahoma!" Jesse said. "This is the Machu Picchu I wanted you to see, Tiger Lily."

The light, early morning rain had disappeared as we went through the turnstiles at the front gate, and if there had been any fog, that shroud had already lifted. I could see the Urubamba River snaking through the valley below us, and majestic mountaintops rising in the distance. Llamas roamed freely on the terraces, jumping from one to the next and grazing, ignoring the humans on the site.

"Can we go look at the place Trista fell?"

"There's nothin' here but the same ole staircase. Same as the past five hundred years."

"But I want to see it."

"You are the gloomiest girl ever. You need to put it behind you. It's gonna wreck this trip if you keep thinkin' on it."

I stared a little ahead, where the Inca houses were. They were made from finely fitted stones, just like everything else on the site, though some curator had added thatched straw roofs, to mimic what they would have had five centuries earlier, when the mountain was a royal retreat. The impulse to re-create a site was natural enough, but it struck me as odd. I didn't need help imagining the site as a thriving city back in the day. What I could have used was help turning my imagination off. There was some other part of my dream that was niggling at me. How could I explain that to Jesse?

"Lil, honey, you need to put that out of your mind," Jesse added, his voice softer.

"Can you do that?"

He nodded. "You just shove it back and close the door. It might try to come out, but you push it harder."

"Let me get this straight. You have a closet in your brain to hide dark thoughts?"

"Not a closet," he answered, the corners of his mouth turning up. "It's more like ... compartments. And if I'm doin' one thing, I'm not thinkin' about the others."

"I wish I could do that. Everything hangs over me like a shadow."

Jesse sighed. "That's not very Ava-like, y'know. She's supposed to be your role model. She definitely had lots of compartments for dark thoughts in her brain, what with all her lousy husbands and boyfriends and the like."

"The compartment for Mickey Rooney must've been little."

That earned a grin. "Now, that's my girl."

"I still want to see where Trista fell," I added, in case he got the wrong idea. "I had a dream about her and ... I don't know, it felt like I was missing something yesterday."

"We're not revising history, right? I mean, we know what we saw. Right, Lil?"

"But what about what we heard?"

Jesse shrugged. "We didn't hear much."

"We did. We heard Len call her a liar. What we didn't hear was her denying that she lied."

Jesse blinked at me. "You got a point there. If I heard it right, she said, 'How dare you judge me.' She was plenty mad, too, from the sound of it."

"Until I saw Len last night, I thought he was the villain in all this," I admitted. "But maybe he was trying to help her. Don't ask me how. But last night I saw Trista in a dream, and it reminded me of something else she said."

"What's that?"

I closed my eyes to picture the scene more clearly. "I can't believe I was ever in love with that bastard. I threw away the best years of my life on him. But don't worry, I'm getting even."

"Get even? How was she gonna do that?"

"That's what I'm thinking about. Let me put it this way: if someone cheated on you, how would you get even with him?"

"I'd bash his head in with a baseball bat. Okay, that's just my fantasy. In reality, when Ted cheated on me with Bit Part, I put his lucky suit in the dryer so it would never, ever fit him again." Jesse stared into the distance. "I don't feel bad about it, neither."

Even though thinking of Trista made me sad, Jesse's confession made me smile.

"What about you?" he asked me. "There was that Lady Architect . . ."

"Yes, I remember. I Google-stalked her for ages. I thought about ways to wreck her life, but I couldn't think of anything that wouldn't make me seem like a nutcase."

"So you did nothin'?"

"No."

"You're kiddin'. Nothing?" He stretched out each letter.

"Except for reporting her to the IRS."

"Aw, now that's my girl. Guess they audited her?"

"It was a little worse than that. She was getting paid for some of her work abroad through a foreign account. One I thought the IRS should know about."

"So what happened?" Jesse's face was beaming with some sort of misplaced delight.

"I don't know. It's not like the IRS gives its anonymous tipsters updates. But the next thing I knew, she was unemployed and moved back to her home state." I shrugged. "She married some guy there, so maybe that was part of her plan all along. It's not like she went to jail for tax evasion."

"We're kinda lame on the revenge front, we are," Jesse said. "You hear about those crazy folks who set up Web sites and stuff. I wish I could do that, but I'd feel like a big jerk."

"Which brings us back to Trista. Len said she called him and said she needed help. He flew her down here. What kind of help did she need?"

"Getting away from a bad boyfriend?" Jesse said.

"Maybe, but I didn't get the sense she was over Len. There was one other thing she said. 'He's already crazy, so it wasn't hard to make him crazier.' How would she do that?"

"I see that Len's crazy, but I dunno. Give him drugs?"

"According to Bastián, Len's already on drugs all the time anyway."

"Whaddya mean, according to Bastián?" Jesse stared at me. "When'd you have this conversation with him?"

"Last night. In the computer room."

"I can't believe it. I leave you alone for an hour and you're off with a thug."

"He's not a thug," I said.

"You have lousy taste in men."

"Look, can we just go back to where Trista fell? I want to make sure that there isn't something obvious we missed yesterday."

Jesse kept his disapproving face on, but we hiked over together. When we got there, after passing through the quarry and Serpent Rock, there wasn't anything to see. There was the staircase, and people were taking pictures of it and the glorious valley below it, but there was no hint that a woman had died there the day before. Jesse walked up and down the stairs with me, but whatever I'd hoped to find never materialized.

"She was high," Jesse said finally. "She was raving. I think that's all we're gonna understand about what was in her head."

We went on to Huayna Picchu, the sacred peak that towered above Machu Picchu, and lined up for tickets to hike to its top. That journey should have felt dangerous, because there wasn't any sort of railing to cling to, just mountain on one side and open air on the other, with a narrow stone staircase in between; instead, it was exhilarating, as if I'd found a pathway up into the clouds. From the top, I tried to pinpoint the staircase below where Trista had fallen.

"Look at that, Machu Picchu spread out in front of you. Isn't it amazing?" Jesse asked, shooting photo after photo.

There was no sign of Trista's life or death, or that she'd ever been on the mountain. It was stupid of me to think that there would be. The tourists who'd just arrived at Machu Picchu that morning would never know she'd been there, or what had happened to her. And as I considered it, I realized that I knew nothing about her, either.

"Jesse, what if that was her revenge?"

"What?"

"Dying."

"Come on, now, Lil."

But I thought of her, heart racing, her hand gripping mine. *Len made me drink something that made me sick. Then he pushed me down the stairs. Tell the police. Promise me.* Had any part of that actually been true?

25

When we finally got back to our hotel in Cusco, all I wanted to do was rip off my clothes and take a long bath with a relaxing glass of wine. Physically, I was ragged. The combination of the hiking, the stress, and the altitude was taking its toll. On top of that, our train had deposited us in Poroy, where buses and taxis waited to take travelers back to Cusco. I'd tried to wake Jesse up, but as usual that was a long process unless you had a pair of cymbals handy. By the time we'd stumbled off the train, the buses had departed, and we'd been lucky to land a driver with a ramshackle Toyota, so we'd had a bumpy ride back to Cusco. At least when we got to our hotel, the clerk, Rosaria, was the same smiling nineteen-year-old who'd been working when we'd first checked in, before we left for Machu Picchu. She greeted us warmly, then found the keys for our room.

"Your luggage has been moved from storage into your suite," she told us. "It is waiting for you. Also, there's a message." She handed Jesse a folded piece of paper.

He stared at it. "What the hell?"

I looked down at the note. *Do not check in. Leave Cusco immediately.* It was printed in a curving, slightly awkward script.

"Who left this?" I asked.

"A man telephoned, and I wrote it down," said Rosaria.

"I asked him for his name, but he said he was a friend and you would know who it was."

That was frustrating. No fingerprints. "Can you trace the call?"

"Um, *trace*?" Rosaria looked confused. I glanced over the counter between us and saw an old beige plastic phone. No call display on that thing.

"That's downright lame," Jesse said, pocketing the note. "Not even like it's warnin' us of danger. No, we're supposed to run away 'cause somebody said *boo*."

"I'm sorry," Rosaria said. "I didn't mean to cause trouble."

"You didn't," Jesse assured her. "Probably somebody's idea of a joke. Hey, is the restaurant open?"

"Sorry, but it is only open for breakfast. But there are many places to get dinner in the Plaza de Armas."

Jesse rolled his eyes at me. *Only lazy tourists eat in the Plaza de Armas,* he'd told me when we'd first come in. We took the stairs up to our new home away from home. This time, the hotel had put us in a second-story suite that was just down the hall from the one we'd first stayed in. It had two small bedrooms, each with a night table and a desk and chair, and a decently sized sitting room in between. Through the window, there wasn't much of a view of town—we were at the back of the hotel, which meant that most of our view was blocked by other roofs—but we could see the night sky and the lights of buildings that went up a hill. That was where the people of Cusco lived; many worked in or near the historic town square, with its hotels and restaurants and grand colonial churches, but the small, mostly flat, part of the city that most tourists stayed in was a far cry from how most locals lived.

"You know what I could really go for right now?" Jesse asked.

"One of those cute animals they have here? Guinea pig? Alpaca?"

"Naw, I'm thinkin' pizza."

"What happened to eating Peruvian cuisine?"

"I reckon I'm an individual with a wide spectrum of tastes."

"You had hot dogs at Machu Picchu," I pointed out. "Also, pizza for dinner last night. I think that those are the only two food groups they have in Aguas Calientes."

Jesse laughed. "You got a scorecard there? Listen, there's a great pizza place that's behind the cathedral and down some street to the right of it."

"You don't know where it is, do you?"

"Sure I do. My stomach will lead."

"Ugh. Pizza again."

"Don't worry, I'll bring you back somethin' else," Jesse offered.

"Bring me back . . . what are you talking about?"

"I'm not gonna say I'm creeped out by that note, but I don't like it. Maybe we should look at rearrangin' our plans. Cusco's okay and all, but Arequipa's a beauty. It's got these volcanoes around it, and a lot of the colonial stuff is made from *sillar*."

"What's *sillar*?" I asked, taking the bait.

"It's this white rock made from ash. It gleams in this amazin' way, like it's lit from within. We're only gonna have a day there before we leave for the Colca Canyon." Jesse had arranged our itinerary like a marathon. "If we leave Cusco early, we could have a few days there."

"I'm not leaving Cusco because of some stupid anonymous warning. That's ridiculous."

"That li'l note really is dumb, ain't it?"

"It's not even a proper threat. It's the kind of thing a kid would write."

"You got a point. But humor me on this, Tiger Lily. I'm goin' out to pick up food. You stay here and have a little siesta."

"I need a bath, not a nap."

"Well, you also need dinner, and this here hotel, while mighty nice, does not have room service. We need food. Then we need to figure out what to do. Maybe we don't change our plans at all. I'd wager that weirdo Len Wolven called and left the message. He ain't exactly a threat to anyone but himself."

After Jesse left, I opened up his suitcase and started unpacking for him. My friend liked to look good, but it wasn't his favorite thing to hang clothing up where it belonged. It wasn't really mine, either, but there was something sweeter about doing it for someone else. It was embarrassingly retro of me, but it fulfilled my daydream of a 1950s-era marriage to Jesse: fun, conversation, maybe some dancing, then home to our separate beds, or even separate bedrooms. The more I'd seen of romantic love, the more that chaste fantasy seemed ideal. Ava Gardner's song from *The Killers* ran through my head. *"The more I know of love, the less I know,"* she'd sung. That was exactly how I felt. All I'd learned over the past year was that I had terrible taste in men. With the exception of Jesse, if I trusted one, it was a mistake. True, I'd been able to trust Bruxton when it came to a professional matter—finding my sister—but the passing of his fleeting interest in me made me relieved that I hadn't put any further faith in him. The last thing I needed in my life was another addict, no matter how reformed.

After I finished sorting out Jesse's things, I moved on to my own case, which I stared into with dismay. What had I been thinking when I packed? Everything in it was black. Looking down at it felt as if I were staring into a black hole. That was exactly how I had been for three months, I realized. Something had shifted in the past two days. It wasn't that my heart was lighter or that I'd come to accept Claudia's death any better. But instead of feeling sad and empty, I was angry. That childish little note was the coup de grâce. I had no plan to let anyone nudge me out of Cusco. It wasn't that I wanted to be there, but there was nowhere else I wanted to be, and the thought that I'd become such a nervous little mouse that a note would send me off and running was infuriating. Tomorrow, I'd show it to Vargas, and if he traced it back to Len Wolven, there'd be hell to pay.

My train of vengeful thoughts was derailed by someone pounding on the door. I looked through the peephole, felt my heart leap, and opened the door. Bastián stood there, breathing hard as if he'd been running.

"Jesse's been hurt," he said.

I grabbed for the door frame so that I wouldn't fall. "What happened?"

"I don't know exactly. I was at the hospital with Charlie and Len when they brought him in. They said he'd lost blood. I came over immediately."

"Where's the hospital?"

"I'll take you. But put on your shoes. And a coat. It's freezing outside."

I couldn't think about anything but getting to Jesse. Bastián pointed out my shoes, then wrangled me into the same jacket I'd been hiking in. I grabbed my bag and keys. He guided me out of the hotel, his hand resting gently on my back. It was cold out, and rain was coming down hard.

"This way," Bastián said, putting up an umbrella and leading me along the street. "Careful of your footing. It's slippery out here, and the drivers are crazy."

"Can we get a taxi?"

"I have a car," Bastián said. "It's this way." He led me past a row of touristy shops and to a small plaza with a church and a fountain I hadn't seen before. "Down here." Bastián gestured at an alleyway. The car was a four-door sedan, and he opened the passenger side first. I moved to get in but the seat was filled with open maps and books.

"Damn it," he said. "I wasn't thinking. Here, take this." He handed me the umbrella. "Let me put that in the back." He marched to the back of the car and unlocked the trunk. I grabbed a bundle of papers and carried them to him.

"Thanks. Just drop them anywhere, Lily," he said. As I did, he grabbed me from behind, pressing a cloth against my face. It smelled sweetly acrid, and the force of his hand against my mouth prevented me from screaming. I dropped the umbrella and struggled, but his arms held me tight. He whispered something I couldn't quite catch, except for *mina*. Then his voice got farther and farther away until everything in front of my eyes melted away with the rain.

26

When I came to, it was pitch-black, but I was moving. Under me, the ground rocked and shook, as if I were in an earthquake. The room smelled of gasoline, but there was something cloying hanging in the air beside it. My head throbbed, and I tried to focus my eyes. Everything stayed just as dark when my eyelids went up as when they went down.

That wasn't the ground moving, I thought. That was my head spinning. Bastián had drugged me; that lingering, sweetish scent was an olfactory remnant of the drug he'd used. My senses were so jumbled that it took me another moment to realize there was something in my mouth. My tongue felt thick and woolly, but I could tell it was pressed up against something. I tried to spit it out and couldn't. When I tried to reach for it, I realized my hands were tied behind my back. It struck me suddenly that my body was crunched into an S-shape and I tried to thrust out my legs, but they hit metal. My scream came out as a pathetic muffled gurgle, like that of an animal about to be put down. I was in the trunk of Bastián's car.

That was when I lost my mind. Adrenaline surged through me as terror took hold. I thrashed around like a caught fish. As I hyperventilated, the gag in my mouth seemed to sink into my throat. I'm going to suffocate, I thought, and for a moment, I must have lost consciousness. I was certain I was going to die. In the darkness, Claudia took my hand. *You need to get a grip, Honey Bear. Trust me.*

I can't! my brain screamed. *I'm trapped!* I was claustrophobic in small rooms; being locked and bound in a trunk was a nightmare for me.

I'm here and nothing bad is going to happen to you.

You can't promise that! my mind yelled back. That was the last thing Trista had said to me on the mountain, and it brought tears to my eyes.

Breathe. Just breathe.

I took a long, slow breath and tried not to retch at the smell. Part of my brain was aware, even then, that my sister couldn't possibly be with me, but it was ignored by the part that remembered being locked in darkness with my sister.

Like music heard in dreams, like strains of harps unknown, of birds forever flown, she whispered.

After our father died, our mother occasionally locked us in closets, sometimes to punish us and sometimes to keep us from prying eyes, like when Child Services turned up. Those were the times that Claudia consoled me. She didn't mind the darkness, the sensation of something awful closing in. For years, she made me recite poetry to her, and she would occasionally reciprocate with a few verses, almost certainly from Poe. Hearing it squeezed my heart tight.

Breathe. Stay with me, Claudia commanded as the car thunked and thudded along. Cusco's roads offered a rough ride, but this was extreme, like an unpaved road out somewhere in the countryside. How long had I been knocked out? I tried to move so that I could kick the lid of the trunk, but I couldn't turn enough to do it, so I banged on the side of the car instead. That made a little noise, but not enough. The car went over more rough terrain, jostling me. There was some kind of cloth under me. It wasn't to make me cozy. It was to make sure that there wasn't a trace of me left in the car for anyone to find later.

Think. No swooning.

There were many times I'd told myself I had my claustrophobia under control. I felt a little shiver every time I got on a plane, yet I'd managed to become a travel writer. It wasn't that all small spaces spooked me, it was the sensation of being trapped. More than that, it was the idea of being at the mercy of a crazy person. That was exactly where I was now.

I can't do anything but hold your hand, you know. You need to do the rest.

Claudia's voice receded into the darkness. When she'd first spoken, I would have sworn she was stuffed into the trunk with me. Now, the voice was tucked inside my head, originating from the same folds of my brain that gave me warnings that a certain street in a foreign town looked too shady to stroll down alone. But that didn't matter, because the words were exactly what she would've said if she were beside me.

Jesse, I thought suddenly. Bastián had lied to me about Jesse being at the hospital, but that didn't mean my friend wasn't hurt. Had Bastián attacked Jesse before he'd come for me? If he hadn't, Jesse would be wondering where the hell I was when he got back to the room. He would have been worried and called the police, and people would be looking for me now.

Time. I needed to buy time.

Because someone's going to rescue you? You've watched too many stupid old movies. I'll tell you one I like. Sorry, Wrong Number.

That sent another shot of adrenaline through me. Claudia didn't share my fascination with old movies, but *Sorry, Wrong*

Number was the exception. *That character, the one Barbara Stanwyck played, she could have saved herself,* Claudia had said to me long ago. *She could've screamed. She could've attacked the guy and fucked him up. But she wanted to be rescued, so she died.*

I'm not going to die, I told myself. The next second, the car suddenly stopped, and the engine went silent. I heard a door open, then heavy footfalls, and a key in the trunk. As it opened, the first thing I saw was the night sky, black like velvet and heavy with flecks of light. Then a bright beam hit my face, forcing me to shut my eyes. Keeping my head down, I opened them a little, and Bastián came into focus. Not that I could really see him; he was a hulking, dim shadow holding a flashlight. He must have stepped back as he opened the trunk, I realized. He must have thought I would do something to him. Coward.

"I bet you didn't enjoy that ride much, did you, Lily?" Bastián asked.

I stared at him.

"I shouldn't expect an answer with you gagged up like that." He came forward, still shining the light in my eyes, and reached down, touched the back of my neck and lifted off the kerchief that had secured the gag in my mouth. I spat it out and took deeper breaths. Then I sat up, feeling the freezing mountain air on my face and throat; it wasn't raining here, but the air was icy. It was a relief after being trapped, but a brief one.

"Where are we?" My voice was harsh from the dryness and fumes.

"We're literally in the middle of nowhere," Bastián answered. "I was told to take you to a place where no one would ever find you. This is it."

27

"What are you doing?" I whispered.

"Just following orders," Bastián answered. "This wasn't my idea, you know. But it's too late to do anything about it now."

"Jesse—he's all right?"

That made Bastián chuckle. "He's discovered by now that you're missing but that's not going to help you."

"This is crazy," I argued. "You came into my hotel. People saw you. There's a security camera at the entrance. You can't get away with this, Bastián. You'll be caught."

"By the time anyone finds you, I'll be long gone," he answered. "Don't make any sudden moves. From what I've read, you know how much this hurts." He pulled something out of the pocket of his jacket. In the glow of the flashlight, I recognized the black and yellow plastic of a Taser. I shuddered at a particularly ugly memory. "Let's avoid that if we can," he added, putting it back in his jacket and lifting my chin with a finger. "I also have a set of surgical knives in the car. Trust me, you don't want me to bring those out."

"Look, if you drive me back now, I won't tell anyone this happened. If anyone asks, I'll say we just went somewhere to talk. I'll say I went with you willingly." I hated the pleading in my voice. I was trying to make myself sound reasonable, as if Bastián drugging me and putting me in the trunk of a car and driving me up a mountain to a deserted place wasn't so bad. And it wasn't; we hadn't hit the point of no return.

Maybe I could convince him. "And then I'll leave Cusco. I'll leave Peru. I won't come back. I promise."

He shook his head. "I'm sorry, *mina*." The most terrifying thing about him was his quiet calm. He wasn't anxious or nervous about killing me. This was just a job to him and he'd done it before, countless times for all I knew.

"I can pay you." I hated myself for pleading, but I was desperate. My hands were tied behind my back; all I had was words. "I don't have much money, but I have some very rich friends. They will pay you whatever you want. Millions in cash." My former fiancé's face flashed through my mind; Martin was dishonest and amoral, but as much as I hated him now, I knew that if I asked him for money, he would give it to me. Claudia's ex, Tariq, would help me, too, and his assistance wouldn't have strings attached. "Do you know who Martin Sklar is? He owns a company called Pantheon Worldwide, and he will pay any ransom you ask for me. Or if you let me talk to him—"

"Whoever he is, he's not as rich as Len Wolven." Bastián's tone was dismissive. "And I'd rather avoid trouble with the Wolvens, so I have to do what they're paying me to do."

"Why?" I cried out. "Why would Len Wolven want me dead?"

"Oh, Lily. You've caused a lot of trouble already. They don't want you around for more."

"But all I did was tell the police that Len was on the mountain when Trista fell. And I don't even think the police really care. Look, I'll leave. Immediately. I'll take the first plane out of here to anywhere."

"It's too late, Lily."

"Did Len murder Trista?" Rattled as I was, I still wanted an answer to that question.

"I don't really know the answer to that. I've worked for

the family for years, but only for the son for the past year. He's such a mess, I wouldn't put anything past him."

"Then why does he want me dead?"

"You brought up his wife."

"Kirsten?" I gulped. "He killed her?"

"Who knows? That was before my time. But I know for an absolute fact Len Wolven murdered his second wife."

That sent a chill through me that was harsher than the cold mountain air. "What are you talking about?"

Bastián chuckled softly. "You had no idea about that, did you? Her name was Marianne. Len strangled her to death not three weeks ago. He was high—that little *culeado* is always high—and he killed her. Or maybe he had one of those weird blackouts of his. I don't know if he puts those on or not. Either way, can you believe it? I had to dispose of her body."

Dispose of her body? That made me shiver. "What did you do with her body?"

Bastián stared at me openmouthed. "I can't believe you just asked me that." He seemed genuinely stunned, then recovered. "Len always needs someone to clean up after him and cover for him. Remember the compact I found at Machu Picchu? Trista had cocaine in it. That's why I was sent to get it back."

That puzzle piece clicked into place dimly, but all I wanted was to get out of this trap any way I could. "I don't care about that. And I don't know anything about Marianne. I don't want to know. Why would Len think—"

"He's unstable. I don't think he meant to kill Marianne. It might have been an accident. I think he might even miss his toy."

"His . . . toy?"

"Marianne was a stripper, before she married him. Red hair, big boobs, just his type, you know?" He reached forward and touched a lock of my hair, tucking it behind my ear. "Just like you're my type, *mina*."

My stomach churned, but I was determined not to show it. "Len's completely out of control, Bastián. Next, he could want you dead. You need to get away from him."

"I plan to. But I can't get away from the entire Wolven family. You have to choose which devil you're going to get into bed with, Lily." He stroked my face. "Len doesn't just want you dead. He wants you tortured before you die."

"Bastián, please listen to me . . ."

"I don't want to do it. The thought of torturing you is terrible . . ." His face loomed close, and suddenly his lips were pressing hard on mine. His tongue probed the inside of my mouth, and one hand moved down the front of my shirt, popping buttons open. He pushed his hand into my bra, squeezing my breast so hard it made my eyes tear up.

"I've thought about nothing but this since I saw you, *mina*," he whispered in a hoarse voice.

"Me, too."

"You have?" His voice was suspicious. He kept his eyes on my face, searching for a flicker of doubt or the hint of a lie.

"I was trying to figure out how I'd manage to come back to South America, to see you when you go back to Chile. I thought you said you wanted me to visit." My tone was slightly injured, as if I might be genuinely hurt to learn he wasn't that into me after all.

"Oh, Lily." He pulled me up roughly so that I was no longer sitting in the trunk, but on the edge of the car. Then, as if he suddenly realized that this wasn't going to work well with my hands chained behind me, he took a key ring off his belt, unlocked one cuff, and let me move my arms a bit. Just as he reached to recuff me, I put my hands on his chest, stroking him.

"You're so huge," I whispered. "Is the rest of you this big?"

"I promise, you won't be disappointed, *mina*."

He started to kiss me again, with the same Neanderthal intensity. He rubbed up against me, and I could feel him getting hard. I also realized he wasn't exaggerating his size. "Wrap your legs around my waist," he commanded. I did and moaned as if it were what I wanted, too. My whole body quivered against him, but that was from the cold, thin air, not lust.

"Do you have a c-condom?" I whispered. I'd been aiming for a seductive tone, but the mountain chill was starting to make my teeth chatter. So much for faux-sexy.

"Yes." Of course he did; he'd been planning to rape me all along, though he wasn't stupid enough to leave fluids behind. Bastián took one hand off me to rummage in his trouser pocket. "Dammit. It's g-got to be . . ." He checked the other pocket. "Here." He handed it to me.

"You'd better warm me up. I'm about to fr-freeze to death."

"I hate it in the m-mountains," he said, nuzzling against me. Was he so arrogant and delusional that he really believed I wanted to have sex with him? My left wrist still sported a handcuff bracelet, but Bastián seemed willing to believe that my ardor was real. "I hate it in this c-country. This last year has been the worst of my life. I can't wait to get back to Chile. Even if I have to st-stay in Santiago, it will be worth it."

The way he whined reminded me of a man I tried hard not to think about. When I was fifteen, a friend of mine betrayed a confidence. I'd sworn her to secrecy about my family, but she'd ended up telling all to the school principal. He'd called me to his office, first commiserating with me, and then making it clear exactly what I would have to do with him so that he wouldn't tell the proper authorities about my mother's alcoholism, abuse, and neglect. But as sickening as it was to have his hands on my body, what was worse was the reassurance he wanted from me. He wanted to hear that I enjoyed what he did to me as much as he did—maybe more—and after a few meetings, I knew all about his thwarted dreams and loveless marriage, too.

"You'd like it there, Lily," Bastián said, surprising me for a second.

"Where?"

"Chile, of course."

Of course, I realized in a rush. If he led me to believe that I might live through this encounter, having sex with him would seem like a reasonable price to pay. "Is it warm there?" I shivered violently, though not from the weather. His hand had found its way into my bra again. Mine had found its way into his pocket just long enough to fumble for the power switch of the Taser and flick it on.

"Let me unzip you, baby," I said, not caring that I sounded like a bad porn actress. "Let me see what you've got for me." I reached forward, dropping the condom. "Oh, no! The condom . . ."

"Right here, *mina,*" he said, kneeling down to pick it up. As he started to rise, I eased off the ledge I'd been sitting on, so my feet were solidly on the ground.

"You know what I want?" I said, reaching for his zipper with one hand, while the other returned to the Taser in his pocket. *Please, God,* I thought. I was about to pull it out of his pocket when I realized I'd never make it. He'd break my wrist before I could fire. There was only one way I could see this working. I started to tug his zipper down.

"What?" he groaned.

"This," I said, pulling the trigger.

28

Bastián convulsed and shouted. The blast of the Taser bent him over; he was down but not out. He braced himself against the trunk with both hands, and I grabbed the lid and swung it down. It caught him on the top of his head, but his skull was too thick to allow even that blow to knock him out. I wanted to run for my life, but there was nowhere on the mountain for me to run to, so I grabbed the lid again and pulled it down. He screamed, and I saw that part of his left hand was caught. While he tried to extract it, I ran to the driver's door. He'd threatened me with the knives he had in the car, and I thought they would be sitting out, ready to use. Instead, I saw the keys dangling in the car's ignition. I pulled on the door, found it unlocked and jumped inside. Immediately I locked it and all the other doors, but my hope of a getaway was dashed by the sight of the gearshift. I hadn't driven standard since I was in high school. There was no way I could do it now, in the dark, on an unpaved, unfamiliar road down the side of a mountain. My instinct was to run from the car, taking my chances with my feet. But before I could act on that impulse, I heard Claudia again.

Breathe. Come on, breathe. You can do this. Just remember the clutch.

The clutch. I put my left foot on it, pressing it all the way down. Gearshift, neutral, that much I remembered. I wiggled it around slightly, working up my nerve, then I turned the key and let out the clutch. What if the engine needed time to warm up? I turned to look through the back window, to see what Bastián was doing, but he wasn't there. Was he lying unconscious on the road? Or dead? Whatever scintilla of guilt was needling my Catholic conscience vanished when I heard him try to open the passenger door. He must have crept around that side, thinking I wouldn't have locked it. When it didn't open, he stood, ranting at me in English and Spanish. I didn't understand all the names he called me, but I got the part about cutting me into a hundred pieces and feeding me to vultures.

I had no choice. Just as I pushed the stick into first gear, he smashed the passenger window with the metal flashlight. Glass shattered and rained over me like confetti. I turned my head and flattened the gas pedal. As the car surged forward my body jerked back hard, and I screamed, thinking that Bastián had somehow grabbed me and pulled me back. But it was the kick from the car, and that first blast of terror was instantly replaced by the sensation I was driving off a cliff. I swung the steering wheel to the left, and somehow stayed on the road, taking a sharp curve and continuing straight ahead.

Down, off the mountain. That was my goal—that and living through this. I had no idea where I was. There was no GPS, not that one would have done me much good, since I had no idea where I was starting from or where I wanted to go, except as far away from Bastián as I could get. It took me a couple of tries to find the headlights. I needed them desperately. The driver's seat was set way back for Bastián's huge frame; that left me sitting on the edge of it as I careened down the side of a mountain. Every ten seconds, I was in imminent danger of colliding with the rock face as the road twisted and wound like a snake. There was no guardrail, just a drop down the side that I didn't want to think about.

I would have sold my soul just then to be able to safely stop the car and get my bearings. Well, for that and a cigarette. Bastián might have had a cell phone I could use; my own tote bag might've been in the car, too, with my own phone, for all I knew. I had no idea what had happened to it after Bastián knocked me out. But as afraid as I was to keep going, I was too terrified to stop.

My temples were pounding. Cold air blew in through the broken passenger window. I knew I was overrevving the engine, going too fast in first gear. Focus, I told myself. It's like that scene in *North by Northwest,* where Cary Grant is forced to drive drunk by thugs. At least I wasn't suffering from double vision. Just don't stall out, I warned myself, pushing the clutch again and shifting gears. Only somehow I missed second and went into third.

I took a hairpin turn and gasped when my headlights caught on a shrine at the edge of the drop. It looked like a white dollhouse with a cross on top of it. Jesse had told me about these markers. It was both a loving memorial and a warning beacon—it marked the spot where another car had dived off the cliff.

The only blessing was that the road was empty. If anyone else had been on it, there would have been a fiery crash. But as I swooped along the treacherous switchbacks, the road got straighter. There were fewer curves the closer I got to the base. But the awful thing was that Bastián, watching from above, could watch my progress. Since he brought me here, it stood to reason that he knew the mountain, and if there were a shortcut down, he might be able to attack me again.

After another treacherous twist, I found myself on a gravel road that was easily twice as broad as the mountainside path. It was a bumpy ride, but it led gradually down and was far easier to navigate. I must be coming up to a town, I thought, a moment before the car plunged into a dense thicket that blocked out the moon and stars. I kept driving, waiting for the bright night sky to shine through again, but it didn't. If anything, the darkness closed in around me. I wasn't driving on gravel now; it felt like a dirt road. It got narrower as it wound along, and I started to despair. Was I going to meet up with the mountain I'd been on? My sense of direction, normally strong, was gone. All I could think to do was to keep going.

29

When the gravel led to a paved road that looked wide enough to be a country highway, I was ready to jump out of the car and kiss the ground. But I was still terrified that Bastián might be just behind me, waiting for me to stop, so I didn't stop even to consider which way to go. There were no signs, or lights. Just a starry sky above and my headlights on the ground. I hoped they would lead me where I needed to go.

I don't know how long I drove before I started to worry that I was headed away from Cusco. The only sign I'd seen named a town that started with a Q and had a really long name that I couldn't catch as I speeded by. *Bastián can't get you now,* I told myself. *He's back on the mountain. Even if he knows its secret shortcuts, he couldn't catch up with your head start.*

And even if that bastard Bastián were following you, he'd assume you'd make for Cusco, Claudia's voice murmured in my head. *You driving in totally the wrong direction? Way to outwit him, Honey Bear.*

"Shut up," I snapped aloud. Okay, I was losing it. I promised myself I'd stop at the next place with a working light. They were few and far between.

That turned out to be a small building with a sign out front that I could not read. *Cañas! Carreteles! Señuelos!* The only item on the sign I recognized: *Cerveza!* Beer. I floored the clutch and hit the brakes. The hard stop jolted me forward and then back in my seat.

"That's what you get for not wearing a seat belt," I scolded myself.

I sat in the car, slowly turning my head and hoping I didn't have whiplash. Then I dusted bits of glass off, opened the door and got out. Shaky as my legs were, I was glad to be standing again. When Bastián had reached inside my shirt he'd popped a couple of buttons, so I was now flashing my bra to the empty parking lot. I pulled my jacket tightly around me and considered my options. The car was a disaster. Bastián wasn't just a sociopath, he was a slob, and the backseat was filled with maps, bottles of water, and empty wrappers. There was no sign of my handbag, or a cell phone. I wobbled over to the passenger side and reached into the broken window to unlock the door. Once I had it open, I reached—gingerly because of the tiny glass particles everywhere—for the glove compartment. There were some extra batteries in there, presumably for the flashlight he'd smashed the window with. No wallet. No money. No phone.

I put the car keys in my coat pocket and started walking across the lot. There were a couple of other cars parked in it, and judging from their dodgy, rusty condition, I didn't have high hopes for the clientele inside. *What was Peruvian for* stripper? I wondered. Bracing myself, I walked around to the entrance.

The reek of old fish hit me before I even had the front door fully open. A bell tinkled, but the noise that grabbed my attention was that of voices.

"I swear, man, there are photos from 1969 that prove it," a man was saying. "It's like the Roswell of Peru. You'll see."

"You're full of crap, pal."

Four sets of eyes turned on me. I recognized the red hat with the dangling pompoms before I recognized any of the faces. "Holy shit, it's goth girl!" one of them exclaimed.

"That is so awesome! How'd you find us?"

"I knew there was a special connection between us," said a guy with matted blond dreadlocks. I recognized him as the weirdo from my hiking group who rambled on about UFOs the night before. The pair of binoculars that had hung around his neck at dinner the night before was still in place. I still couldn't remember his name.

Part of me thought this must be what taking a psychedelic drug was like. All these different compartments of one's brain would dump out the contents into a mess that made no sense. "What are you doing here?" I asked. "And where is here?"

"We came here to see Lake Huyapo," red hat said. "It's, like, UFO Central in Peru."

"Those photos are bullshit," another kid muttered.

"Ye of little faith," blond dreadlocks added. "We're definitely going to have a sighting."

A bunch of stoned college kids in the middle of nowhere, looking for UFOs. Of course.

"And what's this place?"

"Tackle shop. But they've got beer and munchies so we're getting supplied."

"We've been here for a few hours, 'cause it's cold out, and the heat won't work in the car," said another. "The lady who owns this place just went downstairs to get more beer."

"Um, can I ask you a question?" red hat asked hesitantly. "How come you have handcuffs on one wrist?"

In my terror at driving along the mountain road, I'd forgotten about it. "It's a long story," I said. For a split second,

I thought about telling them what had happened. No, it was just too much, so I backpedaled. "It's a goth thing."

They all nodded as if that made sense.

"Did any of you happen to bring a cell phone on your UFO expedition?" I asked.

Red hat gave me his iPhone. I retreated to a corner, dialed the hotel, and spoke with a very agitated Rosaria. It took a while for her to let Jesse at the phone.

"Lil, thank God you're all right. I was worried somethin' sick. Praise the Lord!"

"I'm fine, but Bastián Montalvo—that's Leonard Wolven's bodyguard . . ." I had to swallow hard a couple of times while my stomach heaved. "He attacked me. I don't know where he is now. I'm somewhere near Lake Huyapo with the stoners. They're hunting UFOs."

"You sit tight, Lil. We'll come and get you. I gotta call Vargas. Everyone's lookin' for you. Yeah, yeah, she's fine, thank God."

"Who are you talking to?"

"What? Oh, that's Charlie."

"Charlie Cutler?" I said. A gust of cold air hit me, and I felt as if I might drop any second.

"Yeah. He was real concerned about you, Lil," Jesse said. "Vargas insisted I wait here at the hotel for you, 'cause he reckoned there'd be a ransom call and I'd be the fella they'd want to talk to. Charlie came over to wait with me."

Bastián worked for Len Wolven and his job description involved killing me and disposing of other bodies. Who knew what Charlie's role was supposed to be. I could guess: maybe when a phony ransom demand came in, he was supposed to pay it, to show how the Wolvens were on the up and up. He had access to plenty of money. Look at how he'd tried to pay Jesse and me off.

"Jesse, listen to me. Len Wolven . . ." *Just tried to have me killed* was what I wanted to say. But the words died on my lips as I realized that telling Jesse anything now, while Charlie was there, might get him hurt or killed. "Look, I can't tell you anything right now, not with Charlie there."

"What are you talkin' about, Lil? Are you safe where you are? Should the police head there now or can you hold tight till we come get you?"

"We?"

"Charlie's got a car and driver and—"

"Hold on." I moved the phone away from my ear. "How did you guys get here?" I called out. "Do you have a car?"

"Yeah, sure, it's like an old Dodge Dart or something, but it runs."

"I think I'm the strangest thing you guys are seeing tonight," I said. "How would you feel about calling off the UFO hunt till tomorrow and driving to Cusco now?"

"Um, okay."

"Lily Moore, you are not gonna get driven back to Cusco by a pack of stoners!"

"You're right, Jesse. Hey, who's got the keys?" I called. Someone tossed them to me. I didn't know whether these guys were so tame normally, but they were about as fierce as Chia Pets while stoned. Still, if Bastián were lurking anywhere between Lake Huyapo and Cusco, their company would be helpful.

"Call Vargas and have him meet me at our hotel," I told Jesse. "And tell him to bring a key."

"A key?"

"For the handcuffs."

30 The hospital in Cusco—at least, the one they took tourists to—was housed in an architecturally unimpressive rectangle not far from the Plaza de Armas. Against every objection I made, Vargas dragged me there, swearing that he'd lock me back up in handcuffs if I refused.

"I'm perfectly all right," I insisted.

"We'll see about that," he said. *Testaruda mula,* he muttered a couple of times. I was pretty sure that translated into *stubborn mule.* I wanted to ask Jesse, who was sitting beside me, but his hands were balled into fists and his mouth was pressed into a grim line.

Under the bright, sterile lights inside the hospital, I caught sight of myself in a mirror in the examination room, and felt like backing away. My hair was a torrid black halo and my eyes looked dark and wild, with purplish crescent moons underneath. I looked like one of Bela Lugosi's victims in the original *Dracula.* Dressed in head-to-toe black, with pale skin and a gothic air, I realized I'd unknowingly transformed myself into Claudia's twin.

Strangely, that thought didn't bother me at all.

A tall, somewhat round, young doctor examined me. He had a light touch and spoke English well. "Your wrists have some little cuts, but otherwise you appear quite well," he mused. Until he pointed them out, I hadn't noticed thin skeins of blood from where the handcuffs had frayed my skin. All I could think about was Vargas arresting Len Wolven and charging him with his wife's murder. Well, that and getting Bastián into a cement cell, preferably one that wouldn't see daylight for a long time to come.

After the doctor cleaned and bandaged my wrists, he turned me over to the police. The doctor and Jesse left the room and closed the door, leaving me alone with Vargas. He was as still and stern as he was when I'd first encountered him the day before.

"Tell me absolutely everything from the time you left Aguas Calientes," he ordered me.

"Nothing unusual happened on the train. Jesse and I sat together. We were both tired. He dozed and I . . ."

"You what?"

"I was staring out the window most of the time. Just lost in thought."

"Did anyone speak to you on the train?"

I thought about that for a moment. "No. Just train staff, checking tickets and asking if we wanted drinks or sandwiches. But why would that be important? I know who attacked me."

"Did anyone sit close to you and appear to be eavesdropping?"

Clearly, Vargas was determined to be thorough in the most annoying way possible. "No, I don't think so. Everyone got off the train at Poroy. That was the only stop."

"Then what? A bus?"

"A taxi. We went straight to our hotel. There was a note . . ."

"Yes, Jesse gave it to me. *Do not check in. Leave Cusco immediately.* Please go on."

"There was no food at our hotel, so Jesse went out to pick some up. He was worried about me, so he insisted that I stay in our room. Maybe fifteen minutes later, there was a knock on the door. It was Bastián Montalvo. He works for Leonard Wolven."

"The clerk at reception said he was holding a bouquet of flowers," Vargas interrupted. "He told her he was an old friend of yours, and he wanted to surprise you. We found a bouquet later, down the hallway from your room."

"Bastián didn't have any flowers when he came to my door. He told me that Jesse had been hurt and was at the hospital. He'd come to get me to take me there."

"You believed him?"

"I didn't think twice about it," I said. "I panicked. Part of it was the note. That had worried me. I'd met Bastián at Machu Picchu; he hadn't done anything to make me nervous. If anything, I thought . . ." I'd thought he was someone who might be on my side. When he'd come into the computer room at the resort, he'd told me that Charlie worked for Len Wolven; I wouldn't have known that but for him. From what he'd said—*Unless you wish to create a great deal of trouble for me, please do not tell anyone what I have told you tonight. Not Len and not Charlie. I don't trust either one*—it had seemed as if he were worried he'd revealed too much to me. Had that come back to haunt him? Was that the real reason he was going to kill me?

"What? What is it?" Vargas sounded impatient.

"Bastián took me to his car. There was junk all over the passenger seat, so he opened the trunk to clear it away. Then he grabbed me and held a cloth over my mouth and nose and I passed out. When I woke up, I was in the trunk with a gag in my mouth and my hands cuffed behind my back." It sounded so foolish in the retelling, though the memory of the trunk still made me shudder. That was worse than my mad drive down the mountain, worse even than Bastián's groping me with his hands and probing me with his tongue. He was guilty of kidnapping me, but I was guilty of being stupid and impulsive.

"We are searching the rental car for evidence now. The knives Montalvo threatened you with do not appear to be inside it."

"Any sign of Bastián?"

"Not yet. We are searching. That area has few paths in or out. He cannot escape on foot. He will be found."

I shifted uneasily in my chair, disturbed at the thought of Bastián on the loose. Before I could say anything, there was a knock at the door. Vargas opened it. A young officer was there, and I sat up straight, expecting to hear that Bastián was apprehended. Instead, the cop handed Vargas a bag and left without a word. Vargas set the bag in front of me on the table. "Empanadas. There is a little restaurant over behind the plaza that is open all night for the school. They make the best empanadas. I thought you must be hungry."

It was oddly touching for him to be so thoughtful, especially since his voice was as commanding as ever. "Thank you," I said, opening the bag. I'd thought my appetite was dead but it came back to life with the smell of the meat pie. I took a bite, and then another.

"They are good, are they not?"

I nodded. "What did you mean, that the restaurant is open all night because of the school?"

"We do not have enough schools, or enough room in the schools we have, for the children who need to be taught. So, children go to school in shifts. The school is open day and night."

"That's terrible."

Vargas stared at me with that same forbidding expression he'd worn when I first met him. I felt suddenly embarrassed for my sympathy. It wasn't wanted. I ate in silence, finishing one and then a second. When I was on my third, Vargas spoke again.

"I would suggest that perhaps you should have a further medical examination," Vargas said, studying the wall intently. "There is a female doctor at the hospital. She speaks English."

"The doctor who was in here was fine." I examined my wrists. "He bandaged me up quite well."

"I do not mean that sort of standard examination." He cleared his throat. "Perhaps a more, ah, personal one."

The implication behind his words hit me suddenly. No wonder he was so tense. "Bastián didn't rape me. He didn't get the chance. I Tasered him and hit him with the lid of the trunk. Then I jumped into the car and drove away."

"He did not, ah, violate you?"

"No."

"That is a great relief," Vargas said, letting out a long breath. "I thought it was more serious than you said."

"More serious? Let me recap my evening for you: Bastián drugged me, handcuffed me, and abducted me," I clarified. "Then he told me he was going to kill me, ripped open my shirt, and groped me. He kept threatening me with knives. Just as I got away, he smashed a window so I was covered in glass."

"We will find him. Please be assured about that. Mr. Cutler has agreed to provide us with photographs, documents, and other details. I do not think that this Bastián will be adept at hiding for long. He is not from this country, let alone this region."

"I need to talk to you about Leonard Wolven."

"Yes?"

"Bastián said that he was ordered to kill me, by Len Wolven."

The severe lines on Vargas's forehead deepened into crevasses. "He was *ordered* to kill you?"

"Yes. He also told me his boss murdered his wife."

"Miss Deen was his wife? Did he somehow cause her hypertensive crisis with drugs?"

"No, I'm not talking about Trista Deen. This is about Marianne Wolven, his second wife. Bastián said Len Wolven murdered her about three weeks ago. Bastián disposed of the body."

Vargas stood completely still, staring at me. I waited, but he didn't speak. His glare was so intense, I wondered if he was considering forcing me into a hospital, maybe a mental ward.

"Did he tell you *where* he buried her body?" he murmured.

"No, only that he was the one who disposed of it." I swallowed hard, and the drumming in my head got louder.

"I have been investigating Len Wolven. The police in Lima took a missing persons report on his wife two weeks ago, but they did not take it seriously."

"Why not?"

"The statement was made by telephone from America, by a woman named Elinor Bargeman."

That name rang a bell, but I couldn't say why. Then I remembered, Marianne Bargeman...Marianne Bargeman Wolven. The realization made me gasp.

"What is it, Lily?"

"*MBW*. Those were the initials engraved on a silver compact and a lipstick case. They were lying on the stairs where Trista fell." Trista had been carrying Marianne's things with her at Machu Picchu. That wasn't an accident—they were monogrammed. Had she known what had happened to Marianne, and was that why she was dead?

31

Len Wolven was a patient in exactly the same hospital for foreigners that I was in. He wasn't too sick to be released, Vargas explained to me, as we walked along a hallway and took the elevator up two stories. It was the risk of suicide that kept him there.

"Why not let him kill himself?" I asked.

My question rearranged the expression on Vargas's wooden face into bitter disapproval. "How could you say such a thing?"

I didn't answer, but what I was thinking was this: Len Wolven preyed on women. Last night, I'd pitied him; now, all I felt was disgust and loathing. How many woman were dead because of him? If his life were lost, others would be saved. But what made me bite my tongue was that I wanted vengeance for myself as well. The man had tried to dispose of me, and some dark part of my soul that should have been erased by civilization wanted blood.

As we approached his room, I noticed a uniformed cop standing in the doorway, and a woman sitting in a chair, knitting. She was striking, with shoulder-length black hair, smooth olive skin, and kohl-rimmed, catlike eyes that reminded me of Sophia Loren's. Her lips were painted bright red, and her polished fingers were clacking away on knitting needles, turning bright pink yarn into what looked like a blanket for a baby. Or maybe I was assuming that because she was very obviously pregnant. She looked up as we approached, but her hands kept on working.

"This is the American lady, Miss Moore?" she asked Vargas. Her English was elegant, with just a hint of an accent setting it off. One hand fluttered to her heart. "Thank God she is safe. Miss Moore, you have the deepest apologies of my family. We will do everything in our power to make sure this evil man is caught."

"Lily, this is Augustina Wolven Moreno. She arrived earlier today from Santiago. She is Leonard Wolven's sister."

"Half sister," Augustina corrected him. She held my hand for a moment. "Pardon me for not getting up. At seven and a half months along, I can barely move, or fit through a doorway."

"Congratulations," I said. "Is this your first child?"

"My third. Another girl."

"That's wonderful."

She smiled, and her hands went back to knitting. "I have been in my own little world until today. I had no idea what was happening with my little brother. He is . . ." She shook her head. "There is always disaster swirling around him. Perhaps he cannot help it. But I can promise you, that is all going to change now that I am here. This situation cannot be allowed to continue."

There was a steely determination in her voice that I didn't doubt.

"I will go back to my hotel now that I have seen you're well, Miss Moore. But I would very much like to see you tomorrow. Perhaps we could have lunch or dinner together, if you have time. All I do these days is eat or sleep." She smiled again, but she was gazing at the blanket with a fond, eager expression.

"Charles Cutler is in his room with him?"

"Charlie is *always* there," Augustina answered Vargas. "Well, almost always. He does whatever his master tells him." The way she said it wasn't exactly contemptuous; it was more as if she were speaking of a particularly well-trained pet. But there was no time to ask her to explain. Vargas thanked her and opened the door. He stepped inside, gesturing at me to follow, then shut it behind us.

The lights were on low, presumably for sleeping, but there were enough bulbs burning dimly to see everything in the room. Len Wolven's bed had a curtain pulled around it. If I'd been expecting beeping equipment, I was disappointed; still, that made sense given that Len should have been fine to leave, if the police weren't concerned about what else he might do. There were two chairs on either side of a small window to the outside; Charlie stood in front of it. He turned and nodded to us when we entered. I hadn't seen him earlier. He was wearing a dark suit, and his hands were bandaged.

"Who the hell is it, Charlie?" Len asked.

"Inspector Vargas again."

"Tell him to go blow himself."

"And Lily Moore is here," Charlie added.

"I don't want to see her." Len's voice sounded as if he were on the edge of tears.

If Vargas hadn't stepped forward and pulled the curtain aside, I would have done it, but I almost certainly would have followed that by putting my hands around Len Wolven's throat. He lay there, wearing a hospital gown. I could only see his shoulders, which looked bony. He didn't look much older than a teenager, and his peevish voice made him sound like an overgrown child. "What do you want? I'm trying to rest here."

"Len Wolven, we can do this here, or we can go to the police station," Vargas said. "I promise that you will strongly prefer these surroundings."

Len mumbled something, maybe a curse. He pulled himself into a sitting position, but then dropped his head in his hands, refusing to look at us.

"Where is your bodyguard, Bastián Montalvo?" Vargas asked.

"I don't know." Wolven didn't raise his head.

"When did you last speak with him?"

"I haven't."

"If you are going to attempt a lie, put some effort into it," Vargas advised. "Obviously we are aware that you spoke with him today."

Len sighed, as if this pressure were all too much for him. "He carried me off the helicopter. Then I saw him in the afternoon. Charlie was with us the whole time."

Charlie's eyebrows shot up to the ceiling, but he didn't contradict him.

"Did you speak to your bodyguard about Miss Moore?" Vargas asked Len.

"No."

"Did you have any idea that your bodyguard planned to abduct Miss Moore?"

"Of course not!" Wolven looked up. "What the hell are you suggesting?"

"Your statement is that you did not order Bastián Montalvo to abduct and kill Lily Moore?"

"Why would I do that?" Wolven shouted. "Tell me why?"

I stepped closer to the bed. "Bastián told me that you ordered him to do it."

Wolven's face was purplish, and his eyes darted wildly,

from my hair to my breasts to my mouth, but they never landed on my eyes. His tongue flicked across his lips. "No." His voice was quiet now, a low moan that was almost like a sulky child's. "No, no . . . I'd never . . . I wouldn't . . ."

"You know what Bastián told me? He said you murdered your wife. He said he had to get rid of her body—"

"No!" Len howled. His sobs were punctuated by screams. "You're a liar. He's a liar. You're all plotting against me." For a second, I thought he was going to take a swing at Vargas, but he started to shake violently. "You are all out to get me!"

Charlie ran to the door. "We need a doctor in here now!"

"All I want is to die. Please. Just let me die," Len begged. Then he hit his head against the table next to his bed.

32

Charlie held Len Wolven down while he dissolved into incoherence. Vargas ordered me into the hallway outside the room, but he waited inside with Charlie, taking everything in with his flinty eyes. After doctors gave Len an injection that knocked him out, Vargas sighed and joined me.

"Your friend Jesse is waiting downstairs. I will take you both to your hotel now," he said.

"But what about . . ." I gestured at Wolven's room.

"There is a guard posted here. Leonard Wolven will answer my questions in the morning."

"What is the guard going to do when Wolven decides he wants to leave? Who's going to stop him from leaving the country?"

"I suggest you calm down, Miss Moore."

That only made me angrier. "You weren't the one who was attacked tonight. Len Wolven didn't give orders to have you killed. And now we also know he killed his wife."

Vargas took my arm and pulled me away. I looked into Wolven's room, but all I saw was Charlie's stunned face. His eyes were wide, his mouth was open, but he didn't look surprised so much as guilty to me.

"How *dare* you drag me out of there," I said. "That man tried to have me killed."

"Even if that is the truth, you are not helping yourself."

"What are you implying? Of course that's the truth."

Vargas stared at me for a long time without speaking. "Have you read any Carlos Castaneda?"

I knew the name, but only because I remembered Claudia reading books by Castaneda. She'd tried to interest me in them, but somehow I'd never gotten around to them. "What does he have to do with anything?"

"Castaneda was a Peruvian writer who found great success in your country. He—"

"I don't need a lecture on Peruvian culture. You should be taking Wolven to jail, not standing here talking about literature."

"You need to spend more time listening, Miss Moore. You speak too quickly, too angrily, and you give everything away."

I started to object but he put up his hand.

"It's better to get something worthwhile done using deception than to fail to get something worthwhile done using truth." His voice was so low it was only scarcely above a whisper.

I stared at him, trying to understand.

"That's Castaneda," he added. "Now we will go back to your hotel."

"What are you going to do?"

"I advise you to go to sleep, Miss Moore. You need your rest." He turned and walked away, leaving me to follow in his footsteps, fuming.

33

"Now I've told you everything that happened to me," I said to Jesse. "Tell me about you."

We were sitting together in the little sitting room between our bedrooms. Jesse was sprawled on the sofa and I was beside him with my head on his shoulder and my bare feet curled up under me. As much as I wanted a glass of wine, I was sipping coca tea instead. It was supposed to make me feel more alert but all I felt was angry and deflated. Now that the adrenaline had seeped out of my bloodstream, my bruised body ached and my wrists felt like someone had sliced into them with a dull knife. All that was minor next to the humiliation I felt. Bastián wasn't a very clever person, and I'd fallen for his ruse. Jesse had called him a stupid thug, and he'd been right all along.

"I'm so proud of you, Lil. You're my superhero." Jesse rested his cheek on top of my head. "Can you forgive me?"

"For what?" I was perplexed.

"This was supposed to be three weeks of me and you hangin' out, seein' my favorite country, havin' adventures together. I figured I'd hit on the best doggone plan on the planet, since you'd be writin' about it and I'd be shootin' photos. Figured on us makin' some money, at least breakin' even. Worst case was I'd drag you on a llama trek, and you discover how bad those critters smell when it rains. Seriously, it's nasty. Instead, I dragged you to Peru, it turns out, so you could watch a woman die at Machu Picchu and then get kidnapped the next day."

"Oh, Jesse." I moved my head so that I could look at him. His handsome face held such a hangdog expression that I almost laughed. "Stop blaming yourself. None of this is your fault."

"We're only here 'cause I insisted we come here, Lil."

"We're here because I said yes." I could still recall his happy whooping over the phone when I had. He'd hated the fact that I'd gone back to Barcelona. I wasn't even sure why I had returned, except that I didn't feel like I belonged in New York anymore. But, it turned out, I didn't belong in Barcelona, either. An invitation had come in, asking me on an all-expenses-paid trip to see a newly opened hotel in Doha, and I'd considered going before I realized that the hotel was built by Pantheon Worldwide, the company my former fiancé, Martin, had founded. My world felt at once very large and very small. Large, in that it was lonely and empty, but small, in that it was going to be tough to avoid certain people that I wanted nothing to do with ever again. Jesse's suggestion of coming to Peru had seemed heaven-sent.

I took his hands. "Jesse, you cared enough about me to want to be with me, even when I was the most miserable company in the world. You're the best friend I could ever ask for."

"But that lousy son of a bitch gettin' his filthy hands on you tonight . . . that never should've happened. I shoulda been here. That is my fault."

"Nothing happened," I said. "I promise you, I'm fine." My voice was quiet, but so firm that it surprised me. But I felt the words as I said them, a kind of quiet confidence that I'd been lacking for some time. I was fine. Waking up in the trunk of that car had been a nightmare, but that was behind me. I was alive, and I was grateful. For the first time in months, I felt strong. I'd failed my sister, and the guilt had swallowed me up afterward. Now, something had shifted, though I couldn't quite articulate it. I could only hope that Jesse felt it, this strange energy crackling through me like electricity.

He gave me a shy smile. "I know you're just bein' kind. But thanks." We hugged, and he patted my hair. "Here's the new plan. Let's fly home tomorrow. We'll just go back to New York and—"

"Jesse, there is no way in hell that I'm leaving now."

"But that psycho Bastián is on the loose, and who knows what his boss is up to, and—"

"I'm not leaving Peru until Len Wolven is brought to justice," I said. "Also, my passport was in my purse, and the police can't find it. They think Bastián ditched my bag when he abducted me, and somebody snatched it up. I can't leave Peru until I get a new passport. In case that wasn't bad enough, my money and credit cards are gone, too."

"The money ain't a problem, y'know. But the passport? That sucks. How do we get you a new one?"

"Vargas said the Tourist Police will help me, but it's going to take more time because there's no American consulate in Cusco. Everything has to go through the embassy in Lima. I have to get passport photos taken tomorrow."

"You're the victim of a crime, and you have to get photos?" He was incredulous. "You have to fill out the dumb passport form, too?"

"Yes, but it's worse than that. The embassy will probably need to interview you, too, to prove my identity." I put my head back on his shoulder and closed my eyes. Replacing the passport and taking care of the credit card mess was going to be a lot of fun. I didn't want to think about it now. "You still haven't told me what happened to you. I was worried sick because Bastián pretended you were hurt. But you were probably busy scarfing down pizza."

"Not scarfin' but waitin' on it. It was only when Charlie called me that I realized something was wrong."

I sat straight and stared at him. "Charlie called you?"

"Yeah. He was worried. He thought you were in danger."

34 "You need to explain this from the top," I said. "How did Charlie know I was in danger?"

"I wouldn't say he *knew,* exactly. I came back to the hotel with our food and Rosaria gave me a note with Charlie's name and number. Then she told me you'd gone out with an old friend. I was all, like, *what* old friend? She didn't know his name, but she said he was this huge guy with a shaved head and a scar on his cheek. And he showed up with flowers for you, so that kinda narrowed it down for me, y'know?"

I'd been thinking that the security camera by the door would be what caught Bastián up. I hadn't realized that any human being with eyes would note his distinctive appearance. He was impossible to miss.

"I was kinda concerned, truth be told. I saw how that ape was lookin' at you the other day. But I was thinkin', well, if that's your type . . . I dunno. I guess I was plannin' a little Come to Jesus talk in my head. Your taste in men is seriously flawed, Lil, and—"

I stared him down and he shut up. "Don't get me started on *your* taste in men," I snapped back. "Where does Charlie come into this?"

"So, I went back to the room to have some pizza, and Charlie called again. I mentioned you and Bastián were hangin' out together and he freaked. He said if you were with

Bastián, you were in danger. I told you that fella was a thug, Lil. He's probably massacred villagers back in Chile."

It was tough to get a story out of Jesse with all of his editorializing. "Back to Charlie. What else did he say? Why was he worried?"

"All he said was there's no way you were safe with Bastián. That got me all worried. So I called Vargas and told him you were missin', 'cause by then I realized somethin' was off. I know you like to run off and do your own thing, Tiger Lily, but there ain't no way you'd do that without leavin' me a note."

The confidence in his voice made me smile. "You know me so well."

"I don't know what I'd do if anythin' ever happened to you. I can't believe you coulda been killed tonight. Or you coulda been . . ." He let that thought trail off.

"So you called the police . . ." I prompted.

"Vargas got concerned after I laid it all out for him. I wanted to run out and look for you myself, but Vargas forced me to stay put at the hotel, 'cause there could be a ransom demand. I called Charlie back and he came over from the hospital to wait with me."

"What did he talk about?"

"Lotsa stuff. Nothin' real specific on Len Wolven, but I could tell he doesn't like that punk. He reveres his boss, though. It was like, 'Mr. Wolven thinks this' and 'Mr. Wolven says that.' He's kind of old-fashioned in some ways, that Charlie."

It made me uncomfortable to think of Charlie coming over, almost as if he were a spy sent to keep watch on Jesse. Was that part of the plan? It struck me as odd, the fact that Charlie had called my friend at the hotel more than once.

Why was he so eager to speak to him? It suggested to me that it was all part of a greater strategy, but I couldn't quite figure how it fit together . . . unless Len Wolven's idea had been to get rid of Bastián after Bastián got rid of me. I let that scenario play through my mind. What if Charlie were waiting there, knowing he'd get a call from Bastián saying I was dead? What if it was his job to hand Bastián over to the police? It had been clear to me that Bastián hated Peru and wanted to go back to Chile. Len Wolven must have promised him an exit as a bonus for killing me. But with what Bastián knew about the murder of Marianne Wolven, he wouldn't just want Bastián arrested, he'd want him dead. Something didn't quite fit there. Bastián had knives—he'd mentioned them several times—but there had been no sign or mention of a gun. Unless the police thought he would shoot them, they weren't likely to kill him. Or were they? Jesse's earlier comments about corruption in the ranks of the Peruvian police still echoed in my ears.

"Since we can't leave Peru till you get your passport, you know what we should do?" Jesse asked. His voice was bright with enthusiasm. If he had a tail, it would be wagging. "Call Bruxton and Norah. They'll have some idea what's up."

Norah Renfrew was Bruxton's partner and the other cop who'd investigated my sister's disappearance. She was a smart woman with a sly smile and a fondness for the same old Cole Porter and Moss Hart lyrics I cherished. While I was genuinely fond of her and considered her a friend, calling anyone on the NYPD didn't seem like a helpful move right now. "What are they going to do with the Peruvian police department? Tell them to arrest Wolven?" I couldn't picture proud Felipe Vargas taking direction from anyone, certainly not an American.

"Well, it can't hurt to have our friends on the force talk to the locals. And they'll be able to hunt down information on this little Wolven creep that the Peruvians can't get at. Len Wolven's first wife died in the U.S., right? So let's find out more about that."

35

"The cathedral is closed," an elderly woman in a black dress informed me. "It will be open at ten A.M."

"But I want to go inside to pray," I explained.

"The service is for *Peruanos,* not tourists," she insisted. "Besides, it is in Spanish."

"Pero hablo español," I said, switching languages. "Yo vivo en España. Mira, yo no sé dónde más ir a dar un servicio. Te lo prometo, voy a volver más tarde para la visita turística." *I live in Spain. Look, I don't know where else to go for a service. I promise, I'll come back later for the sightseeing tour.*

I'd tried to sneak into the church, but even though my hair was black, my pale skin was a dead giveaway. My slender build was, too: while my plain black dress and black flats fit in well enough, my lack of significant muscle mass marked me as a person from a place other than the Andes. Most of the native population was short—shorter than I was, in any case—but they were powerfully built.

The woman sighed. "Tourists almost never come to Mass," she said. "The ones who do try to take photographs. No photography allowed inside!"

"I don't even have my camera with me."

The woman gave me a little smile, and I saw she was missing a few teeth. "Go on. God bless you."

The irony was that I hadn't set out to attend Mass. I'd woken up early and decided to get the taking of my new passport photo out of the way. Vanity, which had mostly been a stranger to me lately, had suddenly reared its proud head and made me fix my hair and put on mascara and lipstick. When I pulled on the dress and looked into the mirror again, I felt as if I were emerging from hibernation. It wasn't exactly the old me, but it wasn't the broken, battered zombie who'd been sleepwalking her way through the world for the past three months. The fact that I was wearing black still felt appropriate. Claudia would have liked that, I thought. In the back of my mind, I caught a whisper that sounded like *Go get 'em, Honey Bear.* My sister would have been proud of me for bashing Bastián's head last night. It was my reserved, good-girl side that she'd always disapproved of.

Claudia was on my mind while I had breakfast at the hotel—Jesse was still sleeping—even though I was ostensibly reading a guidebook at the same time, one that was produced by Frakker's, the same company I wrote for. I was still thinking about her when I walked outside into the sunshine. Vargas had given me a very small area in which I could walk freely, which consisted of the Plaza de Armas, the massive town square at the heart of historic Cusco, and a couple of blocks around it. *The police are everywhere in that area,* he had stressed, and he was right. As far as I knew, Bastián was still on the loose. Secretly, I was afraid to venture out on my own after what had happened the night before. I didn't want to leave my hotel, which meant that I actually really needed to go outside. Our hotel was on a street called Espinar that was just a block from the Plaza de Armas. I turned left at the first street—I didn't see a sign but knew it was called Mantas from the map I'd consulted—and followed it into the plaza.

All I'd really planned to do was go to a shop that took passport photos, but I was thunderstruck by how beautiful the square was, even with the seemingly endless rows of tourist shops around it. Even they were tucked inside colonial arcades, with roofs supported by curved archways and slender pillars. Cusco's massive cathedral dominated the plaza with its sheer size. It stood at the northeastern edge of the square, and while the plaza gently sloped up, so that the cathedral stood at the highest part, it got a further height boost from the fact it was built on a stone platform with a broad staircase leading up to it. The church had taken a century to build, starting in 1559. I knew that from the guidebook, but the book had talked mostly about the art collection inside, not the stunning red-brick façade, which rose at either end into bell towers decorated with what looked to me like oversized chessboard pawns.

But what really caught my eye was the Jesuit church that was its neighbor to the southeast. I'd read that a seventeenth-century Cusco bishop had written to the Vatican to complain about its construction, but the crafty Jesuits had completed it just before Pope Paul III told them to stop work on it. Suddenly, I understood the rivalry. Built of a lighter-colored brick, this church, while technically smaller, was more spectacular. Its pair of bell towers were topped with gold domes, its façade was far more ornate, and a tremendous gold dome that must have been built over the nave was clearly visible from the side.

I could have stood staring at it all morning, inhaling the appetizing fragrance of roasted corn from carts scattered around the plaza, if a woman dressed in a brightly colored and embroidered costume hadn't come up to me. "You take picture?" she asked. With her was a snowy white alpaca with a red rose tucked demurely behind one ear.

"No camera," I said.

"All tourists have camera. Maybe camera phone? Just one nuevo sol," she pleaded.

"No, thanks," I said, making my escape. But I wasn't swift enough. A boy caught me before I fled across the cobblestones.

"Where are you from, miss?" He might have been ten. His English was good.

"Canada." It wasn't the first time I'd used that line while traveling.

"Canada! Your capital city is Ottawa. Your national tree is the maple leaf. Your anthem is 'O Canada.' Your national animal is the beaver."

"That's pretty good. How many countries can you do that for?"

"Forty-two. Want to hear? Australia, capital city, Canberra—"

"That's okay. Here." I gave him a couple of coins. As far as acts went, his was a good one.

A girl's voice behind me piped up. "You buy postcards, miss?" There were more kids heading toward me, and I backed away. I knew from experience that standing around a touristy area made you a target. That was especially true in a poor country, though it wasn't necessarily thieves that would surround you. Seeking sanctuary, I headed for the cathedral. Claudia would have done that if she'd been there, I knew. My sister had no use for the Vatican or the hierarchy of the church, but she adored the hardworking members of the Church's lower ranks. She'd told me that the priests and nuns and laypeople were the only ones who saw the homeless as people; since she had been homeless herself at times, that came from personal experience, and it resonated with me. Her sentiment wasn't limited to the Catholic church; it encompassed all faiths, and it had always amazed me that my sister, who didn't seem to care about religion, had such strong sentiments about those who devoted their lives to it.

When I finally talked my way inside the cathedral, it took my eyes a long time to adjust. At first, it seemed as if I had stepped into total, incense-wrapped darkness. Then the glow of a few tiny, flickering yellow candles came into focus. The Mass was being held in a room that would have been a good size for a normal church, but that clearly took up only a tiny piece of the cathedral's real estate. I sat in a pew at the back and sized up the crowd. There was no one particularly suspicious. The parishioners were a mixed lot, many of them dressed casually, as if they were on their way to work.

As I listened to the priest, I looked around. There were large canvases on the walls that couldn't be benefiting from the smoke and incense. When I looked at the congregation again, I noticed a man sitting off to one side, noticeably taller than the others.

It was Charlie Cutler.

My heart seemed to splutter for a moment, before it started pounding. I wanted to run out the door and into the arms of the first police officer I encountered. I must have made a sound, because a couple of older ladies turned around to look at me. I didn't care; my mind was reeling. Had Charlie followed me into the church? No; when I'd come inside, I'd stood in the doorway until my eyes adjusted. No one else had come in after me. In fact, he didn't seem aware that I was there. So, what had drawn him to church today? Guilt, I was certain. He knew exactly what Wolven had done. That was why he'd called Jesse, and why he'd come to the hotel.

The night before, I'd speculated on his motives. It had seemed like part of a plan, though the pieces had to be squashed and twisted to fit together. Maybe that was where I'd gone wrong, I realized. Maybe Charlie wasn't part of any plan at all. Perhaps he'd called Jesse because he knew what Len Wolven was up to, and, in his fumbling way, he'd tried to stop him.

I didn't take Communion, but I watched Charlie do so. He saw me on his way back to his seat, and he did a double take that I took as genuine. For once, I had the advantage of surprise. I stood and walked around the back of the last pew, then up the aisle to join him. "Fancy meeting you here," I whispered.

"Lily." As always, he was wearing a suit and tie. He may have been the only man in the church so attired. He didn't look much like Gary Cooper today, even in the flattering light of the candles. Even if I couldn't make out the difference between which eye was green and which was blue in this light, I could see that he was weary. If I were lining up bets, mine would be on the fact he hadn't slept the previous night, or the one before that.

We sat staring forward, eyes on the priest. His were, in any case; mine drifted over to him from time to time. Then the service ended and we were forced out into the daylight again. The sky was no longer clear; it was as if a gray shroud had been draped over us, though the sun continued to burn brightly behind, forcing me to squint.

"How are you feeling today, Lily?" he asked me.

"Better. You?"

"It's been hard to sleep with everything that's happened."

"I know that feeling." I took a deep breath. "We need to talk."

He didn't seem surprised. "I was going to get back to the hospital, to see if Len is any better. But we could have coffee first."

There were many tiny cafés spread over the plaza, and several occupied balconies on the second story of the colonial arcades. But I looked at them and realized we'd have no privacy, and Charlie would never answer the questions I wanted him to if I didn't get him alone. The problem was, I didn't want to stray beyond the little border Vargas had set for me, certainly not in Charlie's company. I was impatient for answers, but also suspicious.

"Hold on," I told him, going back up the cathedral steps and finding the elderly lady who'd let me inside. She lit up when I asked her my question.

"What was that about?" Charlie asked me when I came back.

I smiled. "Walk with me."

36

Santa Catalina had been converted into a museum, but it was still a working convent. All we'd had to do was walk up the Calle Triunfo beside the cathedral and turn at the first right, but it felt as if we'd entered another world, away from the touts and hawkers of the plaza. There weren't any police around, either, I noticed, though I was certain that I was still within the narrow parameters Vargas had given me. It was too late to turn back now, in any case, and I wasn't going to display any nerves in front of Charlie. There was a large wooden door with thick studs in it that looked as if it had been there since the Spaniards had charged into Inca territory. It was shut, and I knocked on it.

"What is this place?" Charlie asked.

"An art gallery that's not very busy, especially at this time of day."

It took a few very long minutes, but a very petite, wrinkled nun in full habit opened the heavy door and let us inside. The door shut behind us with the solid finality of a dungeon gate. For a moment, I felt as if I'd walked into a trap, then remembered this was my idea. The anteroom was so dark, I could only make out the faintest of outlines. The scent of incense was faint, but it hung in the air here, too.

The nun asked if we had purchased advance tickets, but since we hadn't, we paid admission there.

"Please enjoy our little convent. There is much to see," she said, in English. "Would you like me to give you a tour?"

"No, no," Charlie answered quickly. "We'll just wander around if that's all right."

"Of course." The woman's smile grew fainter. "This was once the palace of the archbishop. Before that, in Inca times, it was Acllawasi."

"Acllawasi?" I said, trying and failing to pronounce the name properly.

"The House of Chosen Women," the nun clarified. "It was a convent, of sorts, for the sun god of the Inca. They lived a contemplative life, weaving cloth for priests' robes and baking foods for special ceremonies. Not so unlike the nuns."

"Very interesting. Thanks," Charlie said.

"In 1975, we became a national art museum. We have one of the very best collections of paintings of the Cusco School. Are you familiar with the Cusco School?" She didn't pause for an answer. "It began after 1534, when the Spanish colonized the area. Cusco had been the Inca capital and, to convert the people to the Church, the Spanish believed it necessary to teach them through art. The Inca did not have a writing system as such, you see. They had symbols in their art that had meaning to them, but not books."

"I've read that the Inca had a record-keeping system called quipu," Charlie interjected. I glared at him. *Really? You want to argue with nuns?*

The nun frowned. "That was a system of string and knots, *not* a writing system. As I was saying, the Spanish wished to convert the native people, so they brought a group of religious artists to the city. It was the first art center set up by Europeans anywhere in the New World. The results were wonderful but, if you are familiar with European religious paintings, you will find some of these works quite astonishing. Even disturbing. They are most vivid." She smiled again. "Let me know if you have any questions after you see the art."

Charlie and I walked down the lone hallway, which led deeper into the convent. It was narrow and dimly lit, but there were religious paintings lining it. We kept walking, our own footfalls making the only noise in the building. Charlie paused briefly at the door to the chapel. It was empty, and the altar stood behind a dramatic wrought-iron grate. I started to walk inside, staring at the delicately painted frescoes that were of crops rather than people—corn, and some others I didn't recognize—but Charlie touched my shoulder. "Let's go upstairs," he said.

The staircase was wooden and creaked under our feet. I guessed that would be an advantage, since we could hear anyone else approaching. On the second story, there were paintings all over the walls, all of them with the same bare-bones description: *Cusco School, XVII Century.*

The nearest room was through a curved portal. My eye caught on a painting of Saint Joseph as we walked through; an infant Jesus was nestled against his cheek, eyes closed. Its serene beauty almost made me forget that I wasn't with Charlie for an art tour. Almost. I shook my head and followed him into the room. It was massive, and filled with towering canvases that must have taken the artists years to work on, given their intricate detail. Charlie sat on a bench and I followed suit.

"I don't often get to visit art museums," Charlie said. "I never have the time."

"Your boss must keep you busy, what with having people murdered," I whispered.

"Lily . . ." Charlie shook his head. "I've worked for Mr. Wolven since I graduated from Harvard Law. That was fifteen years ago. He's like a father to me, and he's a good man. But his son has some . . . issues."

"Issues? That's what you call them?"

"Look, for all I know, you're recording this right now. Maybe you're wearing a wire. I don't want to be paranoid, but I've got to think of Mr. Wolven first. You can understand that, can't you?" His expression was plaintive. "But at the same time, I've sworn to myself that I'm not going to let anyone else get hurt. I need to tell you certain things, to keep you safe. But I'm not going to talk to the police. The sooner you go home, the better."

"Guess what? I can't go home until I get my new passport. Bastián made my old one vanish, along with my credit cards and money. So I'm not leaving Peru for a few days."

"I can give you money. Whatever you want. That's no problem."

"I don't want your money." My voice was too loud, and it echoed back at me. I took a deep breath. "Bastián told me Len wanted me killed. *Tortured* and killed, actually. Did you know that?"

Charlie's face didn't betray much emotion, but he rubbed his forehead with one hand. There were still bandages on his hands, but they were flesh toned and relatively subtle, especially compared to my white wristbands. I wondered how his burns were healing, but I didn't ask.

"I know he talked to Bastián, and I wondered what was going on. He rarely speaks to Bastián; to him, Bastián is just there for protection, not conversation. The man has muscles where his brain should be. I should have been suspicious when Len said he wanted to speak to him, but yesterday was a hectic day. It was only a couple of hours later that I started to wonder. I tried to call Bastián, but his cell phone just went to voice mail."

"Why didn't you just ask Len?"

Charlie stared at me for a moment, his face frozen. There was enough light for me to see his curious eyes, and I felt that they were calculating and recalculating what to answer. "Our relationship isn't like that."

That was an understatement. I remembered how Charlie had tried to calm Len down in the villa a couple of nights earlier, and how Len appeared to detest him. "Has he asked you to kill for him?"

"Len? Never."

"What about general threats?" I asked. Charlie stared at me, as if he didn't understand. Fine, I'd spell it out. "The night Jesse and I came over to the villa, Len told everyone to shut up. And he said, 'I'll make sure someone shuts you up. I can do that.'"

"Len is completely immature. That's a perfect example. The only person he's ever been a danger to is himself."

That brought the memory of Len plunging into the fire back into my mind. Even though I hated him, that was a grim image.

When I didn't respond to him, Charlie turned to the painting in front of us. "Look at that, will you? It's like something out of a nightmare."

I took in the painting. In it was an adult Jesus, bent under the weight of a wooden cross, standing in a vat of grapes. Blood flowed from his wounds into a Communion cup. In the top right corner of the painting, a bearded man in the sky turned a giant wooden screw. *Divine Winepress, Cusco School XVII Century*, read the little plaque under it. My heart ticked faster. It was the ultimate, literal interpretation of suffering for another's sins.

Looking at it, I accepted that Len was in pain; he wasn't faking that. But the women in his life were human sacrifices. First Kirsten—I had no proof there, just an instinct—then Marianne, then Trista. He'd tried to make me into one as well. He reacted the same way afterward, expressing a desire to die. Why didn't he just kill himself if he wanted to die? There were a hundred ways to do it. I could name twenty my mother had attempted before she finally succeeded. The hesitation marks on my mother's arms took the shape of different wounds on Len, but they covered the same territory: a death wish that was articulated, but not heartfelt.

"Charlie, did you know that Len murdered his second wife?"

"I'm not sure I believe that."

What astonished me was that he didn't give me a flat-out denial. Charlie had clearly considered the possibility.

"Bastián told me that Marianne Wolven was dead, and that Len killed her. He said Len strangled her, and that he had to dispose of her body."

"I've heard that story, too. A version of it, in any case," Charlie admitted.

"Weren't you there when it happened? You're almost always with Len."

"Not that week. I'd gone back to the U.S. Len and Bastián were at the house in Lima."

"So you heard about it when you got home?"

"Not exactly. Marianne was gone, and I asked where she was. Len got upset and wouldn't talk. Then Bastián started dropping hints that Marianne wouldn't be coming back, not ever. Neither of them explained what happened. Then Trista

Deen got in touch and Len asked me to fly her down. They hadn't seen each other in quite a while, but he didn't seem worried that Marianne would come back and find another woman in her house." He looked at his hands. "I knew something was wrong, but I hoped that Marianne had just run away. I hired a private investigator in Lima, but he hasn't been able to find her."

I stared at him. "Leonard Wolven killed his wife and flew in his ex-girlfriend to replace her. Then he took her on a sightseeing tour of Machu Picchu, where she died? What kind of sick freak is he?"

"Len had absolutely nothing to do with Trista's death. I'm certain of that. He's innocent of that."

I stared at him, utterly astonished. "And Marianne's death?"

"Please don't get any more involved with this. Mr. Wolven will pay you and Jesse whatever you want," Charlie pleaded. "I will see to it myself that Bastián is brought to justice, but please stay away from the family. I don't just mean Len, I mean Augustina, too. Even if you can't leave Peru for a few days, you could go to another city. What about Arequipa? I hear it's—"

"Listen to me, Charlie. I'm not going to be chased off. I won't take anyone's money. And I'm not going to let the Wolvens off the hook for any of this."

"Then we have nothing to talk about," he said, standing suddenly. "I'm sorry, Lily. Good-bye."

He rushed out of the room. His feet clattered on the old staircase, as if someone were chasing him. I stared at the Divine Winepress, feeling as if my own blood were being drained out of me. I'd talked tough with Charlie, but I had no idea what to do next.

37

When I came back to my hotel, Rosaria was at reception as always. She gave me a bright smile. "There she is," she said. "Lily Moore. It is so good to see you. Have you recovered from your adventure? Did you sleep well?"

"I'm fine, thank you."

"Good, good. There is a lady here to see you."

"Oh?" I turned, looking around the couches in the small reception area, expecting to see Augustina. But the only person sitting there was a solidly built middle-aged woman in a tangerine pantsuit. Her shoulder-length blond hair was carefully coiffed, with tight curls mercilessly sprayed into submission. She stood and squared her broad shoulders. In flat shoes, she stood four inches over me. As she extended one hand, I noticed that her nails were painted coral, presumably to match her outfit and her lipstick.

"I been trying to reach you all morning." There was something aggrieved in her flat voice, as if I'd been dodging her.

"All morning? It's only nine-thirty."

She frowned, her blue eyes narrowing and her blue eyeshadow crinkling into the creases. Clearly she'd expected better manners from me. "I want to talk to you about my sister."

"Who's that?"

"Well, you're a woman of few words, huh?" she said, shifting from one foot to the other and cocking one hip. She was a large woman, but she had more muscle than fat. Big-boned, she would have been called years ago. I thought of the Dorothy Parker story "Big Blonde," but this woman had been crafted from a different mold. She brought to mind an old cosmetics ad, and it wasn't hard to picture her in a tangerine Cadillac. "Is there some place we can go to talk? You know, somewhere private?"

"I'm still waiting for you to explain who you are and why you want to talk to me," I said. She blinked, and I stared at her expectantly. Her coral lips blew out an audible sigh.

"Well, you're about as easy to talk to as a mule with a nail in its head," she huffed.

Without intending to, I smiled. "Are you from Oklahoma?" The only person I'd ever heard use an expression anything like that was Jesse.

"Oklahoma? Are you kidding me? I'm from Texas." She drew herself up proudly. "Look, I wouldn't be here if I didn't have to be, but I think my sister's in trouble."

"Your sister?"

"Marianne."

My heart sank to my toes. "Marianne Wolven?"

"Yeah, that's her. I'm Elinor Bargeman."

My breath caught in my chest. Marianne Wolven, the woman Len had murdered and Bastián had made disappear. Looking into Elinor's clear, no-nonsense eyes, I could see she had no idea of what had happened to her sister. There was concern there, and worry, and the dark circles that spoke of sleepless nights and unspoken suspicions. But lurking there, underneath all of that, was a flicker of hope. Looking at her transported me back to where I'd been three months earlier, when I'd been on a frantic quest for my own sister.

"I'm so sorry," I whispered.

"About what?"

"Her death."

Elinor looked at me in surprise, then shook her head. "Oh, no, honey. You got it all wrong. That wasn't her who fell the other day at Machu Picchu." The way she said it sounded like *Ma-chew Pitch-chew*. "That was just some hussy her old creep of a husband took up with." She pulled a photograph out of her purse. "That's my sister."

I stared at it, trying to think of a way to tell her that her sister was dead. The photo showed me the woman I'd seen in that article online. Pretty face, dyed red hair, well-upholstered chest, and tiny waist. My mouth felt like sandpaper all of a sudden, and even though I was rooted to the spot, I worried that my legs would buckle under the weight of my anxiety. How could I tell her what Bastián had told me? Would she even want to know?

"My sister's gone missing," Elinor added. "So I'm worried about her, and I think you might be able to help me find her."

38

"This sure is some kind of dumpy, rundown country," said Elinor. "I can't figure why anyone'd want to come here. 'Course, I don't really get why folks are in such a hurry to get to these far-off places. They're never as nice as home."

"I think the Inca ruins are a pretty big draw."

"Oh, sure. But we got history in Texas, too. Like the Alamo. They even do re-creations of the battle there. Costumes and everything. Bet they don't do that at Machu Picchu."

We were sitting in the hotel's little balcony café, one story above the bustling street. Below us, children on the street were waylaying anyone who looked like a foreigner. They weren't begging, exactly; instead, they were trying to sell postcards or postcard-sized paintings. The kids couldn't have been older than nine or ten, and watching them go through their spiel again and again brought a lump to my throat.

"I guess you don't travel very much," I said.

"Not if I can help it," Elinor answered. "I hate planes. If you can't drive there yourself, why bother? Only good thing I found in Peru so far is the coffee."

"Really? The coffee I've had here has been terrible. They use—"

"Nescafé! Just like at home," Elinor said, sounding happy. At least one thing about Peru won her approval.

I gave her what I hoped looked like a sincere smile and glanced over the balcony again. Ever since she'd told me who she was, I'd felt a terrible rush of fear. How could I tell her about her sister, and what Bastián had said last night. *Len Wolven strangled her to death.* Vargas had told me not to talk about it, but I wasn't sure that it was right to keep the truth from her. Not that I could claim to know what the truth was.

As if on cue, the waitress came over with two steaming mugs, setting them down in front of us with a smile. "Breakfast?" she asked.

"No, thank you," Elinor said. I ordered scrambled eggs. As the waitress walked off, Elinor started talking again. " 'Course, my sister was always one for traveling. Couldn't wait to leave home. Thought she was going to be an actress, so she went out to La-la-land."

"Hollywood?"

"Nah, Las Vegas."

I sipped my Nescafé and refrained from pointing out that most women who dreamed of acting, at least in films, went to Los Angeles. "She was in a show?"

"Sure, if you call taking off your clothes for strangers a *show.*" Elinor shook her head, though her curls refused to yield, and sipped her Nescafé. There was a bluntness to her that I liked, even though I felt as if I had to bite my tongue around her to keep from telling her the truth. I wasn't sure what I owed her, exactly. There was no mistaking what Bastián had said. But was it better to extinguish her hope early on, or let her find out for herself? When I'd been searching for Claudia, I don't think I would have believed anyone who told me it was hopeless.

"Oh, I see."

"I don't want you thinking it was one of those, you know, sex shows or something. It wasn't anything like that. Just girls wearing lots of rhinestones and nothing else."

"Sure. That's Vegas."

"I'm not some kind of prude, you know," Elinor said. "Not like my mother, God rest her soul. You know who she named us for?"

"Us?"

"Marianne and me. The Dashwood sisters. In *Sense and Sensibility.*" She took another slurp of her pseudocoffee, giving me the chance to wonder what Jane Austen would have made of the Bargeman sisters. "Marianne really went the other way. She's always been a little wild. Not bad, you know. But she has her own ideas about things." She stopped speaking when the waitress carried over my eggs.

"How long has she been married to Leonard Wolven?" I asked.

"Not long. But too long, if you want my two bits."

"How did you find me, exactly? And why did you think I could help you?"

"That Ala-cana-bama-rama character."

"Alcántara?"

"Yeah, you know who I mean. He's a cop in Lima. Only one that would take an interest in Marianne's disappearance." She set her mug down. "When I first called, the so-called cops wouldn't even take a report. Kept telling me 'Call the Yankee embassy' and that kind of stuff. And I did call them, too, but they didn't do nothing. Our tax dollars are being wasted there, let me tell you."

"So you kept calling the police until you happened to get Alcántara?"

"Nah, he found me. 'Bout a week after I started making

calls, I heard from him. He told me I was right to be worried. He didn't try to blow me off. But he and his partner couldn't find Marianne, either, so I'm down here to do it myself."

"Have you talked to Felipe Vargas yet?"

"Yeah. He's useless. He only seems to care 'bout this hussy who died at Machu Picchu."

"Well, the circumstances around her death were strange—"

"That's neither here nor there," Elinor snapped. "Point is, not only did Len take up with that hussy, but he brought her on *vacation* with him. Marianne will cut his head off when she finds out. He's crazy as a betsy bug."

"I think he's a drug addict," I said.

"Oh, he surely loves his liquor. Marianne says he's Dr. Jekyll and Mr. Hyde." Elinor leaned forward, and lowered her voice. "Just before she disappeared, Marianne told me she had discovered his porno collection. You know what it was? Photos and articles about young women who'd been murdered. There was a special section on girls who'd been hacked to pieces." She closed her eyes and shuddered. "Can you imagine the filth in his mind?"

My fork fell out of my hand, clattering to the floor and bouncing, dropping down to the sidewalk. "That's awful."

"Yeah, but the worst part is this. Out of the blue, Marianne tells me she's afraid for her life. She said she was sure he was gonna try to kill her. She seemed to think it would happen any day."

39

"I can't deal with her. You go talk to her," I pleaded. Jesse raised his eyebrows.

"Lil, you're gonna burn a hole in the carpet with all your pacin'. Calm down." He was sitting in the love seat in the sitting room between our bedrooms, in jeans and a button-down shirt, comfortably barefoot and drinking coca tea.

"How can I be calm? That woman is looking for her sister, and her sister is—"

"Her sister is gone. Dead, if that sleazeball Bastián can be believed," Jesse said evenly. "Vargas needs to have a real heart-to-heart with her."

"I can't tell her to go away, but I don't want to be alone with her. Talking with her brings back all of these awful memories." When Elinor had described her sister, I felt as if she could have been talking about Claudia. *She's always been a little wild. Not bad, you know. But she has her own ideas about things.*

Jesse made the long-suffering sigh of a martyr. "So you want me to use my considerable down-home charm on her, that about the size of it?"

"Could you? Maybe you could talk her into going back to Texas."

"She's not gonna disappear, Lil. She's worried about her sis. Would you have left off lookin' for Claudia if someone told you to go away?" He set the teacup down. " 'Course not."

"But I don't want to give her false hope. And I don't want to be the one who has to tell her that her sister's dead."

"Okay, I'm roped in." Jesse stood and touched my shoulder. "She's waiting in the restaurant, right?"

I glanced at my watch. "I left her there ten minutes ago."

"Okay, here's the plan. I'll go have breakfast and shoot the breeze with her. You're gonna come join us when you feel up to it. Then we'll check in with Vargas and see what he wants us to do. Maybe he caught Bastián this mornin'. Any case, we can rent a car and go see Ollantaytambo today."

"Jesse, I'm not going sightseeing. I want to make sure Len Wolven is put behind bars."

"Well, we can't just sit around this pokey li'l room," he complained. "We need to go out somewhere. And I don't like stickin' around here. Bastián knows where we're holed up. What if he comes back?"

That prospect hadn't occurred to me. Being alone in the room didn't seem so appealing anymore. I started pacing again. "Where's Vargas's office? Do you think he's at the local jail? I need to tell him what Elinor said to me." Jesse stared at me as if I'd grown another head. "What?"

"This is the first time I've seen you all hepped up about somethin' since we went lookin' for your sister," he answered. "You've been down in the dumps—anybody would understand why—but it's like puttin' Wolven away has given you a mission."

He was right. I was cruising on adrenaline. The fact that Len Wolven still wasn't in jail was like a tonic for me. I was seething, but somehow that anger was transformed into a desire to act. Instead of thinking about Claudia in a mournful way, I thought of her as I had last night, urging me on when I thought I was going to die. It was as if my sister and I were co-conspirators, for the first time since we were children. And my sister, for all her many faults, hated for injustice to go unpunished. I did, too.

Elinor Bargeman was still sitting at her table on the balcony. She peered at the street below with a laserlike focus and an expression that suggested she thought the people on the street were up to no good. Her leather handbag sat in her lap, one arm resting on top of it just in case someone tried to grab it from her. She looked proud, nervous, and like she was wishing she could be just about anywhere else in the world at that moment.

"Oh, you're back," she said, giving me a sidelong glance. When she caught sight of Jesse, she turned her head and her eyebrows shot up. "Oh, my goodness. You look like a young Gregory Peck."

"Thank you, ma'am. A pleasure to meet you. Jesse Robb." They shook hands and we sat down, Jesse taking my original seat across from her.

"Which side of the Red River you from?"

"The Sooner State, ma'am." Jesse smiled. "My family's been there since 1887."

"Just before the Land Run. Good timing." She shot another glance at me. "Huh. Talk about a lucky girl."

"Oh, I'm the fortunate one, I assure you, ma'am." The bemused expression on Jesse's face was priceless. "So, what exactly brought you all the way down to Peru?"

"Well, your . . ." Elinor looked at my unadorned ring finger. "Ah, girlfriend, probably told you, Marianne Wolven's my baby sis. We're not much in touch these days—haven't been for years, but there's seventeen years between us, so that's no surprise. In any case, she's been talkin' for some time now about her husband's fits."

"Fits?" Jesse asked.

"You know, like talking crazy, acting crazy. I never actually met Len—I wasn't even asked to their wedding—so it's not like I knew this all firsthand. But lately, Marianne's been confiding in me more and more." She twisted her gold wedding band around and looked at the table. "Some of what she told me—well, let's just say it doesn't sit well with me. That Len Wolven might be tall in cotton, but he's got no more character than a rattlesnake."

"Tall in cotton?" I asked.

"That means rich, honey." Jesse patted my hand. He shrugged at Elinor. "She's second-generation Yankee. Anyhow, you were sayin'?"

"Well, Marianne and me haven't been close, but lately she's been kind of desperate and took to calling me almost every day. And then..." Elinor took a couple of deep breaths. "Marianne said she was in danger."

"Danger?" Jesse repeated.

"She didn't say . . . not exactly." More twisting of the ring. She looked at Jesse and blushed, dropping her eyes again. "She made it clear Len's got more kinks than a garden hose. I asked her how she could stay with a man like that, and she said he wasn't like that all the time, just when he was having those fits. Trouble was, he was having more and more of those fits."

"Could he be mentally ill?" I asked.

"I don't really see how, exactly, since the man's running a company that's bigger than Dallas." She caught my look. "The man makes money hand over fist."

"I thought it was Len's father who owned and ran the company. Len's just set to inherit everything."

"Oh, the *father*." Elinor rolled her eyes. "Marianne said he was a mean old buzzard who'd steal pennies off a dead man's eyes. He's a controlling son of a gun. Threatened Len when he married Marianne. Said he might just cut him out of the will if he didn't behave himself. Didn't like him eloping with a Vegas showgirl. Guess he thought his son should be able to nab a princess or somesuch with all that gold behind him." She sighed loudly. "Whole family's worthless, you ask me. Marianne told me the only one who treated her decent was the sister."

"Augustina?" I asked.

"Yeah, that's her. She's the only one who treated Marianne kindly. Only one in the whole family who bought her a wedding present, matter of fact."

"What about Len's mother? Where is she?" I asked.

"Don't know. Len wouldn't talk about her. Marianne found out, through the sister, that the mother hightailed it out of there a long time ago, just left her son and ran. Apparently no one in the family is allowed to say a peep about it."

"Can you explain something to me?" I asked her. "Len married Marianne in Las Vegas. Was he living in Peru then? Or did that happen later?"

"The whole family's like a pack of gypsies. They roam everywhere. Len was sent down here to take the family biz in new directions. He's in the gaming industry." Elinor made a face. "That's his fancy-pants way of saying *gambling.*"

Her answer struck me as off for several reasons. If relations were so poor with his father, would Len really come to Peru to work for him? And if the father was supercontrolling, why would he want his wayward son a continent away? But even more bizarre was the idea that gambling was a money-making proposition in these parts. "Gambling? Then what on earth is he doing in Peru?" I asked. "This is a poor country. That doesn't make any sense."

"Shows what you know, Tiger Lily," Jesse said. "Peru's the second-biggest gamblin' market—pardon me, I mean *gaming* market—in South America."

"What? Where? I haven't seen a casino the entire time we've been here."

"It's mostly online gamblin'. Seriously, Lil."

"That is big business here," Elinor added. "Len set up shop in Lima, because apparently you have to base your company in Peru to take any part of the gaming industry pie here. From here, it's a hop and a skip to the rest of the South American market. Len's got big plans, least according to Marianne. 'Course, the father doesn't really think he's up to the job."

"Why do you say that?"

"On account of that old coot sending his boy toy assistant to babysit Len."

"Boy toy?"

"Charlie Cutler. He's supposed to be the Wolven family's lawyer, but the man is as gay as a goose in pink spats. You met him?"

"Yes," Jesse said. "We have." His voice was just slightly strained, though his expression gave away nothing.

"Well, then you know. Man's a raving homosexual." Elinor drew out every syllable as she spoke, so the word came out *hoe-moe-SEX-you-all.* "You can't trust someone like—"

"I thought you said you never met Len Wolven," I interrupted her. She nodded. "Then when did you meet Charlie?"

"Oh, Marianne told me all about him. He's all fussy, though, like those gay men are."

"Are they?" Jesse's easygoing demeanor had vanished. His voice was softer, but there was a hard edge in it. "God gave them over to a depraved mind, to do those things which are not proper."

"Exactly," said Elinor. She smiled at me. "I do love a man who knows his Good Book."

"Let's get back to your sister," I said. "She actually told you she was in danger? She thought Len was going to kill her?" Elinor nodded. "Why?"

"What do you mean, 'Why?' "

"Why did she think she was suddenly in danger?" I tried to clarify. "She married Len, what, six months ago? And then, one day, she starts talking about him killing her. Something must have happened. Did she find out something about him? Was there something illegal he was involved in? There had to be a reason."

"Well, with her telling me all that, you know, kinky stuff, I thought maybe it had to do with that."

"How would that make any sense?" I asked. "She's been dealing with his kinky demands for months. Before that, she was a stripper in Las Vegas. Kinky is her specialty."

Elinor's hands froze. Her big gold band was caught up at the knuckle. "Well, now . . ." She looked from Jesse to me, obviously uncomfortable. She took a handkerchief out of her bag and blew her nose, making a loud honking noise that turned heads. "That I don't know. I mean, maybe something did happen. Or maybe it didn't. All I know is that my baby sis was scared to death. And I keep hearing her voice in my head from the last time we talked."

"What did she say?" I asked.

"She was crying, I know she was." Elinor's face was pale under her circles of orange rouge. "He's gonna kill me, Elinor. Any day now. Promise me you won't let him get away with it. Promise me."

40

"Well, that wasn't awkward at all," Jesse said as he opened the door of our suite. I looked back down the hall, in case Elinor Bargeman was charging after us. She wasn't, of course; she'd left our hotel to go back to her own, which was just up the street and around the corner. She was going to freshen up and call Alcántara, she'd told us. Only she'd called him *Alakazam.*

"I thought it was tough to sit with her by myself. I didn't realize it would be worse with you there," I admitted, locking the door behind us. "What was that verse you quoted to her?"

"It's from Romans." Jesse still sounded oddly formal, pronouncing every word with a precision that didn't mesh with his normally relaxed demeanor. " 'For this reason God gave them over to degrading passions; for their women exchanged the natural function for that which is unnatural, and in the same way also the men abandoned the natural function of the woman and burned in their desire toward one another, men with men committing indecent acts and receiving in their own persons the due penalty of their error. And just as they did not see fit to acknowledge God any longer, God gave them over to a depraved mind, to do those things which are not proper.' "

"That's horrible."

Jesse shrugged. "It's not all like that. But Saint Paul had a bee in his bonnet on certain issues."

"You're the most religious person I know, and you know the Bible inside out," I said. "But I don't understand how you can be part of something that trashes you for being what you are."

"There's more to it than that, Tiger Lily." He went to the window and stared outside. "The Bible's called the Word of God, but it lives and breathes. It contradicts itself all over the place, 'cause it was written by different folks, workin' at different times, and then Constantine and his gang of pagans who'd just converted to Christianity held a council to decide what went in and what got the boot." He looked at me. "You could use it for any purpose."

"Part of that purpose has been to justify terrible things. Crusades, killings. Slaveholders used it to allow for slavery."

"But it's filled with hope and beauty and grace. Anything that powerful, it can be used for good or evil. Though there are some parts that defy misinterpretation. Love thy neighbor as thyself."

"Quoting Jesus. That I understand," I said. "It's the rest of the Bible I'd get rid of."

"Then you'd be tossin' out the baby with the bathwater," he answered. "And it wasn't Jesus who first said that. *Love thy neighbor as thyself* is from Leviticus."

"Really?" The worst part about discussing religion and the Bible with Jesse was that I always sounded hopelessly ignorant. As much as I mocked people who criticized books without reading them or movies without seeing them, I was guilty of the same thing. Aside from my First Communion training, my religious education was lacking. "Okay, next time we sit down with Elinor, how about you quote her something Jesus said about telling the truth?"

"Why's that?"

"Are you kidding?"

"No. What did I miss?" Jesse cocked his head, suddenly intrigued.

"She's leaving out part of the story. Something happened and Marianne found out about it or confronted her husband about it or something. If she started telling Elinor that she was in danger, there had to be some reason for it."

"Yes and no. Maybe nothin' new happened between them, but she found out about his first wife. What was that thing in the paper about him havin' a breakdown? There's a big part of this story we're missin' out on."

Jesse had a point. "We need more information about Len Wolven."

"Time to call in the cavalry, Tiger Lily."

Let me get this straight," the voice on the other end of the phone crackled. It wasn't a bad connection; it was pretty much the way he always sounded, thanks to the endless chain of cigarettes he smoked. "You and your Okie pal think you've stumbled onto a serial killer doing business in Peru."

"We think he's killed three women, but there could be more. One was in the U.S."

"So he's an underachieving serial killer." I'd almost forgotten what a gruesome, dark sense of humor Bruxton had. "What is he, some kind of drug kingpin?"

"I think he's too busy taking drugs to be running any kind of business, but Jesse thinks he could be a drug lord."

"Peru's the biggest cocaine producer on the continent after Colombia," Jesse called.

"Did you hear that?" I asked Bruxton.

"Say hi to the peanut gallery for me." Bruxton sighed. "By the way, you know what pisses me off about amateur sleuths? You think everything is like a movie."

"What's that supposed to mean?"

"Look, I've never been to Peru, but even I know it's not all cocaine and llamas."

I had to bite my lip to keep from bursting out laughing. Bruxton was being his usual blunt self, and it was good to hear.

"What's he sayin'?" Jesse asked.

"The connection's not that good," I lied. "I'll tell you afterward, okay? I promise." I closed the door to my room.

"Bet he's pouting," Bruxton said.

"You got that right."

"Look, you called me for advice, so I'm going to give it to you straight. I think you and Jesse should get the hell out of there. I don't know who this Wolven character is, but everything you've told me about the situation is bad news."

"Running away isn't an option. My passport was stolen, and it takes a few days to get a new one. Besides, I don't run away."

"Is that your John Wayne impersonation? It sucks," he groused. I felt pangs of guilt. The news I'd held back from Bruxton was what he would've considered the biggest piece of the puzzle: that Bastián had kidnapped me, planned to kill me, and tried to rape me. It was wrong of me to hold that back, but I knew that if I told Bruxton, he would yell at me until he lost his raspy voice or until I went home, whichever came first. Moreover, he wouldn't help me with anything for fear of me getting more deeply involved. Before I could think of anything to say, he added, "Okay, who was the woman who died at Machu Picchu?"

"Trista Deen. She was Len Wolven's ex-girlfriend. He'd jilted her to marry a Vegas stripper."

"Okay, what do you know about her death? Are the cops there doing a tox screen?"

"Yes. What they've said so far is she died of a hypertensive crisis. They said she was high on cocaine. Before she died, she told me that Len Wolven made her drink something, but she might just have been raving at that point . . ."

"Ayahuasca?"

"Excuse me?"

"Tell the cops to check for ayahuasca." He spelled it out for me. "It's a Peruvian drug, and it's ingested as a drink."

"How do you know that?"

"I used to work narcotics, Lily. I told you all about it."

"You did." That was true. He'd told me about those days, and his own battle with drug and alcohol addiction. That had made me feel closer to him and yet increased the distance between us. The addicts I'd known went back to their destructive patterns sooner or later. Even though Bruxton seemed to be managing his demons and resisting their siren call, the fact that he heard one at all frightened me. On some level, he had to be fighting it every day.

"Ayahuasca's got a bunch of fans in the U.S. They think of it as natural LSD. Of course, it's illegal. I've known of several cases where people went into hypertensive crisis after using it. Some of them died."

"So the drug causes that?"

"Not on its own. The combination of ayahuasca and another drug—cocaine would be one—has killed people, though."

I thought I heard something brush against my door. "So, it's possible that Trista . . ." As I spoke, I slipped out of my shoes and padded silently across the floor, opening the door suddenly. Jesse almost fell inside. He gave me a hangdog expression and muttered, "Fine, I'll scoot," before heading over to his room.

"Sorry about that," I said. "You-know-who was at the keyhole."

"There's a surprise." There was the sound of a lighter clicking. "Cocaine and ayahuasca is a bad mix. If that woman was on both, she was crazy. Tell me the rest of the story."

"Len Wolven's first wife, Kirsten, supposedly died in a car crash in the U.S. He apparently strangled his second wife, Marianne, in Lima three weeks ago."

"How the hell do you know that?"

"Someone told me," I muttered.

"What, do people think you're a priest over there? Look, you're nowhere near as good a liar as you think you are, Lily. Gimme the rest. Just no sleepwalking stories this time."

I'd lied to him a few months earlier, and he was determined never to let me forget about that, as far as I could tell. The man held a serious grudge. "Brux, Len Wolven is completely nuts. I saw him try to burn himself up. He's capable of anything."

"What haven't you told me yet?"

"This morning, his assistant offered me money to go away."

"Yeah, that's a sign of a guilty conscience," Bruxton said. "Okay, give me the names you want checked out."

I spelled them out—Len, Charlie, and Bastián, then Trista, Kirsten, and Marianne.

"Sure it's not like I'm busy or anything," Bruxton said.

"I'm sorry, I—"

"That was a joke, Lily. Three women are dead? Of course I'm going to help." There was a long pause. "You sound good," Bruxton said suddenly. "Maybe Jesse was right, and taking that trip was the best thing for you. You're flying back through New York, right?"

"Right."

"So, you planning on visiting at all?"

"I think so."

"Wow, this is like pulling teeth," Bruxton said. "You want to tell me to go away?"

"No, of course not."

"Then can I see you when you come in?"

"I'd like that," I said softly.

"That makes two of us. Okay, I'll call you when I find something."

41

After having such a busy morning, the afternoon was painfully slow. A police officer showed up to help me file my new passport request with the embassy in Lima. I'd already reported my credit cards stolen via the Web in the wee hours of the morning, but I followed up with calls to make sure that whoever had found them hadn't gone on a shopping spree. No one had tried to use them, and I wondered where they'd ended up. As if it weren't bad enough being the victim of a crime, I had to waste hours dealing with the aftermath. Of course, Bastián was still on the loose, and all I could hope was that he was suffering. The blood and tissue the police found on the trunk suggested to me that I'd hurt him seriously, and since hospitals in the area were on high alert for him, it didn't seem like he'd be able to access much medical care. Of course, he or Len Wolven probably knew some doctors who'd do anything for money. Whatever happened, I hoped he was in pain. It was a vile thought on my part, I knew, but a satisfying one.

Hector Alcántara dropped by my hotel to see how I was. He was oozing his Valentino charm again, but it wasn't working on me. When I started asking him questions about Marianne Wolven, he'd smiled and said that for professional reasons, he couldn't answer. "You understand, I'm sure," he said, his expression solemn.

"No, I don't. I mean, I understand that you're looking for

Marianne Wolven. You undoubtedly wanted to talk to her husband after his girlfriend died at Machu Picchu. But why would the Lima police force send you there? Vargas could ask whatever questions you wanted answered."

"This is a very delicate matter, my dear Lily. You do not understand, and I only wish that I could explain. But what I want to know is, how did Bastián Montalvo dispose of her body?"

"He didn't tell me that."

"You see, without her body, this is difficult. All we have is your word."

"I'm telling you the truth."

"You were in fear of your life that night, Lily. It must have been terrible. Perhaps you became confused."

It was hard not to yell at him. "I know what he said. Len Wolven killed Marianne."

Alcántara sighed. "If only we could find this man for questioning."

"Why don't you question Len? He's still over at the hospital, isn't he?"

Alcántara smiled, as if I were too stupid to answer. "I hope you feel better soon, Lily. Do rest up."

After he left, I was restless. Vargas wasn't returning my calls directly, though his subordinates gave me progress updates each time I phoned; those consisted of telling me there was no progress.

"Where is Vargas? Who the hell does he think he is?" I ranted at Jesse.

"Maybe we should get out for a walk. I reckon bein' cooped up like this ain't makin' you feel better."

Since there weren't many places I could go, we ended up back at the cathedral, this time to see its art collection. The same elderly woman I'd talked with in the morning sold me my ticket on the way in. "You came back!" she said, obviously delighted.

Inside, it was still a gloomy place. Jesse dragged me to the back, so that he could introduce me to the masterpiece: a painting of the Last Supper, rendered by an artist of the Cusco School. There was Jesus and his disciples, sitting around a table with a platter of guinea pig.

"Is that supposed to be a joke?" I whispered. "I mean, guinea pig?"

"It's called *cuy* in these here parts, and it's a delicacy. To a native-born artist, that's what Jesus would have had at the Last Supper."

"But that's so bizarre."

"Ha. Just wait till you see Jesus in a lace skirt."

"What?" My voice bounced off the towering ceiling of the cathedral and back at me. A security guard gave us a disapproving glare.

"Hush, Lil. C'mon, this way." He dragged me to an alcove, where there was a smaller canvas of a very unusual Jesus. "The native painters had some ideas fixed in their skulls that Christianity didn't root out. For instance, they thought it was blasphemy to paint Jesus in a loincloth on the cross. To them that was just wrong, wrong, wrong. So they dressed him up in the skirt of the Inca nobility. Topless was okay with them, but the skirt was nonnegotiable."

We stared at it, silently.

"It's actually very beautiful," I admitted.

"You just need to forget what you already know. Or what you think you already know. Open yourself up to what's around you here." He took my arm. "Now I'm gonna show you my favorite thing here."

The cathedral was massive, and we had to walk almost back to the entrance, then make a U-turn, to approach the altar. We stopped at the feet of another Inca Jesus.

"Meet Taytacha Temblores. Lord of the Earthquakes. Or Jesus, to folks like you and me."

"The native people thought Jesus was black?" I asked.

"He didn't start out black. That's from all the smoke and soot." Jesse stared at it admiringly. "Rumor has it that he stopped an earthquake here in 1650. Don't know how it all went down, but it was part of the reason many locals made fervent conversions."

We spent an hour wandering through the cathedral. Then, because we had nowhere else to go, we went to the Jesuit church and paid admission there, too. It was well lit inside, and the gilding on wooden pillars almost glowed. But the most interesting part was following a rickety staircase up several flights and discovering a room of abandoned saints. They were covered in sheets of plastic that had once been clear but now were yellow or brown. A few of them had tears in the plastic, usually in front of the face. Presumably someone had been looking for a missing saint.

"They're all so *little*," Jesse said. "It's like an army of holy midgets."

There was something very sad about seeing centuries-old wooden statues retired with so little glory. "They belong in a museum," I said. "They shouldn't be tossed under a sheet of plastic and left to rot here."

"D'you think they upgraded to bigger, better saints?"

For some reason, when he said *upgrade,* it brought to mind Len Wolven's women. He was rich enough to have his pick, in spite of his lack of redeeming qualities. I hoped that Bruxton would get back to me soon with some report that would explain Len's behavior. Right now, all I had was questions, and leaps in logic. Whatever Alcántara said, I knew Len had murdered Marianne. He had almost certainly killed Trista, too, even if I wasn't able to figure out what happened. And his first wife, Kirsten? That remained the puzzle piece that didn't quite fit. A car accident just wasn't a good way to get rid of someone.

"C'mon out here," Jesse said. The room of abandoned saints led to an open-air balcony overlooking the Plaza de Armas. We were the equivalent of maybe four stories up, with a clear view of the cathedral, the colonial arcades, and the green park at the center of the square. In the middle of the park was a fountain, built on a wide hexagonal base, with six paved paths leading around it. In the section nearest the Jesuit church, I saw three headstones that I hadn't noticed before: one with a ring of plants nestled around it, another with a little white gate, and the last with a giant cross. Everywhere I turned in Peru, I felt as if I were being confronted with death. It was inescapable.

"Jesse, why do you think Len Wolven killed those women?"

"Because he's a sicko, Lil. Why else?"

I tore my eyes away from the plaza and stared at him. "When we were at his villa, and he reached into the fireplace, what did you think he was doing?"

"I dunno. Maybe bein' dramatic or somethin' like that. Like, 'I'm so sad because my girlfriend's dead. I couldn't possibly be guilty. Look, now I'm sufferin'. Poor me!' What did you think?"

"He wanted to be in pain. Maybe he felt he deserved it. As if suffering were his penance for killing."

"Lil, you're lettin' yourself get carried away. It's the midget saints, ain't it? They're turnin' your head."

Maybe he was right. Perhaps the disturbing artwork I'd seen at the convent and the other religious art and icons I'd encountered were nudging something normally buried in a corner of my mind. But I couldn't shake the thought that Len Wolven was a tormented soul, as well as a murderer.

42

The voice on the other end of the phone was languid. "This is Lily? I apologize for not calling you sooner. I had planned to, but then ended up napping for two hours this afternoon."

"That's all right, Augustina. I'm glad you called. I've wanted to talk to you."

"Yes, we must talk. Could I persuade you to have dinner with me tonight?"

I hesitated for a split second. Augustina's brother had tried to have me killed. Did I really want to run the risk of that happening again? Then, as if reading my mind, she added, "My little brother won't be there. He is still in hospital, feeling sorry for himself, as he always does. I know everything he's done must make you want to run away from my whole family, but I would very much love to see you."

"Where would you like to meet?"

"Could you come to my hotel? I hate to trouble you, but in the condition I'm in it's hard to move around a great deal, especially with the altitude here."

I'd found it tough to deal with thin air; it would be brutal to do so while pregnant. "That's fine," I said.

"You will bring your handsome gentleman friend Jesse, won't you? I only met him briefly last night. I would love to see him again."

She offered to send a car for me; when I declined, she gave

me directions to her hotel. I wondered what she would think of Charlie's offer to pay me to go away if I told her about it.

Jesse had wandered out to buy water and soda while I was on the phone, and by the time he came back, I was dressed for dinner. He grinned when he saw me. "What's Ava Gardner doin' here, and what did you to with my Tiger Lily?"

I was wearing a black dress with a fitted bodice and a full skirt. It had ended up in my suitcase presumably because of its somber hue. If only I'd thought to pack some heels. "I suggest you take a very quick shower and get dressed in your finest," I said. "Augustina Wolven is expecting us for dinner at eight."

"What on earth made you accept that invitation?"

"She said her brother isn't going to be there," I explained. "It's just us having dinner with her at her hotel."

"Lil, I heard some interestin' stuff from Charlie last night. Seriously, Augustina Wolven isn't someone you want to hang around with."

"What did Charlie say about her?"

"Just that we should steer clear of her."

"Oh, Charlie's just the person I'd take advice from right now," I deadpanned. "He's completely trustworthy."

"He's a good guy. I really believe that. And if he says avoid Augustina Wolven, well . . ."

In spite of that, he got ready for dinner. While he did, I called Vargas and left a message. Technically, Augustina's hotel was a few blocks out of the green zone Vargas had given me; I didn't like playing by his rules, but given what had happened the night before, I would have been foolhardy not to. The cop I spoke to chuckled. "That is the richest part of town. I think you'll be fine," she told me in Spanish.

Jesse suggested taking a taxi, but I wanted to get there on

foot. It was all uphill on cobblestones, but walking on a chilly night helped me clear my head. By the time we got to the hotel, I was composed.

At least, I thought I was. Strolling behind the cathedral and through the Plaza del Tricentenario and the Plazoleta Nazarenas had shown me how elegant Cusco could be. This part of the old city was dramatically elevated, both figuratively and literally. Jesse and I had to climb a series of steps to reach Nazarenas, which left me feeling a little breathless, even though I'd acclimated, at least mostly. But Augustina had said she was staying at a hotel, not that she'd rented an entire villa. It was only a two-story house, but the wrought-iron gate in front of the heavy wooden door suggested a lavish interior. When we pressed the buzzer, an elderly man with stooped shoulders answered and ushered us inside.

The interior was more beautiful than any place I'd seen in Peru. The walls were painted deep red, and two cabinets filled with pre-Columbian artifacts faced each other just inside the archway. Were they real? I barely had time to wonder: on the walls just beyond were a series of portraits in gilded frames; from the way the subjects were dressed, I guessed that they were two centuries old. Ornately carved wood furniture set off the space, and carved wooden columns reminded me of what I'd seen in the Jesuit church, minus the gold leaf.

The villa was laid out like a classical Roman one. I realized that as the man led us to an open-air courtyard at its center. There were trees around its perimeter, so that you could almost forget that you were in a building, and space heaters gave off enough warmth to feel cozy. Augustina sat at a glass-topped table, with a glass of what looked like orange juice in front of her. Her knitting needles clacked away, but instead of the fuchsia blanket, now she was working on a little pink hat.

Given the ostentatious wealth of her family, it seemed almost comical that she would knit her own baby clothes, yet there was a sweetness about it I found touching.

"Lily! Jesse! Thank you for coming," she called, setting aside the knitting to pull me down to kiss my cheeks. "You look so beautiful," she purred. She shook Jesse's hand. "I cannot drink alcohol in my condition, but we have absolutely everything here. What would you like to drink? Perhaps champagne?"

"I'll take a pisco sour, thanks," Jesse said, sounding a little grumpy.

"I'll have one as well. Did you already finish knitting the blanket?" I asked.

"Yes, just an hour ago. Of course, I had to start something new immediately." She smiled in response to my quizzical look. "When I found out I was pregnant again, I had to quit smoking—how do you say it?—cold turkey. So I needed something to do with my hands. I must always have something to do with my hands. With each pregnancy, I knit like a demon, but I never have time for it normally."

"Are your daughters here with you?"

She shook her head. "They are in Santiago with my mother. She lives with us, so it is not disruptive for them. She is a wonderful grandmother. My father, on the other hand . . . well, would you believe he takes no interest in his granddaughters? I am not sure he knows their names, although I do send him photographs. In any case, I was not sure how long I would have to be here, or what state I would find my little brother in. I'm not really supposed to travel now, but I decided it was necessary, given the devastation my brother has caused."

"Did your husband come, too?"

"No, he is in a remote corner of Australia at the moment. We lived there for a year, to oversee some of my father's interests, then moved to Santiago, also for my father's interests. Franco is a mining engineer specializing in rare minerals. He could literally get blood from a stone." Her haughty, catlike face spread into a broad grin. "My father relies on him heavily for some of his most difficult operations. But Franco will be home in time for the baby to arrive."

She chattered along quite rapidly while a servant got us drinks; her English was easy to understand. "I realized I was very thoughtless," she said. "I should have checked the menu with you. Do you have any food allergies? No? I am so glad. One of my daughters has a tree-nut allergy. Half the children at her nursery school have some kind of intolerance or condition. It's so hard for the little ones, because of course they want to share food. Ah, well. By the way, your dress is stunning, Lily. Is it a vintage designer piece?"

"It is vintage, but I don't know who designed it. It doesn't have a label."

"Did you know that some of the best designer vintage can be found in South America?"

"Really?"

"Upper-class South American women, who tend to be very glamorous, have a long history of going over to Europe to buy clothing. They have original Dior and Givenchy and Lanvin dresses up in their attics. Even some Chanel and Schiaparelli. There is a Peruvian woman who has opened up a shop in Toronto, in fact, selling such dresses."

"Divine Decadence! I know exactly the place you mean. It's lovely." It was a stunning shop, though one that I couldn't afford. I was used to unearthing treasures on cluttered racks in stores that reeked of mothballs, not paying thousands for a single dress. Still, it didn't hurt to look.

"Well, I can't fit into anything there these days, but . . ." Augustina looked up and the smile slid off her face. I'd heard the clacking of shoes on the tile, but only when I turned around did I see that Charlie was there.

"Yes? What is it?" Augustina asked, her voice brusque and businesslike. "Is it my brother? Has something happened to him?"

"Len is fine, just resting. I thought I would join you for dinner."

"Did you? I think you should be at the hospital in case my little brother needs anything, Charles."

"Why don't we call Mr. Wolven and see what he thinks, Augustina?"

She smiled, but her eyes narrowed to slits; the antipathy between them was palpable. "I am certain you don't need to consult my father on where to have dinner."

"Good evening, Jesse, Lily. Good to see you both." Charlie was acting as if our meeting this morning hadn't happened. "I suppose you've been talking about Len."

"Why would we waste our time doing that?" I asked.

Augustina broke out into peals of delighted laughter. "I had been hoping for a graceful way to bring the subject up, because I owe Lily an apology from the bottom of my heart. My whole family does. I do not pretend that I know or understand what is going on with my little brother. We have never been close, and we did not grow up together. You may already know this, but my mother was my father's third wife, and Len's mother was his fourth."

"You don't look at all alike," I commented.

"We couldn't be more different."

"I don't think it's Len's behavior you need to apologize for, Augustina. It's Bastián's," Charlie interjected.

"Len is family, so he is my responsibility. Bastián is nothing but a lowlife. The police will find him, and—"

"Did you tell Lily that Bastián worked for you for four years?"

Augustina frowned. "Before my father assigned him to my brother? No." She glanced at me. "My father has a bad habit of assigning and reassigning people work according to his whim. As a matter of fact, that is what he did with Charles here. Charles worked for my father for years and years. Started showing up at all of the family gatherings. You would almost have thought he was an adopted son. And then, one day, he banished Charles to Peru to take care of Len."

"It was not a banishment, Augustina, I never called it—"

"Yes, quite right. You told my father he was sending you into exile. What, you didn't realize that my father would tell me that? Do you think your complaints to him are confidential?"

Charlie appeared stunned. If his face had registered surprise at some of my accusations at the convent that morning, now he was flummoxed. "Mr. Wolven makes his decisions with precise logic." His words came slowly, as if his lawyerly brain were in retreat.

"I am sure he would say there is a logic to it, but it is annoying," Augustina said. "To be fair to Bastián, when he worked for me, he never caused any trouble."

"So he mysteriously went bad just recently?" Charlie's tone was mild, yet mocking. He was back on comfortable ground.

"You want the truth, Charles? Let's get this out in the

open. I believe Bastián did what he did because my brother *ordered* him to."

"Is that what you think?" Len Wolven stepped out from behind a pillar. He was wearing the same pants and shirt he'd been wearing when he'd tried to set himself ablaze in Aguas Calientes. The scorch marks and tears made him look like a castaway on a pirate ship.

"Len!" Charlie stood. "What are doing here? You're supposed to be resting."

"I heard you on the phone. Plotting with my father as usual. Doing what you do best, Charlie." He turned to Augustina. "So where are my darling little nieces? It's been, like, forever since you've let me see them."

"They are at home with my mother in Santiago."

"Don't you worry that you'll come home and find that she's eaten them?"

"You are *revolting*," Augustina snapped. "I know you have had yet another mental breakdown, but you will *not* come into this house and speak of my mother in this way."

"It's not your house. It belongs to my father, which means it's all going to belong to *me* one day. Not you." He surveyed the courtyard. "Nice to see everybody gathered here. All the people plotting against me gathered in one place . . ."

"No one is plotting against you, Len," said Charlie.

"That's pretty funny, coming from my father's puppet. You ever have a thought of your own, Charlie? Or did you think it would make him happy if you just checked those at the door when you started working for him?" Len asked. "It's why he likes you so much, though. You're his favorite dog." His dark eyes fell on me. "I can't believe I fell for what you said. You were plotting against me all this time, you bitch."

"That's it. You're gettin' your clock cleaned out, you little freak." Jesse got up and strode across the room. Len's eyes widened in panic and he ducked behind the column and around part of the courtyard, away from my friend's reach.

"How typical," Augustina chimed in. "The alcoholic, drug-addicted little coward who likes to hurt women, just like his father, won't face a real man."

That last taunt was too much for Len. He grabbed a vase and threw it at his sister, missing her by inches. Augustina didn't flinch as it shattered; her expression was coldly superior, as if she were watching a child she detested having a tantrum. Len moved toward her, but Charlie intercepted him, holding him back while Len yelled. He broke free and turned over a tray of crystal glasses before Jesse punched him in the nose. Len put his hands up, cradling his face, but that didn't stop the blood. It gushed down, staining his shirt. I couldn't see his nose, but I was positive Jesse had just broken it. Len sobbed as if his heart had fractured instead, and Charlie led him out of the courtyard, murmuring about taking Len back to the hospital. The crying continued until the heavy door slammed shut, and then everything was quiet.

Jesse stood by Augustina, rubbing her shoulder.

"I am so sorry. That was terrible. I hope you do not mind, but I think I must lie down in my room. Jesse, would you mind helping me? My room is just down a hallway, on the first floor. I couldn't climb stairs, you see. I hope you will both stay for the cook's dinner, though." Augustina was chattering again. Even though she was leaning on Jesse's arm, she threw her other around me as she went past. "I am so embarrassed of my family," she whispered. "The name Wolven is appropriate, because we *are* like wolves."

43

When I took the staircase up to the second floor of the villa, it was only because an elderly servant directed me to the bathroom up there. Listening carefully, you could still hear Len Wolven shouting and carrying on just beyond the front door. I didn't want to encounter him again, so I rushed up the stairs as quickly as I could. At the top, I felt dizzy and breathless, and belatedly remembered you weren't supposed to run up stairs at eleven thousand feet above sea level unless you were from the Andes. Lesson learned, I thought.

Which door led to the bathroom? I wondered. There were several black-painted wooden portals along the hallway. I grabbed a handle and turned it. The ornately carved wooden door swung in, and I groped a stuccoed wall for a minute looking for a light switch.

When it flickered on, chaos was immediately apparent. Clothes were strewn over the bed and the floor, as if some unruly teenager were calling it home. A collection of stupid-looking hats covered an antique dresser and I realized this had to be Len Wolven's room. There were some designer women's shoes on the floor, but I guessed those belonged to one of his dead female companions. There was also paper lying everywhere. Blue file folders lay empty, their contents unleashed and kicked around. Envelopes were separated from letters. The place looked like a tornado from the American Midwest had mysteriously touched down.

I stepped gingerly, wondering if there was broken glass mixed into the debris. There seemed to be a lot of that around the Wolvens. Given what I'd seen, the surprise would be if there weren't dangerous shards lying around.

My snooping instincts were keen, but I had no idea where to start in such a mess. Fighting my urge to pick up the papers, I headed for the en suite bathroom. It was massive, decorated with ornate blue and white tiles and with a white Jacuzzi at one end. There weren't any papers lying around here, but it looked as if someone had dumped the contents of a giant toiletry kit on the marble countertop of the vanity, letting them spill over onto the floor. There were lotions and potions of all descriptions, mostly Creme de la Mer products with names like the Lifting Face Serum and the Body Refiner. That was all Trista's, I guessed. Then I picked up a jar. Cellmen Intensive Revitalizing Skin Care Cream for Men, it said. The murderer was a preening metrosexual on top of everything else? That shouldn't have surprised me, but it left me shaking my head.

A lone prescription bottle, with Viagra written on the label, sat on the Jacuzzi. After an extended shudder, I opened the medicine cabinet. That was the treasure trove. Seroquel, read the first label I saw. Len Wolven's name was on it, too. There were at least a dozen bottles. I wasn't sure what Seroquel did, but apparently it needed lots of company, at least according to the doctor who was prescribing all this stuff. The labels had names on them—Depakote, Tegretol, Geodon, Nimodipine—but nothing I recognized until I pulled out Lithonate. That rang a bell somewhere . . . Lithonate, as in lithium? Was Wolven bipolar? I thought of his mood swings, from weeping depression to outsized rage, and it suddenly fit.

I stared at the bottles, wondering if it would be wrong to take them with me. Reluctantly, I put them down and settled for scribbling the names down. How could anyone take this many pills and still be standing?

Stepping out of the bathroom, I wondered how long I had to explore before any of the servants noticed that I was here. Kneeling, I reached for a red envelope with *LEN* printed on it in block letters. Inside was a card with a painting on the front: a woman wearing a broad choker, her head twisted to the side in a pose that would only be possible if her neck were broken. I recognized it instantly as Gustav Klimt; while some people saw his paintings as beautiful, I'd always seen his female subjects as mutilated. The inside of the card had only one sentence, also in block letters: *I KNOW WHAT YOU DID.*

Staring at it, I realized there was a reason for Len's paranoia. He was being blackmailed. Crazy as he was, he wasn't imagining that.

I picked up a few scattered pages, but they appeared to be from random files, one about a mine in Chile, another about a corporation called Betsson, then a series of photocopied news stories from Brazil. I didn't understand Portuguese very well, but I could tell that the stories were about a suggested ban on online gambling in Brazil. I grabbed up a bunch and leafed through them until I found one that caught my eye.

> *My dear Mr. Cutler,*
> *Our search for Mrs. Marianne Wolven continues. After a careful search of available credit and banking data, we can say with confidence that our investigation was correct: none of the accounts in the name of Marianne Wolven or Marianne Bargeman have been*

accessed since the date in question. Our agents have circulated her photograph but there have been no credible sightings (your increased reward dramatically increased the reports of sightings, but none of these has withstood scrutiny). The tourist card that was registered when she entered Peru is still officially registered as "open," meaning that her stolen passport has not been used by anyone leaving the country. This strongly suggests that she remains in Peru, though there is a possibility that she has made a land crossing (whether voluntarily or by force, as you suggested). As we have previously discussed, Ecuador, Colombia, and Brazil are unlikely destinations for various reasons, but both Chile and Bolivia would be possibilities. Would you prefer for us to now expand the scope of our operations? Please advise at your earliest convenience.

Best regards,
Xavier Alcántara

The letter stunned me. Xavier Alcántara? Was that a relative of Hector Alcántara's? How could it not be? I wasn't ready to consider all of the implications as I stood there in Wolven's bedroom. I folded it and tucked it into my bag. Moving quickly to the door, I shoved it open and stepped into the hallway, stopping to make sure no one had seen me, and rushed down the stairs.

"Tonight takes the prize for weirdest dinner ever," Jesse said. He was sitting across from me at a little restaurant we'd found on a narrow street. The sign out front called it the Moni Café-Restaurant. Inside, there were just a few simple tables and chairs, only a couple of which were occupied, and two women cooking in the open kitchen, which stood in the center of the room.

"I don't even know where to begin," I answered. "Though I don't think you can call it dinner, because we didn't eat anything."

"Ha. I was gonna make a joke about you draggin' me into a vegetarian restaurant." Jesse pointed to a sign I hadn't noticed at first.

"Wow. That is a first, for both of us."

"Yeah, but after that scene at Casa Wolven, it's pretty tough to call anythin' else weird. I swear, Lil, I was thinkin' I'd have to smash my glass against something just to be part of that party. Augustina might just be a crazy diva-lady, but Len Wolven is a total nutjob."

"I think he's manic-depressive," I said. "I found a lot of prescription medications in his bathroom. Check out the list of what he's got."

Jesse looked at it and whistled. "There's no way one body could take all that, is there?"

I shrugged but didn't answer. One of the cooks came over

to take our orders—a corn-potato-quinoa curry for me, and a pasta dish with eggplant for Jesse—and then we waited until after she brought us our pumpkin cream soup and some bottled water to pick up our conversation again.

"Charlie said somethin' last night about how screwed up Len is. He reckons it has to do with his mama runnin' out on him when he was a little boy, and that's why he always needs to have some chick around."

"Oh, thanks. You just brought back the memory of the one pill I didn't write down. Viagra."

"Okay, now my brain needs a bleach bath. Eww. So, you think he's as sexually rabid as Elinor Bargeman said?"

I reluctantly considered that. "I think the quote was, 'Leonard's got more kinks than a garden hose.'"

"Them Texans talk kinda cute. Too bad the Longhorns suck."

"The Longhorns?" I asked.

"College football team. They got a war with the Sooners that runs back to 1900. We call it the Red River Rivalry. By the way, this soup is incredible."

"I know you're trying to distract me from the thought of Len Wolven's sexual escapades, but college football isn't going to do it. Do you remember back at the Inkaterra, when Vargas said Trista hadn't had sex recently?"

"Lil, do I have to fill you in on how conservative that fella is? No offense to him, but no Church-approved boy-girl relations *don't* necessarily equal no sex."

"Good point." I pulled out the letter and the red envelope I'd found on the floor of Len's bedroom and handed them over. "These, you have to read. Len's room was chaos. Clothes, hats, but most of all, paper was everywhere, like he'd dumped out a file cabinet."

Jesse pulled out the card, opened it and frowned. "Blackmail?"

"Looks like it. Read the letter."

He scanned it, raised his eyebrows, then went over it again. "Son of a gun. Alcántara."

"A relative of Alcántara's, I'd guess. I wonder if that's his angle in all of this. He's got a relative who does private investigations, and he uses his police credentials to assist."

"That would make a lotta sense. It would also explain why Vargas acts like Alcántara is poison."

"What do you think of the rest?"

"I don't think Charlie knows what happened to Marianne Wolven," he answered. "He may have his fears, his suspicions, his worries, but the bottom line is he just doesn't know."

"I think he *does* know, Jesse. But he's determined to keep his blinders on at any price."

45 When I called the U.S. embassy in Lima the next morning, I got the runaround. First, they claimed not to have the police report for Cusco; then, when they found it, they claimed they hadn't received my application. I spent the better part of the hour being transferred from one careless bureaucrat to another, until I lucked out and got a woman who'd read the police report. "You poor girl," she said. "I will make sure everything is completed for tomorrow morning."

Jesse and I had already had breakfast at that point, and we'd started arguing early about what to do with the day. I couldn't imagine being too far from the phone, in case the police found Bastián or something else about Len Wolven came up. In the back of my mind, I worried a little bit for Augustina, though I had no doubt that she was tough and quite capable of taking care of herself. But she was heavily, uncomfortably pregnant, and therefore less able to, say, run if her demented half brother attacked her. I refused to go outside until I got an e-mail from Bruxton, and one arrived just after ten. *You want to give me a call?* it read. I did.

"Hell, that was fast. Next time I want to hear your voice, I know what to do," he said. I could hear him chewing gum, which meant he was somewhere inside the NYPD precinct on the Lower East Side, where he couldn't smoke.

"Just the facts, Detective Bruxton, just the facts."

For a second, I thought he might be smiling that crooked nonsmile of his. "Why do I put up with you again?" he asked.

"You like being led astray."

"I hate when you're right. Okay, Kirsten Wolven died in a car crash, like you thought. Leonard Wolven junior—yeah, yeah, I know he's not technically a junior, but humor me—was injured in the crash, but not bad."

"What caused the crash?"

"Junior. Blood alcohol level probably put him on Mars. Car ran off the road, met a tree. Junior got arrested for vehicular manslaughter and DUI, but the charge got watered down to nothing. Junior didn't even get probation, just a fine and time in a rehab center. Though that was interesting."

I swallowed the bait. "What does *interesting* mean?"

"Took him three tries to get through one stint in rehab. Twice, Junior had to be rushed to the hospital. The records are sketchy, but it looks like he tried to kill himself."

"With a drug overdose?"

"Nope. Slashed his wrists, then the next he drank some kind of cleaning product. I can probably find out details, but that'll take time. This is all I got now. Couple other things real quick: three other miscreants on that list you gave me."

"Who?"

"Marianne Bargeman. You told me check-kiting. I'm seeing credit-card fraud, solicitation, minor drug possession . . . lots of penny-ante shit. She some kind of scam artist? She's not too good at it from what I can tell."

"I really don't know."

"Okay, then there's Trista Deen. Possession, possession, intent to sell, possession, public intoxication, possession, possession. You seeing a pattern here?"

"She was really into drugs?"

"Bingo. Now, best for last. Charlie Cutler."

"What about him?"

"Arrested for aggravated assault seven years ago."

"What? Who did he assault?"

"His father. Can't tell you much, except that the father wouldn't drop the charges. Cutler pled out, got probation and rage-management counseling. His father took out a restraining order against him. Cutler violated it three weeks ago."

"What did he do?" I remembered Charlie telling me that he'd been back in the U.S. recently; that was why he wasn't certain what had happened to Marianne Bargeman. While Len Wolven was strangling his wife, Charlie was in the U.S., apparently terrorizing his own father.

"No assault this time, just a violation of the restraining order. Cutler's supposed to stay at least two hundred feet away from his father. Nice."

My mind was reeling. Charlie, who'd seemed so reasonable and measured and sane, had beaten up his own father?

"Earth to Space Cadet Lily. Are you with me? Where'd you go?"

"I'm here," I breathed.

"What, is this fucker somebody special? Let me guess. He's probably all polished up and looks good in a tux. I see he went to Harvard." He pronounced it *Haah-vaaahd*.

"Brux! No, definitely not. I'm just in shock. Of all the crazy people I'm dealing with here, I thought Charlie was the least crazy."

"Shows what you know," Bruxton muttered darkly. "Probably looks like Tyrone Power."

That was my first clue that he was jealous. I'd admitted my Tyrone crush to him when I was still in New York. If I hadn't been completely in shock about the revelations about Charlie, I might have laughed. "Would it make you feel better if I told you that a woman I met here described him as gay as a goose in pink spats?"

"No shit? That's a great line. I'm stealing that."

"Thanks for looking all this stuff up, Brux. I really appreciate it."

"Yeah, well, you can show your appreciation when you come back to town." His voice was too gruff and brusque to be suggestive, and I wasn't sure whether I wanted him to be.

"I will," I promised. "Say hi to Norah for me, will you?"

"Yeah. Lily? Just keep yourself safe, okay."

"I will."

I hung up the phone and lay back on my bed, staring at the ceiling. Aggravated assault? Charlie? I couldn't get over that he'd hit his own father. What kind of man would do that?

Maybe the kind of man who'd be willing to hurt other people.

There was a knock on my door. "Lil?"

I sat up. "Come in."

"You ready to go yet? Sittin' around this place is makin' me stir-crazy. Never could stand bein' cooped up. Let's go out."

"I just spoke with Bruxton. Guess who has a record for assault?"

"Len Wolven."

"No. Brux just told me—"

"Augustina Wolven?"

"No, it's—"

"Elinor Bargeman? She looks like she could win a calf-tossin' competition."

"No! Stop guessing! It's Charlie."

"Charlie?" Jesse's body froze, but his eyes blinked over and over. "No way."

"Seven years ago he assaulted his father, and his father pressed charges. The father has a restraining order against Charlie."

"I don't believe it. You need fresh air, 'cause if you believe it, well . . ."

"Do you think Bruxton is lying about it? Maybe Brux is setting Charlie up for a fall?"

"No, but someone else is," Jesse suggested. "He's a real gentleman. C'mon, we both saw him rescue that creep Len. I bet Len or somebody else did something, and Charlie took the fall for it."

"Let me get this straight: you think Len assaulted Charlie's father, and then Charlie took the rap? How does that make any sense?"

"Nothing about this situation makes any sense," Jesse muttered. "The whole thing stinks."

46 Finally, I gave up on arguing with Jesse. He had a way of wearing me down with his eternal cock-eyed optimism. It was annoying, to say the least, to have it applied to Charlie Cutler, of all people. I refused all sightseeing offers but agreed to go out for a walk around the Plaza de Armas. We'd exhausted its main tourist options already by visiting the cathedral and the Jesuit church, and so we walked around a few times, never stopping for long because the ladies with tricked-out alpacas and kids hawking postcards were out in full force.

There was an interesting series of archways to the north of the cathedral, and Jesse took pictures of everything in and around them. If you stood at the right angle, they framed the Jesuit church perfectly. We followed the steps up to the lovely Nazarenas plaza, and found we were peering over a paved schoolyard. There were high walls around it, and a series of brightly colored murals on them, most of which were of sports scenes, including one of tennis. On the side of a mountain to the south, someone had carved *Viva El Peru Glorioso*.

"Look, another message for the UFOs," Jesse joked. We headed back toward our hotel, stopping in our tracks at the corner below it, when we saw Elinor Bargeman in a bright yellow suit coming toward us. Fortunately, she didn't see us; instead, she turned and went up the steps to our hotel.

"You know what? I just don't have the energy to deal with her today," Jesse said.

"Me, neither." That admission made me feel guilty, but there it was. There wasn't anything I could do for her. Sooner or later she would have to accept Marianne was gone, but even though I'd gone through a similar journey, I didn't know how to make it any easier for her. Somehow, I couldn't see her accepting anything, including advice, from me.

Needing somewhere else to go, Jesse dragged me along a broad avenue called El Sol. "Did you know that Cusco gets more sunlight than any other city in the Inca Empire? That's why they made it their capital. Of course, they didn't have a writin' system . . ."

"Really? What about quipu?" I asked, remembering something Charlie had mentioned at the convent the day before.

"Holy moly. You know about quipu, Lil? That's awesome."

Thus began a lecture on knots and cords and threads that lasted until we got to the Temple of the Sun. We were well beyond the boundary prescribed by Vargas, but since there were tourists and police everywhere, it didn't seem dangerous.

"So, this was called Qorikancha by the Inca," Jesse explained, shifting gears. "See this whole courtyard at the front? The whole thing was covered in gold. The temple? Also covered in gold. Every part of the Inca Empire had to send gold here in tribute. There were statues, but even the walls were gold. And it took the conquistadors only a few months to melt it all down and ship it home."

The Spanish had torn down the Inca temple, replacing it with the impressively grand church and convent of Santo Domingo. As we lined up to buy tickets, Jesse went on about its history. To say my friend loved playing the tour guide was a massive understatement. By the time we got inside and he started explaining the astronomical significance of the site, we had a crowd of tourists around us.

"The Spanish knew not to mess with some of that stuff, even though they tore down everything else," he said. "There's a wall over this way . . ." A flock of people followed. "See the trapezoidal shapes? Those line up perfectly with certain constellations on significant dates."

"What's a trapezoid?" a stranger asked.

"Okay, see this shape that's kinda like a rectangle, but it's wider at the bottom than the top? That's a trapezoid. The Incas used it over and over in their architecture. Their doorways are all trapezoids. Same with their windows and niches. Everything they designed was made to resist earthquakes. The colonial stuff here's been knocked down a bunch of times. This wall? Never."

We finally shed the crowd when we got to the courtyard. Surrounded by more archways, columns, and colonial arcades, its walls covered by giant paintings in gilt frames, the courtyard made people stare in wonder, snap photos, or both. "You've lost your students, Professor," I teased him.

"Fickle bunch they are," he said, pouting. "Well, at least I got my captive audience."

By the time we wandered back to the Plaza de Armas and had a late lunch, it was closing in on four in the afternoon.

"There's no way that Elinor Bargeman is still waiting in the lobby," I said.

"Yeah, shows what you know about Texans. That's a stubborn race of people." He shook his head. "Look, you go in first. I'm gonna buy up some postcards for the folks at home. If you haven't got rid of her by the time I get back, I'm gonna tiptoe by and pretend I'm sick, okay? You can tell her I got food poisonin' or whatnot. She'll buy that."

"Chicken." I went inside alone. Rosaria was at the desk. There was a group of three Asian men sitting in reception, drinking coca tea. "Any messages for me?"

"Yes. Señora Bargeman was here for almost three hours. That lady is so . . ." Rosaria shook her head in frustration. "She hates everything about Peru. The food, the weather, the children selling postcards. She wanted me to tell her what the risk of earthquake was."

"I'm sorry. Anyone else?"

"Señor Vargas, but he said no news. Sorry."

"Thanks, Rosaria."

I took my key and went up the stairs. Inside the suite, I discovered that the maid had left the window of the living area open. There wasn't much of a view—mostly it was the roofs of other buildings surrounding the Plaza de Armas—but a powerful breeze streamed in. I went to close it partway and heard a strange click.

"Don't move or I'll shoot," Len Wolven said. He stood in the doorway of my room. In his hand was a gun, and it was pointed at my head.

47

"We need to talk, Lily," Wolven added. "You're going to tell me the truth."

"Then put that gun down."

"No way. You don't give the orders around here. I do. You'll do a handstand if I order you to."

"I can't talk with a gun pointed at me."

"Yes you can, Lily. You'll talk just fine."

He was casually dressed in jeans, a black windbreaker, and a ball cap, and he looked oddly relaxed. His nose was taped up, and there was raccoonlike bruising around his eyes. That didn't seem to bother him; there was a little smile on his face, as if something amusing were under way. My eyes darted around the room, and I wondered what I could use as a weapon. There was a lamp on a table. Could I reach it before he got a shot off?

"You're wondering what you can use to disarm me," Wolven observed. "You're clever, just like Charlie said. But you wouldn't be able to hit me before I shoot you, so you may as well stop thinking about it."

"What do you want?"

"I told you. The truth." Wolven's voice was as casual as his attire, and I wondered what drug he was on now.

"You want the truth?" I asked, my fear giving way to my fury. This was a man who brutalized women, and I imagined that he savored the power he had over them before they died.

At that moment, I'd never hated anyone as much as I had him. "I think you have a split personality. Part of you is a deranged psychopath. The other part is little boy who hides behind his father's coattails."

"Don't you dare talk to me like that." He raised the gun a little higher, closer to my face. We were both breathing hard, as if we were running a race instead of standing perfectly still. His face was flushed and feverish, and I imagined mine looked much the same.

"How did you get into my room?"

"It's easy to walk into any hotel here when you're white. There's not even a security guard during the day. And I know how to pick a lock." That last line was spoken with obvious pride. "Now, you're going to answer my questions. Are you working with Bastián?"

"*Working* with Bastián? He tried to rape me."

"Yeah, and you magically got away from him, a guy who weighs two-forty and can bench-press a moose." He grinned. "Nice try."

I held out my wrists. I'd peeled the bandages off that morning, but there were still red welts scarring my skin. "You think I'm lying about this?"

"Some damage that will heal up later is a small price to pay, I'm sure. It makes you look more convincing to the police, no doubt." Len's thin lips tightened. "Who told you what to say?"

"Are you high? Because Bastián talked a lot about you, and he said you always were. He also said he hated working for you and would do anything to go back to Chile. Even your henchmen hate your guts."

"Bastián thinks he's going back to Chile?" Len blinked furiously and suddenly looked less sure of himself. His gun hand quavered. "Is that really what he said?"

"Yes. Why does that matter?"

"It explains everything. Maybe not everything, but a lot." He lowered the gun partway, so that it was pointing at my chest. "I figured you were working with him, but you're just a dupe. I was wondering how Bastián got you into this. With your sister dying, you seemed like a really weird choice for a business partner. But I get it now."

"Get what?"

"Why Bastián told you I killed Marianne. Because your sister's dead, and you're a mess from everything that happened to you. You'd believe anything. Then you'd go tell the police and get me arrested. And the whole time, you'd be too clueless to figure out what's really going on."

"Here's what I see going on, Len. Women around you die. Trista died. Marianne died. And Kirsten died."

"Don't say her name."

"Which one? Trista? Marianne? Kirsten?"

He rubbed his eyes with the back of one hand. Tears were rolling down his cheeks. "I killed Kirsten," he whispered. "I didn't mean to, but I did. I'd give my life for hers in a second if I could. I never meant to hurt her."

"Is that why you tried to kill yourself after she died in the car wreck?"

His jaw dropped. "Nobody knows about that."

"You know how you've been looking me up, and finding out about my sister? I've been looking you up, and finding out about you and your family."

"You can't. My father makes sure that nothing reaches the media. Unless someone goes blabbing to them, like Trista did, those vultures get nothing."

"How about you tell me why you tried to kill yourself after Kirsten died?'

Len's face twisted in anguish. If he hadn't been holding a gun on me, I would've felt sorry for him.

"You killed Kirsten by accident," I said, as gently as I could. "You felt guilty afterward, and you wanted to die?"

He nodded. "It was my fault she died. She was pretty wasted, too, but she told me I was too far gone to drive. I told her she was nuts . . . But she was right. After the car flipped, we were both conscious for a couple of minutes, but I knew she was fading. I was holding her hand when she . . . when she passed away. I should've died. Not her."

It felt harsh to pepper him with questions when he was reeling, but I felt that I had no choice. He was still holding a gun on me. "What about Trista?" I prodded.

"I feel sick about what happened to her," he murmured.

"What was the drug you gave her? Cocaine and what else?"

"We took ayahuasca together. Do you even know what that is?"

"It's a hallucinogen, like LSD." Mentally, I thanked Bruxton. He was the only reason I'd even heard of the drug.

"You need to read what William S. Burroughs and Allen Ginsberg wrote about it," Len said. "It's a completely spiritual experience. Or it's supposed to be, if you do it right. Look, when Trista and I were a couple, I took every drug going. It kind of helped with the pain, for a while. But then I stopped, because I knew Kirsten would hate what I was doing to myself."

He sounded childish, yet oddly sincere. "Trista was a hard-core addict, wasn't she? Why did you fly her down to Peru?"

"She called me, completely out of the blue. Said she kept having this dream about me, that she was falling and that I would save her life by catching her. I believe dreams are a portal to—" He stopped suddenly. "You don't care about any of this, I bet. But I thought I could help Trista. She needed to get herself right and I thought I could somehow make her see what her path should be."

"And the way to that path was through ayahuasca?"

"You don't get it, Lily. Your sister was a heroin addict, and you think all drugs are the same. When my father sent me down to Peru, I felt totally lost. He said it was time I acted like a man and learned about the family business, but I knew he didn't trust me. That was why he sent Charlie to watch me. I didn't have a choice. Same with Bastián. Those two didn't want to be with me any more than I wanted to be with them. Charlie was spying for my father, and Bastián was spying for my sister. And Marianne . . ." He sighed, and his shoulders sank.

"What about her?"

"I only came to Peru because my father swore he'd cut me out of his will otherwise. Marianne didn't want that. But she hated it here. She complained all the time . . ." His voice faded. "But I discovered I loved Peru. It was the first place that felt like home since my mom died. I heard about ayahuasca, and I went to a shaman to try it. It opened up my mind, and it made me remember all these things I'd forgotten. These things my family wants me to forget. Especially my father."

"Like what?"

"You don't want to know." Len's eyes were unbearably sad. "If I told you, he would kill you."

"You already tried to have me killed," I pointed out.

"I swear to God, I didn't. And I didn't hurt Trista, either. Not on purpose. I told her she couldn't take any cocaine or alcohol or even caffeine before or during her awakening. Before using ayahuasca, I mean. Your body has to be pure. But she lied to me. She was on all kinds of shit, but she pretended she wasn't. That was why she died."

"There was a cut on her hand. What did you do to her?"

"Trista was using my wife's things. I tried to pretend that didn't bother me, but it did. When we were on the mountain, she pulled out Marianne's compact. She'd loaded it up with cocaine. I lost it when I found out."

"You hit her?"

"No. I threw it on the ground. She grabbed it, but the mirror broke and cut her hand. She tried to put it away, but I took it and threw it down the staircase. Then I threw the lipstick case. I figured she might have coke in there, too. She went running down the stairs and I took off. When I cooled off, I came back, but you and your friend were there."

That was a strange confession, but it fit what I knew. Len had given Trista a hallucinogen; the coke was hers. She had lied to him. That snippet I'd heard of their argument, before Trista collapsed, suddenly made sense. Even if I didn't see how giving someone a psychedelic drug was "helping" them, Len truly believed he had been.

"What about Marianne?" I tried to keep my voice soft. "Was her death an accident?"

"No! I'm sure I didn't hurt her. I love her."

That stopped me cold. "You're *sure*? Don't you know?"

"I can't be positive. I had a blackout."

"You mean you passed out because you were using drugs?"

"No. I have blackouts whether or not I'm on anything. I had one at Machu Picchu, too. What I told you about running to get help, and getting lost, that was all true. By the time I got to the entrance, my head was exploding. I blacked out for a long time that day."

"You've seen a doctor about this?"

Len nodded. "The blackouts started when I was a kid, but they used to be just for a few seconds. Now, they can go on for twenty minutes or more. I don't know what I'm doing." His eyes looked wild and haunted. All of those pill bottles I'd seen suggested madness that was kept under wraps, but not under control.

"My father blames my mother. He said the blackouts only started after she ran away and abandoned me." His voice was getting softer, as if he were retreating into a story he'd told himself over and over. "When I was growing up, I'd ask him where she was, and he'd say, 'Remember, son, I'm the parent who didn't abandon you.'"

"But a moment ago you said your mother died."

Len's eyes widened. "Don't! Don't ever say that again, not to anyone. My father doesn't think I know. He tried to keep it from me. But a little part of me remembered . . ." He took a few panicky breaths, trying to collect himself. "He lied to me. He pretended she left us when she'd been murdered. He said it was my fault."

"How could it be? You were a child."

"He said they were so close before I was born, but then I changed everything." He gulped. "My father took me to doctor after doctor. He wanted me to forget what had happened. That was when the blackouts started. It was like my brain would short-circuit sometimes. It's been happening ever since."

He seemed caught between a vivid reverie and a dialogue with his demons. I took a little step back, toward the door to the hallway, and then another.

"You had a blackout, and then Marianne was dead?" I asked. "Is that what happened?"

"Lily, I would never have killed her. If she's dead it's because someone else murdered her. Not me." He was terribly agitated again. He closed the tiny bit of distance I'd created between us and lifted the gun so that it was in my face again. "Someone's using you to plot against me. You. Augustina. Trista. Charlie. I see it now . . ."

There was a sound of a key in the door.

"Don't!" I shouted. "Don't come in! Get help!"

The door flew open and Jesse sprang into the room. Len turned, taking aim at Jesse's head. I grabbed his arm just as he fired the gun. The force of the shot torqued Jesse's body. My friend turned his head back, staring at us with a stupefied expression frozen on his face. He raised a hand to his wound just as scarlet petals bloomed on his shoulder.

I screamed, holding on to Len's arm so he couldn't fire again. He pivoted, hitting my face with his elbow and shoving me back. I clawed at him as I went down, drawing blood from his throat in two long red tears before he sprinted out of the room.

"Jesse!" I scrambled to my feet.

"I felt bad 'bout leavin' you to face that Texan lady alone," he said. The stain on his shirt was growing by the second. He sank to the ground, his face perplexed, his voice disbelieving. "Did that fella just shoot me?"

48

It took all of my restraint not to attack Vargas when he arrived at the hospital. Instead, I shouted at him, "How could you let this happen?"

Vargas looked as stern as he always did. "How is your friend?"

"How do you think he's doing? He was shot in the shoulder. There's a bullet in his body and he's lost a lot of blood."

"I am very sorry. This is a terrible thing."

"What I want to know is how Len Wolven ended up running around free with a gun," I demanded. "Why wasn't he locked up?"

"From what I've been told, he was released from the hospital into the custody of Charles Cutler and the Wolven family with the understanding that he would be effectively under house arrest in his family's villa. Only, he managed to slip past the officer who watched the house."

"How would he get a gun?"

"According to Augustina Wolven, a gun is missing from the collection in the house."

"So, you let Len Wolven, who's killed several people, walk into a house with weapons and arm himself? Then you let him stroll over to my hotel, hold me at gunpoint, and shoot Jesse?" I was incredulous.

Vargas sighed, but before he could answer, the doctor returned. He was a young man with a slender build and a hairline that was already receding. He'd been assigned to deal with me because he spoke English, but we'd ended up talking in Spanish. While discussing Jesse's medical condition, we'd had to switch back to English because I didn't know the Spanish terms for things like bullets and body parts. The doctor nodded at Vargas, clearly recognizing him.

"Can I see Jesse now?" I asked.

"Yes. Please, this way."

We were back at the hospital where I'd been treated after Bastián abducted me; it was the same one Len Wolven had burrowed into, hiding from the world and the consequences of his actions. I wondered if there were any traces of him left that I could burn in a bonfire. Then I saw Jesse and all thoughts of vengeance disappeared. He was sitting in bed in a private room with white walls and red-patterned curtains, and he gave me a lopsided grin.

"Honey, I forgot to duck," he deadpanned.

My eyes were watery and I held back a sob. Even though he was hurt, it was an incredible relief to see him there, sounding like his usual charming self. "How long have you been sitting there, waiting to quote Ronald Reagan?"

"Hey, I gotta amuse myself somehow."

I sat on the edge of his bed, putting my hand on his good arm. "So, how do you feel?"

"They gave me somethin' to take the edge off the pain and *yeehaw*." He yawned. "Okay, maybe I'm just sleepy." He eyed the doctor. "That's normal, right?"

"Absolutely," the doctor affirmed.

"Anyhow, the main thing is, I'm fit as a fiddle. Bullet didn't get anywhere near my vitals. So praise the Lord. I'll be up and around in no time." He looked at Vargas. "You catch that no-count little bastard who can't shoot straight?"

"We are working on that."

" 'Cause if you don't, I'm gonna do it myself. And the results ain't gonna be pretty."

The doctor cleared his throat. "Excuse me, but there is one complication we should discuss."

"What's that?"

"Mr. Robb still has the bullet in his shoulder."

"What? Why haven't you taken it out?" I demanded.

"A bullet? Like President Monroe in his shoulder?" Jesse asked. "That is so cool."

"Are you insane? There's nothing good about having a bullet in your shoulder!"

"It's no big deal." Jesse tried to shrug and looked pained. "James Monroe got himself shot at the Battle of Trenton in 1776. Had the bullet lodged in there the rest of his life. Didn't bother him none. 'The best form of government is that which is most likely to prevent the greatest sum of evil.' Always liked that fella."

"Unfortunately, it would be most unwise to allow the bullet to remain in the shoulder," the doctor said.

"Why?"

"A retained bullet acts like a foreign object in the body," the doctor explained. "It causes mechanical problems and it destroys cartilage. Over time, the bullet would begin to dissolve, and that would lead to periarticular fibrosis, chondrolysis, or hypertrophic arthropathy."

I stared at him blankly, not knowing what those medical terms meant in English, either.

"Also, it could cause lead poisoning," the doctor added.

"Well, why don't you take the bullet out, then?" I asked.

The doctor looked from Jesse to me and sighed. "The traditional techniques would result in heavy blood loss, neurovascular complications, and a very prolonged recovery," he said. "For this reason, we recommend arthroscopic removal."

"There a doc in these parts who can do that?" Jesse asked.

"In Lima, yes, but in Cusco, no," the doctor said. "Of course, you could have the surgery in America, instead. But flying in your condition is not ideal."

"Truth be told, doc, I'd rather have surgery in the good ole U.S. of A.," Jesse said. "But do I need to stick around here to testify in court?"

"We will take a statement from you, and videotape it," Vargas said. "Normally, that does suffice. We will have to discuss this further." Jesse yawned again and Vargas nodded. "Perhaps tomorrow."

"I'm fine. I don't need any shut-eye," Jesse said. He yawned. "Okay, maybe just a few winks."

I kissed him on the forehead, promised to be back soon, then let the doctor shoo me out of Jesse's room. Vargas followed me into the hallway.

"We need to speak privately, Miss Moore."

"Oh, you're right about that. Why the hell didn't you call me back this morning? Why wasn't Wolven in custody? Where were your cops who were supposed to be watching him?"

"We will discuss all of that," Vargas promised. "But first, there is something more pressing."

"What?"

"You are in grave danger. You need to leave Cusco. Ideally, leave Peru."

"And leave Jesse here?"

"I understand that you do not want to leave your friend," Vargas said. "But this is a matter of life and death. Augustina

Wolven says she is certain her brother will kill you if given the chance. She has made a sworn statement to the police. This is not something you can ignore. Len Wolven wants you dead."

49

"You aren't going to scare me away," I told Vargas as he dragged me out of the hospital. "And I don't trust any of the Wolvens. Augustina probably just wants to get rid of me to protect her brother."

"She would not have gone to the trouble she did if she were trying to protect him. The Wolvens normally do everything they can to sweep a mess out of sight. Her statement, yours, Jesse's, together they ensure Len Wolven will go to jail."

"Blood is thicker than water," I muttered. That was true: even when I'd thought Claudia might be guilty of a crime, I was willing to cover up for her.

"Nonetheless, the threat to you is real, Lily."

I looked up and down the street. It seemed peaceful enough, but I knew I'd been caught unawares twice now. There had been madness in Wolven's eyes when he'd approached me with the gun in hand. If Jesse hadn't barged into the room, Wolven might have shot me. At point-blank range, there was no doubt I would have died. The thought should have chilled me, but instead I felt defiant. Twice, I'd had to go to morgues to identify a body: the first, when my mother died, and then in January, when the police thought they'd found my sister's body. Suddenly I pictured myself on that mortuary slab, eyes closed and a sheet covering my naked body. Not yet, I thought. Not for a long while, if I can help it.

"We will go to your hotel so you can pack. Then the airport," Vargas said. He opened the door of a black sedan for me, and I got inside. The driver, a uniformed officer, nodded at Vargas, who told him, "Calle Espinar."

"It's fine to take me back to my hotel," I said. "I need to pack up some things for Jesse. But I am not being chased out of Cusco because you and your cops are so incompetent that you can't catch Len Wolven."

"The man is extremely well connected," Vargas said. "The Wolvens have many friends in high places."

"Which means there's nowhere I can go to escape," I said. "Look, the Wolvens have a company with tentacles all over the world. They have people everywhere. Where am I going to go to be safe from them? I am *not* relocating to Antarctica. And even if I could get away, I'm not leaving my friend here alone at their mercy."

Vargas was silent for a long while after that, though he came into the hotel with me and watched me pack an overnight bag for Jesse. When he spoke again, it was to insist that I put all of my own things in my suitcase. "You must leave Cusco for your own safety."

"Have you listened to a word I said?"

"Yes. You are a stubborn, bullheaded young woman."

I gave him a sidelong glance. He couldn't have known that I'd told Claudia, countless times, how stupidly stubborn and willful she was. It was almost funny that the shoe was now on the other foot.

"I'll change hotels," I offered. "But I'm not leaving Cusco."

"Yes you are. You will be at a private casa just outside the city."

That I could accept. "All right. What's this place called?"

He frowned before he answered. "Casa Vargas."

. . .

Back at the hospital, Jesse had already charmed the nurses. It was no surprise: he spoke good Spanish and was an unrelenting flirt. When I walked in with his dinner—spicy chicken from a restaurant he'd told me we had to eat at—I discovered a pretty nurse with long black lashes and full red lips trying to feed him. Jesse glanced at me and grinned, and I rolled my eyes.

"If only she knew," I said, quietly in English, and kissed him on the cheek.

She mistook me for a girlfriend, and sat back with her arms crossed, appraising me. "Demasiado flaca," she muttered, then made a humphing noise and clipped away on surprisingly high heels.

"Did she just call me too skinny?" I asked Jesse.

"Never mind her. Is that for me?" he asked with obvious glee, then took a deep breath. It did smell delicious. "Yum."

"I also have your toothbrush and your cameras." I set the shoulder bag on a chair.

"What about my conditioning shampoo?"

I stared at him. He wasn't joking. "I believe that's in there, too. Along with your shaving oil."

"You're the best, Lil. Thanks."

"It's the least I could do, considering that I got you shot." I sat on the bed.

"I'm the one who went barreling into the room, guns blazing. Only I forgot my guns at home. This is what happens when you got no way to defend yourself." We locked eyes for a moment, our old argument about gun control hanging in the air. The irony was that I now felt like a hypocrite, given what I was willing to do when I was looking for my sister. Jesse was too much of a gentleman to mention it. "That Wolven creep ain't turned up yet, has he? Or psycho Bastián?"

"No. Vargas has talked to Charlie a couple of times, but no one has found either of them. The thing is, I don't trust that Charlie would turn Wolven in. I think he'd get his boss out of the country, given the chance."

Behind me, Charlie said, "I hope I'm not interrupting anything." I almost tumbled off the side of the bed. Charlie stood there in neatly pressed chinos and a dark blazer, with a giant floral arrangement in his hands.

"Hey, Charlie," Jesse said, waving with his good hand. "Thanks for droppin' by."

"I can't tell you how sorry I am, Jesse." Charlie came over, setting the flowers on the bedside table and rearranging everything to make room for them. "I would have come over before, but the police wouldn't let me. Hello, Lily. How are you?"

"I'd be fine if Len Wolven and his minions didn't keep trying to kill me."

Charlie didn't respond to that. "How are you feeling, Jesse?"

"I'm countin' my lucky stars. It's real thoughtful of you to come by."

I stared at Jesse, wondering if there was some piece of sarcasm lodged in there, but he was looking at Charlie with warmth. Suddenly, I felt like an awkward interloper. Charlie glanced at me, as if to check whether I was still hanging around. But I wasn't going anywhere. I wasn't sure why, but suddenly, I disliked him with a force out of proportion to the situation. I'd always been a little bit jealous of Jesse's boyfriends, the same way he'd been jealous of mine. But with Charlie, suddenly, I felt like I was watching him zero in on his prey.

50

If Vargas hadn't come to collect me, I probably would have stayed in Jesse's room all evening. But he came in, told Charlie it was time to leave, and then let Jesse and me talk a little longer before insisting that it was time to go.

While we drove to the Vargas house, I tried to picture what it must be like. In my mind's eye, I saw a big, empty building that was silent as a mausoleum. It would be formal, probably immaculately clean, and I'd be afraid to sit down. When we pulled up in front of the iron gate, my worst suspicions were confirmed. Vargas was grim as a jailer, and his house would undoubtedly reflect that quality. I braced for bars on the windows and cold concrete floors. Instead, a woman opened the front door. The light behind her illuminated her short, broad-shouldered silhouette, but as I got closer, I could make out the streaks of gray in her long, black hair. A few steps closer, I saw the smile on her face.

"Buenas tardes, señora," I said.

"Welcome, Lily!" she called gaily. "You are so late! You must be starved with hunger!" She reached for both my hands. "I am so delighted you're here." She pressed my hands together, gently, so it looked as if we were about to say a prayer together. "You are such a tiny girl. Like an Inca wren. Have you seen one yet on your visit?"

"Not yet."

"It is a lovely bird, but with the most delicate tiny bones.

They are quite rare—you can only find them in three valleys in Peru and at Machu Picchu. They always bring good luck."

I was, at five feet six, easily five inches taller than her. But Señora Vargas was solidly built, not at all fat, but with solid muscle. The Andean build was like that: shorter, more muscled, more powerful. The people had adapted long ago to the thin mountain air.

"It's so kind of you to let me stay here."

"Of course! Felipe told me about the danger you are in, and about your friend, Jesse. How is he now?"

She kept up a steady stream of questions and chatter as she put her arm around my waist and led me inside. Her husband trailed behind us, like a sullen storm cloud. I'd pictured his wife as a female counterpart to his stolid, stoic nature. Instead, he'd married a charming chatterbox. I guessed things had a way of evening out.

While Señora Vargas settled me into a chair and fussed over me, I looked around. The Vargas home wasn't quite as large as I'd pictured, but it was grand. The Spanish colonial style showed in gorgeous details, from the exquisitely patterned tile to the carved columns, and even the covered balcony I'd caught a glimpse of at the front of the house. But it didn't feel stuffy. If anything, it was relentlessly cheery. The furniture was plushly upholstered, and there were little knickknacks on every surface. The wall in the entryway was a sea of framed photographs, and even in the dining room, I spotted a few in silver frames. Vargas had mentioned a son who was away at university. I thought I spotted him in many a snapshot, alongside a girl I took for his sister. She was a couple of years older than the boy.

"I've made an *olluquito con charqui*. It's a traditional Andean stew," Señora Vargas said. "It's good for you."

"I know that I'm imposing by being here," I said.

"It is good that you came here. Felipe told me all about this crazy foreigner, Wolven. It is madness. And these criminals are still walking free?" She turned her dark eyes on her husband.

"We are looking for him," Vargas murmured. He was seated across from me at the table.

"What are you doing, sitting there now? Go out and look for him!"

"That is what my men are doing."

"You should not be resting until you find him," Señora Vargas said. "He is an earthquake. Everything shakes before him."

They said grace quickly once the food was on the table. I took a spoonful of the stew. It consisted mostly of meat and something called *olluco,* which was like a potato but crunchier, and some onion and spices, all served over white rice. Hearty was an understatement. "This is delicious. Thank you for going to so much trouble for me."

"It is no trouble at all. Your friend will be able to leave the hospital soon?" she asked.

"Assuming that there are no complications," her husband answered. "The bullet is still in his shoulder."

Señora Vargas crossed herself. "So he will have surgery in front of him. Poor man. He is your, ah, fiancé?"

"No. Jesse's my friend."

"Not your boyfriend?"

I laughed. "No. He's my best friend in the world. He's like a brother to me."

"We have an old Quechua saying: 'Just as you love others, they will love you.'" She smiled at me. "The older I get, the more I take heart that you can find more family on this earth."

"That's lovely. I'll remember that."

"Felipe told me that you had come here to get over the sadness of your sister."

I froze and my spoon almost slipped out of my hand. Vargas really did tell his wife everything, apparently. She went on.

"It is a blessing you have such a good friend to open your heart to." She patted the back of my hand. "I was very sad to hear about it."

There was a long pause. "It's still hard for me to talk about," I said finally, not looking up.

"It was hard for me, too, when my daughter died," Mrs. Vargas said. "I promise you, your heart will grow lighter in time. The memory will make you smile, rather than cry."

"Your daughter?" I glanced at Vargas, then at his wife. His eyes were downcast, and stared into his stew with an intensity that at least matched my own of a few moments before. But his wife looked at me with a tender expression. She wasn't smiling, but there was kindness there.

"Isabella died almost four years ago. We were devastated," Mrs. Vargas said. "I wanted to crawl into the grave with her and have them bury me, too." She touched the gold locket at her throat. "It was not at all what people described to me. They would say it was a loss, like they had lost a piece of themselves. For me it was like . . ." Her eyes went a little out of focus, as if she were zeroing in on something inside her mind's eye. "Like I had fallen into another world, one in which everything was out of place. I was out of place. I was a ghost wandering through my old life."

"I'm so sorry," I said. Vargas continued frowning at the table. His wife seemed at ease with the subject, but he clearly wasn't. My heart went out to him, unexpectedly and suddenly.

I could feel the truth behind Señora Vargas's words, but I couldn't have articulated such sentiments any more than her husband could.

"I say this because I want you to understand. You will have better days ahead." She sighed. "It must be very hard for your family now. How are your parents taking it?"

"My parents have been dead for many years," I said. "It was just Claudia and me."

Señora Vargas's face looked stricken. "Both of your parents are dead?"

"My father died when I was thirteen. My mother when I was eighteen."

"But you have cousins? Aunts, uncles?"

"No. My parents didn't have any other relatives I know of. They were born in Ireland. They might have had some family there, but they weren't in touch with them."

"You poor thing. I am so . . . I feel terrible for mentioning it." She shook her head. "I want to help people, but I forget that everyone has their own tragedy, and their own reasons for speaking—or not speaking—of it."

"It's all right," I said. "I don't mind." Strangely, for the first time, that was true. Was it because I couldn't imagine how awful it would be to lose a child? I wasn't sure, but I felt relaxed with them, and when Señora Vargas refilled my plate, I didn't object. It had been a very long time since I'd been under a mother's care.

51

"I hope that what my wife said at dinner did not disturb you," Vargas said.

"She was being kind. I know that."

"She does not understand that grief takes root in different ways. She thinks it is like a season that passes, not a seed that is planted, one that grows with time."

We were sitting in a covered patio, drinking pisco. Vargas had lit a lantern behind us, but that left our faces mostly in shadow.

"I'm sorry about your daughter."

"Thank you."

I was tiptoeing up to my real question, about what had happened to Isabella. But I stopped suddenly, teetering on a cliff. It was a sore point with me when people pried into my life, and I owed Vargas the same space I craved. I stepped back from the ledge and sipped some of the liqueur instead.

"What do you expect you will write about Peru?"

"I don't know. Some articles, I guess. Even if Jesse and I were on our planned itinerary, I wouldn't be seeing enough to write a guidebook."

"Is that your ambition? To write another guidebook?"

"No," I admitted. "I do them because they pay pretty well, at least if you can spin them off into other books and articles."

"So, you write a book you do not care much for, so you

can write more things you do not care for." He took a drink. "Have you ever thought that you are capable of so much more?"

His words made me uneasy. It wasn't what he was saying, but that fact that he was echoing something Claudia used to harass me about. "Oh?"

"You are a very determined young woman. I have not seen your writing, but I have seen your nerve. I believe you could be a real journalist."

He was blunt, but he wasn't trying to insult me. And it wasn't an unreasonable question. Growing up, I envisioned myself as a serious journalist, a fantasy that was fed by movies like *His Girl Friday* and *Call Northside 777*. But serious journalism didn't pay, at least not for a freelancer starting out. I'd fallen into travel writing by accident, and I kept at it because it paid the bills and gave me a sense of freedom that would be hard to match. I didn't feel like explaining any of that to Vargas, so I said, "Thanks for the vote of confidence."

"I have a more important question for you. Why would Leonard Wolven want you dead?" Vargas glanced in my direction, and I saw the edge of his face in the lamplight. "A great deal has happened in a short time, but have you stopped to think about that?"

"I'm not sure what to believe anymore. In my hotel room, Len swore he hadn't tried to have me killed, and I believed him."

"You are not thinking about my question. Let me put it plainly. Why would *Leonard* Wolven, the father of Len, want you dead?"

I froze. "He—what? I've never met him in my life. He doesn't know me."

"Leonard Wolven, the one from Montreal who spends most

of the year in Palm Beach, Florida, spoke to Bastián Montalvo by telephone just hours before you were attacked," Vargas explained. "I do not believe this is a coincidence. As a matter of fact, I do not believe in coincidences at all, Lily."

That revelation shouldn't have stunned me, I realized. What had Augustina said the night before? *To be fair to Bastián, when he worked for me, he never caused any trouble.* And then Charlie had come back with, *He somehow went bad just recently?* Augustina's next words had been, *You want the truth, Charles? Let's get this out in the open. I believe Bastián did what he did because my brother* ordered *him to.* But what if it hadn't been her brother who'd ordered my death, but her father?

"From what you said in the car, and your report to the police, Len Wolven held you at gunpoint, trying to force you to admit to conspiring with Bastián. Isn't that correct?"

"Yes. He denied sending Bastián to kill me." Turning the scene over in my mind, I looked at it from new angles. "I still think he's crazy, though, so—"

"What if he was telling the truth? Could his father have ordered your death without the son's knowledge? Of course he could. But Bastián fails to kill you and you return, telling everyone what Bastián admitted to you: Len Wolven murdered his second wife, Marianne, the one who has been reported missing in Lima."

The idea whirled around my head. It made sense in a horrifying way. Len Wolven was self-destructive, there was no doubt about that. When I'd glimpsed his face on Machu Picchu, I'd thought he was terrified. He had tried to kill himself at least twice after his drunk driving caused his first wife's death. The conversation I'd had with him in my hotel room, at gunpoint, was the longest I'd had with him, and it had made me see him as an overgrown child. He might be clever and sneaky, sly enough to get his hands on a gun, but a criminal mastermind he was not. He had shot Jesse in a moment of panic. From what I'd seen of him, Len lacked impulse control; that trait paired up with access to unlimited funds was a recipe for destruction.

"Leonard Wolven—the father, I mean—is a very intelligent man. He has built an international business and made himself incredibly rich. But I wonder how smart he really is," Vargas mused.

"Why do you say that?"

"Perhaps he thinks he is infallible, like the pope. Ordering your death to protect his son would be a terrible miscalculation on his part. It seems impulsive. I do not believe that those who succeed in business or much else are without restraint."

We sat quietly again for a while, drinking and staring into the darkness. Vargas had opened my mind to new and even more unsettling possibilities. I had been able to accept that Len Wolven was crazy and wanted me dead. What if his father, who pulled all of the strings behind the scenes, was the one who wanted me out of the picture? That was much more dangerous. I wasn't afraid of Len, but the faceless specter of his father was another matter entirely.

"You need to make sure Jesse is safe," I blurted out. "What if the father wants him dead, too, so that he can't testify against his son?"

"I assure you, I have already thought of that, and there are several guards in the hospital. But as more people are drawn into this, there is less risk to each. Killing one no longer fixes the problem, and killing all is unfeasible."

"Easy for you to say."

"Let me ask you about someone else: Charles Cutler."

"I don't like him and I don't trust him."

"This is not female jealousy, is it?"

"What?"

"I saw him tonight with your friend Jesse. There is an, ah, interest there."

"That's what I thought, too," I admitted.

"Charles Cutler is a much more interesting man than he would have us believe," Vargas said.

"Did you know he has a criminal record in the U.S.?"

Vargas made a strange sound that was like a bark. "The stubborn mule has good sources. Yes, I know. Now, tell me how many men have you seen who are so self-effacing in the service of another man? In another age, when Lima was still the City of Kings, Mr. Cutler would have been a courtier. He serves, without being unctuous. I find him fascinating."

"He seems to revere his boss—not Len, the father. I get the feeling that Charlie would do anything for him." I took another drink. "Charlie keeps offering me money to leave Peru. He's more upset that my passport was stolen than I am."

Vargas leaned toward me, his face half illuminated in the lamplight. "Miss Moore, the next time someone offers you a bribe, I suggest that you take it."

"Why?"

"Because whoever pays you is giving you a great deal of information."

"Charlie?"

"Charles Cutler does not have much money of his own," Vargas said. "So if he has access to a large sum of money to make bribes, it does suggest something interesting about the trust the senior Leonard Wolven has placed in him."

52

Comfortable as the guest room at the Vargas house was, I couldn't fall asleep. The events of the past few days, and my talk with Vargas that evening, swirled around inside my head like a tornado. Everything had happened so quickly: a woman's death on the mountain, my kidnapping, Jesse's shooting. Every day brought a new disaster.

Then there was the mystery of Marianne Wolven. Had Len Wolven really killed her, or had someone else committed a murder to frame him? When I'd first encountered him, I'd assumed his paranoia was from mental illness, drug use, or the combination of the two. But everything I'd heard about his father—which came from a variety of sources—was making my heart thaw out a little. Len's family—at least, his father—was monstrous. And his mother's death was ominous. *He pretended she left us when she'd been murdered. He said it was my fault. He said they were so close before I was born, but then I changed everything.* What kind of sadist taunted his son with accusations like that?

Bastard. The rich are different from you and me, Honey Bear.

That they were. I sat up in bed and turned on the light. There was no one there but me. I was in a pretty bedroom with terra-cotta walls, ornately carved furniture, wrought-iron fixtures, and a wooden crucifix over the bed. I stared at the crucifix, noting that Jesus wasn't wearing a standard-issue loincloth but a larger swath of fabric that tied at one side like a sarong. Apparently, even the modern-day descendants of the Inca weren't comfortable with sacrilegious nudity.

Lying down again, I left the light on. I needed to think through what had happened but events had spiraled so fast that I'd barely been able to catch my breath. What did I know? Leonard Wolven had come from money and had built a leviathan of a company that reached into all corners of the globe. He had two children, neither of whom seemed to care much for him; Mr. Wolven may not have minded that, since he didn't treat them any better than chess pieces. I remembered one of the online articles about Len Wolven. It had called him the sole heir to the family business. Why wasn't Augustina inheriting half? She wasn't an illegitimate child; her mother was Leonard Wolven's third wife. What had first struck me as old-fashioned sexist thinking at work was reframed as something more sinister by what Len had told me when he'd held a gun on me. *I only came to Peru because my father swore he'd cut me out of his will.*

Was that how life was in the Wolven family? You did something that the father didn't like, and he cut you out? Had that meant Augustina would have inherited the business instead? Or was there someone else who might benefit from all of this?

The only other person I could think of who might stand to gain was Charlie.

Len had accused Charlie of spying on him for his father. Augustina had said that Charlie acted as if he thought he was Mr. Wolven's adopted son. Charlie had been unfailingly loyal to Mr. Wolven, doing everything that was asked of him. Could that extend to murder?

Elinor Bargeman had made it clear that Mr. Wolven disapproved of Len's marriage to Marianne. What if Charlie had been told to get rid of her? His cold eyes came to mind. He could kill; I was certain of it. This was a man who'd attacked his own father. Murdering a Vegas showgirl would be nothing for him. The fact that Charlie had been suddenly out of town when Marianne died grated on me. That timing didn't seem coincidental. If Bruxton hadn't told me that Charlie had violated a restraining order in the United States at that time, I would have doubted whether he'd even left Peru. Still, the fact that he was out of the country didn't mean he hadn't arranged for Marianne's death. It signaled that he had an accomplice.

Something else bothered me: Len didn't believe he'd killed Marianne, but he didn't actually *know*. The murderer had exploited Len's blackouts, leaving him agonized by the fear that he might actually be guilty. No matter how evil and sadistic the father was, I didn't believe he'd ordered up that kind of hell for his son. No: if Charlie had set up Marianne's death that way, he was playing his own angle.

Charlie had the father's trust, as well as access to information and money. If anything happened to the elderly Leonard Wolven in Palm Beach, would Charlie end up running the company in his absence? If that were true, was that an incentive for Charlie to get rid of his competition? He'd struck me as ambitious, but if that were true he was downright Machiavellian.

Was Vargas right about Mr. Wolven? I wondered. Had the family patriarch ordered my death? Or could that have been Charlie's initiative as well?

The house phone started to ring, once, twice. Then silence. Had someone answered? I pulled on my slip and opened my door a crack. There was the low grumble of Vargas's voice. I listened but couldn't make words out. I covered up with a warm, blanketlike robe his wife had given me. I waited a moment, hearing a commotion in the room across the hall. Señora Vargas was talking, but I didn't recognize the language. It was low and guttural, not at all like Spanish. I opened my door and stepped into the hallway.

"Is everything all right?" I called softly. Jesse was at the top of my mind. Had there been a complication at the hospital?

"No, it is not," Vargas called back. The light was on in his room, so his wife must have been awake, too. He came into the hallway. "Len Wolven has been found."

The way he said it chilled me. "Been found?"

"The young man is dead. He committed suicide tonight."

53

We didn't hear the full story of Len's death until the next morning, and it was short on details. Len had somehow made his way to Lima; no one was sure how. But he'd shown up at the office of Xavier Alcántara, the private investigator Charlie had hired to find Marianne. To say the meeting hadn't gone well was a huge understatement; Len, drunk or high or both, had accused Xavier of hiding his wife's whereabouts, and then of actually murdering Marianne to frame him. Len had warned him that there was no going back now, because he'd shot a man in Cusco. After that, Len had stormed out, saying he was going to the police. Xavier had followed him out of the office, then down a few blocks, through a place called the Parque del Amor and along a Pacific Coast beach called Costa Verde. Len had walked along a popular pier, toward a restaurant called La Rosa Nautica, and jumped in the water. Then, according to Xavier's report, Len had thrashed and screamed in the water, finally going under and not resurfacing.

"Are you kidding?" I asked Vargas when he related this to me. "That's not a suicide. That's a ruse. Xavier Alcántara is probably in on it with him."

"One would be suspicious about that, particularly since there is no body," Vargas agreed. "Also, because no one with the name Alcántara can be trusted."

"Is that why you dislike Hector so much?" I asked. Vargas

just stared at me. "You can't hide it. I've seen you two together."

"Hector was the police officer in charge of investigating my daughter's disappearance. From the beginning, it was clear that nothing would be done unless I hired his brother Xavier to privately investigate the case as well."

"So that's how he works it. I'd wondered."

"We paid and paid and Xavier strung us along like fools with a sighting here and there. Then he would go investigate, and we would pay for his trip to Buenos Aires. It went on like that for months."

"And then they found her?"

"No. They never did. The only reason Isabella's body was discovered was because the American man who drugged her and killed her bragged to a friend about it. He was proud of committing a perfect crime." Vargas turned away and left the room.

Jesse's reaction to Len Wolven's apparent suicide was subdued. "Poor pathetic varmint. I wish I could've wrung his scrawny neck first." But he brightened up as we discussed the odds of Len's conspiring with the Alcántara brothers, realizing that he probably had a good chance of still getting to hurt Len before we left Peru.

My suspicion only deepened when I went to the Wolven villa in Cusco. There was music playing in the house—I recognized it as Verdi's Requiem—but Augustina smiled when she saw me in the doorway of her room.

"Lily! Thank you for coming. Sandor! Come put these beautiful flowers in a vase! Lily, thank you. You are so thoughtful. How is Jesse?"

I handed the flowers I'd brought to the servant. "He's

uncomfortable but determined not to show it. I can't wait to get him home. How are you feeling? I'm sorry about your brother."

"Thank you. But, you know, it is for the best if he is finally at peace. His life was nothing but sadness and pain. He was always a tortured soul." She was knitting again, another blanket from the look of it, this one a soft peach color. "I was thinking about you and Jesse. I will need to fly to Lima to make arrangements for my brother's funeral and—"

"Funeral? But I thought they hadn't found Len's body."

"Oh, well, they haven't yet. But no doubt they will. We will have to do a funeral Mass."

I stared at Augustina. There was absolutely nothing mournful about her.

"As I was saying, I must fly to Lima, and I thought I would take you and Jesse there, then send the jet to New York. How does that sound?"

"That's very generous of you. It would be much easier to get Jesse home that way." It was increasingly obvious that Augustina wanted rid of Jesse and me. Whatever her agenda was, we weren't supposed to hang around for it. I suspected that it had to do with Jesse's shooting; if he left and the case were closed, Len could resurface at some point without going to jail. Still, no matter how suspicious I was of her, I couldn't turn down the offer of a private plane to New York.

I asked Augustina where Charlie was, and that brought out a frown. "Upstairs, in his room. I told the staff to hide his razor blades."

"Why?"

"He failed my father. Don't you know what that means? He wants to commit ritual, what do you call it, seppuku? Yes, that's what he wants to do now."

I went upstairs. At the landing, I could hear drawers slamming. It wasn't coming from Len's room, but from across the hall. I knocked on that door. No answer. I tried the handle and it swung open. A cloud of whisky fumes greeted me at the door. Charlie knelt on the floor rummaging through a drawer. He wore a full suit but no socks or shoes, and his tie was askew. It was as if he'd gotten dressed on autopilot, skipping a step or two along the way.

"Charlie?"

When he looked up, his eyes were swollen and so bloodshot that I could barely see his mismatched irises anymore. He mumbled something I couldn't understand.

"Vargas told me about Len," I said. "I'm sorry, Charlie."

His chin dropped to his chest and he made a gasping sound. "How could he die?" He continued rummaging.

Since I wasn't at all convinced Len was dead, it was tough to answer. "I don't know."

On the dresser was an almost-empty bottle of scotch, which he reached for.

"I think you've had enough for now, Charlie." I pried it out of his grasp.

"He never had a chance at life," Charlie said. "Len was so screwed up. His whole life. I watched him grow up, you know. He was a good kid."

"He shot Jesse," I pointed out.

"He was out of his mind. He knew someone was out to get him, and it made him paranoid. He couldn't help it."

Staring at him, I wondered if he were a terrific actor. Mostly, he'd struck me as a controlled, emotionless presence; could he really transform into a sloppy, overwhelmed drunk at Len's death? Then again, maybe this wasn't really about Len so much as Mr. Wolven. Augustina could be right: if he'd been sent to watch the boss's son, and the boss's son died, Charlie really had failed.

"Len was mentally ill, wasn't he?" I asked.

"Why would you think that?"

"Aside from the way he acted? There are more than a dozen prescription pill bottles in his room," I pointed out.

"Len only got into trouble when he went off his pills," Charlie said. "I was supposed to make him take them. Otherwise he would do crazy things."

"You were making him take all of those drugs? There's no way he needed all those pills."

"Mr. Wolven had taken him to all kinds of doctors. They came up with a regimen for Len."

"Including Viagra?"

"Some of the pills had side effects," Charlie mumbled, putting his head down again.

No wonder Len hated having Charlie around. The man wasn't just Mr. Wolven's eyes and ears; he was more like Len's jailer.

"Those pills could be causing Len's blackouts."

Charlie eyed me suspiciously. "You don't know what you're talking about."

"Yesterday, when he was in my room, Len told me the blackouts only started after his mother died and his father started taking him to doctors."

As the words came out of my mouth, I remembered that Len had told me not to mention his mother's death to anyone. The family line was that she had run off; I wasn't supposed to cross it. Charlie's red eyes appraised me; he wasn't as drunk as he was pretending to be. Whether he was really distraught, I still couldn't tell. He was fully aware of what I'd said and what it meant, but he didn't comment on it at all. He looked down at the drawer again.

"What are you looking for?" I asked.

"Trista was a thief," he said. "At the house in Lima, she started picking up things of Marianne's and acting like they were hers. I'd take them back from her when I could, but I had to be subtle about it."

"The lipstick case and the compact. Engraved with *MBW*. I saw them at Machu Picchu."

"There were other things. Marianne's diary. Trista would read it aloud sometimes, just to upset Len. It was here. I know it was." He rooted around a little more. "But it's gone."

"Maybe you put it somewhere else." I tried to sound calm. "Why don't you sit for a bit?"

He stood, bracing himself against the dresser. I'd convinced myself that he was a criminal mastermind who'd preyed on Len Wolven's weaknesses, but I was revising that opinion. He dropped on the edge of the bed and put his head into his hands.

I went past him and picked up a bottle of water from his nightstand. Opening the top, I said, "Here, drink this."

"Why?"

"Because it isn't alcohol." There was another bottle of whisky by the bed, tilted on its side; some was pooled on the floor under it. "How much have you had to drink?"

"Don't know. I drank a lot, but then I threw up." He held the bottle against his forehead, even though it was room temperature.

"You're not used to drinking, are you?"

"Just wine sometimes."

I took a deep breath and ducked into the bathroom, grabbing a cotton washcloth and running it under the tap. While I waited for the water to cool, I opened the medicine cabinet, in search of aspirin. There was nothing inside it but a razor, a styptic pencil, and two vials filled with white powder. *That can't possibly be what I think it is,* I thought. Charlie using cocaine? Even with him exhaling whisky fumes, I didn't believe it.

I turned off the tap, wrung out the cloth, and walked back to him. "Here," I said, dabbing the cloth on his forehead and neck.

"Thank you, Lily." His voice was soft as a whisper, but oddly formal as always.

"You need something to eat. Something has to soak up that scotch."

Charlie sighed. "Jesse said you were the kindest person he'd ever met."

"Jesse is prone to exaggeration." I stood there with my arms crossed. As much as I was fascinated by Charlie's personal demons, I had more important questions for him to answer. "Len told me about the ayahuasca yesterday: what it was, what it did for him, how he gave it to Trista because he thought it would help her . . ."

"Ayahuasca is legal in Peru." It was good to know that some part of Charlie's brain was still intact.

"But cocaine isn't."

"What do you want, Lily?"

"I knew someone had to be supplying Trista with drugs," I said. "I thought it was Len. If not him, Bastián. But it was you, wasn't it?"

"You seem to have made up your mind about that already, Lily."

"What I'm wondering is why anyone wanted her dead." I stared him down. "Without naming names. You're a lawyer. You should be comfortable with hypotheticals."

"Very well. Trista was a monster. She called Len just after Marianne, um, vanished, and convinced him to fly her down to Lima. I was still in the U.S. then. It wouldn't have happened if I'd been on the scene. But by the time I got back, she was in the house, and she was making Len's life hell. She talked about Marianne all the time. She raided her closet and her jewelry box. She knew exactly how much she was upsetting Len, and she was doing it deliberately. Then there were these mysterious cards that started appearing in the mailbox. They said the same thing: 'I know what you did.' Pure evil."

"But why?"

"They had a bad breakup, that was all Len would say. I know Mr. Wolven had steered Trista into jail at one point—not on some trumped-up charge, but drug possession. I supposed she was bitter. But her anger was corrosive on Len. He wouldn't force her to leave. It was my idea to arrange the trip to Machu Picchu, just to get her out of the house. Len loved the idea, because he thought that would be the perfect place for her to be 'reborn,' as he put it."

"And the cocaine?"

"Speaking completely hypothetically, now. That could have been suggested by another person familiar with her drug history. That is all I have to say about it."

The way he said it wasn't hypothetical at all. Mr. Wolven had ordered her death. But what struck me then was the memory of Trista's voice on the mountain. *I threw away the best years of my life on him. But don't worry, I'm getting even.* She had been torturing Len in her own way. *He's already crazy, so it wasn't hard to make him crazier.* She'd known exactly what she was doing to Len.

"I suppose you're going to the police with this," Charlie said.

I shook my head. "No. I thought that you might have killed Marianne."

That caught him by surprise. "Why?"

"Because I don't believe Len did it."

Charlie exhaled a long breath. "That thought tortured him, day and night. He asked me, so many times, did I think he was capable of killing someone."

"It's a funny coincidence, you being away when Marianne disappeared. Why did you go back to the U.S. that week?"

"It was . . . personal time."

"It's too late to be cryptic now, Charlie. What happened?"

"My mother died, and I went back for her funeral. Only, my father wouldn't let me go to the funeral. He'd thrown me out of the family years ago, and he said I'd never be welcome back." He rubbed his eyes. "He didn't know that my mom never stopped talking to me."

"Why did he disown you?"

"Why do you think?"

"I don't know." At various times, I'd tried to pretend I didn't have a sister. But, in each case, I craved contact with her after some time had passed. "Sometimes my sister would drive me insane because of her drugs, and I'd stop talking to her."

"It was nothing like that. When I was fifteen, my father found me with another boy. He got angry a lot, but I'd never seen anything until that day. My mom had to stop him from killing me. Then he sent me away to one of those camps."

"Camps?"

"You know, the kind that are supposed to cure gay people."

"That's awful."

"So I pretended. For years. Until I just couldn't anymore. When I told him, my father punched me. When I didn't punch him back, he told me I was a pussy. He kept hitting me until I shoved him back, and then he called the cops and told them I'd assaulted him. He never let me in the house again. Told the family never to mention my name to him, that I was dead. Only my mother disobeyed him." He lifted his head, as if the memory of her gave him strength. "She couldn't see me very often, but we talked. Mr. Wolven understood."

"All these years you've worked for him, and you still call him Mr. Wolven?"

That got a hint of a smile. "He told me once, early on, to call him Leonard. I said that would be like me calling my father by his first name. It wouldn't feel quite right. But Mr. Wolven is the father I always wished I had. He's the most honorable man I've ever known." He closed his eyes. "And now I've failed him. Len is dead and it's my fault."

54 Elinor Bargeman was lying in wait for me when I got back to my hotel. "Well, there you are!" she said, struggling to uproot herself from a sofa. "You're as hard to track down as frog fangs."

"Elinor, I don't know if the police have been keeping you up to date with what's happened, but—" I was about to tell her about Jesse, but she interrupted.

"I know all about it. I'm so thrilled! And, by the way, I told you so."

"You told me . . . what, exactly?"

"That the police would find my sister. And they have! Ala-baba-whatever-his-name-is got a lead on Marianne in Lima. I'm flying out today."

"What do you mean, he got a lead?"

"Somebody saw her. At a restaurant, I think he said. He's got to go there and do some legwork and whatnot, but I know he'll find her this time. I can feel it, like a sixth sense, y'know? Marianne's just around the corner."

"Elinor, are you paying Alcántara money?"

"Well, not exactly. His brother's a private eye, so I hired him to help out on the investigating."

Listening to her made my head hurt. "You can't believe anything he says. All he's doing is ripping you off."

"No one takes advantage of me!" She raised herself up to her full height. In her bright purple pantsuit, she did look fearsome. "I'm not some fool who was born yesterday."

"I've met someone who paid Alcántara and his brother to find his missing daughter. They strung this man along for months, getting more and more money out of him. They bleed people dry, and they don't find anyone."

"Well, that's not what's happening here. You'll see. Give me a call tomorrow, why don't you? I'm staying at some fancy-pants place in the center of Lima. The Grand Hotel."

"The Gran Hotel Bolívar?" I asked. It was where Jesse and I had planned to stay in the city, before our trip was cut short. Our stay in Lima was only going to be long enough for me to swing by the U.S. embassy and pick up my replacement passport.

"Yeah. That's it."

"Look, I'm not trying to upset you, but I want you to be prepared for the worst. If what I've been told is true, your sister was killed by . . . someone. You need to be realistic about this."

"Listening to you is like trying to scratch my ear with my elbow. I don't know why I'm wasting my time. Good-bye, Lily." She stormed out of the lobby before I could answer. Watching her retreating back made me feel oddly wistful. There was something sweet about living in hope, even if the hope was completely misguided. In a way, I envied her.

The next day, Vargas took Jesse and me to the Cusco airport. It wasn't a long drive from the hospital, but it was a depressing one. As we got farther from the well-touristed parts of the city, Cusco got shabbier. You could see row after row of cheap houses clinging to the side of a mountain. It wasn't a shantytown, but it looked decrepit. Some of the kids begging in the Plaza de Armas undoubtedly came from its scraggly alleyways. I wondered where the alpacas roamed when they weren't wearing roses, because there didn't seem to be any place for them to graze.

"It was actually pretty thoughtful of Augustina to offer us a ride. How often do you get to fly on a fancy ole private jet?" Jesse grinned at me. "Well, you bein' a hoity-toity travel writer, you're used to luxury, but us photographers are used to lyin' in the mud for hours to get the perfect shot at sunrise."

"Woe is you. You don't even have to develop film anymore. A few snaps and you're done."

"Yeah, well, at least I gotta go to a place to take those snaps. Not like a travel writer who can sit in their living room and write about an entire country they never even set foot in!"

Vargas didn't say much, but at the airport he pressed a little square of tissue paper into my hand. "May God keep you safe, both of you." He gave us a little hand wave that was unusually effusive for him, then turned and walked away before I could hug him.

"That fella doesn't do emotion well," Jesse commented. I opened up the tissue and found a sterling silver cross on a delicate chain. It didn't look new and I had a feeling I knew who it had belonged to. I slipped it on without explaining any of that to Jesse. "Wow. I guess he did pick up on how much you like jewelry, Lil." I hadn't told him about Isabella Vargas; I didn't think I'd be sharing that story for some time.

Augustina and Charlie were already on the plane. They were sitting as far apart from each other as they could, Charlie staring moodily out the window and Augustina knitting a pale green sweater. The cabin was more like a living room than a plane, with intricately embroidered black leather seats that faced each other and some couches topped with white and red cushions. There were plasma screens in every part of the cabin, and a red carpet with a golden sun woven into it.

"Jesse! How do you feel today?" Augustina was clearly still in high spirits.

My friend's arm was in a sling, but he smiled. "Just fine, thanks. I'm much obliged to you for letting us fly with you."

"It is the least I could do after all the trouble my brother caused for you."

Charlie looked over. "Don't you dare speak about Len that way."

She rolled her eyes. "Would you like a drink? The attendant will be back in a moment."

She was less chatty today, but Charlie was completely subdued. During the flight, he just stared out the porthole, looking grim. He didn't even speak with Jesse.

The trip to Lima was only an hour. Midway through the flight, a phone call came in. All I heard was Augustina's side of it. "Hello? Yes? What are you talking about? No, that is not possible. Absolutely not. Who the hell gave that order? Really? We'll see about that." She hung up. "Get me my father's office on the phone," she snapped at the attendant. He dialed for her, then spoke so quietly into the phone that I couldn't hear him.

"I am sorry," he said to Augustina. "He is not available."

"What? Give me that phone!" She dropped her knitting and grabbed it. "Hello? Yes, tell my father this is his daughter calling. What? I don't believe this!" She let off a string of curses and hung up, then turned to Jesse and me. "I must apologize. I don't understand why, but this plane is being grounded when we get to Lima."

"Grounded?"

"I'm sorry. My father . . . I don't know what he's doing. But don't worry. We will get you to New York soon."

55

A private car was waiting for Augustina and Charlie at the airport in Lima. "I will be in touch," she said, giving me a hug. "I hope to get this all straightened out soon, perhaps even by tonight. Good-bye!"

I'd called the Gran Hotel Bolívar, so at least Jesse and I had a place to stay. It didn't take long to get a taxi. Our driver was a man in his sixties, very slender and short but able to lift our luggage into the back of a station wagon before either of us could offer a hand. He threw a ratty blanket over it and ushered us into the backseat. "Lima's safer than it used to be, but you don't want to look like a rich Americano in these parts," Jesse commented. As we drove along, I saw that the neighborhood beyond the airport's impressively bright, shiny borders wasn't a shantytown by any means, but it was decrepit and derelict. Groups of young men huddled on curbs watching cars as if ready to pursue and pounce like jaguars.

"Do you think he'll be all right?" Jesse asked me.

"Who?"

"Charlie." My friend looked concerned. "He's had a couple of hard blows recently, first his mom and now this. That'd be tough for anyone to take."

"You don't really think Len Wolven is dead, do you?" I asked.

"Not really, but I sure think Charlie does."

I'd also called the U.S. embassy, locating my sympathetic

friend and discovering that my passport was ready. But the hotel and embassy were a half hour's drive apart, so we went first to the Gran Bolívar. Jesse was in good spirits, but there was no arguing that having a bullet in his shoulder was causing him pain and fatiguing him. The hotel sat at one side of the Plaza San Martín, a pretty five-story 1920s-era confection with a whitewashed façade, rounded corners, and scalloped edges around the windows and roof. It was as if the designers had hoped to suggest extreme voluptuousness, as if the hotel were the Mae West of her era. And maybe she was; I knew it had been a favorite of Ernest Hemingway's.

One sign that Jesse wasn't doing so well was that he ignored the 1920 Model-T Ford that sat inside the lobby. That would have been his thing to see, while I was more impressed by the stained-glass dome above us, seemingly held aloft by marble pillars. But Jesse didn't care about the car; he sat down while I checked us in, and then we took the elevator up to our suite. It had a similar layout to the one we'd shared in Cusco, with a bedroom on either side of a sitting room, but the space was larger and grander, with towering ceilings and a wrought-iron balcony overlooking the plaza.

"Naptime," Jesse said. "I'm kinda wonderin' if maybe it wasn't so bad for ole President Monroe 'cause bullets were smaller back in those days. Stupid shoulder." He disappeared into his room, and I wondered if it wouldn't have been smarter just to have him catch the next flight back to the U.S. while we were still at the airport, even if I couldn't go with him. Too bad it was too late for that.

I looked at the room-service menu, but decided that it made more sense to grab lunch from a café and eat in the taxi on the way to the embassy. Hunger had crept up on me. Maybe I was making up for all the times I hadn't been able to eat over the past few months. I wrote Jesse a note, in case he was so sleepy that he forgot about my passport. Then I went down the hall and waited for the elevator. In the lobby, the first person I saw was Elinor Bargeman in a shiny red pantsuit. She was pacing under the dome with a cell phone in her hand.

"Lily?" She smiled when she recognized me. "Am I glad to see you! I been hoping someone I know might walk by. I just hate sitting all alone in my room."

"Hi, Elinor. How are you?"

"Excellent. Guess what? I'm gonna see my sister this afternoon."

"You are?"

"Yep. That Xavier Ala-boom-bah says he's gonna take me to her."

"Well, that's great." I tried not to sound as dubious as I felt.

"Only I got to pay him more money first. These Peruvians will rob you blind if they get a chance." She looked at her cell phone and then at me. "He was supposed to call me to give me the address Marianne's at, but I'm still waiting."

Her voice had an edge to it, as if she were starting to realize she was a dupe.

"You gave him the money already?"

"Yep. First thing this morning. Hector Ala-whatnot came by to pick it up. What do you think the holdup is?"

"Oh, Elinor." What could I tell her?

"I mean, if you told somebody who'd been waiting for weeks to find out her sister's okay, you wouldn't be so mean about making her wait, would you?" She took a couple of gasping breaths and, for a terrifying moment, I thought she was going to burst into tears.

"Have you tried calling him?" I asked.

"Yep. He's not even answering his phone. I can't quite make heads or tails of it."

I could: the Alcántara brothers had just collected a windfall from Elinor, and that would probably be the last she would see of them.

"You could go to Xavier's office. Do you know where it is?"

"Sure. I had to go there once before." She started pacing again, glancing at the cell phone. "But I'd best stay put. He's gotta call me sooner or later."

Watching her, I realized for the first time how scared she was. In Cusco, I'd thought of her as a giant annoyance, kind of a brightly hued spider that took up residence in my hotel lobby, waiting to pounce on me each day. Now, I saw that she was just a frightened woman, someone who'd never left home before but was suddenly compelled to travel a continent away, to a country she didn't know or understand, because she loved her sister. She didn't speak the language or know the customs, and she had no one to help her out. She was powered entirely by sheer doggedness and faith. What she lacked in knowledge she tried to make up for with determination and grit. For the first time, I felt as if I understood her, even admired her. When I'd been searching for Claudia, I'd only had to return to my hometown; Elinor was without friends in a foreign country, at the mercy of a pair of con men.

I worried for her, imagining her devastation when she found out the truth. But maybe Elinor was one of those people who could sustain hope indefinitely; if Marianne's body were never discovered, there was no reason to give up. Maybe that was for the best. Who was I to challenge that? If I were being honest, I'd have to admit that I carried an illusion with me. When I heard Claudia's voice, I thought of it as my sister communicating with me, instead of acknowledging that it had to have come from a place in my own brain. She was so firmly lodged there that she seemed like a separate person, a blend of memory and imagination that was real in my mind. Maybe she existed elsewhere in the cosmos, too; for all I knew, that was a distinct possibility. But what mattered most was that I could convince myself she was near me. Memory or spirit, angel or devil, that was incidental. She was there, alive, in my mind.

I couldn't say any of that to Elinor. What came out of my mouth instead was, "Do you want me to go with you to Xavier's office?"

She stopped in her tracks. "You would do that?"

"Yes. I have a bad feeling that he's not going to have the information he told you he has, but maybe we can get your money back at least."

"I don't care about the money. I just want to know she's okay."

We got into a taxi in front of the hotel. After Elinor gave the driver directions, she settled back into the seat. "You know, you're not half as snooty as I thought you were in Cusco."

I looked out the window at the square. This was going to be the longest cab ride of my life.

56

For reasons I couldn't explain, my stomach was tied up in knots by the time we got out of the cab. It wasn't from the drive or from Elinor's conversational skills, and it certainly wasn't the neighborhood. The driver had taken us for a little spin on a highway that edged along the shores of the Pacific, and while I suspected that wasn't necessarily the shortest route, it was lovely. Miraflores itself was beautiful; it looked expensive, not so much trendy as comfortably settled. There were colonial mansions behind ornate gates and new apartment buildings with uniformed doormen. Xavier Alcántara's office was in a shiny glass structure with an unobstructed view of the ocean.

"He's doing all right for himself, ain't he?" Elinor said.

"I think he's been running this racket for some time."

"But he's supposed to be a former police officer. He must know something about finding people."

"Maybe he does, but I think he knows a lot more about taking advantage of people."

"Well, he ain't gonna take advantage of me. Not today, not ever." She stormed into the foyer and accosted the guard on duty. When she started to explain who she was, I interrupted.

"Please tell Mr. Alcántara that we're new clients. Or we'd like to be."

The guard rang upstairs, spoke with someone, and sent us up.

"That was smart," Elinor said. "You sure you're really second-generation Yankee?"

The door to Xavier's office was solid wood, with his name in gold. Of course it wasn't real gold, but the thought of him ripping off people like the Vargases and Elinor made my blood pound in my ears.

"Can I help . . . you. Oh. What do you want, Mrs. Bargeman?" Xavier was maybe five years older than his brother and fifty pounds heavier. His hair was just as wavy and black, but there were purplish bags under his long-lashed eyes. He wore a crumpled suit that he had, conceivably, slept in at least once. No one would ever call Xavier pretty, though he was wearing a cologne with a distinctive, woodsy scent that was surprisingly attractive and oddly familiar.

Elinor pushed her way inside and I followed. We were in a small office with a pretty view of the water through floor-to-ceiling windows; from the outside, the mirrored building had seemed tacky, but from the inside, it had a certain charm. There was a closed door that I guessed led to another office; maybe Hector worked out of there, too, or someone else did.

"What do you think I want?" Elinor demanded. "You told me you found Marianne. I gave you the money you wanted. Now tell me where she is!"

"It's not that simple." Xavier closed the door and scratched his neck. When he exhaled, the booze overpowered the cologne. "You have to wait."

"I've been waiting for the past two weeks! Where's my sister?"

"You know, some people aren't too eager to be found," Xavier said. "Who's your little friend, by the way?"

I gave him a glare that was supposed to freeze him in his

tracks, but he smiled at me. His teeth were yellowish and decaying.

"This is Lily Moore," Elinor said. "She's a friend of mine, and she wants to see Marianne, too. So you might as well give us the address, because otherwise I'm gonna call in the police."

"My brother works for the police, Mrs. Bargeman. I don't think you'll get too far with them."

"You listen to me, you two-bit shystering weasel. I paid you and your brother money. Now you're gonna take me to my little sis, 'cause, Lord knows, I been worried sick about her even before she vanished."

Xavier looked at her, and then he laughed so hard his belly shook.

"You are just a silly, spoiled woman," he said. "Go back to your hotel and wait for my call. If you don't do what I say, you will never see your little sister."

Elinor's open, earnest face went blank. Then she reached into her purse and pulled out a gun.

"You don't want to talk to me? Fine. Talk to my new friend." She held the gun up to his head.

"Where did you get the gun, Elinor?" I asked her, my voice shaking.

"Internet. Where else?"

Xavier's face was purplish, and he was choking back tears. "No guns! I hate guns. Put it away. Please!"

"No. Not until you tell me where my sister is."

"I can't!" he cried.

"I'll put a bullet in your head and the only fools you'll be leading around by the nose'll be down in hell."

"Elinor, maybe you should put the gun away," I said. "His brother is a cop."

"I don't care if his brother's the King of China. I'm not leaving here without an address."

"B-but I don't have an address!"

"Then it's a bullet," Elinor said. "I sure hope he likes the taste of lead."

"I'll take you there!" he yelled. "I can! I'll take you to her." There was a foul smell emanating from him. I knew exactly what it was; I'd had to clean up my mother enough times after she'd passed out drunk.

"Well, that's a mite better," Elinor said, lowering the gun. " 'Course, we're gonna have to put a diaper on this big crybaby."

She was only joking about that part. Instead, she made Xavier take us down to the parking garage underneath the building, where he had a big black SUV. We got inside—me in the driver's seat, and the two of them a row back. I was glad to see the automatic transmission. Even though Xavier was making little gasping sobs behind me, I felt like I could handle this.

He told me to take the highway by the ocean. "How come you can take us there if you don't know the address?" I asked him.

He didn't answer. In the rearview mirror, I saw Elinor reach over and poke him. "Well?"

"It's a new development," Xavier mumbled. "There are no street addresses yet."

"Yep, we got that in Texas, too."

Driving on the highway was the least disturbing part. After Xavier told me when to turn off, he gave me a couple of miscues that had me driving in circles. Finally, he figured it out. But when we pulled up in front of a house in a new subdivision, I immediately suspected a fraud. The house didn't just look unoccupied; it was still under construction, just like the rest of the neighborhood. I had a sneaking suspicion I knew how this was going to play out: Xavier would go into the house and no one would be there. Marianne must have moved on, he would say. Maybe he'd invite us to look around. Then he'd hightail it out of there, leaving us stranded.

That was my best-case scenario.

"You two go ahead. I'll wait with the SUV," I said.

"It's safe enough here," Xavier answered. "Come on."

He was urging me to go inside? Oh, he was definitely planning to ditch us. But as they walked ahead, toward the house, I saw him fall behind, eyeing Elinor's purse, where the gun was stashed. Xavier grabbing the gun was an even worse scenario.

"I'm coming," I called. I would have to keep an eye on both of them.

Xavier was knocking on the front door as I approached. We waited. No answer.

He knocked again. "It can take a while."

Another black SUV drove by. It slowed down, but kept on going.

Then the front door swung open. Elinor walked in, then Xavier. I didn't see the man who shut the door behind us until my eyes adjusted to the dim light of the foyer. The first thing I noticed was that he was large enough to fill the doorway. There was a bandage on the top of his head and bruising on his face.

"Bastián?" I whispered. With his wounds and the deep scar running down his face, he could have escaped from an old horror film. One of his hands was wrapped in bandages, like a mummy.

"Who's that?" Elinor asked.

I grabbed the knob, but Bastián leaned against the door, keeping it shut with his weight. "You're not going anywhere, *mina*."

57

"The other one's got a gun!" Xavier said. "It's in her purse."

Elinor was already fumbling for it.

"Let me go, now!" I said. "Elinor, call the police!"

"You want to see your sister?" Bastián asked her. "No police."

"He was there when Len Wolven murdered your sister. Bastián disposed of her body!"

"What are you going on about? I'm right here."

The woman's voice wasn't familiar to me, but her face was. Marianne Wolven was a very beautiful woman, with a mass of bright red hair and flawless golden skin that made her look like a cross between Rita Hayworth and a lioness. Her figure was surgically enhanced, and not at all subtly, with cartoonishly large, buoyant breasts and a nipped-in waist above narrow hips and long legs.

"Marianne!" Elinor ran to hug her. "I been worried to death about you."

"I'm sorry, El. I never thought this would go on so long."

I was so stunned that all I could do was stare at them. Bastián moved away from the door so that he was beside me, and I didn't even try to make a run for it. I was transfixed by the scene in front of me. Marianne was alive?

"I'm going to go clean up," Xavier mumbled, disappearing

downstairs. I hoped, for his sake and ours, that there was a shower and a clean set of clothes down there.

"What happened to you, girl? Where you been all this time?"

"It's a long, crazy story," Marianne said. "Anyone want something to drink? There's bottled water and Diet Coke in the fridge, plus some bottles of wine. The Peruvian stuff tastes like shit, though."

"The mouth on you!" Elinor chided. "Cut that out, child."

"We're a long way from Armstrong County, El."

"Well, manners travel wherever you go . . ."

As she led us farther into the house, I couldn't hold back. "What is going on here?" I demanded. "Bastián told me you were dead."

"Why the hell would you do that, Bastián?" Marianne asked. She looked genuinely perplexed.

"It's what I was instructed to do."

His answer shocked me. "Instructed?"

"Exactly. I was never going to kill you, Lily. I can't believe you thought I would."

"You drove me up to the top of a mountain in the middle of nowhere and said you were going to kill me. You said you had knives!"

"I had to be convincing. Look, my job was to make you believe you were in danger of dying. Then, I was to tell you that Len Wolven had murdered Marianne, and make sure you believed it. After that, all I had to do was let you go. Your job was to spread the word that Len had killed Marianne, which is exactly what you did."

"You tried to rape me!"

"That wasn't rape!" Now Bastián was indignant. "I kissed

you and you kissed me back. You were moaning. You liked what I was doing. Your nipples were hard."

"They were hard because we were on top of a mountain. I was freezing!"

"I was going to let you go after you slept with me! Instead, you attacked me and I lost part of a finger." He held up the bandaged hand. "Do you want to see what you did?"

I knew I shouldn't feel bad about it, but the wound made me squeamish. "But . . . you were in a death squad. In Chile."

"How old do you think I am? I was in high school when Pinochet held a referendum on restoring democracy in Chile. My family were Pinochet supporters, true, but—"

I stared at Bastián as if seeing him for the fist time. That hungry, feral look was still in his eyes. He rubbed my arm with his good hand. "You *have* to sleep with me now. You mutilated me," he whined.

"Look, I don't care what all went on between you two," said Elinor. "But Lily, I'm just gonna tell you that if you leave Jesse for this knucklehead, you're trading down big-time."

"Get the hell out of here before I mutilate the rest of you," I said.

Bastián cringed. "I have nowhere to go."

"Just go away," I hissed.

He stormed down the hallway, slamming the front door behind him.

"Well, good for you," Elinor said. "Now, baby girl, I want to hear what happened to you. Was somebody holding you prisoner?"

"No, El, it's not like that. I've been, um, working."

"Working? How's that?"

"It's like a top secret project." Marianne smiled. "Ain't that something? But I have to lie real low. No leaving the house, ever. Basically, I been living in the basement." Her face tensed up. "Actually, we should go down there now. Come on, it's real nice."

She led us down the stairs. She wasn't wrong: the basement was set up like a luxury apartment with pale wood paneling and curved, feminine furniture. It didn't have any natural light, but it was filled with showgirl amenities. "There's no phone or nothing, but I got a TV and a tanning bed!" Marianne said. "There's an iPod, magazines, food, booze, all that stuff. Look at all the DVDs I got."

My eyes took it all in. There were boxed sets of DVDs, each dedicated to a different actress: Marilyn Monroe, Sophia Loren, Ingrid Bergman, Rita Hayworth, and Ava Gardner. There was a video-game console next to a series of cases that promised tennis, golf, and salsa lessons, among other things. My eyes went back to the DVDs. *Gaslight.*

"But it's been real tough," Marianne said. "I was glad when Bastián showed up, 'cause at least then I had somebody to talk to. It's real weird being all alone, y'know?"

"Who's paying you to stay here?" I asked.

"What?" Marianne said. "I don't know what all you're talking about."

"Marianne, your husband has been tearing himself up because he thinks you're dead," I said. "Somebody wanted him to think you were killed. Actually, they wanted him to think he had murdered you."

"That's crazy talk," she answered, glancing at Elinor, who was frowning at both of us. I didn't want her to bring out the gun in her purse, so I tried to keep my voice calm.

"Marianne, your husband killed himself last night. He did that because he thought he was responsible for your death."

"No. That's a lie!" Marianne's full lips opened and closed like a guppy.

"It *is* a lie," Xavier said. He'd cleaned himself off, at least somewhat, in the bathroom, and was lounging in the doorway. "Len isn't dead. He paid me to tell that fable."

"Then where is he?" I asked.

"Look, I don't give two hoots where he's at, but I do care that my baby sister's been on the lam. Don't you tell me you been working. Save that for somebody who doesn't know you. You've broken your marital vows to shack up with some man, haven't you?"

"No, Elinor." Marianne sighed. "I'm getting paid a million dollars each day I hide out."

"A million dollars each day?" Elinor and I said in unison. "U.S.?" Elinor added.

"Uh-huh."

"But honey, you married a rich man," Elinor said. "Why'd you live in a basement for money?" She squinted at the wall. "Is this like one of them reality shows?"

"Look, Len is supposed to be this rich guy, but it turns out he gets an allowance from his daddy. A tiny pittance of an allowance, if you follow me. When I use a credit card to buy some nice things for myself, next thing I know I got this lawyer standing on my doorstep with a postnup agreement. A postnup! Do you believe that?"

"But you told me you were in danger," Elinor said. "Life and death."

"I was! Charlie made it clear if I didn't sign away my right to absolutely *everything*, I'd be pushing up daisies under a cliff. And then Tina started telling me all these stories about Len and, well, when she offered me the money, it seemed like a good time to hightail it out of there."

"Hold on," I said. "Tina? You mean Augustina? Len's sister? She offered you money to hide out here?"

"Yep." Marianne bobbed her head.

I'm not sure who was more stunned: Elinor, at the revelation that her baby sister had, in fact, never been in danger, or me, at the realization that Augustina had orchestrated everything from day one. That moment of sheer dumbfoundedness gave Xavier his chance. I saw him reach for Elinor's purse, and then the gun was in his hand.

"*Putas,*" he spat. "Ordering me around. Humiliating me." He hadn't been joking about his fear of guns; even though he was the one holding it now, his hand trembled violently. "Keys!" he shouted. I realized he wanted the keys to the SUV, and I held them out. "Put them on the stairs," he ordered. I did, walking them over and then backing away with my hands in the air, feeling faintly ridiculous. "I'm going to get even with all of you," he said, moving to the stairs.

"What'd I do to you, Xavier?" Marianne asked.

"Not you. The other two. Especially the *vaca gorda.*"

Elinor was watching Xavier through narrowed eyes as he crept up the stairs, and I could only hope she didn't understand that he'd just called her a fat cow.

"Don't follow me or I will shoot you," he pledged. "All of you can stay down here." He opened the door at the top, and I heard him say something in Spanish. Then there were two gunshots, and Xavier's body came tumbling down the stairs. He was already dead, and the expression seared on his face was one of absolute bewilderment. Two men I'd never seen before came down after it, each one holding a gun.

"Come up one at a time," called Charlie. "Don't make any sudden moves."

58

I was the first to step around Xavier's body and walk up the stairs. "What do you think you're doing?" I asked Charlie when I reached the ground floor.

"My job," he said, not looking me in the eye.

"Did you know Marianne was here all along?"

"I had no idea. Mr. Wolven wanted Xavier watched after what happened with Len last night. Just in case . . ." The words died on his lips. "I shouldn't tell you anything. You know too much already for Mr. Wolven to let you live."

"So what are you going to do?" I asked.

He stood, staring at me, while another man put a needle in my neck. The colors in the room turned gray immediately, and I felt myself start to spin. "Catch her," Charlie said, and then the fog rolled in, obliterating everything.

When I came to, I was sitting in a chair in a dark room. There was a ringing in my ears that wouldn't stop, and my whole body felt leaden. How was I managing to sit straight? I wanted to call out, to see if anyone else was there, but my mouth felt as if someone had filled it with cotton. It took me a few moments to realize that I was shackled to the chair. My arms were secured by thick metal bands and my ankles were fastened to the legs of the chair. I was trapped.

Suddenly I was suffocating. I couldn't move and I couldn't

pull air into my lungs. I was caught up in an undertow, and it was dragging me down. Panic overwhelmed me.

Why do you do this to yourself?

I'm chained to a chair!

The panic. You do that to yourself. Breathe, you fucking idiot.

Another voice came to me in the dark. *You just need to forget what you already know. Or what you think you already know. Open yourself up to what's around you here.* Jesse had said that when we'd been walking through Cusco's cathedral together. At the time, he was just trying to make me look at art and culture in a different way, but his words reverberated in my mind now.

I tried to, even though my heart was pounding. Bits of what had happened were coming back to me. Marianne Wolven was alive after all. How was that possible? It was a fact, even if I couldn't wrap my mind around it. Tina. Augustina. That was who had convinced her to disappear in the first place. She'd promised Marianne money to vanish.

What else did I think I knew? And what else was I wrong about?

Bastián had tried to kill me. No, he hadn't. Bastián had abducted me, told me lies about Marianne Wolven—lies that I was expected to repeat—and had tried to coerce me into having sex with him. But I was always supposed to live through the encounter. Live and repeat lies to the police. Vargas had made me look at the night differently, by presenting the possibility that the elderly Leonard Wolven had wanted me dead. But it wasn't him at all. The person who'd put Bastián up to it had to be Augustina.

It was her, all along, I realized. She'd played all of us as if we were instruments in a symphony. I was still trying to put it all together when the door opened and someone shone a bright light in my face.

59

"Lily Moore," said a man with a raspy voice I didn't recognize. "Finally, I get to see you in the flesh. I have been waiting for this."

The light moved so that it shone on the wall and I turned my eyes forward. In front of me was a man in a wheelchair. Under a jaunty fedora, his face was deeply creased, but his sharp cheekbones still stood out. His eyes were sunken into his head, with the lids only half open, as if he were ready for a nap. But there was nothing else about him that suggested drowsiness. His body, though noticeably thin in a dark suit, seemed ready to pounce. His hands clenched the arms of his wheelchair so tightly that corded veins stood out.

"I should introduce myself. My name is Leonard Wolven. We haven't met before, but I know all about you, Miss Moore." Harsh as his voice sounded, his manner was smooth. There were two men with him, neither of whom I'd seen before, and he gestured to one to move him forward, closer to me.

"Where am I, and why am I chained to this chair?"

"You're in no position to ask questions, Miss Moore, but I will indulge you. You are in my home in Lima. You are chained to that chair because we're going to play a little game."

"A game?" His tone was mild, but his words were ominous.

"You are quite the little game player, yourself," Wolven said, studying me. "Only your game was to spread lies about my son."

"That isn't—"

"You told everyone that he murdered Marianne. You drove him out of his mind with that."

"When Bastián abducted me, he told me Len had murdered Marianne. I didn't realize he was lying. I didn't know I was being set up."

"My son always had a sensitive, high-strung nature. He couldn't even have pets when he was a boy, because if anything happened to them, he blamed himself. Once he found a baby robin that had fallen out of its nest and died. Len cried for days about it. He wouldn't let anyone take it out of his room." Wolven cleared his throat. "Tell me, Miss Moore, what was it that led you to join the plot against my son? I'd assumed it must be because you and Bastián were sleeping together, until I discovered you'd maimed him."

"You know I never plotted against your son. You've looked into my background. You know I came here with a friend, and you know I did that because my sister died." I'd come to Peru to escape my nightmares, only to fall into a family drama that resembled a horror movie. "It was your daughter, Augustina, who has been plotting against your son all this time."

Wolven sat there, looking at me for a long time, without a word. "I do not take accusations against my family lightly."

"It's not just an accusation. I didn't realize what was going on until we were inside that house. I thought Marianne was dead, but Xavier Alcántara led us to her. She told us that it was Augustina who had offered her money to vanish."

"Yes, I've heard this same story from that trashy stripper and her sister. I'm surprised that you would throw your lot in with them, Miss Moore. They were obviously conspiring with the Alcántara brothers against my son."

"That's insane. I'd never encountered any of those people until I came to Peru. This is a conspiracy that's been going on for months, not something that cropped up overnight." I took a deep breath. "It was Augustina who planned everything. I can prove it."

"Famous last words, Miss Moore. No, don't say another word." He cut me off as I started to speak again. "I have my own way of getting to the truth. It's my own lie-detector system. Very simple, really. But so effective." To one of the men, he said, "Bring the rest of them in."

We waited in silence. Finally, there was the sound of an elevator door opening. I heard Augustina before I saw her. "I can't believe I'm being dragged down to the basement in my condition," she complained.

"Please find a chair for my daughter," said Wolven. "I wouldn't want her to be uncomfortable."

"What is *she* doing here?" Augustina said when she saw me. She didn't comment on the fact that I was secured to the chair; perhaps in the Wolven family, this wasn't such an uncommon sight.

"Miss Moore is going to tell us the truth. Ah, there's a chair for you. Sit down, Tina."

She sat in the metal chair but didn't look pleased about it.

Marianne came in next, flanked by one suit and followed by another who carried a metal chair like the one I was in. Wolven pointed for her to sit and she was strapped into her chair just as I was in mine. She looked from me to Augustina, but when she opened her mouth, her father-in-law snapped, "Not a word, unless you wish to have your tongue cut out."

We waited in silence a little longer. The elevator sounded again. This time, it was Bastián who came in, his hands tied behind his back and flanked by two guards. Another man brought up the rear, carrying another metal chair. Bastián sat, and the men shackled him to it.

Next, Charlie walked in, carrying a revolver.

"That's the .38 from my desk?" Wolven asked him.

"Yes, sir."

Wolven held out a gnarled hand. Charlie gingerly placed the gun in it.

"Careful, sir, it's loaded."

"Thank you, Charlie." Wolven opened the cylinder and slowly, painstakingly extracted five bullets. Then he spun the cylinder and handed the gun back to Charlie.

"Ready to begin, sir?"

"No, Charlie, we're waiting for one more guest to play."

Charlie looked around, as if mentally accounting for who was there. "Hector Alcántara?"

"Unfortunately, Mr. Alcántara jumped out a window rather than be taken by my men," Wolven said. "I believe he is still clinging to life in the hospital, but that could change at any time."

"Not Elinor Bargeman?" Charlie whispered. His voice echoed through the room.

"She is of no consequence."

Charlie looked around again. That was when a guard brought the last guest into the room. It was Jesse.

60

"Everyone in this room had a role to play in this plot against my son," Wolven announced, after Jesse was strapped to a chair. We were sitting in a rough circle. I was on one side of Wolven, and Augustina was on the other. Marianne was next to her and Jesse next to me, with Bastián between the two of them. All but two of the guards had left; the pair that remained had retreated to two corners of the room. Charlie stood behind Wolven, holding the revolver. Of those sitting, only Augustina and Wolven himself weren't tied down.

"You all know what Russian roulette is, of course," Wolven said. "My game is a variation of that. I like to call it Truth Comes Out. It comes out, you see, whether you want it to or not. There is nothing quite so clarifying as a gun against your head." He smiled at all of us. There was something absolutely mad about him, yet he was calm and collected. It was his absolute authority and certainty that chilled me most; watching him, I felt as if the rest of the world had fallen away, and all that mattered was this one-man Inquisition.

That was a terrible thought just then, because the darkness and bleakness of the room made me feel as if the walls were closing in. For all intents and purposes, I'd walked into a real-life version of Edgar Allan Poe's "The Pit and the Pendulum." Only instead of burning walls, the ones around me were freezing, and the pit at the center of the room was the shadow cast by Leonard Wolven.

He sat bolt upright in his wheelchair, his claw hands holding tight again to the armrests. "The rules of Truth Comes Out are simple," he said. "I ask all of the questions. If I don't like the answers I receive, Charlie will take that gun, put it against your head—or some other body part, if I see fit—and press the trigger. Do you understand anything of the law of probability? There is a one-in-six chance of a bullet ending up in your brain. That probability does increase as the game goes on."

He smiled that eerie, tight smile again. "None of you speaks out of turn. None of you asks a question. None of you attempts to influence another's answer. Do I make myself clear?"

The pit was absolutely silent. Even Augustina looked disconcerted.

"You may answer that," Wolven said.

There was a hushed chorus of yeses.

"Miss Moore, why don't you start us off? When my son came to your hotel room in Cusco a couple of days ago, what did he talk to you about?"

"Len said that he'd believed I was plotting with Bastián, but then he'd realized that I was just being used." My voice was rough from the dryness of my throat. "I couldn't understand that, because I'd thought Bastián was going to kill me the night he abducted me. It wasn't until I saw him this afternoon that I discovered Len was right—Bastián abducted me to feed me lies about Len. It wasn't designed to get Len arrested, because there was no body and no proof. It was designed to make Len want to kill himself, just as he'd tried to after his first wife's death."

"No theories, Miss Moore," Wolven chided. "Did I mention that when I spelled out the rules?" He froze for a moment, as if in thought. "Perhaps I did not. You will restrict yourself to direct answers to my questions, and to statements of fact. Now, was there anything else my son said to you that afternoon?"

"He told me about his first wife, Kirsten. He told me that he'd felt responsible for her death, and that he hadn't been able to live with himself afterward. He told me that he'd tried to kill himself more than once—by cutting his wrists, by drinking poison—because he felt that he deserved to die for causing the car crash." I'd conflated the little bit that Len had told me with details I'd gotten from Bruxton, but together, it was a potent combination. Augustina's catlike eyes narrowed at me before watching her father for his reaction. Wolven's breathing had become ragged, but he didn't say a word. I took that as a cue to continue.

"Len told me about what happened with Trista on Machu Picchu. He said that his plan had been for them to take a Peruvian drug called ayahuasca together. He thought it would help open her mind. He didn't know she was using cocaine at the same time. He said the combination was deadly."

"Very interesting, Miss Moore. Did my son mention me?" Wolven's eyes were bright, even in the dim light of the cell.

"Yes. He said you'd made him come to Peru."

"And?" Wolven prompted. "What else?"

"He said you threatened to cut him out of your will if he didn't go."

Wolven cleared his throat. "Anything else?"

I had the awful sense that this was the real purpose of his questioning: vain and arrogant, Wolven cared less about what had happened to his son than what his son might have said about him. "That's all."

Wolven looked at the others. "Now you'll see what happens when someone lies to me."

"I haven't lied!"

"You talked to Charlie about your conversation," Wolven said. His tone was hectoring now. "You told him that my son mentioned his blackouts to you. Is that correct?"

"Yes. Len did mention blackouts. He said he'd had one the night Marianne had died . . . not that she died, I mean, but Len thought she was dead . . ." I was embarrassed by my own fumbling for words.

"My son mentioned his blackouts without mentioning me?" He was aggrieved.

"Yes. I did ask him what caused the blackouts, and he said you'd taken him to doctor after doctor but no one had an answer."

"And did he tell you when the blackouts started?"

"He said they started after his mother d—"

"Bastián's trying to get out of his handcuffs!" Charlie shouted. "Guard, come here." One of the silent men came out of a shadowy corner. "Watch him. If he tries that again, shoot him."

"I didn't do anything," Bastián said. "You're a fucking liar, Charlie."

"Trying to escape is against the rules, in case that somehow wasn't clear." Wolven coughed. "No, that was quite clear. Charlie, the gun."

61

Wolven put out his hand and took the revolver. "Let's see if this is your lucky day, Bastián." He braced his elbow on the armrest, gripped his wrist with his other hand, and pointed the gun at Bastián. "One-in-six chance..." he said as he took aim.

The gun fired with a crack that reverberated through the room. Bastián screamed and doubled over, then threw his head back in agony. The bullet had gone into his stomach; blood was running over his shirt, down his leg, and onto the floor.

"Sorry. I was aiming for your head." Wolven's voice was cool. "Guards, take him out. He's too much of a distraction like this."

The two guards took him out, and two more came in, retreating to the corners. Wolven's game of Truth Comes Out clearly wasn't foreign to them.

"My hand," Wolven said, gripping it. "That really hurt."

"Father, you can't just shoot people," Augustina said. "The girls liked him. He used to take them to school every day when we were in Australia."

"Don't talk out of turn, Tina. You'll cause others to break the rules." Wolven looked at me. "Pray, continue, Miss Moore. When did my son say his blackouts started?"

I tried to keep my voice calm, and it came out as a whisper. "Len said his blackouts started after his mother deserted the family. He said they'd gotten longer over the years, some-times twenty minutes or more." It hadn't escaped me, what Charlie had done. It had been on the tip of my tongue to say, *after his mother died.* I knew I wasn't supposed to mention her death, but this Inquisitor had rattled me. I couldn't let that happen again. Bastián had taken a bullet for me, however involuntarily. The next one-in-six odds would be my own. "Len described it as his brain short-circuiting. He also said that it had happened that day at Machu Picchu, when he'd run to get help and got lost." It sounded as if I were rambling, but drowning the room in detail was as good a strategy as I had at that point. "He also said he believed Augustina was plotting against him. He said the blackouts made him vulner-able." That was stretching things only slightly, and it was es-sentially true. I waited for the command for the gun to be pointed at me, but it didn't come.

"Thank you, Miss Moore." Wolven was still toying with the gun, and every pair of eyes in the room was on him. He'd loaded another bullet into the cylinder and spun it; after snapping it back into place, he handed the weapon to Charlie.

"Now, Miss Bargeman. I want to hear from you. Why were you living in the basement of a house, and letting my son think you were dead?"

"That was Tina's idea." Marianne's voice was hoarse.

"You are a liar," Augustina said. "But that is what I'd ex-pect of a whore."

"Quiet, Tina. Answer the question, Miss Bargeman. Why?"

"It was the postnup and Len acting all crazy all the time and him taking that weird drink and having visions. I didn't mind the marijuana, but I wasn't having none of that weirdo stuff." Her words tumbled out like hailstones. "I told Tina how miserable I was and she said she had this supersmart idea and I asked her what and she said I needed get away for a while. She said Len was wacky and you never knew what he might do next, and actually I might get a big settlement if anything happened to him, but even if it didn't she'd pay me a million a day to stay outta sight—"

"That's enough, Miss Bargeman," Wolven commanded. "You admit to plotting against my son. You knew his mind was weak, and still you did this to him. Charlie! The gun. Place it against Miss Bargeman's right temple. That way I can enjoy the best view."

Charlie moved into place. "No, no, no! Please, Mr. Wolven. I didn't mean any harm to come to Len. I'm so sorry! I swear on my momma's grave, I'm so sorry." Marianne dissolved into tears. Wolven watched her for some time. There was no other sound in the room but her sobbing.

"Do you have a handkerchief?" Wolven asked Charlie. "Give it to her."

"Thank you," she mumbled, then blew her nose with a loud honk. "I'm so sorry. I'll never forgive myself."

"One in six. Charlie, please proceed."

"No!" Marianne screamed, eyes wide.

Charlie fired the gun. The empty click was as loud as a firecracker going off.

"Hmm. Again," Wolven said.

"Sir?" Charlie looked at him. In the shadows, his face was heavily lined; he'd somehow aged two decades in a few minutes.

"Pull the trigger again. No, don't spin the cylinder. The odds are now one in five."

"Our Father, who art in heaven . . ." Marianne whispered.

"Keep your prayers to yourself or I'll have one of the

guards shoot next. That will take your odds to one hundred percent, Miss Bargeman."

A vein pulsed in Charlie's temple, and he paused to brace himself.

"Now, Charlie."

Charlie hesitated, then pulled the trigger. Another resounding click.

"Your lucky day, Miss Bargeman," Wolven said, his tone acid. "Well, Augustina, you have been accused by both Miss Moore and Miss Bargeman. What do you have to say for yourself?"

"They are both liars who are conspiring against me." There was heat in her voice as she answered, but it was evenly applied. None of the ragged, bitter edge of true rage, just the affectation of a seasoned performer. "They want to excuse their own crimes against my brother. Miss Moore may simply be crazy because of her dead sister, but that sleazy whore Len married is a con artist. She set this up herself. We all know her record with the police. Honestly, this story she tells? Ridiculous. A million dollars a day to hide in a basement? Please."

"What did you promise Trista?" I called out.

All eyes turned on me. "What about Trista?" Wolven asked.

"I talked to her after she collapsed at Machu Picchu. You know what she said? Len had abandoned her, but then he came crawling back, just like Tina said he would. She mentioned you by name, Tina." I looked at Wolven. "That was why Trista just happened to call Len when she did. It wasn't a coincidence. Tina had told her exactly when to call. Just as she had her torture Len with anonymous notes that said 'I know what you did' on them."

"Well, Tina?"

"This is insanity." Augustina crossed her arms over her belly and stared at me. Her face was as cold and haughty as it had been in Cusco when Len had thrown a vase at her, but her hands were twitching. "Oh, the baby," she said suddenly.

"What's wrong?" Wolven asked.

"I was cramping earlier and I . . . Ow! I must call my doctor. In fact, I think I will go to the hospital, just to be safe. I must leave now." She sprang up from her chair and made for the door with a swiftness and agility I hadn't seen from her before. When she knocked, a guard opened the door, let her out, then poked his head inside. Wolven shrugged and the guard shut the door.

"The plot thickens," Wolven said. "Charlie, put the revolver against Miss Moore's temple. Either side is fine."

Charlie hesitated in front of me.

"You haven't spun the cylinder, have you? One-in-four odds for you, Miss Moore." He frowned. "Just pick a side, Charlie."

"That's enough!" Jesse's voice was loud enough to make me catch my breath. "This game is bullshit. You know full well your daughter plotted and planned against your son. You better get comfortable with that, 'cause it's the bald truth. You holdin' court like you're the Great Inquisitor doesn't cut it, and it ain't gonna bring him back from the dead. And you know what? You got no one to blame but yourself. What sick excuse for a human being keeps a torture chamber in his basement, or makes up a game like this?"

"Charlie, I've changed my mind. Put the gun against Mr. Robb's temple instead."

"All these riches you got, and this is the best you can do?" Jesse taunted. "This sorry-ass kangaroo court? You know,

I should thank you. You explained something in Matthew's gospel I never quite got. 'It is easier for a camel to go through the eye of a needle, than for a rich man to enter into the kingdom of God.' "

"The gun, Charlie."

"See, I always thought God loved everybody. Why hate on rich folks? But I see it now—when rich folks set themselves up like God—"

"Charlie! Stop standing there like a moron. Point the gun."

"I can't, sir."

"You . . . what?" It seemed to be the first time Wolven had ever heard those words from Charlie.

"He's already been shot," Charlie said. "I can't shoot a man who's already got a bullet in him."

Wolven's mouth stayed closed, but his head tipped so far back that his hat fell off. It hit the floor with a muffled thud.

"You know this isn't how we play the game, Charlie," Wolven said. "But you can take Mr. Robb's turn. Step into the center, in front of me. Now point the gun at your own head. What were we at? One in four?"

"Yes, sir. One in four." Charlie's voice was quiet.

"Good. Now pull the trigger."

Charlie didn't hesitate. The sharp click filled the air and for a moment my body sagged with relief.

"Again, Charlie. We're at one in three. This is where it gets very exciting."

"Yes, sir." Without missing a beat, Charlie fired the gun again.

Click. Empty.

Wolven nodded, as if he had ordered up this afternoon's entertainment and felt he was getting his money's worth. "It's your lucky day, Charlie. Let's see how you do with one in two. I wouldn't bet on a horse with those odds, but I like to see them played out."

"No," I said. "Enough. You can't—"

"Yes, Miss Moore, I can. Go ahead, Charlie."

Charlie didn't speak this time, but he kept his eyes on Wolven as he fired the gun. The click sounded slightly different, a little louder, almost harsher, as if metal were grinding up against metal. Or maybe that was an illusion, because time had stopped, and the beating of my heart was almost as loud in my ears as the fall of the hammer.

Empty. Charlie stood there. He didn't look relieved. His face was a bland mask, but his body swayed slightly as if he'd taken a punch to the chest.

"Good, Charlie. Again."

"Stop!" I shouted. Wolven's sly face turned my way. Charlie stood straight, the gun still next to his head. "You didn't ask me the most important question."

"Most important question?" The Inquisitor was taken aback. In his private hell, people pleaded and suffered and died. They didn't tell him he'd failed to ask a question. I could feel every pair of eyes in the room on me, even the guards' in the dark corners.

"About Len. He's still alive."

62

We took the elevator up. Wolven was seated in his wheelchair, and the lone guard who pushed it for him didn't speak. I had a fleeting fantasy of grabbing his gun and shooting Wolven, but then the elevator doors slid open. There were servants and guards everywhere. They murmured in English, and I wondered if Wolven traveled with a platoon accompanying him.

The house was possibly the grandest villa I'd seen, outside of a museum. I was led through rooms and hallways filled with priceless art and antiques, but I didn't really see any of it; all I really felt was the grim, cursed presence of Wolven beside me.

The guard wheeled Wolven onto a balcony on the second floor. *Balcony* wasn't quite the right word, because it was more like a giant, sweeping patio suspended in midair. Wolven gestured where he wanted to be placed, next to the wrought-iron railing that overlooked a manicured lawn and what looked, at a distance, like a koi pond. A female servant brought him a blanket to cover his lap and a pack of cigarettes. He placed one in his mouth and let her light it for him, then waved her away. He seemed even older and more decrepit than he had in the basement pit. There were purple crescent moons under his eyes, and pink, scaly patches of skin on his face, neck, and hands. "Miss Moore. Take a seat."

There was a chair directly across from him and I took it.

He offered me a cigarette, and while he lit it for me, all I could wonder was whether he saw my hands shaking. I felt as if I were awaiting a verdict. Instead, I got a question.

"What did Len really say to you, Miss Moore?"

"I told you that already."

Wolven looked at me again for a long time, just as he had in the basement when I'd accused his daughter. It was a look that gave me goose bumps and made little hairs on the back of my neck creep up. "There's more. There's always more."

I look a long drag. "It's not flattering."

"Do tell."

"Len said you blamed him for the fact that his mother left. He said you claimed you and she were close before he was born, but then he arrived and that changed everything."

"Mmm. What did that make you think of me, Miss Moore?"

"It made me sad for Len, and for you. It was awful to think that you could have a happy family, but instead you were jealous of your own son."

Wolven's eyebrows shot upward. "Here I was, thinking you would say anything to get free of me. I thought you would flatter and smile and try to charm me." He studied me intently again, then smiled suddenly. "You're a perfect little beast. If I were twenty years younger, I would keep you in a cage." He lowered his voice. "You won't believe this, looking at me as I am now, but you would've enjoyed it."

Repartee failed me then. I puffed on my cigarette and gave a look I hoped was worthy of Ava Gardner in *The Killers*.

"Tell me about my son," he commanded.

"He's alive. Xavier Alcántara said so before he was killed. He said that Len had paid him to tell that story, and that he was alive."

"Is that all?" Wolven exhaled a stream of blue smoke with

obvious displeasure. "That man is full of shit. Pardon my language. I know my son is dead."

"You're not sorry for playing Russian roulette with me, but you apologize for swearing?"

"In some ways, I'm old-fashioned, Miss Moore. Sometimes, I'd like to think gallant." My lips must have twitched, because he added, "You must think me an old fool."

"No. It's just that, before I came to Peru, I thought I was lonely. I had no idea."

Now Wolven was without words. He lit another cigarette with the embers of his last.

"Why do you insist your son is dead?" I asked.

"My son can't survive on his own. If he were still alive, he would have called me for help by now. He wanted to die. He must be dead by now."

"Listen to me. I was in a room with your son when he had a loaded gun in his hand. If he'd wanted to kill himself, he could have. He had the means. He had opportunity."

"He's never gone this long being out of touch before. He always needs something from me. He has to be dead."

"Mr. Wolven, you've looked into my background, so you're aware I know something about suicidal people," I said. "Your son, for all his capacity to hurt himself, wasn't like that. Len doesn't want to die, Mr. Wolven, but he doesn't know how to live."

"You think he's out there, somewhere?"

"Yes. And I think you should leave him alone."

He was quiet again, though he lit me another cigarette when I finished the first. The silence stretched on until I broke it. "What I don't understand is this: you knew your daughter wanted to hurt your son, since he was supposed to inherit everything. You had to have known that."

"So why didn't I see what was happening sooner? My daughter is very much like me, Miss Moore. Years ago, she made me a promise, which was that she would never lay a hand on her brother to harm him or hire anyone to physically hurt him. Tina kept her word about that, you see, but she found a loophole." He sighed. "I thought she would learn a lesson from what happened to her own mother."

"What do you mean?"

"My third wife was an actress—not a very good one, but a very beautiful one—from Spain. She was hopelessly jealous of my fourth wife."

"Maybe she wasn't jealous so much as furious that, as soon as you had a son, you disinherited her daughter," I pointed out.

"You have it the wrong way around, though your point about the inheritance is well made. Tina's mother was responsible for what happened with Len's mother . . ." It was odd listening to him, realizing that most people didn't exist as individuals in his mind, just appendages. "Without going into details, I suppose Tina's mother thought she should give Len's mother a reason to leave me before she had any more children with me. It was one thing to have the inheritance divided in two, but not three ways or more. I disinherited Augustina because of what her mother did. I know that was harsh, but there was an odd justice about it."

"Justice?" I tired not to choke on the word. "Why punish the daughter for what her mother did? Why not just punish your ex-wife?"

"Oh, I did. My former wife did not go free. The world became her prison."

"I don't understand what you mean."

"She was an incredibly vain woman," he explained. "Her appearance was everything to her." His voice gave me chills as I began to realize exactly what he meant. "From what I understand, she has not let anyone but her immediate family see her face in a quarter century."

It took every bit of my nerve not to flee from Wolven then. I'd felt that Len was insane, and I'd seen inklings of craziness in Augustina's operatic emotions, but the coldly calculating mind that was in front of me was the worst of all. Wolven believed he was justified in everything he did, and there would be no convincing him otherwise. His brain was ordered by unbreakable rules and an unshakable confidence in his own honor. I couldn't run from him, but I could leverage his need to be viewed as gallant.

"You know now that I never did anything to harm your son, don't you?" I asked him.

"Yes, Miss Moore. I apologize for my error. It's never easy to get to the truth."

"When are you going to let me go?" I asked him.

"As much as I'd like to keep you in that cage, you are free to fly when you wish."

"And Jesse." It was a statement, not a question.

"Good riddance to him."

"And Elinor?"

He nodded, granting that.

"And Marianne?"

"No. I have to draw the line somewhere. That amoral trollop should die."

"Augustina kept telling me how violent Len was. She told Marianne the same thing. And she made her think her life was in jeopardy." I didn't care that Marianne was a greedy scam artist willing to leave her husband in exchange for money; I had a feeling her biggest disappointment would be in failing to get her promised millions.

"What will you do with these people if I let them go with you? Start a circus?"

"Maybe. What will you do about your daughter?"

"I have no idea. Dealing with my children is my worst nightmare. They know I won't kill them, so they're not afraid of me."

I didn't even try to set him straight on that one. "One more thing. Will you get a doctor for Bastián?"

"Tell me, Miss Moore, do you feel pain every time a baby bird drops out of a nest?" He crushed his cigarette against the railing.

"You'd be surprised how tough I can be, Mr. Wolven."

EPILOGUE

The drive to the airport was eerily silent, given how many people were inside the huge SUV. One of Wolven's guards drove us. Charlie sat next to Jesse, in what seemed to be companionable silence. Elinor and Marianne sat at opposite ends of one row, each staring out the window as if overtaken with longing or, quite possibly, regret. We stopped to pick up the luggage we hadn't unpacked and again for my passport. It wasn't as if we had a flight to catch, exactly. Leonard Wolven had promised me a private plane to make the trip back to New York. It had come at the expense of a promise I was already trying to forget. *One day I'll call for you, and you will come to see me. It could be next month, or I could be on my deathbed. But I will call, Miss Moore.*

I'd agreed only because I was worried about Jesse. He should have been back in New York already, and in the care of a surgeon. Thinking of the lead bleeding into his system made me light-headed. It was a fortunate thing that Wolven hadn't realized just how desperate I was.

At the airport, I felt as if I needed to give my friend some measure of privacy to say good-bye to Charlie, but they both kept following me. Finally, I turned to Jesse. "Would you mind letting me talk to Charlie in private for a minute?"

"Sure thing. I'll be, uh, just over there." He loped off.

"I don't know how to say thank you," I said. "You saved

my life, and you saved Jesse's. Everyone in that room is alive because of you."

"You got yourself out of there. Mr. Wolven is genuinely fascinated by you."

"You know I screwed up, Charlie. If you hadn't interrupted me and given up Bastián, I'd be dead now."

"Maybe it makes up a bit for the pathetic excuse for a warning I left at your hotel in Cusco before you checked in." He looked rueful. "When Mr. Wolven spoke with you privately, did he say anything about Len's mother?"

"Only obliquely. He blamed what happened with her on Augustina's mother."

"He would." Charlie looked exhausted, but he gave me that crooked smile. "Len's mother had an affair with her predecessor's brother. Tina's mother introduced them, of course. That was why he came down so hard on her, and Tina."

"He killed his wife and her lover?"

"He hacked them both to pieces, Lily. He has a map in his office in Toronto. It's on the wall, marked with little gold and silver dots. When anyone asks him about it, he says it's a treasure hunt he once did for his son. The truth is, it shows where he buried them. Bits of them." That made me shudder. *Torture porn*, I thought suddenly. Elinor had talked about Len's collection of articles about murdered women, especially ones who'd been dismembered. Charlie went on. "Len's just starting to remember. Whatever his father did to tamp it down, it's bubbling to the surface. I can't imagine what will happen when the truth comes back to him. There's going to be a quake that's off the charts." Charlie cleared his throat. "I probably don't need to tell you this, but don't put anything you don't want Mr. Wolven to see in an e-mail, and be careful about phone calls."

That was a chilling reminder of the man's reach. "What about you?" I asked him.

"Well, I guess I've learned I'm lower down the totem pole than I realized. I'm trying not to take that as a comment on my job performance." He was trying to keep things light, but tension squeezed his voice.

"I'm sorry. I know you thought of him as the father you never had, and he—"

"After everything I've done for him, he thinks I'm as disposable as last week's newspaper. I've just been given the ultimate memento mori."

That was an even more brutal assessment than what had been on the tip of my tongue, but it was impossible to argue. Wolven's moods were mercurial, and while I'd experienced his clumsy attempt at charm, I'd witnessed something so bleak and cruel it left me quivering. "How could you stand working for him for so many years?"

"Maybe it's hard to believe, but Mr. Wolven would never hurt either of his children. I guess I deluded myself into thinking that he saw me as one of his kids. Isn't that the most ridiculous thing you've ever heard? How could I be such a fool?"

"You got a raw deal with your birth family, at least with your father. There's nothing foolish about looking for a replacement." I wished I could say something that would help make sense of it all in his mind. Instead, I shared an identical, elemental need for family that would never be satisfied by the one I'd been given at birth. I thought of what Señora Vargas had said. *Just as you love others, they will love you.*

"Lily, I was willing to do anything Mr. Wolven wanted. Trista's dead because of what I did." He shook his head. "I don't know what I'm going to do. Mr. Wolven thinks everything is back to normal, but I can't go on living the way I have."

I threw my arms around him. It took a moment, but he hugged me back. "I'm going to leave you alone with Jesse now," I said, pulling away.

"I can't remember the last time anyone hugged me."

"Maybe you should try it again soon." I kissed his cheek lightly. "Good-bye, Charlie."

I moved off without looking where I was going, and ended up on the edge of a hornet's nest. Marianne and Elinor were facing off a few yards away, and they had already attracted an audience. The pair took turns standing and yelling, and there was a lot of finger-wagging and head-shaking and pointing.

"What did you just say to me, little girl?"

"I wouldn't waste my time repeating anything to you 'cause you're not gonna listen to me, just like always!"

"Don't think you're too old for me to slap you down, missy, 'cause I will. You're just looking to plow up snakes."

"You think you're better than me, Elinor? Let me tell you something. Dirt shows up on the cleanest cotton . . ."

Other people found it amusing; I knew that it was, but it also brought tears to my eyes. *That would be Claudia and me, if my sister were alive today,* I thought. In my mind, I transformed her into a force for good, but if she were still alive, I didn't believe our relationship would have been anything other than what it was. She would still have lied to me and stolen from me, and I would have talked down to her and cursed her out for being so reckless. Occasionally, there might be a moment of grace that made me think things could be better. I touched the silver necklace Vargas had given me, and longed to have my silver bracelet, waiting for me in New York, around my wrist again. I'd thought Jesse was hopelessly sentimental for talking about Claudia in heaven, but he was also the one who said she'd be kicking my ass from there, and he was right.

I lost track of time watching them battle back and forth. Jesse was able to sneak up behind me and put his good arm around my shoulders. "Here's what I don't get," he said. "You saved our lives from a crazy megalomaniac billionaire who wanted us dead. You make him see that everythin' is his daughter's fault. Then, you make him put us on a private jet back to New York. You're possibly the smartest gal on the planet. At least, the craftiest."

"I try."

"So what I don't get is why you turned the plane into the yokel express. Who the hell said they could come on board?"

"I was worried Wolven would change his mind about letting them go," I admitted.

"Texans. There is just nothin' you can do with them folks."

On the plane, Jesse and I sat next to each other, even though there was plenty of room to spread out. At first, I thought he might sleep the whole way, since he put his head back and closed his eyes. But after a while, he started talking. "You know what I want to do when we go home? After I get the surgery done, I mean—holy hell, I can't wait for that. I want to see that movie again. *Gaslight.*"

"Why that one?"

" 'Cause we just had a real-life viewing of it." Jesse opened his eyes. "I never watched any of those old movies thinkin' stuff like that could happen. To me, it's all an escape from real life. I mean, when you watch those old films, do you ever stop and think, 'Oh, yeah, I lived through that last week'? Holy hell. *Gaslight.*

"Frightening as it is, at least *Gaslight* has a happy ending," I pointed out.

"I think hangin' around me has finally turned your head, Tiger Lily."

"In what way?" I took the fresh drink the flight attendant held out to me. My second or my third? I couldn't remember, and I didn't care.

"You don't watch out, you'll turn into a cockeyed optimist, too. Don't tell me it can't happen. You're the one who invited that pair of lulus on the flight."

I laughed. "Remember, I've got you reading Poe now. Your world is about to get a lot darker."

"So can you really recite all that verse? I remember Claudia once sayin' how you could just rattle it off the top of your head."

Setting my drink down, I started to recite. " 'Take this kiss upon the brow. And, in parting from you now, thus much let me avow—You are not wrong, who deem that my days have been a dream.' " Something stirred in the back of my mind, and I heard my sister's voice. *You are such a fucking show-off.*